The
Wartime
Nursery

BOOKS BY LIZZIE PAGE

The War Nurses

Daughters of War

When I Was Yours

The Forgotten Girls

The Wartime Nanny

SHILLING GRANGE CHILDREN'S HOME SERIES

The Orphanage

A Place to Call Home

An Orphan's Song

The Children Left Behind

An Orphan's Wish

THE WARTIME EVACUEES SERIES

A Child Far from Home

Lizzie Page

The
Wartime
Nursery

bookouture

Published by Bookouture in 2024

An imprint of Storyfire Ltd.
Carmelite House
50 Victoria Embankment
London EC4Y 0DZ

www.bookouture.com

Storyfire Ltd's authorised representative in the EEA is Hachette Ireland
8 Castlecourt Centre
Castleknock Road
Castleknock
Dublin 15 D15 YF6A
Ireland

ISBN: 978-1-83525-974-0
eBook ISBN: 978-1-83525-973-3

To Aunty Becky – and all the wonderful caregivers who transform the lives of little ones every single day.

'Wartime nurseries have been provided at the cost of the Exchequer as an aid to war production. Their purpose has been to enable women with young children to help in the war effort and where these facilities are no longer required their continuance for this purpose at the cost of the Exchequer cannot be justified.'

Mr Henry Willink, *Hansard Parliamentary Debates*, 21 December 1944

1

SEPTEMBER 1939

Lydia

Lydia Froud and her two best friends, Francine Salt and Valerie Hardman, walked from the house they shared in Romberg Road to their school, each of them carrying one piece of luggage. Bringing up the rear were Lydia and Francine's mothers. Valerie's mother wasn't there; she had already said her goodbyes and gone to work.

Even in the street, nine-year-old Lydia could smell her mother's perfume. Not only did she smell the sweetest, but she was the prettiest of all the mummies and Lydia wanted to be just like her when she grew up. Today, however, her mother's nose was red and shiny when she wasn't pressing it into a hand-kerchief.

'Silly me!' Mummy kept saying, and 'Ignore me,' and 'My goodness, I don't know what's come over me!'

Usually, Lydia's mummy was happy-go-lucky, giggly almost. But today, the headteacher greeted her with, 'You look like death warmed up, Mrs Froud.'

Some of the mothers left their children at the school, but

Lydia's didn't. Mummy walked with them all the way up to the railway station, ignoring the teacher's hard stares and the head-teacher's hints. At the station, Lydia's mother put her slender arms round Lydia and said, 'I love you more than all the tea in China.' She squeezed her so tight Lydia could feel the buttons of her coat digging into her chest and for the first time in her short life, Lydia felt fear. This was so unfamiliar to her that she didn't know what to do with it except to push her mummy away.

'Mummy!' she whispered, 'You're hurting me!' and her mummy pulled back and apologised.

On the train to the countryside, Lydia and Francine, who was also nine – 'a young nine', Mummy often said – played cat's cradle and dice and with Margaret-Doll while Valerie, who was older than them both by two years, although you'd think it was twenty sometimes, stared out of the window or chatted, but with the adults not the other children.

Lydia was no longer scared. She would do anything for a day off school – she was not one for sitting at a desk – so she was full of glee at this out-of-the-ordinary event. They hadn't been on the train for long before Lydia had swapped their name tags for fun, asked the teacher if they could get their suit-cases down from the overhead shelf (no, they could not), if they could eat their sandwiches yet (will you just sit still for five minutes?). Boys had thrown paper aeroplanes at them and kicked them and Lydia had told on them and got them into trouble.

Once they'd passed Reading station, and the rocking of the train on the tracks grew monotonous and Francine had fallen asleep, Lydia's enthusiasm started to wane.

'Are we there yet?' she asked repeatedly.

'We'll tell you when we're there!' snapped the teacher.

Lydia made an 'ooh, strict!' expression at Valerie, who wouldn't meet her eye.

It was late afternoon when they were there and, feeling grubby and tired, Lydia could feel the fear returning. They were led to a hall, a church hall, that looked a bit like their school gymnasium, and Lydia told herself, 'Don't be a scaredy cat.'

Valerie had given Lydia her suitcase in exchange for her pillowcase, and now she was looking at Lydia like she regretted it. She wanted some of Lydia's fruit cake but Lydia was determined to hold on to it – not because she liked fruit cake particularly, but because it reminded her of Mummy in the kitchen, putting it in the oven, her cheeks pink as rose petals.

They hadn't been there for long when a lot of adults came in another entrance, and went to the opposite end of the hall and surveyed them all. They were lined up like two opposing teams in football and Lydia wanted to giggle or blow a whistle or something. Then some of the adults broke away to examine the children's side more closely. They strode up and down in front of them, and this time it was like they were in the butcher's and, for some, these cuts of meat were not up to their standard.

'It's like being in a zoo,' one teacher said sympathetically. 'Don't worry, it'll be over soon.'

'Chin up, girls,' said another. 'Big smiles.'

'Why?' asked Lydia. She knew they had been evacuated. She knew this meant going to live in the countryside. She did not know why that meant they should smile at strange adults in a church hall. She wished she had asked her mummy more questions about this. Once again, she felt uneasy about her mummy's tears. It was so unlike her.

The teacher felt her hair. 'Because they're going to decide whether they want you or—'

'Not!' finished Francine in that mawkish way she had. Lydia's mum said Francine was like a girl in a Hitchcock film, permanently scared.

Lydia wasn't a baby and, anyway, most of the looks she was receiving were approving. She kicked her feet and did a cheesy grin, but kept tight hold of Francine's hand. Valerie was the other side of Francine, holding her other hand. The teacher didn't ask Valerie to smile and you couldn't tell if Valerie was scared or not. Lydia's mummy called Valerie 'self-contained'.

Francine asked Valerie to make up a story like she did at home and she launched off into one of her elaborate tales. Lydia puffed her cheeks with air, then slowly released it. She wished she could tell her mummy all about this. Her mummy would have said, 'Be kind, Lydia!'

'Do they separate?' people kept asking. 'We can only take one.' Or, 'She's such a lovely little thing.' Or, 'She reminds me of Little Bo-Peep.'

Lydia fluttered her eyelashes.

'Poor baby, so far from home...'

Lydia got Valerie to retie the bow in her hair. She didn't want anyone to think she was messy.

Some of the children were led off. Even Colin the kicker was selected. The fact that the three of them wouldn't separate was causing the hold-up, apparently. There was a man walking around in wellington boots and he licked his lips noisily. She held Francine's hand tighter so she didn't squeal. Mummy would have told her she was a good girl.

A smiley lady said apologetically, 'I haven't got room for three, doves.'

'We're not doves,' Francine whispered to Lydia.

'I was hoping for older ones,' another said. 'Kids who can pull their weight around the home...'

Another man grinned. 'If I were looking for someone decorative, you'd be it.'

Lydia preened. The adults discussed things over their heads. Lydia used to listen in to adult conversations but found that they were just as dull as anyone else's. Nowadays, everything was about the war. Nazis, Hitler, Zeppelins and bombs. Conscription. Rationing. Daddy spoke at length about how some men – like him – had to protect the people at home. Mummy went on about shortages and making do with what they had – nothing new there!

Another woman was looking at them. Something about her commanded attention. She was tall and held herself straight. She was somewhere between thirty and sixty, she supposed. Lydia's guesses at people's ages sometimes made her mummy cry with laughter.

There was a discussion and then a decision. It seemed the woman was prepared for two young ones, not three and not... Head low, she and Valerie engaged in a muttered conversation.

Lydia heard Valerie say, 'We're not actual sisters...' and she felt hurt even though it was true. She stuck out her bottom lip. Why could Valerie never lie?

Valerie was separated from them. Her face fell, although she covered it up; she too was trying to be brave. Privately, Lydia thought it might be for the best – three *is* a crowd sometimes. Mummy said that too.

Valerie squeezed Francine and then Lydia.

'It'll only be for a few weeks,' she said urgently. 'Then we'll be home. Don't worry...'

'I'm not,' Lydia whispered.

The woman who had won them said Lydia and Francine were to follow her. She wasn't half as pretty as Mummy but she was strong, carrying both their cases, one in each hand. She apologised that she had let her driver go, just the week before.

Francine and Lydia looked at each other, both thinking the same.

She had a driver?

As they walked, Francine wrinkled up her nose because of the country smell. There was no pavement, so they had to squeeze close to the hedges and listen for traffic. A load of sheep came towards them, and both of them pressed against the hedges, while the woman chatted to the man in a flat cap who was with them and told him that these were her evacuees.

'You won't find much better than Bumble Cottage.' The man winked at them.

'Bum!' whispered Francine, making Lydia chuckle. The woman pretended not to hear.

'Come along, girls. Enough dawdling.'

And then they were in front of a house with honeysuckle and ivy and a path, wriggly as a worm, with trees just bursting with leaves, so heavy that the branches were overflowing with them. There was a dog too, an elderly dog with a moustache and beard, sleeping on the doorstep and a shiny bell with a tug-rope, like a church bell but smaller, and the door was bright red.

'This is my home.' The woman's lips twitched. 'And yours too.'

Francine whispered, 'Oh my God,' which was not allowed, she could get a smack for that, but Lydia couldn't be shocked because she was thinking it too.

It was perfect.

2

SEPTEMBER 1939

Lydia

Lydia Froud loved living at Bumble Cottage. What wasn't to like?

She enjoyed having her own bedroom, not having to share with her little brother, one-year-old Matthew. Francine had asked to share, but Lydia was relieved when their host mother, Mrs Howard, said they had a room each. Lydia already shared with Margaret-Doll, who slept next to her on the pillow.

Mrs Howard had a twelve-year-old son, Paul, and he came and stayed but only for holidays and high days. He was at a boarding school. When Lydia first heard that, she thought it was a *boredom* school and wondered what made it different from other schools. Then, once she understood, she wondered if he had been sent away – evacuated – because Bumble Cottage was unsafe, but Mrs Howard corrected her. He had been sent away for a different reason.

'What reason?' Lydia persisted, all kinds of scenarios running through her head. Was he bad? Was he a prisoner?

Mrs Howard made a tight-lipped expression when she didn't like something. 'For his education.'

'Why?'

'That's enough, Lydia. I made the decision a while back and I am happy with it.'

Paul wasn't interested in the two little girls from London who were occupying his home. He had tennis and fishing and fighting with the boys in the village to contend with. And he was used to being away – since he was six. To Lydia, he seemed impossibly grown up. So she and Francine had the run of the house, the garden, the village. She had never felt so free, so uncontained in her life. It was like she'd grown wings.

Mrs Howard enrolled her and Francine into a private school, St Boniface, and largely left them to it.

Most of the other evacuees were at the local village school. Lydia missed her old friends' attention – even if the attention gave her bruises on her shins or tangles in her hair – but she liked St Boniface. The girls at St Boniface weren't sure about her and Francine's cockney accents at first, but Francine always managed to win people over with her sweet nature. Lydia wasn't sure how she herself won people over, but she usually did, eventually. She also toned down her accent somewhat – it wasn't difficult. She overheard a teacher call her a chameleon, which she supposed was another war-word.

Lydia was an ordinary student. One teacher said she was exasperating because if she applied herself then she'd be an all-rounder, but Lydia felt being an all-rounder sounded dull. She and Francine were able at netball but Francine didn't have a competitive bone in her, and Lydia didn't like getting sweaty. She had also attended a dance class in London, but the children who were good had been learning since they were five and, at nine, Lydia had decided she was past it.

In the playground she made friends with Betsy and Flora, who liked the skipping games that she enjoyed, though they didn't want Francine to join in, which was awkward. Lydia was a good enough friend not to tell Francine to go away, but not a good enough friend to include her. She felt torn between the old and new, and the new was so shiny and fresh... Fortunately, Francine was so mild-tempered that she always forgave Lydia by the walk home after school.

Lydia's mother and Mrs Salt had visited only about a month after they'd first arrived, and you could see how impressed they were with everything: not only by what they said, but by their raised eyebrows and hushed, reverential tones.

'Ooh,' her mummy cooed. 'This *is* an experience!'

'How the other half live, eh!' said Mrs Salt.

'They'll become snooty ladies!' Mummy joked.

'They won't want to talk to us!' said Mrs Salt but you couldn't tell if she was joking or not.

At going-home time, her mother had cupped Lydia's face in her hands and searched in her eyes. 'I know it's special here, Lydia,' she said and then paused. 'But never forget I love you!'

'Course not, Mummy!' Lydia laughed. 'How would I forget that?'

Valerie Hardman – Lydia's friend who they'd been separated from when they were evacuated – was also in Somerset, but she went to the school where most of the other evacuees had gone. She had been taken in by the Woods family, who owned the local hardware store. Whenever they visited the shop, Valerie was hidden behind the counter and moping, even though she got the entire run of the place and all the watering cans, buckets or nails she could ever want.

Mrs Howard had suggested they visit her more often.

'I thought you three were inseparable, back in London!'

Lydia had shrugged.

'She does seem lonely,' Mrs Howard continued, but you

couldn't touch anything on the shelves and Valerie never looked pleased to see them anyway.

At Christmas, after just three months away, Lydia and Francine took the train back to London. Francine was so excited she couldn't sit still and kept opening and shutting the windows, but Lydia was full of concern. She was excited to see her mummy, and Daddy too, but she didn't want to be made to stay back in London – that was happening a lot.

When they got back to the house in Romberg Road, Francine was crying and laughing at the same time. She was so relieved to be back, and Lydia understood that for the last few months Francine had been pretending that she was happy, but she was not herself, not like Lydia was. And Mummy was weeping again too, as she ran out and hugged her.

'I'm so glad you're back where you belong!'

Lydia couldn't speak. She buried her face in her mummy's blouse, inhaling her perfume. Francine was hustled away upstairs to her family's flat and Lydia was taken into theirs. Daddy was at work and so was Valerie's mother, who lived in the basement flat below.

'We've been making it look pretty!'

There was a tiny plant strung with paper rings and that was their Christmas tree. Her mummy regarded her with her eager expression.

'You're not cold? I try not to put the fire on in the day.'

'It's only for a while, isn't it?' Lydia gazed around, trying not to frown. 'I'll cope.'

Everything in London was 'make do and mend'. Everything was make do and mend in Bumble Cottage too, but the starting point there was so much higher. Make do with just one house-keeper rather than a fleet of staff. Make do with a room of your own rather than one shared between four.

Lydia missed everything about Bumble Cottage. Even silly things that you mightn't notice like the furniture, or the cutlery, the starchy tablecloths. She missed the things you definitely would notice – like the gigantic Christmas tree that had taken three men to carry inside. And she'd had to stand on a box to put the star on top.

Here, Matthew was always whining about something. Mummy didn't lose patience with him though – she was always sweet; everyone said she was 'so good with little ones'. She asked Lydia to play with Matthew, while she fried eggs. Lydia felt awkward. *She* was not good with little ones – she found their unpredictability and their demands tiresome. Still, she rolled a ball across the floor to Matthew like he was a dog and he squealed happily. Mummy put her hands on her shoulders and said, 'My best girl is home!' and then in a choked voice whispered, 'I can't believe I've got both my children under one roof again!'

When Daddy came back, he said gruffly, 'Your mother's missed you,' and Lydia's first thought was: what about you? He must have read her mind because then his face broke into a rare beam and he admitted, 'All right, I did too...'

She wasn't too old to walk up his legs, holding his hands to do a mid-air roly-poly. She was *nearly* too old to sit on his lap as he read the newspapers, but he said, 'Just this once.' And Mummy watched them, her flushed face full of fondness, just like Lydia remembered.

Lydia knew she was lucky to have them, but that didn't mean she wanted to stay with them. She was secure in their love. It was like something she put in a pocket and carried around with her. It wasn't something she wanted to stare at all the time. It wasn't how she wanted to live. No, thank you. Not when she'd tasted the finer things in life...

A few days after Christmas, Francine decided she was going to stay in London rather than return to Bumble Cottage, which was a surprise to no one. Naturally, Mrs Salt was over the moon.

'Francine is such a homebody,' Mummy sighed. Lydia nearly said that she too was a homebody, but it was not this home her body yearned for. There was a leak in the flat and you had to keep walking round the tin bucket and ignoring the constant noise. Daddy said water-dripping was a torture method, but he thought it was funny. The carpet was thread-bare. At Bumble Cottage, the carpets sank as deep as their mattresses. Didn't Mummy notice these things? Why didn't Daddy get paid properly for his important job? Lydia resented *The Times* newspaper for treating her daddy so badly.

'Do you want to stay here too, darling?' her mummy whispered as she brushed her hair with Lydia squidged against her. 'I could probably persuade Daddy...'

Lydia hummed and hawed, like she was considering it, yet she had no urge to stay. It was like the air was different in London. It bewildered her why anyone would choose to live in a poky flat in the smog-filled city when elsewhere there was space and colour and light.

At Bumble Cottage, there was a bicycle with a basket she could borrow. The St Boniface school blazer was a good colour for her complexion, and the blouses were soft on her skin. Things didn't fall apart. She didn't want to hurt her lovely mummy with her pretty blue eyes and her worried smile. Lydia adored her, and she knew she was adored, but there was no way round it: life was better in Somerset.

3

SEPTEMBER 1940

Emmeline

Mrs Neville Froud – Emmeline – was at home in her flat at 67 Romberg Road, London, thinking about what rations she could eke out for tomorrow's breakfast, writing a letter to her daughter Lydia in Somerset and sewing a hat for Lydia's Margaret-Doll. Emmeline was not adept at dressmaking, but she enjoyed sewing outfits if they were smaller than her hand.

Her son, Matthew, was 'sorting' the laundry. This amounted to him pretending socks were worms or throwing underwear up in the air. Her husband, Neville, was fire-watching that day. He was doing it for more than three times a week now, and he went straight there from his day job at the newspapers, so she hardly saw him, but if she said anything about it he got even more crabby than usual.

She was just about to put Matthew to bed when there was a cacophony of noise. And then a wail of sirens. Ever since war had been declared, they had been waiting for this – rehearsed for it even, gas masks at the ready – but it still seemed unreal.

Emmeline moved quickly, surprising herself. She grabbed

Matthew, still clutching a sock, and raced upstairs to bang on the door of the Salts' flat.

'It's time! Mrs Salt! Cooo-eee!'

Francine Salt – who had been back in London since last Christmas – opened the door looking petrified, so Emmeline tried to contain herself.

'Ready for an adventure!' She took Francine's hand and Francine held her little sister's Maisie's hand, and Emmeline ran, carrying Matthew, out to the shelter in the backyard.

It was probably only a few minutes, but it felt like ages before Mrs Salt joined them with baby Joe and toddler Jacob. She had been packing her bag of biscuits and making sandwiches.

'We've already had tea!' exclaimed Emmeline. Sometimes it was hard to get your priorities right, but this was getting your priorities wrong.

'An army marches on its stomach,' Mrs Salt said.

'We're not an army and we're not marching,' retorted Emmeline.

Mrs Salt wiped her forehead, her eyes tired. 'It's going to be a long night.'

For the first time, Emmeline felt grateful that Lydia was still away in Somerset. She had wanted to get her daughter back ever since she had sent her away. The fact that nothing had happened all year had somehow made it all the worse. They had been pushed to keep the children away. Pushed or encouraged or obliged. Everyone phrased it differently.

'It wasn't for me,' said ten-year-old Billy from down the street, who was a law unto himself. 'Countryside stinks.'

He wasn't the only one: plenty of the children at the school came back – Emmeline saw them running around in the street, all cock-a-hoop – and each one felt like a kick in the teeth – Lydia should be home with her.

'Weren't you evacuated?'

'No one wanted me,' snotty Alan Gold said. 'Dunno why.'

Handing him a handkerchief, Emmeline thought she could hazard a guess.

'Ma wanted me back,' Mary Roberts said with a shrug. 'Cos she's got another bun in the oven.'

Mrs Salt had never liked being separated from her eldest daughter, Francine, and had wailed for most of the autumn until Francine returned at Christmas, and then Francine refused to get on the train or Mrs Salt refused to let her on – depending on who was telling the story. But Neville was adamant that Lydia had to stay in the countryside – he was as determined as he was last September. He had not wavered, not once, and Lydia didn't seem too unhappy there either. It seemed it was only Emmeline who didn't like the arrangement.

She put a brave face on it, but it was agony having a young daughter living halfway across the country. Her instincts were crying out to mother Lydia and yet on a day-to-day basis she could not. She had to make do with letters, the occasional telephone call from the box on the street and their rare visits instead. It reminded her of a time when Neville's mother had taken newborn Lydia out in the pram while Emmeline's breasts ached to feed her. When they finally returned long hours later, Emmeline said she couldn't have her on her own again.

Now hours had become weeks and months. Lydia didn't need her like she did back then, but Emmeline still needed her daughter. She had to funnel her mothering energy into Matthew, who was too young to be sent away, or the four Salt children, Francine, Maisie, Jacob and Joseph, known as Joe. Matthew – bless him – hardly knew his own sister, so she talked about her to him all the time. 'Wonder what Lydia is doing today?' or 'I bet Lydia would like that!'

Lydia would not have liked the air raid shelter.

Emmeline would have had more children if she could have, but Neville told her she was lucky to have two. She enjoyed the

company of children, and the funny things they observed. 'Out
of the mouths of babes,' she liked to say.

Since Mrs Salt was too distressed to partake in a conversation, Emmeline got out the dominos and sat with Maisie and
Francine while the little ones had their bottles and watched
with big eyes. Six dots on the six: 'You can't put five dots on the
four, Maisie, that's not fair!'

Maisie kept wanting to give up. Francine giggled non-stop.
They debated whether it was a game of luck or skill.

'Does it matter?' Mrs Salt interrupted. Their arguments
irritated her and she didn't hide it 'It's still win or lose.'

It did for the girls.

They had been in the shelter for about an hour when there
was a horrible battering on the door. Emmeline and Mrs Salt
looked at each other warily before opening – surely it couldn't
be Nazis already! – but it was only Mrs Hardman, who lived in
the basement flat below. She'd been out working and now she
flew in, all askew, in her bus uniform, before dramatically
collapsing on the floor.

'It's hell out there,' she said, covering her face with her
hands.

4

Lydia

Lydia had been living in Somerset for just over seven months when she got *the* best present that she'd ever had. If you rolled all her Christmas and birthday presents together, over every year she had been alive, they would never, ever add up to this.

'He's not just for you, he's for Paul too,' Mrs Howard said. 'You understand that, Lydia? LYDIA?'

Lydia was already on the carpet, entwined with the dog. He was black and white, medium-sized and had the waggiest of tails. Mrs Howard had got him from the kennels down the road, and he was a good boy. The Smarts, who owned the kennels, thought he would do for them. Cassie, Mrs Howard's elderly dog, had died not long after Lydia and Francine had moved in and Lydia had been devastated.

Rex was another mark in the Somerset Good, London Bad sheet that Lydia kept in her head. She didn't blame her parents for not getting a dog – 'How could you keep a dog in a flat? It would be so unhappy.' That was just life. But she *could* demand that she stay in Somerset, especially now she had Rex to look after.

Lydia walked Rex for miles. Sometimes she walked so far, she didn't know where she was, but when she said 'home', Rex would take her back to Bumble Cottage. He knew where home was.

Lydia was not allowed to feed Rex from the dinner table but, if Mrs Howard left the room, she did it anyway. It was hard to resist those little eyes staring intently at her. So, despite Mrs H, Rex usually sat at her feet, intently, waiting for crusts.

One morning in September, after Lydia had been in Somerset for one year, Mrs Howard was too preoccupied with the newspapers to tell her off about Rex. She was making faces at something she was reading over her home-made marmalade.

'I have some bad news,' she said presently.

Lydia swallowed. If Rex was going to be taken away from her, she would run away.

'It looks as though the Blitz has started.'

'What's that?' Lydia relaxed and scraped butter along the toast.

'London is under attack.'

Some of the boys at school were crazy about 'King Kong'. She pictured that giant beast standing over London, picking up people and squeezing them or crushing things under his massive feet. Paws. She imagined St Paul's Cathedral, Romberg Road, and her school in ruins and Mummy...

'We'll wait for news – if Francine or your mother and Matthew want to come here, do let them know there's a place.'

'Did you hear that, Margaret-Doll?' Lydia whispered to her friend on the seat next to her. 'London is under attack.'

5

Emmeline

Emmeline hardly slept in the shelter. Not only was Matthew grumbling in his sleep, she wasn't used to being such close proximity to so many people either. The Salts were bundled together but Francine kept leaning her head on hers, so Emmeline had felt obliged to keep still.

She kept reminding herself how good it was Lydia was away. Lydia would *definitely* have hated this. She didn't like small spaces, crammed spaces, small children, dominos, bombs... She was much better where she was and, in a ridiculous way, Emmeline felt relieved that the year away hadn't been for nothing. For the first time, the evacuation made sense. She was saving her from this.

The next morning, they packed up and went back into their house, which she was pleased to see looked exactly as usual – Emmeline didn't know what she had been expecting, but it wasn't that. Everything felt strange. Everything felt brighter that morning, technicolour or vivid. They had made it through the night!

Neville was already back too, standing at the kitchen window in his fire-watching cap and jacket. He looked wonderful; she had never been so glad to see him, and she thought maybe he would kiss her and hold her tight like he used to.

But Neville was exhausted and Emmeline's exhilaration at being alive soon wore off.

'The Germans had had a field day,' he said.

She thought *field day* was a strange way of putting it.

They'd attacked just when everyone had been imagining they wouldn't. It was going to go on for a while now, he predicted. Maybe it was the start of the invasion? Maybe it was the start of the occupation? Neville had spotted fires all over East London. The way he talked! If it weren't for him and his eagle eyes, the whole city would have been destroyed.

But then Neville told Emmeline she and Matthew had to leave London – now, as soon as possible, or he'd send Matthew away without her.

That got her back up. Ordering her around like he was Lord of the Manor and she was a scullery maid? She didn't take instructions well from anyone, but from her husband? Never.

'What's wrong with the shelters?' she asked, and he laughed grimly.

'What's right with them?'

Then she said, 'Why don't I just hop on a train and find a place near Lydia?' but Neville, who was usually the more inventive one of the pair, insisted that she evacuate through 'proper channels'.

'It's probably going to be like this for months, Em.'

'So I'll find a little house to rent.'

'You're not going to be able to find anything! Plus, how could we afford it?'

Then, even though he'd hardly slept, he had to go to work at the newspaper office, which cut the conversation short –

although it wasn't a conversation, it was a monologue, and Emmeline had hated listening to it.

All day Emmeline cooked and cleaned and tried to occupy Matthew. If she wore him out then he'd sleep better, and, if they were going to have another night in the shelter, the more worn out he was the better.

That evening, Neville came home, had forty winks in the armchair, then almost immediately went off for more fire-watching. There was no kissing or cuddling. The idea that everyone was having wild 'we could be dead tomorrow' romances did not apply to their household.

Emmeline was too worried to write letters. And yes, the dreaded sirens went off again, and again they clamoured out and across the yard, although this time Mrs Salt didn't bring any supplies (this time Emmeline had hoped she would) and they were all in their nightgowns and housecoats. Mrs Salt's husband had joined up a long time ago, so she couldn't ask her if Mr Salt was being more romantic than usual.

She wouldn't have said there was a party atmosphere the first night, but there definitely wasn't the second.

Maisie Salt started singing 'London's Burning' and got told off.

'Everyone's singing it!' she protested, tears in her eyes, after her mother slapped her on the thigh.

Emmeline didn't want to tell Mrs Salt that she and Matthew were considering evacuating, because her dear friend was already on the edge, and she couldn't have her in hysterics, not in this confined space.

'How about we sing "Oranges and Lemons"?' she suggested.

Everyone agreed this was a good one, although Mrs Salt scowled at 'here comes the chopper to chop off your head,' and when they'd finished, she muttered, 'What is the matter with the world?'

.   .   .

First thing on Monday morning, Emmeline dragged Matthew across town to the council to find out if there was still a chance of evacuation through Neville's preferred 'proper channels'. Some people had relatives to go to – indeed Emmeline had a beloved aunt, but she was in Coventry and Neville had shouted, 'Not Coventry! Think of all the industry there – it's a sodding target, that is!' so that was out the question.

'I wish we could go near Lydia...' she said.

'I wish you'd just get on with it...' he replied.

It was her first time in town since the bombing had started and to be fair, she could see Neville's point: the bomb damage was horrendous, the dust clouds, the ruins, and the growing despair. Maisie hadn't been wrong either: London *was* burning – here was the aftermath. The ambulances and the police cars, the rubble, the fallen masonry. Two children walking briskly along without shoes. A woman, her head in a bandage, grimly gripping a cat. A distressed elderly woman pushing a pram full of clothes and books.

Emmeline didn't know how to help – was she even in a position to give help? No, *she* needed help, and that made her feel ashamed.

The council would be worrying about rehousing those made homeless; she and Matthew wouldn't be a priority. She had a habit of leaving things too late and then making poor decisions in a panic. Why hadn't she learned her lesson?

She wasn't the only one at the council and she and Matthew had to queue. People chatted in the line, but it was chatting with an edge, since everyone was a rival in a way. This one's son had joined up this morning, that one's husband was joining up next week. This one had twins and a baby on the way and that one had elderly parents to worry about.

Matthew was well-behaved but he wasn't *that* well-behaved, and soon people were looking sternly at them both.

'Shhh,' Emmeline whispered, wishing she had brought the pram. He was whining because his legs were aching.

And then it was their turn.

'Yes, pregnant women and young mothers with children are still being evacuated,' the woman across the desk explained wearily. She was impervious to Matthew's large eyes and golden curls. 'I mean mothers with young children. Your age is not relevant.'

She didn't even bother to cover her mouth when she yawned, and Emmeline had a surprise glimpse of tiny teeth and wet tongue.

'Have you anything in Somerset?'

Emmeline imagined a simple place near Lydia in the West Country. She had grown to if not love, then no longer resent that part of the world for taking her Lydia. The idea that Lydia would be in peril, far from her, dogged Emmeline constantly. Her imagination took her to countryside accidents involving tractors or bogs or some archaic malady – smallpox or typhoid.

There wasn't much to do that way but it would be a great sanctuary, she couldn't deny it. And she didn't need a whole house. A bungalow or even a caravan would do. She remembered the Mrs Howard that Lydia lived with had a barn that doubled as lodgings. What about there? She could invite Lydia to teas after school. Sunday walks after church. Before too long, Lydia would move in with her.

'There's nothing west,' the woman said, examining her papers.

'Nothing in the whole of Somerset?' Emmeline couldn't believe this.

'It's bursting at the seams with Londoners. And there's a problem with people coming back and forth and we don't know where they are.'

'Oh?' Emmeline felt like this was a veiled accusation of her, even though she had no intention of going back and forth.

'Where do you have then?'

'We have spaces in Norfolk.'

'Norfolk?'

Last year, Emmeline had half-hoped Lydia would be allocated there. Norfolk wasn't too far, and now Emmeline imagined a pretty seaside village with cobbled streets that curved onto golden sand. Matthew could paddle in the sea or go crabbing and get sand in his trouser legs. And perhaps she could get a little job working in a seaside gift shop? She would persuade day-trippers to buy sticks of rock or cloth parasols or picture postcards or fudge or...

'All right,' she agreed. 'Norfolk it is.'

The woman carried on flipping through papers as though she hadn't spoken.

'So this family have said they will take one mother with one child. Here...'

She pushed an address over the table: Old Rectory, Fincham.

Emmeline backtracked. 'I'm after my *own* place. Matthew and I, we don't want to live with a... a family. We want to live by ourselves.'

She fiddled with the clasp of her purse. She hoped the woman could read her subliminal message: *I can afford to pay. For a month – at a push.* She didn't respond, so Emmeline said it aloud.

'That probably won't be enough, I'm afraid.'

'Why not?'

More yawning.

'Cover your mouth,' Emmeline wanted to say.

'It's evacuation. It could be months, years even. It's not a...'

'Holiday, yes, I know that.'

'So if you are sensible, you'll take up the free lodgings in

Norfolk. I've sent my mum, my cousins, my grandfather to Wales. They've got everything they need.'

'But I don't want to live with a family,' Emmeline said quietly. She knew she sounded spoilt, like Lydia when you offered her anything but crumpets, but it was important to get this across, especially if she wasn't to become one of the shameful 'back and forthers'.

She had kept her own house for twelve years, a decent home, she didn't want to go and live in another woman's house. She wanted room for her and Matthew to grow and for Lydia to join them one day, if possible. At the same time, she understood that beggars can't be choosers, but she did not want the woman to say that to her. She did not see herself as a beggar yet she could feel the phrase was on the tip of the other woman's tongue. Instead, she said the other phrase Emmeline was tired of hearing, 'No one wants to be at war either, but we are where we are.'

Emmeline sighed. 'We'll take it.'

'They're sending us to live with a family in Norfolk,' Emmeline told Neville early that evening. She wanted him to say, 'On second thoughts, stay back. The shelters are fine,' but he didn't.

'They didn't have any places we could have to ourselves,' she added. Would he not respond to that?

He puffed on his pipe. She had told him plenty of times that it made him smell like an old man, but he didn't care.

'Norfolk?' he eventually snorted. 'Can't think Hitler will be interested in Norfolk. More sheep there than people.'

Was this a joke? Emmeline didn't like it whatever it was.

'They bombed Norwich in July. Lots of people died,' she said.

'You'll be in the countryside though,' he said. 'Not the city. Isn't that the point?'

'*You* want us to go,' she said stiffly.

'I don't *want* you to go,' he said. 'You s*hould* go.'

'Should I ask Lydia's host if she can take us?'

'You can't do that – she's doing more than enough for us!'

'I know, but...' Emmeline felt suddenly overwhelmed. Her family were spread all over England. 'How can I look after you all when I'm halfway across the country?' she asked quietly.

This time, Neville spoke gently. 'I don't need looking after, Em.'

It felt like the carpet was being pulled from under her. What *was* she if she wasn't looking after them? What was her purpose? Did she even exist if she wasn't washing his clothes or planning dinners?

He noticed her despair. 'Matty needs looking after most. He needs you.'

'I can do that here, though. Together.'

He rested his pipe on the glass ashtray, then got up and squatted at her knees.

'I fear London will fall.'

A shiver went through her. 'But *you'll* be here.' It came out in a sob.

'It's for the best. One of us needs to defend the city but not both of us.'

They cuddled and, when she cried, he stroked her back and kissed the top of her head, and there was something about this closeness that made her feel better. This was what she needed.

Before he left for fire-watching, his face pale as the moon, Neville brought her a rare cup of tea and said, 'You were so tired,' which made her feel happier too, even though he spoiled it a bit when he added, 'Don't say I don't do anything for you.'

6

Emmeline

There had been servicemen everywhere since last year, so Emmeline had thought she was used to it, but still it was something to see all the people in uniforms, the blues, the greys and the greens, at the railway station. One of the blues helped her down the station steps with the pram.

'It's like a bloody tank,' he complained, sweating.

'I did warn you,' she said, smiling, and he mock-grimaced.

Another helped her plant the pram at the end of the carriage.

They'd got rid of Lydia's pram after the miscarriages, when Emmeline didn't think a pregnancy would keep again, and then Neville came home with this one, and she was so delighted with it. She used to lift the hood up and down, proud of its smooth mechanism when nothing else was working. Now she could only see it as a sign of her new reduced status – she was someone who had to be helped in these impossible times.

They had sandwiches, sausage rolls, then Emmeline peeled an orange. The smell took over the carriage and she felt guilty.

Matthew ate it all, leaving none to offer around. It was increasingly hard to get oranges now.

Despite Matthew, some of the servicemen made eyes at her. Emmeline had always had plenty of attention and she was accustomed to ignoring it. She and Neville were childhood sweethearts and, although he seemed to have forgotten the sweet bit in recent years, Emmeline took her wedding vows seriously: when young men asked her if she liked dancing, which they invariably did, she always gave the same reply: 'Yes, with my husband.'

The servicemen looked so young to her now, too – perhaps that was what was different, Emmeline thought. First the reservists, and then conscription had kicked in. The thought of Matthew going off to fight one day was chilling. That was the problem with having sons. It was probably why Neville, who was that rare man who didn't mind having daughters, had wanted to stop trying after Lydia.

Emmeline patted her son's head and was glad of his small body wrapped around her. Then they had barley sweets and a chunk of dark chocolate Mrs Salt had given as a farewell gift.

Emmeline had put the suitcase up on the overhead rack where she could keep an eye on it. It was Neville's and they'd rowed about it last year. She'd wanted Lydia to take it, he'd insisted Lydia take a pillowcase to Somerset instead – 'It's lighter,' he had argued, and she had acquiesced. Emmeline sighed to herself. She tried not to be negative and to conjure up memories of a loving Neville, but the only ones of those she had felt very old. He was good in front of people, he said the right things: 'My family are everything to me,' but in private she might as well not be there. Hopefully, her not actually being there would make a difference. Absence makes the heart grow fonder, they say. *Something* had to...

·   ·   ·

After she'd broken the news about leaving to Mrs Salt and the children, little Maisie Salt had asked her *why* they were going and Emmeline had been lost for words. She didn't want to say Nazis, bombs, etc, because of what it implied for Mrs Salt's decision to stay put, so she said she just wanted to try out somewhere else for a while.

'What is in Norfolk that isn't here?' asked Maisie, master of the unanswerable question.

'It's flat,' Emmeline said. 'There are canals. And geese.'

'And *that's* why you're going?' Maisie pressed. 'Because it's flat. Canals. Geese?'

Mrs Salt was shaking her head over Maisie's: *Don't tell her.* So Emmeline tickled Maisie to stop her persisting, which worked, since Maisie was a ticklish little thing.

Before they left, Emmeline had a row with Mrs Hardman, Valerie's mother. Emmeline told herself it had bubbled up out of nowhere, but it was probably a product of all the fear and resentment and exasperation that was whirring in her stomach.

In the past, Emmeline had felt sorry for Mrs Hardman since she was bringing up Valerie on her own. Mrs Hardman seemed like the poor relative, struggling to get by on her umpteen cleaning jobs. But now she worked on the buses, she was *contributing* to the war effort, while she, Emmeline Froud, had become the drain on the war effort.

All Emmeline had done was to point out how lucky Mrs Hardman was to be able to stay in London, to have a respectable job, to have purpose, but her remarks had not gone down well. As Emmeline sat on the train, Matthew's curly head in her lap, she thought, *what did I do that for?* It wasn't Mrs Hardman's fault that she felt as though her life was travelling in the wrong direction.

—————

7

Emmeline

You wouldn't know the country was at war here; the only sound was the buzzing of the cicadas and the distant ringing of church bells. Emmeline and Matthew got off the train at its final destination, Thorpe station, and then got on a bus to Fincham, another final destination. It was hard to believe they were only one hundred-odd miles away from London.

The bus driver helped her with the pram and the luggage and, since he was being so helpful, she asked if he knew where the Old Rectory was. He went on a convoluted explanation. Emmeline pretended she understood, but in London it was all which building, or which shop, to turn at. Here it was trees and rivers or paths you mightn't notice but which were definitely there.

'You've been a great help,' she lied. She had to cut him off otherwise it would be dark before they even got started.

Matthew insisted on walking, so she hoisted the suitcase into the pram. She hated that she might look like one of the refugees in the photographs in the newspapers. This wasn't her – it wasn't her life.

Matthew was slow, but determined. She did eventually come upon a house that might be it, but she decided it couldn't be this one; not only was it massive but it was set on its own like a church or a school. Perhaps it was divided into flats, like their house, she thought, before realising there was a little wooden sign that said THE OLD RECTORY.

As they stood on the doorstep, Matthew was making odd noises, even for Matthew.

'Shhh,' she told him.

'Mama!' he grumbled.

'Not now, darling!'

She was reluctant to ring the bell. She suddenly felt as though ringing it would be starting a new story, a new chapter of her life, and she wasn't ready. She had only just got used to her old life... She reached out though, tugging the cord, and at that exact moment Matthew threw up. It must have been the journey and all the food she had been stuffing him with to keep him quiet.

'No!' gasped Emmeline. That sound, like soup splashing, made her want to retch too. She fumbled in her handbag for a handkerchief. 'Matthew! Why didn't you say?'

Of course, the front door had to open then. A smartly dressed man – all collar and three-piece suit – surveyed them, opened his mouth to greet them, then noticed the puddle of vomit next to them.

'Ah...'

'I'm so sorry...' Emmeline began, horrified. 'It's all my fault!'

The man grimaced but sympathetically. The house had a lord-of-the-manor look about it, but he did not have a lord-of-the-manor look about him. He was not half so intimidating as the house had led her to expect.

'No need to apologise. These things happen. You must be

our lady from London, and, hello, young man, you must be feeling rotten!'

'Are you the butler?' Emmeline asked. She had read enough stories to know that the inhabitants of houses this size employed staff.

'Not quite, this is my house.' He stifled a laugh. 'Mr Davenport, pleased to meet you.'

He wasn't very tall, although he gave the impression of height. He was lean, with chiselled features, although his eyes were slightly crossed, as though he was looking at his nose.

Everything Emmeline had prepared to say disappeared.

'Let's clean you up,' he said, flicking Matthew's chin. 'Welcome to the Old Rectory,' he added, looking at Emmeline.

He led them into a bright kitchen that was about the size of Emmeline's entire flat and called out, 'Mabel?'

No one came.

Emmeline stared around at the flagstone flooring and the latest equipment. A wood fire was burning and the room felt warm and... safe. It might not be with Lydia, but it could be worse.

'I suspect Mabel has gone for the day. She's our maid. I don't think she'll stay here long now everything is up in the air once again.'

He directed Emmeline to the sink and left the room. She deftly stripped Matthew and washed him down. Mr Davenport came back with a large blanket and wrapped him in it.

'There, little fellow.'

Matthew crawled into Emmeline's arms in the blanket. Mr Davenport insisted he'd make her some tea, so she sat still with Matthew heavy on her. He filled up the kettle and set out the cups and saucers. No man except for Neville had ever made Emmeline tea before and it felt incredibly intimate.

'What an introduction,' he said.

She felt like crying suddenly. The stress of the last few days, the parting from Neville and concern for Lydia, was wearing heavily on her. But she wouldn't cry. She steeled herself. She had to stay strong.

'Why did you offer us a place?' she asked.

The money would clearly make no difference to this family and, although it was the rule that if you had a spare bedroom then you helped the evacuation, Neville said the wealthy had ways of getting out of the rules that everyone else had to live by.

'We wanted to provide sanctuary,' he said. 'It's important to us.'

'But you didn't take a child last year?'

'Well, we didn't want to...' he hesitated.

'Actually look after it?' Emmeline finished for him.

He grinned at her. 'Something like that.'

They both laughed. Emmeline decided she liked him.

He said they had already had a mother and two girls to stay September to December last. 'Mrs Saunders, Alice and Nelly.' He sounded pleased that he'd got the names right. 'Father joined up and they needed to get out of the city. Mrs Saunders was a headmistress. We arranged it privately through friends of friends. This time, as you know, we went through the official channels.'

'Where are they now?'

'They went back,' he said. 'Against our advice, I might add. They missed their father, grandparents; they missed their school. We kept the room for them for a while, but they said to offer it to someone else – so we did.'

Emmeline felt nervous about this information. She felt as though she and Matthew might be compared to this other family and found wanting.

'Might they want to return now the bombings have started?' Emmeline was still uncomfortable using the word Blitz – *a German word!* – no one else seemed to stutter over it like she did.

'We did ask,' he said. 'They're going to stick it out.'

'What if they change their minds?'

'You're here now!' He gave her another liquid smile.

The kettle whistled. With concentration, he poured the hot water into the teapot, and they sat in companionable silence waiting for the tea to brew. Matthew snored gently.

A woman burst in. 'Look, you must answer these before you go to London—', then she saw Emmeline and stopped herself. 'Hello, you must be our new mother?'

Matthew woke up, lifted his head and stared around him in surprise.

'Yes,' said Emmeline awkwardly before launching into the speech she had been going over in her head on the train. 'I'm Mrs Froud from London and this is Matthew. Nice to meet you. We are grateful.'

The woman was thin, also smartly dressed, and had an air of education or superiority, Emmeline couldn't tell which – or perhaps they were the same.

Her glasses dangled on a string over her flattish chest. She put them on and took them off regularly; she seemed older with them on, younger with them off, although she was probably about the same age as Emmeline. She said, 'Mrs Davenport,' loudly and Emmeline was about to correct her, 'No, I'm Mrs Froud,' when she realised the woman was introducing herself.

She looked down her nose at Emmeline, but she was tall, so that was probably how she looked at everyone. Her dark hair was pulled back into a bun like Mrs Salt's, but, where Mrs Salt had hundreds of tendrils curling around her forehead and cheeks, Mrs Davenport had not a single stray.

'And what do you do?'

'What do I *do*?' What she did had never occurred to her before, but it was clear the woman was expecting something. 'Mrs Saunders was a headmistress,' she thought.

'I look after my children.' For the first time, it felt inadequate or slight.

'Of course. Very good.'

Matthew continued to look puzzled, his mouth wide open. If Emmeline were alone with him, she would have said, 'Shut your mouth or a bus will drive through it.' She tried to wave over it so he would close it, but he pushed her wrist out of the way.

'What did you do before having children, Mrs Froud?' The woman leaned back in her chair.

'Rose,' warned her husband, 'this isn't an inquisition.'

'There has been no security protocol, nothing,' Mrs Davenport said imperiously.

'I doubt Mrs Froud is a Nazi spy,' he said. 'Nor this tiny boy.' He smiled at Matthew. 'You're not, are you?'

Matthew took aim and pretended to shoot him – 'Pow!' – and Emmeline was about to squeal, 'No, Matthew!' but Mr Davenport laughed and then pretended to die gruesomely from a gunshot to the chest. He collapsed on the floor and Matthew jumped down and patted his cheek and he got up, and clasped Matthew round the middle and tickled him.

'If you are here to spy on me, you won't find an awful lot.'

Mrs Davenport still looked annoyed. 'Mrs Froud?' She raised her thin eyebrows expectantly.

'I once worked in a chemist.'

Before she met Neville. After she left school. Ten months of freedom that she had been too stupid to know what to do with.

'A pharmacist?!' Mrs Davenport's interest was finally piqued.

'Not exactly,' said Emmeline. 'I was a sales' – she didn't want to say 'girl' to this woman – 'assistant.'

She'd used a till, stacked the shelves, served mothers with children and dreamed of having children of her own. She had been in such a hurry back then. Always dreaming of a home and family of her own. She had no idea how hard 'domestic bliss' would be for her to achieve, nor that a war would come along and knock everyone off course.

'I see.'

'My husband, Neville, works for the newspapers,' she added brightly. In Romberg Road, where most husbands were blue-collar workers, Neville's office job impressed – or at least, she thought it did.

'Really? A journalist?'

'Finance. Pardon me, but why would you think I would spy on you?'

Mr Davenport laughed again. 'Exactly!'

Mrs Davenport sighed as though she had the entire world on her shoulders and no one to help. 'Because of his job...'

Emmeline's mind whirled. She felt like she was turning over cards in order to find the ace. What job could Mr Davenport possibly do that he would be worth spying on, she wondered? For some reason, she had thought he might be a golfer; there was something about him – was it the tanned complexion? – that suggested he was outside a lot. Was golfer even a job? Unlikely, she thought. Maybe he was a man of the church – or a business owner or a...

Mrs Davenport put her hand on her husband's shoulder. 'Mr Davenport is an MP.'

'An MP?' repeated Emmeline. 'The military police!'

'My dear Mrs Froud,' Mrs Davenport drawled as though Emmeline had said something hilarious, 'he's a Member of Parliament!'

Emmeline tried to think what Neville had told her about Members of Parliament. Mostly that they were warmongers, cheats, cowards, liars and fools. And their wives? Simpering, strident Lady Macbeths, hollow, vacant or bored.

Emmeline had never met a Member of Parliament before. In fact, until today the poshest people she had ever met were

Mrs Lester, the headmistress of Lydia's school, and the bank manager. Oh, and Mrs Howard, Lydia's Somerset host, of course. This evacuation was showing her people she had only known from a distance up close, and, she supposed, vice versa. For all she knew, she was the only working-class woman they'd ever met who didn't work for them.

'I didn't realise...'

'There's no reason you should have,' Mr Davenport said kindly.

'But there is a reason there should be a protocol before they send any Tom, Dick or Harry to stay in our house,' Mrs Davenport said, glaring at her husband.

Emmeline smoothed down Matthew's hair. She understood what Mrs Davenport was getting at. 'We can look for somewhere else.'

'Nonsense,' Mr Davenport responded. He communicated something with his eyes to his wife and then turned to Emmeline and bowed. 'If you're a security threat, I'm the king of Siam. You're welcome here, Matthew and Mrs Froud.'

Once Matthew woke the next morning, Emmeline quickly got him dressed, then swept them out of the house. She felt horribly aware that she was a grown woman creeping around like a criminal, but she didn't want to wake up the Davenports. She didn't want to interfere with their lives, she wanted them to praise her to their friends: 'They're quiet as mice! We don't even know they're here.' She wanted them to say, 'We have a lovely family from London. So stoical, so well-mannered.'

'We're going to explore!' she said, trying to pretend both to herself and Matthew that it was an adventure and not a self-imposed exile. Further from the house, though, it felt like she had taken a deep breath of freedom. She could taste the country wind. Thank goodness, Matthew seemed to have recovered from his sickness. She had apples and crackers left over from the journey and they had a picnic breakfast.

After they had walked some more, they saw an imposing-looking building behind a tall wall. She couldn't work out what it was at first and then she saw signs for hospital. She and Matthew followed some young women walking up a long dirt track. Another hospital, she wondered? None of the women were pushing prams or stooped over toddlers. Some whipped past on bicycles.

'Where are you going?' she asked one girl who had stopped to coo at Matthew's curls.

'The factory.' She had the slow local accent.

'Where?'

'Up there.'

Emmeline couldn't help feeling jealous, and she hated herself for it. Jealous of factory girls. Jealous of bus conductors. Next, she'd be jealous of the scullery maid!

The girl linked arms with a friend and hurried away, apologetic at cutting the conversation short. Some of the other women were singing.

'Mummy, I need a wee.'

Matthew ran in a circle. Emmeline wondered if he was going mad. She turned back the way they'd come, against the crowds of women.

Back in Fincham village, she saw the bus stop where they had arrived yesterday and a few shops that weren't yet open. It was an attractive place, but there wasn't much to write to Lydia or Neville about.

Emmeline was about to set off back to the Old Rectory when she saw a woman on a bench, dwarfed by a large pram. It looked like the same model as Emmeline's. The woman's hair was pulled back, but you could see it was the loveliest colour of buttery toast. Something about her reminded her of Lydia: the tilt of her head, the upturned nose, or the set of her mouth maybe.

Emmeline suspected she was from London too. She was wearing a pea-green coat, which was so different to what people were wearing here. As she grew closer, though, Emmeline realised the woman was crying, and she didn't know what to do. It seemed rude to interrupt a stranger in distress, but on the other hand... She was just girding herself to go over, to offer her a friendly face, when the woman got up and proceeded away at speed, the pram's wheels turning fast.

When Emmeline got back to the house, there was a young woman in the kitchen in an apron and scullery cap. When she saw Emmeline, she squealed. 'There you are!'

This must be Mabel.

'I love babies,' she said, in lieu of introductions, and kissed Matthew and pinched his cheeks. Matthew, who didn't usually let himself be squidged, let Mabel. She had a knack for children, Emmeline saw instantly.

'They were waiting for you,' Mabel said when Matthew could tolerate the squidging no more.

'Who?'

'The Mr and Mrs. They expected you to join them for breakfast, it being your first day.'

Ashamed, Emmeline hurried to apologise. She hoped the Davenports didn't think she was ungrateful. Or a bother.

She found them in the drawing room, calmly reading newspapers. This room was like an office, with the desk as a centre-piece and piles and piles of papers.

'It's quite all right,' Mr Davenport said mildly at her expla-nation. 'We should have told you.' His hair was swept back and his collar open: it felt like more face, more body, was being revealed. It was disconcerting. He was a handsome man and didn't fit what Neville had told her about MPs. She wondered what other things Neville had got wrong.

'I just assumed you'd come down, instead of traipsing around the town,' said Mrs Davenport. Emmeline couldn't tell if she was being told off or not.

She apologised again, but Mrs Davenport merely shrugged as if to say, 'It's your life.'

Over the next few days, Emmeline tried to get used to her new situation. Each morning, she woke up, not knowing where she was; even when she opened her eyes, her brain didn't catch up. When she realised where she was, she felt a mixture of sadness and hope. She looked at Matthew's sleeping face and felt nothing but tenderness, but seeing him, loving him, made her miss Lydia more. Matthew reminded her of Lydia's absence.

It was strange too being in someone else's house, in someone else's kitchen. She believed two women in one kitchen was rarely a good recipe, but fortunately Mrs Davenport was not in the kitchen. Another woman, Mrs Robinson, appeared briefly to make their meals, with Mabel serving up and tidying away. Mrs Robinson was not interested in Emmeline or Matthew – she had fifteen grandchildren of her own – *fifteen!* But Mabel couldn't get enough of Matthew and was always grabbing him for a cuddle, which Emmeline adored her for.

The house was big, but not big enough to disappear in. When they were home, Emmeline felt the presence of the Davenports deeply; she could sense which rooms they were in, their movements, even their moods. Only when they were both out could she relax. The house was full of antiques. Even the bathroom, even the cupboards, must be treated like they were precious artefacts. Emmeline lived in dread of Matthew destroying something. He was not a particularly clumsy child, but like most small children he had scant idea of consequences and could easily stain a table, chip a wall or something without meaning to.

'We're borrowing,' she reminded him frequently. 'Nothing is ours.'

She didn't think he understood, but maybe he did because one of his first phrases was 'must share!'

Neville had been gung-ho about their staying with another family, but he didn't know what it was like to be a constant guest. He didn't know what it was like to be a mother without a home of her own. Emmeline didn't like to complain in her letters, so she told him that she was making the best of it, but she hoped he could read between the lines. Mostly she asked him questions, which in his short letters back he avoided answering.

'We've got ants.'

'Did you take my lighter?'

'Do you remember the old couple from next door who moved to that place in Crescent Road? They died in a bomb attack last night.'

'I bet the royal family will leave London next. Rats and sinking ships come to mind.'

She didn't know which was worse: his practicality or his doom. When she next saw him, she decided, she would ask him to be a bit more loving. Some men managed it – or so she'd heard.

'Will you have a trunk sent up?' asked Mrs Davenport one time when they crossed paths on the stairs.

'I... no. This is it,' Emmeline said, a crimson heat spreading over her face. At home, the Frouds were regarded as one of the more well-to-do families. She hadn't realised that, in the world outside Romberg Road, she might be regarded as impoverished.

'I might have a few old things—'

'No, thank you,' Emmeline said firmly. She didn't know what Mrs Saunders, Alice and Nelly had done, but she wasn't having her host's hand-me-downs. Children, yes, because they were changing size all the time. Not *her* though.

Mrs Davenport pulled her face again, and said, 'If you change your mind...'

Fincham was flooded with women and children seeking refuge from the bombing of the cities, but Emmeline quickly realised that there was not much for any of them to do. Mrs Davenport told her where children liked to play but when they got there they found that the whole area was fenced off. It had been turned into a training ground or artillery range. Other public spaces had been, as in London, turned into vegetable beds, with KEEP OUT signs all over the place. The nearest town was King's Lynn, but it would cost an arm and a leg to get there.

Each day, Emmeline left the house early with the twin aims of getting out of the way of her hosts and tiring Matthew out. Other women walked through the village pushing their prams or holding on to a toddler's sleeve – doing the same as her, she supposed. They all looked like outsiders. It was their grey faces and city-style clothes that marked them out as Londoners, she decided. She hoped to see the sad lady in the pea-green coat again and resolved to talk to her if she ever did.

8

Emmeline

Emmeline and Matthew had been in Norfolk for less than a week when they were invited into the drawing room to listen to Churchill's speech on the wireless. Emmeline felt that she was in the strange position of being neither staff nor member of the family – some kind of hybrid role. The Davenports had initially invited her to join them for dinner, but they ate at irregular times, mostly late, and Emmeline liked to feed Matthew early, so it was with some relief – certainly on Emmeline's part – that it was decided that she should eat with Matthew in the kitchen.

Mr Davenport poured her a sherry. It was her first, but she didn't say that, and she didn't like the taste and she didn't say that either. Another man was there that evening; he was introduced as Mr Reynolds. He was one of those unfortunates who have a five o'clock shadow from midday, which made him look slightly scruffy – which was probably why he overcompensated with his very smart clothes. Even Emmeline could tell that his tailored suits were excellent quality. He shook hands with her and then Matthew, who hid his face behind his fingers and then scratched behind his ears.

Matthew sat on her lap to listen. The prime minister's voice boomed from the wireless, so loud and so clear he might have been with them in the drawing room.

These cruel, wanton, indiscriminate bombings of London are, of course, a part of Hitler's invasion plans... Little does he know the spirit of the British nation, or the tough fibre of the Londoners.

Emmeline felt stirred but also slighted – did she not have the tough fibre? Should she have stayed back in London and done her bit? She thought of Mrs Hardman from downstairs, clip-clipping off to the buses, full of determination to keep London moving. She thought of Mrs Salt 'I'm not letting Mr Hitler get the better of us,' resolving to endure it as best she could. And here she was... a runaway, a nothing, a rare Londoner who was fibre-less. It was one thing to send your child away, it was quite another to send *yourself* away too.

It was as though Mr Davenport understood that; once they had switched off the wireless, he said gently, 'You see – you did the right thing coming here.'

Emmeline gazed back at him, grateful that he had sympathy with her dilemma. 'Thank you,' she whispered. 'I do feel torn...'

'I can imagine—'

Mrs Davenport interrupted: 'Which line did you help with, darling?'

Emmeline looked between them in surprise.

'All of it, I expect,' said Mr Reynolds, clapping his friend on the back.

'I certainly did not!' Mr Davenport laughed. He was a man who laughed easily. 'Churchill already knew everything he wanted to say and he was determined not to deviate from that, no matter what I suggested.'

'I don't believe that,' his wife said, glasses on.

'I told him to mention the hospitals. He didn't,' Mr Davenport said. 'He always knows what he's going to do and does it. He's the greatest orator of our time – any time.'

'I'm sure you had some influence.' Mrs Davenport patted her husband's sleeve, then winked at Mr Reynolds. 'You mustn't understate your role.'

Emmeline bounced Matthew on her knee self-consciously. She hadn't realised the Davenports were that powerful. Mr Davenport knew Churchill? Mr Davenport was *friends* with Churchill?

The new prime minister was that rare thing that she and Neville agreed on: their greatest hope. Their last hope, even... The idea that Mr Davenport was in his inner circle was intimidating. Mr Davenport might even have mentioned her to the great man. She nervously tousled Matthew's hair, then saw something jump in it. She shook her head – *unlikely* – but then saw something leap again. She parted the curls, to find that the hair was riddled with moving dots.

Lice.

Emmeline whipped her hands off her son and put them down by her sides. *Not here!* She couldn't think what to do or say. The night before they came away they had spent it in the shelter. Maisie Salt had been holding Matthew, her plaits in his face, his hair. She would bet he had caught them from her.

It was past Matthew's bedtime, so a good excuse to get away. She bid everyone a good night and hurried off, ignoring their surprised expressions. As she was in the kitchen preparing Matthew's milk, Mr Davenport came in with the empty sherry glasses.

'Everything all right with this little fellow?'

It was embarrassing – first sickness, now lice. What were she and Matthew going to bring to Norfolk next? A plague of locusts?

Matthew was scratching his head with increasing aggression. How had she let it get this far? It was this incredulity that made her say it: 'I'm afraid my Matthew has got lice,' she blurted out. 'I've only just realised.'

'Ah.' He winced. 'What a bother.'

'I'm sorry,' she said. 'My Lydia never got them, so I didn't expect that he would.'

'It happens a lot – so I'm led to believe.' He smiled. 'I'm no expert.'

He had walked towards the drawers of the dresser. Now he took out a pair of scissors.

'Do you want to or shall I?'

Neville would never have assisted. All things to do with the children had been left for her and her alone.

'If you wouldn't mind...'

She held Matthew on her knee and Mr Davenport cut off his baby curls. He was gentle.

'Hold still,' he said, and 'There! You are *such* a sensible chap!'

Matthew cried silently like he was losing part of himself, which maybe he was. His curls were what made Matthew Matthew. With his hair short, he looked big and unwieldly and reminded her of the newly shorn soldiers she had seen on the train. She had been holding herself together all these days since the bombings began, but again, Emmeline wanted to cry. What if Matthew had passed them on to Mr Davenport or Mr Reynolds or –God forbid – *Mrs* Davenport?

The tendrils lay scattered on the floor. Emmeline collected them up with the dustpan and brush. Always better to be busy.

'I think he looks handsome,' Mr Davenport said, even though Matthew really didn't. He must be saying it to be courteous.

'If the politics doesn't work out...' she said. He gazed at her quizzically and she wished she hadn't started. '...You could always... become a barber?'

He threw back his head and roared. He was, thought Emmeline, a most *unusual* man.

Over the next few days, Emmeline learned that Mr Davenport had been the MP for King's Lynn constituency for five years – since 1935. He had stood in the by-election, which was uncontested, after his predecessor, his father-in-law Rupert, had died of heart failure.

And no, he did not play golf.

Mr Reynolds was his electoral agent and he was at the house a lot. He wasn't just concerned about Mr Davenport at election time, he was his support all the time, a right-hand man, a wingman, and a friend of the family. He was serious – roaring with laughter was not for him – and usually deep in conversation with Mr or Mrs Davenport about the local political party.

Mr Davenport had a secretary in his office at the Palace of Westminster, but here they all chipped in: replying to his letters, arranging his Norfolk appointments and meetings with his constituents.

One time when they were talking, a phrase kept coming up: 'This town is safe,' 'That town is not safe,' 'Nowhere in Norfolk is safe...'

'It's not safe?' repeated Emmeline. 'You think the Nazis might come here?'

Since the evening in the kitchen the previous week, she had felt less guarded around Mr Davenport. It was strange how accepting he had been of the lice. She knew Neville would have been disgusted, both by the lice and by her poor parenting.

Mr Davenport smiled at her. 'By "safe" we are referring to votes,' he said. 'And yes, there is a possibility the Nazis might attack– deliberately or accidentally – but Fincham is safer than many places.'

'I don't understand – how can any seat be "safe" vote-wise?' Emmeline asked.

'If it's not safe, it means you can't predict which way they'll go. Voters who chop and change. Voters who don't have much allegiance to any particular party.'

'Isn't that a good thing?' ventured Emmeline. 'It means people vote according to what they think is right rather than tribal allegiances.'

She had been going to add, 'My Neville says,' because she thought that would give more weight to her opinion, but she realised that was probably quite tribal too. Anyway, she didn't know what Neville thought on this matter – he'd never mentioned it. It just seemed to her the way it should be.

'Well said.' Mr Davenport raised his eyebrows at Mr Reynolds. 'There is that...'

Early the next evening, Emmeline was on her way back to the house when the factory girls poured down the track. Still laughing, still linked arms, still singing.

She'll be coming round the mountain when she comes!

Had they been laughing, linked arms and singing like that for the last twelve hours? Again, Emmeline felt suffused with envy. She was a nothing now – not even looking after her own family, while everyone around her was making a contribution.

'He's sweet,' a girl with red hair said, peering into the pram.

'Wish I had a baby, then I wouldn't have to spend all day tying knots,' her friend said.

'Ha! You love it really.' The redhead poked her in the arm.

'What do you actually do?' Emmeline asked. 'In that building up there?' She had been wondering for days.

The girl who wished she had a baby tapped the side of her nose. 'We can't say, can we, girls?' She was delighted to have a secret.

Emmeline laughed along. 'It's like that, is it?'

The girl made more of a fuss of Matthew and then said, 'You could work there too.'

'Really?'

'I don't see why not... you've got hands, haven't you?' She held up her own, waggling her fingers.

'Yes...' Emmeline could have burst with gratitude. What a kind young woman!

'No, she can't,' her friend the redhead said incredulously. 'She's got the babba.'

'Oh, yes!' The girl said, looking crestfallen. 'Sorry! What was I thinking?'

Together, they strutted away.

'Thank you for considering me,' Emmeline called after them, the girl's words 'She's got the babba' were ringing in her ears.

9

OCTOBER 1940

Lydia

By the time Lydia wrote to say that there was a place at Bumble Cottage if they wanted, it was too late. A postcard had come from her mother with a new address. Her mother and brother had been evacuated to Norfolk – wherever that was – so that was that.

Mum said she missed Lydia more than she could put in words. She described the Old Rectory and the town at length, and then mostly it was about Matthew. Lydia liked her brother, but she wished Mummy would write about something else.

Lydia also received a letter from Francine saying don't worry about us, the shelter in the yard is great: 'Safe as houses.' And that she was reading *The Princess and the Pea* and the pictures were funny! Lydia thought this book was too young for Francine, but it was typical: Francine could be quite immature at times and, unlike Lydia, she never cared if people thought so. Francine included drawings, of monsters and mummies (the Egyptian kind) and planes dropping bombs. In a postscript, Francine asked if Lydia ever saw Valerie, and that made Lydia feel guilty, since she hardly thought about their mutual old friend at all and, given she was so nearby, she should have.

It was strange that her mother wasn't in a place where Lydia could picture her. But Lydia was relieved that no one else was coming to live with them. Since Francine had gone back to London, Lydia enjoyed being the only child in Bumble Cottage (Paul still came and went but he was irrelevant). Margaret-Doll was more than enough company. She laughed at the right time, made funny jokes and she knew all the swear words.

In Somerset, Lydia felt like a princess, and, if there were peas, she neither noticed nor cared.

10

Emmeline

It was getting colder. Emmeline wondered how she was going to get through the winter if these meandering, meaningless days continued. Matthew liked being outdoors, but a destination or a purpose was vital. He needed friends and she needed company. She had always thought she was a versatile sort; now she realised that maybe she was actually a city girl rather than a countrywoman.

It was still not safe to go back. Things were worse. Every night, London was being attacked, particularly the docks near where they lived. There was talk of opening up the undergrounds as shelters. Neville wrote, 'They need to do something – this government are a disgrace!'

Sitting on her usual bench at the edge of the shops and overlooking the former park, Emmeline knitted some gloves for Lydia and some tiny mittens for Margaret-Doll. She had already done Matthew's winter bits – when he wore them all at once, he looked like a ball of wool himself.

Matthew was nearly asleep when she turned the pram back

towards the Old Rectory. She had filled another day with fresh air and nonsense, but nevertheless it was done. Three weeks down, no one knew how many more to go. As she tried to sneak towards the stairs, Mr Davenport called her into the drawing room.

'How *are* you?' he asked heartily. It was as though he were looking for something more than the usual 'fine', but Emmeline wasn't sure how honest she should be to her host.

'No more headlice, at least,' she said.

'Glad to hear it!' He grinned. 'I must say – the next day, I felt a little' – he scratched his head – 'itchy!'

She covered her mouth with her hands. 'You didn't?'

'I did! It was all in my mind though.' He lit a cigarette. She watched him blow the smoke out of his mouth. 'Anyway, I was wondering about you, not the lice.'

'To be honest, I feel a little useless,' she admitted.

He hadn't expected that. 'Useless? How?'

'I would like to do something,' Emmeline explained. 'Everyone is helping the war effort except for me.'

She didn't say *exactly* what she thought – which was that she felt like a louse – a parasite living off the efforts of others.

'I often feel like that,' he said.

'*You* do?!' she asked, her voice shrill.

'Absolutely. I spend much of my time dealing with badgers, traffic and other local issues. These are important but I would prefer to be a part of the nitty-gritty...'

'You are though, aren't you?' She recalled the conversation about Churchill's speech.

'Sometimes,' he said lightly. 'And you *are* also doing something, aren't you?' he continued.

Emmeline tried to figure out what he meant.

'The most important job in the world, isn't it?' he said, stubbing out his cigarette.

'What is?'

'Being a mother. Bringing up the next generation?'

Emmeline smiled. 'Yes, in many ways, but...' She loved Matthew and loved looking after him, but she also felt it used only ten or twenty per cent of her skills. What was supposed to happen to the remaining eighty per cent of her? Was it supposed to shrivel up and drop off?

'I suppose I feel I should contribute more...'

As she spoke, Emmeline wondered if Mr Davenport might find something for her to do – a touch of filing perhaps, answering the telephone, or she would be more than happy to help in the kitchen. Yet he didn't get the hint – or, if he did, he didn't say.

Later that evening, Mrs Davenport came to find Emmeline in her room.

'I hear you're feeling bored,' she said, towering over her.

Bored wasn't the word Emmeline would have used, but she felt encouraged, if a little embarrassed. The Davenports had clearly been discussing her and this might mean they had a solution in mind.

Mrs Davenport handed her some papers. One side was blank but on the other there were paragraphs of typewriting.

Emmeline gingerly took them. What were they asking her to do? To help? At last!

'The boy is welcome to do crayoning on this.'

'Oh?'

'They're not confidential,' Mrs Davenport reassured her, although, of all things, this one hadn't occurred to her. 'You could teach him the alphabet. I hope that helps' – she bit her lip – 'kill time.'

She was trying to be kind, Emmeline supposed, but it was a kindness where she got to decide what was wrong and she got to decide a remedy. This sort of kindness was not what Emmeline needed.

The following day, Emmeline was sitting on her usual bench with Matthew, trying to read a newspaper. She felt a sense of obligation to know the worst of what was going on in the world. No one's efforts, no one's sacrifice should go unnoticed, so she pored over the deaths.

I, Emmeline Froud, have noticed you. You were in my thoughts.

The news was increasingly dire – no wonder Neville's letters were so melancholy. There were lists of city streets affected. Names and ages of people buried under rubble. Children lost. Houses burned down. Families made homeless – and they were the lucky ones. Great Britain felt lonely and isolated as a nation, and Emmeline felt lonely and isolated as a mother.

One good thing – the war cabinet had finally decided the underground stations would soon be open as shelters, and the decision was being welcomed by Londoners. Neville would be pleased.

Matthew was picking up leaves. Sometimes Emmeline suspected her son was advanced, and imagined him working in a laboratory, developing the weapon that would end all wars. Other times, she thought he was slow, that he would never get a job and she would have to help him tie up his shoe laces until the day she died.

'That's ambitious.' A voice cut into her thoughts. A woman was pointing at the paper and grinning. She had short brown hair and sharp cheekbones like actresses in films. That was probably the only similarity though, since she had purple eyebags and half her teeth were missing.

'What is?'

'To think you'll be able to read with a little one at your feet—'

Right on cue, Matthew shouted, 'Mummy, I need a wee!'

'In a minute.'

He'd already gone behind the bushes twice.

'What's in the news anyway?' Now Emmeline noticed the pram.

'Blitz continues... Same.'

That was what it felt like now. Waiting for bad news.

'Is this your bench?' the woman continued.

'It's *our* bench,' Emmeline said, budging up so the woman had room to sit, and was rewarded with a toothless smile.

Her name was Mrs Burke – 'Call me Dot' – and Emmeline said, 'Oh, in that case, please call me Emmeline.' She found the immediate use of first names a little too familiar for her liking, but she supposed that was the way things were now. The war was sweeping away the old social frameworks.

Dot had also been evacuated from London, although she'd come in the first wave, which meant she'd been here since last September – over a year now! She liked the family she was staying with, the Ingrams, but, like Emmeline, she struggled to fill her time.

'It's so dull, yet it feels criminal to say that when so much is going on.'

'Doesn't it!' Emmeline exclaimed. Finally, someone understood!

'You just want to do something, don't you?'

'You do!' Emmeline said excitedly. 'I do! We all do!'

'I wish I were fighting.'

Fighting? thought Emmeline. *That's a bit much.*

She couldn't imagine actually fighting. Agitated, she stood up, and walked round the bench. Then she peered into her new friend's pram. To her surprise, there were two children in there.

'Hettie and Pat,' Dot introduced them. One was curled up

asleep with her arm resting on the other. The bigger one lay with her eyes open and a kind of shocked, disapproving expression. They reminded Emmeline of kittens.

'Hettie sleeps all day and Pat sleeps all night – so that's me buggered,' Dot said cheerily.

Matthew rushed over with some bramble he'd found.

'Gosh,' said Emmeline distractedly. She wanted to listen to Dot. Apart from the Davenports, with whom she was always on best behaviour, Dot was the first grown-up she had talked to properly since she'd been transplanted here four weeks previously, and she had a sparkle in her eyes that reminded Emmeline of her old friend, Mrs Salt.

'Life is difficult with three under three.'

'Three?' Emmeline gasped. It might have been rude, but she couldn't help it.

'I'm pregnant. Peter was on leave early summer.' Dot sighed. 'He only has to look at me to get me in the family way.'

Emmeline squinted at her.

'To be fair,' Dot continued, 'he didn't *just* look at me.'

They both laughed.

'Come on then,' Dot said.

'What?'

'Showtime?'

'Huh?'

'Don't tell me you just sit here all day?'

'Not *all* day,' Emmeline corrected her self-consciously. 'Just... most of it.'

Dot shook her head in mock dismay.

'You haven't discovered the Lane Picture House?'

'What's that?'

'It's the best picture house in West Norfolk. Actually, it's the *only* picture house in West Norfolk. But it's less than fifteen minutes from here...'

. . .

The cinema opened every day at midday and Emmeline couldn't believe she'd never noticed it before. It offered a skeleton service, the manager explained, there were no usherettes to show you to your place, no ice creams or marsh-mallows. Any problems – Emmeline agreed there wouldn't be – and they were to find him upstairs, running the projector.

The audience was mostly women with children, and a few old men in mackintoshes. Today the film was *Rebecca*. Emme-line found it hard to concentrate; she felt this conflict – a tug of war – between the Emmeline who wanted to watch the film and the mother who needed to tend to Matthew's needs. At first she covered Matthew's eyes at the kissing parts and the fighting parts, but soon she stopped bothering. Matthew wasn't inter-ested. He preferred to nap or play with paper fans or pretend he was shooting the people in the row in front. The film was nearly at its end when Matthew decided he needed a wee.

'Wait five minutes,' Emmeline said, smoothing his short hair. It was still hard to get used to.

'Need now.'

Emmeline remembered how impatient she had been for her babies to speak, until she realised it would only mean their commands and demands became stronger. She missed the end of *Rebecca* and she still felt vaguely useless, but it was wonderful to have a new friend *and* a place to go with her.

'Same time tomorrow?' Dot said afterwards as they came out, blinking, into the blue-sky day.

'Absolutely!'

11

Emmeline

It was through Dot that Emmeline met Marjorie – the crying lady in the pea-green coat. When they were introduced, Emmeline was going to say something about seeing her before, but thought it might embarrass her. Emmeline would be mortified if she were caught sobbing in the street.

Marjorie was only nineteen. She was closer to Lydia's age than to her own, Emmeline realised, and this seemed incredible. The poor girl. She had three babies and their names were Della, Deidre and Derek.

Was it twee to have them all have the same initial, Emmeline wondered? Why did parents do that? Emmeline prided herself on Lydia and Matthew's names which she considered both modern yet slightly different. She didn't like the thought of there being another child in their school called Lydia or Matthew. She loved the 'y' in Lydia and hated it when people (Neville!) called her Lyds as though she were part of a saucepan set.

Marjorie was originally from Whitechapel, only five or six

streets along from Emmeline. Marjorie's husband had died at
Dunkirk. She knitted as she talked, and the needles clacked as
though applauding everything she said. Poor fella. He had only
been twenty-one as well. He'd been evacuating on the beach
that fateful day when an aircraft fired on him. She'd been told
he was very brave.

'I'd rather he was less brave and more alive.' She shrugged.

'He served his country,' Emmeline reminded her. 'That's
special.'

'I told him not to,' Marjorie said flatly.

Emmeline couldn't think of anything else to say. With her
Neville, one of the few men of conscription age still at home,
perhaps it wasn't her place to say anything.

'But the family you stay with are kind,' Dot piped up. 'The
Hazells are lovely people. They're just up the road in
Shouldham.'

Marjorie nodded mournfully.

'That's good!' Emmeline said. She wondered if she would
describe the Davenports as kind. Maybe, but not warm –
although when she thought of Mr Davenport roaring with
laughter over one of her silly jokes, she did feel heat in her
cheeks.

'You've got your hands full,' she said to Marjorie, who
agreed dolefully.

'I can't even walk down the street without someone telling
me that.'

Emmeline tried again. She was used to dealing with bleak
people – Mrs Salt had the blackest humour– and she liked the
feeling you got when they finally cracked a smile.

'I love your coat,' she said, and this time Marjorie met her
eyes.

'I saved up for it – it's lasted six years already.'

'And you're brilliant at knitting!' Emmeline added. And

Marjorie's faint smile grew stronger, and the needles clacked louder.

'You don't really mean it!'

'I do!' insisted Emmeline.

Marjorie knitted scarves, gloves, socks, all for the war effort.

'It's the only thing I'm good at,' she said, giving Emmeline an appreciative look.

'One thing is better than nothing!' Emmeline said.

The next day another woman joined them – Dot knew everyone! Emmeline was pleased. From her experience of Lydia, Francine and Valerie, she considered four a better number than three when it came to friendships.

The new woman was Christine and she used to be a nurse. Dot said bitchily that she worked that into any conversation, but Christine took the ribbing affably, and anyway Emmeline couldn't blame her for talking about it. Being a nurse was amazing. Christine's daughter was called Anna (a name Emmeline approved of). Anna was four, older than Matthew, and sadly she didn't seem interested in him at all. Emmeline suddenly missed Valerie, who would always lie down with the smaller children and tell them a story. Lydia would if she felt like it, but Valerie would help even when she didn't.

'How are the family you stay with, Christine?'

Christine muttered something about upstanding people before pointing at Matthew.

'What happened to his hair?'

'Nothing, I just prefer it short,' lied Emmeline, since they'd only just met and, while Dot didn't judge, she had a feeling this Christine might.

'Nits then?' Christine said bluntly, which made everyone laugh.

Christine's Anna didn't have nits but she did have bed bugs while Dot's two were prone to worms.

'Ooh,' said Emmeline, thankful that at least Lydia and Matthew hadn't succumbed to those.

Clack-clacking away with her knitting needles, Marjorie said dolefully that hers got all three.

'Not all at the same time?' Emmeline asked when they'd stopped laughing.

'Sometimes,' Marjorie said. It was good to see that smile again.

Dot preferred magazines to newspapers, and she especially liked the five-minute romances. 'That's how long my Pete does romance for!' she said, and grinned.

She read them the headlines as the women rolled the prams back and forth and did their best to stop the children from crying.

'A casualty of the war – long-term relationships.'

'Maybe it will *improve* relationships,' mused Emmeline, thinking of Neville and his cups of tea. He was good at hand-holding. It was other husbandly things he was less keen on.

'How?' Dot wanted to know.

'Maybe absence makes the heart grow fonder?'

'Do you miss your Neville?' Dot asked. She was terribly direct.

'A bit,' Emmeline said although it wasn't really true. She missed Lydia so much, it felt like she didn't have much left to miss Neville. Plus, he was a grown-up, perfectly capable of looking after himself, whereas Lydia was just a child.

'If Americans come, there will be a lot of marriage "casualties", I swear,' Dot continued.

'Why would that be?' Emmeline asked, picking at the scarf she was knitting. She could never knit a straight line.

'Have you met any Americans?' said Dot, swooning.

'Have *you?*' Emmeline responded.

'Hundreds. Girls, you're in for a treat!'

And then everyone traipsed to the Lane Picture House because it was growing chilly and they had the whole afternoon to get through as well. They were watching *The Philadelphia Story* when a bird flew across the auditorium, just below the ceiling. It must have swooped in while the doors were open. Now it panicked and flapped in front of the screen. The children panicked too. The older ones flipped off their seats and chased it, shrieking.

The manager switched off the film, then came into the auditorium, shouting at the poor out-of-place bird. He was even muttering about shotguns as they all filed out. Emmeline hoped the bird would find an exit too but mostly she wondered what on earth they would do in the afternoons if they didn't have the cinema.

12

Lydia

Mrs Howard had volunteer groups round most days and, if they were still there after school, Lydia had to come in and talk with them. Mrs Howard said it was 'practising the social niceties'. The ladies were sweet to Lydia and said lovely things, whether she was in the room or hiding behind the door to listen. Sometimes Mrs Howard went elsewhere to do her work, packing, buying or selling things for the war effort, planning raffles or tombolas or the putting on of a play, and on those occasions she would come home with a small treat the ladies had sent– a jam tart was especially appreciated, a cheese scone less so.

Lydia had gone from a child indifferent to animals to being mad about them. She named every horse, every sheep she saw. She ran out of names and had to call them George 1, 2 and 3. If anyone suggested she couldn't tell them apart, she would get annoyed. Of course she could! If she saw a rabbit squashed by the road – and this happened plenty – she was inconsolable. She was certain she and Rex understood each other and would often tell Mrs Howard or her friends Rex's views on a thing.

'Rex hates the colour pink.' Or 'Rex thinks "How Much Is That Doggy in the Window?" is a terrible song.'

Lydia also enjoyed being the only evacuee in St Boniface school. It was pleasing to be her own person rather than one half of a whole, which was how she and Francine had been seen. She was no longer 'one of the girls from London' but 'Lydia, the pretty one'. Much as Lydia loved Francine, it was heavenly not to have to look after her. It was not that Francine held her back, more that Lydia had been obliged to hold herself back for her.

She was invited to play at the houses of some of the girls after school. Like Bumble Cottage, Flora and Betsy's drawing rooms were full of oriental rugs and sideboards worth polishing and cabinets that needed tiny fiddly keys and oil paintings of a grandfather and 'that's our second cousin, Lord such-and-such'.

Betsy's grandparents had a castle in Scotland. 'It's not exactly a castle' – Betsy squirmed apologetically – 'more a manor house?'

Flora's parents asked what part of London Lydia was from, and she said, 'Romberg Road.' They didn't know it, so then she said, 'Near St Paul's Cathedral,' and Flora's mother said, 'Potty married there!' *They had a friend called Potty?*

Betsy's mother knew the king and his wife. 'Wonderful people, lovely family.'

Racking her brains for something equally impressive, Lydia said, 'My friend's mummy is a bus conductor.'

'Fascinating!' Betsy's mother said in a strangled voice.

Betsy's father was at war. Lydia said what her father always said – 'War makes heroes of some' – but everyone expected her to finish the sentence and she didn't know how it ended, so instead she excused herself and went to the lav.

Despite the shortages that were now ravaging the country, Betsy and Flora had an endless supply of new clothes and shoes, but they were used to that so it wasn't exciting for them.

Even though her mother had instructed her not to ask for things, Lydia did, and Mrs Howard never shuddered or looked panicked like they did at home, but said, 'Certainly.' Sometimes she came back with two or three of the desired items, 'so that you have enough,' she would say.

'Are you happy here?' Mrs Howard said regularly, checking on her. Lydia would nod and make Margaret-Doll nod too, for emphasis. She would make Rex nod too, but he was often asleep in front of the fire, one paw slung protectively over the other.

One day, after she'd been for another visit at Betsy's, she gave a different response:

'I would like a house like this when I grow up.'

'Ly-di-a,' Mrs Howard began. She was obviously trying to pick her words carefully, like picking out raisins from a bun. 'If you work very hard, I don't see why not.'

This didn't make sense to Lydia. Neither Betsy's mother nor Flora's mother had jobs. And although Mrs Howard was always busy, it was mostly for the war effort, not a job as such. It seemed like for someone like Lydia working hard was essential, whereas for someone like Mrs Howard, or Betsy and Flora's mothers, beautiful homes and leisurely lives just dropped like manna from heaven.

It felt like everyone Lydia met nowadays was wealthy. She couldn't *not* notice it. Mrs Howard put on a play and, at the theatre, the cars pulled up and deposited wealthy people on to the pavement. *Paved with gold*, Lydia thought to herself. Dick Whittington might have done well to stay back home. One of them was the director's car. It was sleek and black and shiny, and had a little silver lady on the front bonnet. The director asked her if she wanted to go for a spin round the block. Spin meant ride, Lydia deduced. She hadn't been in any kind of car before, never mind one as beautiful as this. Francine was the car-crazy one of the three of them, and for once she was sorry Francine wasn't there to enjoy it.

It smelled of leather and polished wood and everything expensive. She was no longer just a princess; as soon as she was in the passenger seat, Lydia felt like a queen. She asked if she might wind the car window down.

'Are you too hot?' he asked, and she said she was, even though it was more that she wanted to wave to the poor people who were walking and to make sure that everyone saw her, *going for a spin.* 'Go ahead,' he said.

'I want one of these when I'm older,' she said.

She thought he'd say something about working hard as well – Mrs Howard was relentless about education – but he just smirked, taking his finger off the steering wheel and pointing it at her face. 'You're pretty enough,' he said.

Lydia didn't know what this meant, but she knew it meant *something.*

13

Emmeline

Spending time with the other mothers was transformative for Emmeline. They didn't just change her day – they made it. How different a place looks when you've got friends! The routine helped, too.

In the mornings, the mothers sat outside and read newspapers or magazines and worried about the war – at least, Emmeline did; the others were more fatalistic. In the afternoons, there were the films despite occasional bird-interruptions. Dot especially loved the cinema and could jabber about the stories for hours although Emmeline found it hard to quell the feeling that she should be doing something more constructive.

After the film, they'd go back to their usual bench. While the others chatted, Emmeline fussed over the children. And that was when Marjorie usually joined them, late.

'I can't get them out the house any quicker,' she complained. 'One always starts crying or needs their nappy changed or needs a drink.'

'I can come and get you,' offered Emmeline. Poor Marjorie's

woes reminded her that her life wasn't so bad after all. But Marjorie said it was all right.

Anna went off looking for bugs to squash and Hettie, Pat and Matthew threw leaves at each other, so Emmeline was left with Marjorie's Three D's, as she secretly called them. She knew they drove Marjorie to distraction, but they were lovely, curious children. She cuddled Della and did nursery rhymes with Derek – his favourite was 'Three Blind Mice' – and chased after Deidre, who, much to Marjorie's chagrin, had learned to walk at only eight months old.

'What did you do before you had them?' Emmeline asked Marjorie.

'Nothing.'

'What did you *like* doing?'

Marjorie gestured her knitting. 'Always loved making things. Mum said I could have been a dressmaker.'

Della winced away from the sun. She was the sweetest baby with her flushed cheeks.

'She's crying again,' Marjorie grumbled, but Emmeline rocked her, thinking she really didn't cry as often as some.

Derek and Matthew were racing around and neither spoke much. She sometimes worried that Matthew was slow, but was Derek too? Deidre, the big girl, shook at loud noises and wet the bed. Now she too rested against Emmeline.

Marjorie thanked her and added, 'I just don't have the energy for anything.'

'It's different when they're your own,' Emmeline said. 'Other people's children are interesting.'

The women talked about the families they were living with. Christine's family thought the war was God's will, which made for some awkward exchanges. Marjorie's family, the Hazells, were very patriotic. Dot's had a spare room and the authorities had told them they had to have evacuees whether they liked it or not.

'They don't mind,' she said. 'But they wouldn't have chosen it.' She eyed Emmeline. 'I bet I know why the Davenports wanted you there.'

'Why?' Emmeline thought suddenly of Mr Davenport's expression as he inhaled on his cigarette.

'It looks good, don't it? It's all about reputation with posh people like that.'

'They're not interested in how it looks,' scoffed Emmeline, but Dot grinned at her knowingly.

Emmeline's new friends were surprised to find out that she had another child, which made for an awkward conversation.

'Why didn't you go to hers?' asked Christine, eyes narrowed.

'Because a place came up here,' Emmeline said uncertainly. Everything had happened so quickly – the bombing, Neville's haste, the council woman's insistence – she still wasn't entirely sure how she had ended up in Norfolk and not Somerset. Christine's question hurt too – it wasn't an accusation of bad parenting, at least, she hoped it wasn't, but it made her feel guilty nevertheless. She doubted she would ever not feel tortured about the separation from Lydia – it felt like a terrible price to pay to keep her safe.

'It must be awful,' they chorused.

'What's your girl like?' Marjorie asked shyly.

Emmeline considered this, smiling. Her darling girl. Lydia's letters were the highlight of her life. She was full of funny tales, all told in her sweet handwriting. Emmeline could imagine her racing around the garden with the dog, or tongue stuck out as she wrote her letters. Emmeline could talk about her daughter's hobbies: playing with Margaret-Doll, her favourite foods – nothing – what she liked best at school – break time – but it was difficult to describe Lydia's essence now they had been separated for so long. Was she still as bold and funny and forthright as she used to be? Emmeline felt awful that she couldn't be certain who her daughter was now, not really.

'She's pretty.'

'Of course she is – just like you,' said Dot encouragingly.

'And cheeky.' That was the wrong word, but Emmeline couldn't think of the right one. 'She is changing all the time,' she added.

'You must be worried about her?'

'Worried sick,' said Emmeline, although the truth was, those first six months without Lydia she had cried most days, but now, over a year later, she realised her daughter was not only safer in Somerset than she was elsewhere, but she was probably *happier* in Somerset than she ever had been in London. She worried about her relationship with her daughter but not her daughter's well-being. It was a bitter pill to swallow, but it was true. The evacuation had been a leap of faith and Emmeline was fairly sure Lydia had landed well, and that made it easier to bear.

After the group had found out about Lydia, Emmeline became the one who, in their minds, knew all the answers and had experienced everything. She did her best to be encouraging, yet she didn't really know more about bringing up children than any of them. Children were all different, there was no one answer to their problems. And she was no oracle – it seemed to her that the more she learned, the less certain she was about anything too.

One evening, Mr Reynolds asked Emmeline into the drawing room.

'You don't mind being photographed, do you, Mrs Freud?'

'Froud.'

'Sorry, Mrs Fraud.'

Emmeline felt that to correct him twice was a step too far. 'What is it for?'

But Mr Reynolds was already rushing towards the telephone in the hall, shouting. 'Lawrence, Rose, we're in business. She said yes!'

The newspaper put them on page three. There was a photograph of Mr and Mrs Davenport on the sofa, Emmeline with Matthew on her lap in the armchair and everyone looking deadly serious: 'Victorian family arrangement,' Mr Reynolds called it. Matthew had had one of his nosebleeds earlier that day and mostly Emmeline was nervous that he might bleed over the soft furnishings.

The headline was: *Everyone needs to do their bit.*

The article said:

Lawrence Davenport, MP for King's Lynn, has not shirked his domestic responsibilities. 'Caring for evacuees is a national service.

'The people in the cities are our brave hope for the future – we want to tell those who are staying and guarding our capital, "Your wives, your children are safe with us".'

When Dot saw it, she just shook her head knowingly. 'Told you!'

'It's not like that,' insisted Emmeline, although this time she did wonder...

14

NOVEMBER 1940

Emmeline

The women had just been to see *The Thief of Baghdad* and were sitting on their usual bench. Whereas the other mothers thought nothing of spending hours staring at the screen, Emmeline struggled to enjoy it now. If at first it had seemed a harmless solution to the boredom, now it felt like a setback.

Nearby, some elderly men were trying to dig vegetable beds. It all seemed depressingly too little, too late, Emmeline thought. The Atlantic convoys were getting blasted into smithereens. She wouldn't let herself think about the young men in the merchant navy. There was huge worry that the country wouldn't be able to keep feeding itself. Neville was beside himself. She wished she could just read the weekly magazines like Dot and Marjorie instead of having this ridiculous urge to inject horrible war stories into her veins. It never made her happy.

She was lost in her own thoughts when Marjorie asked, 'Do you think we could take care of each other's little ones one day?'

'If you need a break, Marjorie,' Dot said, 'Let me have them for you.'

Good grief, Dot was heavier every time Emmeline turned around. Emmeline remembered those months when your body was no longer your own but all in subservience to the growing baby. Dot walked with a waddle now. And Hettie and Pat were a handful too – Hettie in particular. Emmeline wondered if Hettie was always like this or if she was anxious about the new arrival, or missing her dad. (Dot said she was always like it.)

'I couldn't put that on you!' said Marjorie, staring at her bitten nails.

Christine, who helped out her host family a lot, apologised but said she couldn't commit to anything.

Which left Emmeline.

She mumbled something vague, 'I'd be happy to, but...'

She couldn't *possibly* bring more children to the Davenports' house. She and Matthew had been there six weeks now, and she felt like they were overstaying their welcome. On first impressions she had thought the Davenports were close, a happy couple, but now it seemed she was mistaken even in that. They were rarely in the same room, and she had seen one walk out of a room upon realising the other was there. It wasn't just Neville whose public face was different from the private reality. Matthew was already confined enough as it was. 'Don't touch this. Take your hands off that!' It was like living in a museum. The thought of entertaining Marjorie's three children there, adorable as they were, was laughable.

'If only there was a place I could leave them. Just for an hour or two,' Marjorie continued.

For goodness' sake, Marjorie, Emmeline thought. *We're ALL struggling here.*

'That's what mothers-in-law are for,' said Dot dryly. She didn't get on with hers, and the women were often regaled with tales of how old Mrs Burke was a berk who refused to pick up the girls, and how nappy-changing or bottle-giving was completely beyond her.

'They'll be at school soon,' Emmeline offered.

'Two years, ten months for Hettie, three years and ten months for Pat,' said Dot. 'Not that I'm counting.'

'I don't think I can last that long,' Marjorie said under her breath.

Emmeline was going to say something else but they were interrupted by Hettie, who had scraped her knee again, and who reported that Matthew was trying to climb a tree and Anna was eating berries and… Emmeline thought Hettie was a tittle-tattle, but then remembered fondly that Lydia could be like that, too.

Oh, lovely Lydia, she thought. Emmeline had stopped thinking she and Matthew should be in Somerset and instead, started thinking that Lydia should be in Norfolk with her, not miles away with some strange woman who, according to Lydia's letters, quoted Shakespeare at her night and day. How long would they be parted for?

Although Emmeline was anxious that Mrs Howard would become a replacement mother, Lydia seemed remarkably unsentimental about her host. But still, ever since that conversation with the other ladies, Emmeline had lost confidence in her bond with her daughter, and feared the precious yet fragile threads she and Lydia had wasn't going to withstand many more years of separation.

Those were the things she worried about, not getting an hour or two away from the children.

The following morning, just as Emmeline was getting ready to take Matthew out, there was a loud rapping on the front door. Mrs Davenport reached it first, but Emmeline was only seconds after her. There was a man on the front step who Emmeline didn't recognise.

Mrs Davenport gave Emmeline a severe look, as though she personally had summoned him to call at this ungodly hour.

'Mr Hazell,' she said frostily. And Emmeline realised she knew the name. 'To what do we owe the pleasure?'

Mr Hazell twisted his cap between gnarly hands. 'Excuse me, Mrs Davenport. Mrs Froud, I know you and Marjorie are friends... I just wondered if she was here.' It was the man of the house where Marjorie was staying. Apparently, Marjorie had told the family she was going to post a letter late last night, but hadn't been back since. The children were with his wife. Mr Hazell was trying to find her.

'Are there other friends?' Mrs Davenport asked Mr Hazell, 'Don't the London girls' – *girls*? They were the same age as her – 'spend a great deal of time at the Lane Picture House? Is it possible she could have fallen asleep there?'

'That's an idea,' Mr Hazell said, but you could tell he didn't think so.

'All this beautiful countryside and they like to lock up themselves and their children with all the germs.'

Emmeline flushed, but didn't say anything.

'Absolutely, Mrs Davenport,' he said deferentially, but his face was pained as he thanked them and left.

'I'm sure it's nothing,' said Mrs Davenport to Emmeline as she turned back upstairs.

Emmeline put Matthew in the pram, grabbed her coat and hurried out after Mr Hazell, who was standing in the road, deliberating.

'Do you think she's gone to London?' she asked.

'And left the kids with us? Doubtful,' he replied.

Emmeline wondered aloud if Marjorie might be at Dot's, but Mr Hazell said of course, he'd already checked there. She had heard he was a lovely man but right now, he was grim-faced, unfriendly and using his walking stick to bash on the bushes.

'Where do you think she's gone then?' she persisted.

'She's been down lately,' he said. 'I don't know what she'll do...'

Emmeline gulped and said she'd go to check in the park. She told him about their usual bench, but he didn't seem to be listening.

She left him but his panic stayed with her. She felt a sizzling feeling of fear, as she marched through the streets, to the usual bench and then through the park. Other people appeared to be searching too.

'Marjorie?'

Someone thought she was shouting for a dog: 'I saw a Jack Russell running in that direction,' they said.

She thought of Deidre wetting her knickers, Derek wanting 'Three Blind Mice': *See how they run.* Della crying for her mummy.

Come on, Marjorie. You've had your fun, time to get back to your family.

Emmeline went into the more wooded area beyond the park. She walked faster as she grew more concerned. Sensing she was not to be trifled with, Matthew was quiet too. Each time she called out 'Marjorie!', she was surprised how desperate her voice sounded. The other people were calling out for Marjorie now as well, and she saw Mr Hazell in the distance, still whacking bushes with his stick.

And then she saw something and the fear caught light.

Marjorie's pretty pea-green coat, only six winters old. Emmeline nearly cried out in excitement, but the excitement quickly turned to fear. She hurried into where the trees were at their most clustered, towards the other green, like a camouflage. The pram jiggled up and down and Matthew laughed. And there she was, her friend, lying on her side on the ground, among the leaves.

'Marjorie. What did you do?'

She was breathing, but unconscious. Emmeline knelt by her, stroked her hair, murmuring, 'I'm here, Marjorie,' between shouts for help. How childlike Marjorie looked now, her long lashes resting on her cheek, her hair stuck to her face, one arm under her, the other stretched out as though reaching for something.

And next to her there was a bottle of alcohol, empty, and then Emmeline saw a folded piece of paper. Hands trembling, she unfolded it. There weren't many words.

I can't do it any more, sorry.

'Marjorie. MARJORIE!' she shouted at her, then: 'She's here!' she called again. 'Please hurry!'

It didn't sound like her voice. There were other seekers nearby, but they didn't seem to have heard her yet.

'Here, someone, anyone...'

She tried to shake Marjorie awake. *Please, Marjorie.* She was hot and cold and upside down and everything was slip-sliding out of her control.

Finally, someone called back. People were on their way.

'Help is coming.' She raised Marjorie's head, but her friend just flopped back in the long grass.

15

Emmeline

Emmeline wanted to go in the ambulance, but it was too chaotic
and she had Matthew to worry about as well. Mr Hazell and
maybe one of the other seekers went though. Marjorie hadn't
woken, even as they loaded her up. Please God she would – she
had to. Someone she didn't know sidled up to Emmeline and
said, 'Thank goodness it wasn't too cold last night, or she might
have frozen to death.'

Emmeline was too overwhelmed to speak. She didn't think
there was much to thank goodness about. The ambulance man
had told her that Marjorie had taken an overdose of some kind
and was extremely poorly.

And then Dot, white as a sheet, and her children appeared
and she and Emmeline looked for a café to sit in and have some
hot tea, but there wasn't one open. They spent a while on their
bench, but neither could find anything to say. Dot felt terrible
and Emmeline didn't want to upset her any more, not in her
condition, so she told her to go home to bed.

Emmeline took herself, Hettie, Pat and Matthew back to

the Davenports'. She used the back door, to avoid scrutiny. She
fed the children in the kitchen and then ate some toast herself,
surprised how hungry she was. She was relieved that the
Davenports were out. Mabel must have heard something was
amiss because when she arrived, she took the children straight
off to shell some peas.

Emmeline couldn't help reliving the moment she had
spotted Marjorie among the trees and then the moment,
seconds later, when she realised something was badly wrong. It
was like something from a film. She couldn't help wondering if
she should have done something differently. But what?

Later, she took the girls back to Dot's. Both were subdued.
Dot looked even more drained than before, if possible. Emme-
line, always alert to the possibility of disaster in pregnancy, said,
'You don't think you should get checked at the hospital?' But
Dot insisted she was fine.

Back at home, Emmeline got into bed. She was still shivering; shock rather than cold, she supposed. Matthew crawled in
beside her and she patted him – and herself – to sleep. She kept
waking to that vision of poor Marjorie on the ground. An overdose of tablets? What on earth was going through her head?
And her children – what about them?

The Hazell family were distressed the next morning, as
Emmeline had anticipated. She had brought apples and pears
for them from the village shop. Marjorie's three children were
sitting in the living room amid a mess of boxes. They didn't even
look up when she arrived. Mr Hazell was sixty, Mrs Hazell was
fifty-eight. While Emmeline had heard only good things about
them, it was clear they hadn't signed up for this. Emmeline
looked at her hands rather than look at them. She felt partly to
blame. She should have taken Marjorie's exhaustion more seriously. Marjorie was such an inexperienced young woman,

plucked from all that was familiar and dumped in the middle of nowhere, with three tiny, demanding shadows. While some women could cope, not everyone could.

'It's too much,' Mrs Hazell said tearfully. Emmeline helped her feed the children and then washed up after them. The children seemed to be behaving as normal, but you never knew.

'I'll try to organise something,' Emmeline promised.

'Thank you,' Mrs Hazell said.

'It's too late for that,' said Mr Hazell.

'Not at all!' Emmeline reassured her. 'Me, Dot and Christine – we'll all chip in.'

Perhaps they could come here, she thought. She would happily keep an eye on the children – she just needed a place to do it.

'It's all decided,' Mr Hazell interrupted her thoughts, rubbing his chin. 'The council said she'll go in an institution. They're taking the children today – they'll go into care.'

Emmeline's heart sank. In the other room, she could see the children holding on to their blankets. Della was sucking her thumb.

'Is there no al...?'

He wrung his hands apologetically. 'We can't. And they said that's for the best.'

Oh, Marjorie!

16

NOVEMBER 1940

Lydia

There was a new class at school called 'etiquette including elocution'.

No one could work out what it was. Electrician? Execution? But then Winnie Coates-Black, whose father was a viscount, said with authority that, 'It will be about being a good girl, being the sort of girl nice boys want to marry.'

Mrs Howard had cleared her throat at the 'Lydia does not join in enough' comment in her school report and Lydia was already in trouble for not signing up to netball, singing, drama or hockey but this was a class that Lydia actually liked the sound of, so she put her name down.

The etiquette teacher might be a German, the buzz went around the school. There was talk of boycotting the class, sabotaging the lessons. Further reason to go and have a look, thought Lydia. The class was held in the library. Lydia arrived too late to get her and Margaret-Doll the favourite window seat but in time to catch her first glimpse of her new teacher, Miss Picard, explaining that she was not German.

'She would say that, wouldn't she?' hissed Winnie Coates-Black

'I'm Swiss!' Miss Picard continued firmly.

'Like the cheese with holes in it?'

'Like the cuckoo clock,' Betsy said, making cuckoo signs with her fingers.

'Like someone from Switzerland,' Miss Picard shrugged. 'And I have enough of this –one more word and you're out.'

Only eight girls had signed up and Miss Picard took an interest in Lydia right from the start.

'Pretty as a picture,' she said as they filed out on the first day, and Lydia noted – how could she fail to note it? – that she didn't say the same to anyone else. Miss Picard herself was far prettier than a picture – far prettier than anyone at St Boniface – she was dark-haired with cherry-red lips and white skin, and it wasn't that she *wore* her skirt suit, it was more like she had been poured into it.

'She has a great body... for a German,' the girls agreed after the class. It was like a kidney bean. Up until Miss Picard, Lydia had had no awareness of bodies being good or bad; they just were. Now she understood there was a hierarchy and Miss Picard's body stood at the apex.

Margaret-Doll had endured infinite train rides, being shot like a gun, hide-and-seek games, swimming in puddles and riding dogs. But she had weathered all of it and Lydia loved her for it.

In the second 'etiquette lesson', though, Miss Picard said it was unedifying for a young lady over the age of eight to play with dolls. Although she didn't know what unedifying was, Lydia realised with a burst of clarity that Margaret-Doll's days as her constant companion had come to an end.

'Time to put away childish things,' Miss Picard added to ensure that her point was understood.

Lydia and Betsy looked at each other. Lydia knew that at home Betsy was never without Fogel, a scruffy, worried-eyed teddy bear that used to be her grandmother's. Betsy pulled a yikes-face.

Straight after the lesson, Lydia squashed Margaret-Doll into the wastepaper basket under the teacher's desk and covered her with scrap paper. It was hard walking home without her, but she did it. Firsts were rarely easy, she knew that. If she wanted to be 'edifying', whatever that was, she had to do it.

In bed, she thought of Margaret-Doll crying in the classroom, and she put the pillow over her head to stop the noise. She could manage without her in the day, it was just when everything was dark, her absence made her heart ache.

Two days later, the school's elderly caretaker limped over to Lydia, smiling his toothless smile.

'Miss Lydia!' he called as she backed away. 'Didn't you know you lost something?'

'No...'

He thrust Margaret-Doll into her arms.

He was watching her expectantly, so she scolded Margaret-Doll. 'There you are! You naughty girl, you mustn't get lost again. Thank you!'

She took Margaret-Doll home, and this time she buried her in the back garden of Bumble Cottage, deep enough so that neither Rex nor hungry foxes would uncover her. She cried a little as she covered that hard face and soft body in mud, but she knew she had to be a grown-up now and, if this was what it took, this was what she'd do. She didn't ask Betsy what happened with Fogle, but when she next went round he was not at his usual place tucked under the sheets, little worried face on the pillow.

. . .

'Girls, good posture is at the heart of everything,' Miss Picard explained in the next lesson.

The heart of everything, Lydia faithfully copied down in her smudgy book.

'Health, wisdom, beauty...' Miss Picard paused, lowered her voice. 'Sex appeal!'

'Ooh la-la!' chorused the girls.

When Lydia got home, she asked if she could go into the library and Mrs Howard looked up delightedly as if to say, *at last*.

Mrs Howard often quoted from plays, which to Lydia's ears made her sound quite unhinged. She was always talking about reading opening your mind, books being the gateway to different universes and education – not posture – being the most important thing. She often came chasing after Lydia with a book she ought to read and then a few days later would ask, 'How are you getting on, Lydia?' and Lydia would have to admit she hadn't made any progress. 'Not even the first chapter?'

Not even the first line.

Then Mrs Howard might blink or say things like, 'I do think it will be beneficial,' or 'You can take a horse to water but you can't make it drink.'

'Would you like a recommendation?' she said now, enthusiastically, following Lydia into the room.

'I need to practise my walking, so it has to be heavy but not too heavy.'

'I see,' said Mrs Howard in a clipped voice, retreating.

Lydia chose three thick books and went around the house, back straight, head up. Rex begged for attention, but she ignored him.

Think about walking across the ballroom for your first dance! urged Miss Picard in her mind.

This was a great thought.

Think about your presentation to the king.

This was a thought that had never occurred to her before.

Think about walking down the aisle to your future husband!

Now this, Lydia was more practised at. Back in London, she had invented a game: 'I'm getting married in the morning!' It involved her as the bride and any willing boys as the groom. Two days before the evacuation, she had married Leonard, and had been annoyed when he announced he was evacuating not with the school but with his family. But this was child's play; what Miss Picard offered was adult, tangible and real. Lydia could see her future possibilities and she liked them.

They still did the strange walking, even after the pronunciation classes began. Miss Picard had a weird accent, but she knew everything about how to say words.

'After me, everyone: "The rain in Spain stays mainly in the plain".'

That seemed unfair, thought Lydia, although she was also secretly glad that she wasn't one of the plain girls who got rained on.

'How now brown cow.'

Lydia exaggerated it to the point of mockery, but far from annoying Miss Picard, she was held up as one of the best.

The teacher tapped the desk. 'You are my protégée, chérie,' she said, her eyes fixed on her like Rex's when he was after crusts. 'The poor leettle girl from the city...'

17

Emmeline

All Emmeline could think about was Marjorie. For that moment, even the war, even Lydia! was relegated to the back of her mind. She and Dot met at the usual bench. It was cold and rain was threatening.

The first thing Dot said was, 'Do you remember what she asked? If we could look after the children?'

'I do,' Emmeline said quietly, rubbing her arms. She also remembered how dismissive she had been about it. *For goodness' sake, Marjorie, we're ALL struggling here.*

'We could alternate perhaps – looking after them – so she has time off.' Dot suggested.

'I can't have people at mine,' Emmeline said, thinking of Mr Davenport looking up from his papers smiling when Matthew burst in. That smile would disappear eventually though. 'It's a place of work.'

'And I can't at mine.' Dot had sighed. 'It's not fair on the Ingrams. Poor Marjorie,' she continued, 'some people aren't cut out for motherhood.'

'Some people just need a break,' corrected Emmeline. 'If only...' She paused, thinking. 'We could do it if we had a place.'

'What?'

'A place we could look after small children...'

'Like a nursery?'

'Not *like* a nursery. An actual nursery.'

'Don't be daft,' Dot said, but she said it in a kind voice. 'Ready for *The Philadelphia Story* again?'

'Let's not go – let's talk about this. There's all us women floating around the town, when we could, if we got all our talents together, we could do something!'

It wasn't just about Marjorie, it seemed to Emmeline. It was about all the mothers here, all mothers everywhere. It was about Lydia, Francine, Maisie, Valerie – when their turn came – it was important to put systems in place for them. She wasn't just trying to alleviate her guilt – although there was that – she wanted to make things better. And, somehow, she thought, maybe she could. It was like she could see a flicker of light on the other side of the door, if she could just push through. It might be that other people were pushing too – if so, all the better!

And it meant that Matthew and the pram and all that represented was NOT an obstacle but an assistance. Despite being a mother of young children, she could help – in fact, it was *because* she was a mother of young children that she could help. They could be useful!

Dot looked cynical. 'How? Ask the council to set up a nursery? You might have noticed, they've got bigger fish to fry right now.'

'No, we *don't* ask. We do it, we'll set one up. By ourselves!'

Dot sniffed. 'Have you ever set up a nursery before?'

'No.'

'Have you ever set up *anything* before?'

Emmeline remembered arranging a charity tin at the pharmacy and the drama it had entailed – that was the extent of her organising.

'No.'

'Have you even worked with children before?'

'Not *worked*, but I've had two of my own – and so have you.'

'Then why you?'

'Why not me?' she replied excitedly. Dot shook her head as Emmeline went on: 'I've looked after small children for years. We can't leave it to someone else. Remember what Churchill said?'

'He's always saying stuff.'

'He said, "What is good enough for *anybody* is good enough for us."'

'So?'

'So I'll find a place. And if I do, you'll help.'

'Sure,' agreed Dot lazily.

Dot said if they weren't going to the cinema, she was going back home for a sleep. Emmeline wandered around the town with Matthew. She saw other women and other children in her situation mooching around too. They were not just sending people escaping the London Blitz. Many cities were being targeted so now there were women and children from Coventry or from Birmingham in Norfolk too – and all might be looking for something to fill their time.

That day, Emmeline appraised everything through new eyes, with a singular purpose. There was the hospital, the cinema, the factory, the churches, the post office, the pub. All large enough as a place where they could look after small children, yet none of them quite right. Besides, all of them were already in use; she needed somewhere that wasn't. If Marjorie's downfall had taught Emmeline anything, it was that she would not be a shrinking violet any more. Not when she could be useful.

Dot didn't believe her; Dot thought she was building sandcastles. Emmeline wasn't. She was building *real* castles. She knew it wasn't what people were used to. She knew it would be unusual for her, a mere wife and mother, to press forward with such a scheme – and yet she knew: it *could* work. She would be the anybody.

18

Emmeline

The day after she saw Dot, Emmeline had woken up before Matthew, and with excitement – *more* than excitement; a sense of purpose or direction that she hadn't felt in a long time, perhaps ever. By the time he'd woken up, she was ready for action. Maybe he was surprised by this vibrant new mother – she certainly was.

She wheeled Matthew to the Town Hall. Would the council help them? It was not just finding a venue, it was funding too, thought Emmeline, but she wasn't ready to worry about that yet. Baby steps, she told herself, and the aptness of the phrase made her smile.

'I need to speak to someone about the use of a hall,' Emmeline said gaily at the front desk.

The receptionist swiftly brought her back down to earth.

'Whatever for?'

'We're hoping to set up a nursery.' Emmeline explained. A 'we' felt better than an 'I'. A 'we' gave it gravitas, she hoped, although at six and a half months pregnant, Dot was not as reliable a 'we' as she might have been. The 'hoping' sounded weak though. Next time, she resolved to say, 'We ARE setting up a nursery.'

The receptionist stood up straight – which took an effort; she was elderly and her back was curved like a seahorse.

'Who is "we"?' she asked in a booming voice that echoed off the walls. Emmeline was glad no one else was there.

'My... my friend and I,' said Emmeline.

'Why?'

'Uh... so...' Now this was something she should have rehearsed. 'So that mothers can leave their babies with us and go off.'

'Go off?' The receptionist tilted her head. 'What will they do while their babies are with you?'

'Uh...' Emmeline kicked herself for her poor preparation. 'They might work.'

'Work where?'

Emmeline had not thought of this. 'In the nursery, for example.'

'That's a bit odd,' the receptionist said.

'*Some* of the mothers,' Emmeline corrected herself. 'The others will be free to do what they want to do. It would be their time, after all...' She paused. 'But actually, I don't think that's the pertinent question, is it? – I just want to know if the council might know a place where we could set up a nursery.'

'You are welcome to talk to Councillor Arscott.' The receptionist lowered her voice to a conspiratorial whisper, which was just as loud. 'But I can tell you, he'll not like it. Innovation is *not* his forte.'

Emmeline had heard the Davenports talk before about this councillor and suspected they held a similar view.

'He doesn't like children much,' the receptionist added. 'Still, go in. I'll watch this little chap.'

She held out a barley sweet for Matthew, who was instantly won over.

Emmeline knocked on Councillor Arscott's door.

A voice called, 'What now?'

Bracing herself, Emmeline entered the office, and found a man with very little chin and too much nostril behind a desk. She told him that – as he was probably aware – dozens of women with children had turned up in the town and they were struggling without their homes and especially their kitchens, to attend to.

He blinked at her and twitched his nose and it occurred to her that he looked like a cartoon rabbit.

'So, my great friend (great? they had only met three weeks earlier!) Mrs Burke and I had an idea... to open a nursery!'

He held up a flabby palm.

'Stop right there.'

'Yes?' she said breathlessly. She felt surprised that she had nearly got it all out in one go. It was because it was so heartfelt and so true, she supposed.

'We're fighting Nazis right now.'

You're not, she thought but she didn't say that; instead she said, 'Exactly!'

'Mothers and children are NOT a priority.'

There were a billion ways to respond to this. Unfortunately, Emmeline's hot head took over.

'Mothers and children aren't *ever* a priority, are they? What do you think our husbands are fighting for, if not the well-being of mothers and children?'

'Why not get a nanny?'

Emmeline hadn't expected that.

'Ordinary women can't afford nannies!' she blurted out. 'Hardly anyone can!'

'Then why have children in the first place? Good grief, girl!'

This was not the conversation Emmeline had anticipated,

but still she persisted. He had got right under her skin, this man who knew nothing of a woman's struggle. 'Are you suggesting only upper-class families should have children?'

'I'm suggesting your childcare issues are not for my council to solve. Good day.'

Emmeline hovered for a moment, then backed away. *Loathsome man.* In the entrance area, Matthew and the receptionist were deep in conversation about Matthew's favourite subject: *choo-choos.* (This was, alas, his only subject recently.)

'No good?' the receptionist asked, looking up.

Emmeline shook her head and the receptionist shrugged. The shrug said, *He's always like that.*

Emmeline thanked her for her time. She wasn't only down-hearted, she felt like she had been exposed as an idiot. If she looked at it from the receptionist and Councillor Arscott's point of view, she saw it could be seen as a ridiculous idea: she had been in a town she didn't know for just a few weeks and here she was, trying to challenge the way they did things.

Matthew didn't want to leave and Emmeline had to pull him away with him kicking her shins.

'What is the matter with you?' she demanded, embarrassed. She decided to head to her usual bench and drown her sorrows in Dot's tales of Americans – 'You've heard of French kissing, but have you heard of American kissing?' It was a good thing Matthew was too young to understand. Dot was so bawdy that sometimes Emmeline felt like covering her own ears, never mind the children's.

'Hang on.' The receptionist was hurrying after them. Emmeline thought maybe she had left something behind, but when she caught them up she pinched Matthew's cheek and called him 'ducky'. 'For what it's worth,' she said, catching her breath, 'I think it's a good plan.'

It wasn't worth much, Emmeline thought, but it was

encouraging. Goodness knew she needed a boost after the humiliation.

'Don't you live with the Davenports?' the receptionist continued.

'Yes.'

'I knew I recognised you from somewhere! You were in the newspapers! Nice photograph.'

'Thank you,' Emmeline said, wondering what that had to do with anything.

'Well then!' the receptionist went on as if all was obvious, 'why don't you approach the Right Honourable Gentleman for help?'

Emmeline had never heard Mr Davenport addressed like that before. Neville wasn't impressed that she was staying with a Member of Parliament. 'Self-interested so-and-so's', he had written, although privately, Emmeline thought that epitaph might well belong to him ('It takes one to know one,' as Emmeline's aunt used to say). Neville hadn't even asked which party Mr Davenport belonged to, he just said they were all the same, out for themselves, and he seemed aggrieved at Emmeline, as though she had a wealth of homes to choose from and had deliberately selected this one to aggravate him.

The receptionist, by contrast, seemed to be suggesting that living with an MP might just be a good thing.

'I don't think...'

'He was one of the ones who insisted on the evacuation.'

'Did he?'

'Big supporter of it, he was. And he helped open up the underground stations as shelter from the Blitz in London.'

'I didn't know that.' Emmeline was impressed. While she admired her host, and appreciated that he was close to the seat of power, she hadn't realised he was *that* influential. Neville might like him, she thought, if he let himself (which he most likely wouldn't).

'If anyone can help, the Right Honourable Mr Davenport can...'

She sandwiched one of Emmeline's hands between both of her own.

'Another thing – if Councillor Arscott thinks it's a bad idea, then it's probably an excellent idea. Keep going.'

19

Emmeline

The first hurdle was actually *finding* Mr Davenport. Mrs Davenport was often at home, Mr Reynolds was sometimes at home, but Mr Davenport was rarely there. Emmeline was more likely to find him in the newspapers than in the drawing room. The government were voting all the time. It was non-stop war measures: rationing. New powers to local authorities. Lighting. Health. You name it, they voted on it. He was as elusive as the Scarlet Pimpernel, she told Dot, who liked a cinematic refer-ence above all else. And when he did come home, he was exhausted. He was as tired as a cartoon dog, though she didn't share that one with Dot. Although Neville said that Members of Parliament were work-shy, Mr Davenport wasn't.

He would undo his tie and sit in front of the fire with his papers on his lap, cigarette smouldering in the ashtray, and then snore until Mrs Davenport insisted, 'Time for Bedlington', which Emmeline understood to be how the upper classes referred to their beds. It was strange to see the intimacies of another marriage up close and it made Emmeline reflect on her own.

About a week after her visit to Mr Arscott, she found Mr Davenport leafing through the newspapers, drinking sherry. He saw her hovering by the door and called out, 'Come in, Mrs Froud. No need to stand to attention.'

After she had thanked him, buoyed up by the receptionist's remarks, Emmeline took the plunge. 'I have something to ask...'

'Go ahead.'

He looked serious, although his eyes were slightly more crossed than usual.

'We are setting up a nursery,' she blurted out.

'Oh?' He was visibly taken aback.

'And we could do with some help.'

Her explanation had improved since the conversation with Councillor Arscott. It was more succinct and less apologetic.

'Many mothers have poured into town and they are strong, capable women. If their children could be looked after sometimes, they might be able to lead more fulfilling lives themselves. The thing is' – Emmeline checked if he was listening. Amazingly, he appeared to be – 'There is nothing to do here. Except watch films, and if I have to sit through *The Thief of Baghdad* again, I might explode.'

'I'd hate for you to explode, Mrs Froud,' he said.

Emmeline blushed. She did get carried away, but that was because she felt so passionately about this. Meanwhile, he tapped his teeth with his pencil.

'I can take Matthew for a walk sometimes to give you some respite.' He was thinking aloud. 'If it's usefulness you're after, you can help me with campaigning if you like. That's always helpful!'

She was bright red now. The thought of knocking on doors with him, or going to one of his political events, was *not* what she was after (although it did have a certain appeal).

'I haven't explained properly. It's not for me or Matthew, it's for *all* the mothers here. And not only the evacuated mothers. We need to contribute, we want to contribute.'

He paused for a moment. She could see he was considering. And then the verdict came down like a gavel.

'I think – Mrs Davenport and I have discussed this at length – a mother's place is in the home.'

Emmeline's heart was thumping.

'Like the Nazis? Kinder, Küche, Kirche?'

He smiled. Sometimes she got the feeling he really did enjoy talking to her, and that he liked it even more when she disagreed with him. He shook his head, his eyes on her. He had long eyelashes for a man. 'Not like that, no.'

'Don't you think,' Emmeline ploughed on, 'it's important to contribute if one *wants to* contribute?'

'How would you contribute to a nursery? Are you qualified in this field?'

'I will manage it!'

Emmeline stared around the room for further inspiration. Her eyes alighted on his plate, where a half-eaten sausage and some pickle sat. 'I can also cook,' she said, hands on her hips. 'I am an excellent cook.' This was an exaggeration. Neville used to joke that he wasn't sure if she was trying to poison him on purpose or by accident.

He laughed again and there was something about it that went to the core of her. It was like he saw her as a fascinating creature that he'd found in the wild and wanted to keep.

'I already asked Councillor Arscott—'

'You did?' he asked, and now there was an edge to his voice.

'I don't think he quite understood,' she admitted.

'I bet he didn't.'

It transpired that Councillor Arscott and Mr Davenport disliked each other intensely. Emmeline didn't know what this meant for her plan but she had absolutely caught his attention.

'I can't promise anything, but I will give it some thought.'

Emmeline couldn't believe it. She wanted to jump into his arms. To have him, he who was always voting, always writing, always exercised by the future of the nation, take her ideas seriously was like nothing she'd ever experienced before. It made her feel amazing.

A few mornings later, Emmeline was in the garden, hanging out her and Matthew's clothes on the line, pegs in her mouth. Matthew was digging in the mud nearby when Mrs Davenport came out. Her hair was covered by a patterned headscarf and it suited her. Usually she had a sharp look of Wallis Simpson about her, but today she looked softer, more like Princess Elizabeth.

She always went to a wives' club or strategy meeting on Thursday mornings.

'Mrs Froud?'

Emmeline pulled the pegs from her mouth. Mrs Davenport took a step back – she did make Emmeline feel grubby sometimes.

'Yes?'

'My husband is a busy man. He is also a dreamer who has a tendency to get – how shall I put it? – waylaid by ridiculous schemes.'

So this was what it was. Emmeline pegged another blouse onto the line before replying. 'I'm not sure what you mean?'

'I mean, kindly refrain from putting pie-in-the-sky ideas in his head.'

'Pie!' yelped Matthew from the lawn.

'Shhh!' Emmeline felt ashamed of her shabby clothes and her noisy son, but she wasn't going to back down on her idea. 'I don't know what you are saying.'

'I think you do.'

Emmeline tried again. 'Nurseries aren't pie in the sky. They're to enable mothers of young children to' – she wasn't going to say anything about Marjorie – 'live.'

'That's as maybe,' Mrs Davenport said placidly, putting her glasses back on. 'But that has nothing to do with my husband or I.'

Emmeline couldn't argue this point. She stood and watched Mrs Davenport strut off, her headscarf flapping slightly in the breeze. Emmeline realised that, while her host saw herself as kindness personified, she would never let kindness get in the way of her life.

Later that evening, things turned again. 'Mrs Froud, are you here?' Mr Reynolds called from the drawing room. 'MRS FROUD?'

Alarmed, Emmeline hurried downstairs, Matthew in her arms chewing on a carrot. Mr Reynolds' stubble was back – you could almost tell the time by it.

'There's no harm looking into it, is there?' Mr Davenport was saying, while Mrs Davenport glared at her shoes.

Mr Reynolds looked sceptical. 'As long as it doesn't take you away from your true purpose.'

'What is my true purpose?'

'Come on,' scolded Mr Reynolds.

Mr Davenport smiled. 'My purpose is to represent my constituents – and Mrs Froud is a constituent.'

'Only temporarily,' said Mr Reynolds, and Mrs Davenport murmured, 'Exactly.'

Emmeline swallowed. *Was that a threat?*

Mr Davenport went on: 'The point is, there is a possibility of a nationwide roll-out of wartime nurseries, and I happen to think it's an excellent idea—'

'You've never mentioned it before,' said Mrs Davenport, stubbing out her cigarette.

He winced. 'I can't say I thought it was a priority before.'

There it was again, Emmeline thought. Men in a man's world doing things for men. Women's lives are *never* a priority.

'But I've thought about it since,' he continued. 'We've an emergency fund that we can use – and we can reward the councils who set them up. And we can task Norfolk Council with it.'

'Councillor Arscott won't like that...'

Mr Davenport grinned. He clearly saw this as a positive. 'How can he say no? He won't want to be seen as unpatriotic, will he?'

'Well no, but...'

'What's more' – Mr Davenport was warming to his theme – 'You know the bicycle factory up the slope?'

'Who doesn't? – I nearly broke my ankle on one of their bone-shakers.'

'It's not a bicycle factory any more...'

'In-te-res-ting,' Mr Reynolds said, making the word sound long and almost exotic.

A factory that once made bicycles no longer makes bicycles. And this was relevant how?

'This could be the thing.'

'Definitely. It's a win-win situation.'

'You think it will go down well with the local party?'

'I think it's the right thing, whether they're on board or not.'

'I'm not sure I understand?' interrupted Emmeline, feeling more than ever like she was missing something.

'The factory needs workers desperately. The hospitals need workers too, and they have also told me married mothers would be ideal.'

'Ideal?' Mrs Davenport repeated, still looking sceptical.

Mr Reynolds stood up and then he spoke like he was giving a speech to a crowd, his chest out and his head high:

'The Right Honourable Mr Davenport, MP of King's Lynn, understands what the people of this country want – and right now, we want to win the war by any means possible. As soon as it's over, mothers back to the home and hearth, but for now, the wartime nurseries will make it possible for children to be cared for and for mothers to support the war effort.'

'Wartime nurseries?' repeated Emmeline. The phrase felt both familiar and not. It was as though it were being imposed on her, but it was exciting too – as though they were making progress.

'What do you think?' Mr Davenport prompted.

'I don't know,' she said. Things were moving forward, yet she was clearly no longer in the driving seat.

He raised one eyebrow at her. 'Mrs Froud, *I* think your idea is genius.'

20

Lydia

Mrs Howard had on her most serious face, so Lydia ran through the many things she had done recently that might be seen as 'bad'. She had – or rather Rex had – torn up a newspaper, leaving a trail of ripped paper around Bumble Cottage. She had run after the postman in slippers, and she had received a detention for chatting in maths. On the plus side, Betsy and Flora were saying that she was Miss Picard's favourite, which Lydia denied (although secretly she agreed – it was obvious; Miss Picard got her to distribute papers, got her to answer questions, got her to model hats).

But it was none of those things – in fact, for once it had nothing to do with her.

Mrs Howard had offered Valerie a place, here, at Bumble Cottage.

'I didn't have much choice,' she said, in her telephone voice. 'I regret not taking her sooner. The poor girl has suffered so.'

Lydia's heart sank, and she rearranged the bow in her hair to give herself time to adjust. Valerie was an old friend, along with Francine, she was her oldest friend from London, and she did like her, but she also liked having this magical kingdom all to herself. Bumble Cottage was her domain and she was not keen to share it. She felt a bit like when Mummy had first told her she was having a baby: *Aren't I enough for you?*

Then Mrs H said since Valerie was older, mightn't she have the bigger room, but Lydia must have looked so outraged that Mrs H changed her mind: 'Absolutely right, you were here first, Lydia!'

Valerie had come to stay with Lydia once before, years ago, when Mrs Hardman was poorly, and Lydia's parents had instructed her not to be mean. They'd told her it was hard to only have one parent, like Valerie, and yes, it was tiresome... Yet before too long she'd seen both parents come under Valerie's spell. She'd asked Mr Froud about his work and Mrs Froud about cooking and Lydia had felt like piggy in the middle trying to catch a ball that kept sailing over her head.

'When's she coming then?' Lydia asked, telling herself to show interest.

Mrs Howard squinted at her wristwatch. 'In about five minutes.'

Mrs Howard asked Lydia to cut some flowers from the garden. Lydia didn't know what they were beyond that they were purple and pretty. And actually, it was a sensible request; Lydia appreciated the time on her own. Valerie would fit in fine, she reminded herself. And she wouldn't be any bother to Lydia. They were different types. And at least Valerie was easy-going and she always used to share her things if you asked. And there was plenty of room in the house – it wasn't as though they would be on top of each other. And she would always be Rex's number one.

Back inside, Mrs H was still fretting.

'You WILL welcome her, won't you, Lydia? I remember

you girls said that you were like sisters on the day you came to Somerset.'

Lydia assured Mrs Howard that of course she would welcome her old friend.

When Valerie arrived at Bumble Cottage, Lydia realised she was not the same girl as the one Lydia had known in London. Gone was the quietly confident young woman who took care of everything and everyone. Instead here was a jittery mouse. New Valerie was drawn and edgy. Even her face seemed tense. She was pale, with purple bags under her eyes, and she was thin – so thin she looked like she would snap. Lydia had thought being in the Woods' hardware store all day might be tiresome, but now she realised it must have been worse than she had previously imagined.

Valerie didn't meet your eye any more. She had bruises all over her legs and hollow cheeks.

A few days after she arrived, Lydia heard Mrs Howard talking about Valerie to her friends while they did their volunteering. Mrs H said, 'Unsurprisingly, given what she's gone through, she's subdued right now, yet she's a wonderful creature, full of potential.'

Someone must have asked about 'the other one', for she heard Mrs H say, 'Lydia is a doll.' Unfortunately, the word doll only reminded Lydia of Margaret-Doll, who hated the dark and would be freezing outside.

Lydia found herself in the unusual position of explaining to Valerie what they could do and what they couldn't. Where they could go and where they shouldn't. Where Valerie should put her belongings. It was clear Valerie had had nothing new since they'd left London. Her shoes had holes in the soles. Her skirts were stained and too short. For this, too, Lydia was inclined to feel sorry for her.

Valerie was clever, though. She just cottoned on to things straight away. Lydia had to think three or four times, she had to turn information around in her hands. Once she realised it was allowed, even encouraged, Valerie liked reading in the library and listening to the wireless. Lydia found this dull. She preferred to be on the move, with Rex by her side.

Valerie missed her father, who had died when she was little, although she didn't talk half as much about her mother. Lydia missed her parents too, but she didn't feel compelled to be with them, or even to talk about them. It was enough that they loved her and they were there in the background. She thought Valerie was a bit babyish in that way.

When Paul came back, the balance in the house tilted again. Lydia had hardly been aware of his presence previously; he was fun and silly and mealtimes were jollier when he was about, but that was it. Paul's interests were not hers. He liked fishing, tennis and painting – she didn't – and the wireless – she really didn't.

Lydia might not be as bookish as Valerie, but she still noticed things, and she noticed that Paul and Valerie had a rapport. However different they were in many ways, in other ways they were like peas in a pod. It started with that ridiculous radio show *It's That Man Again* that they were both fans of, but it grew to envelop everything. Together they even connived over a new name for the dog, which outraged Lydia. She would never call the dog T.Rex, whatever they said. She wrote about it furiously to Francine, who didn't comment and instead sent back drawings of dogs and dinosaurs, bones and skeletons.

21

Emmeline

Emmeline, Mr Davenport, Councillor Arscott, Matthew, Dot, Pat and Hettie and the vicar huddled in the Church of Our Lady in Shouldham. Emmeline was praying, but she doubted anyone else was. Mr Davenport had his eye on the church hall, which was the square building next door. It was ten metres by ten metres and was like a garage, brick and basic with one small window, lots of tatty signs about what was forbidden (eating, walking, eating while walking) and a massive wooden Jesus on a cross.

First impressions were: it wasn't bad. It would be safe, it would be compact, and they could turn it into something lovely. A spot of polish and a cheery poster here or a cuddly toy there. A bed for dollies, a tea service for bears... She could imagine Della, Derek and Deidre bursting in, pulling off their coats, sitting cross-legged there. She could picture Deidre crayoning, Derek jumping from that platform, little Della sleeping if they put cots over there. And Marjorie beaming as she picked them up at the end of the day: 'Thank you, Emmeline. I'm feeling more myself—'

Her reverie was interrupted by Councillor Arscott.

'This isn't a good time to be chasing women's rights.'

He waggled a finger at her and then at the headline in the newspaper he was holding. *Thousands seek shelter in the Underground* it read.

'Exactly what I thought,' the vicar joined in cheerily. 'During the Great War, the suffragettes suspended their campaign to get behind the country.'

'Mrs Froud here could learn from that,' chirped Councillor Arscott.

It struck Emmeline how easily men like Councillor Arscott and the vicar pronounced on women's rights. No skin off their noses, was it?

'But it's not just about *women's* rights,' Emmeline said. She appreciated the language around this issue was important. Men did not legislate for women. If they thought the nursery plan was just about women, they wouldn't get behind it. She had to sell it differently.

'It's actually about betterment of society.'

Mr Davenport looked at her, impressed. She raised an eyebrow back. *Two can play this game.*

Councillor Arscott was not so easily won over.

'In the middle of the war! My dear woman, how is that going to look?' He broke into a mirthless laugh. 'Our boys are *dying* in Europe. Our cities are being decimated. Let me be clear, the timing of this vanity project is all wrong.'

'When is the timing right?' Emmeline enquired.

'When we're not at war?' suggested the vicar.

Councillor Arscott loved that:

'Exactly!'

Mr Davenport interjected. 'You misunderstand. The women *want* to contribute to the war effort.'

'That's right,' agreed Emmeline. 'So the timing HAS to be now.'

Emmeline continually surprised herself with how strongly she felt about this. What had started as perhaps a way to atone for Marjorie had gained momentum like a rolling snowball. Yes to helping lonely mothers. Yes to getting women who wanted to work to work. Yes to helping the factories increase production. Yes to helping the hospitals care for patients. Yes to the *principle* of the thing. There were jobs that needed doing – and there were people who needed jobs. And, if creating a wartime nursery stopped her from missing Lydia and being hurt by Neville, that was *another* positive. In a way, she was doing this *for* Lydia – so that her girl would never be in poor Marjorie's position in the future. In a way, she rationalised that she was doing it for Neville too. She'd be a better wife if she had purpose, wouldn't she? She wouldn't be left dwelling on his faults all the time. There were so many benefits to it – she struggled to think of any disadvantages. Although clearly Councillor Arscott and the vicar could think up plenty.

Mr Davenport was talking about the factory. He kept saying, 'They are no longer making bicycles,' in a grave tone.

'And the mothers want to work there!' Emmeline added.

'All of the mothers, Mrs Froud?' the vicar enquired in a mocking tone. She did not like this man at all. 'All of the mothers are anxious to spend their days on an assembly line?'

Emmeline was still hazy about the exact nature of the work at the factory, but she didn't doubt it would be arduous. And she didn't doubt either that some of the mothers she saw in the street, the park and in the cinema would NOT be up for it. But many would be.

'Some of them.'

'Let me be clear, whatever the factory is making, I'm against nurseries,' Councillor Arscott pronounced. 'Children should be with their mothers at all times.'

He grinned smugly at them. 'Or with Nanny. I have fond memories of Nanny Parker-Hughes.' He paused. His eyes brightened as he reminisced. 'She loved feeding ducks. It's a shame there aren't more women like her around any more.'

Emmeline looked at Mr Davenport. He seemed to be struggling to contain himself. 'It's marvellous you had a good experience,' he said finally. 'But *you* don't have to go to the nursery,' he said. 'It's not for you. The point is that this hall is available – I understand it's empty all day?'

'Not all day,' corrected the vicar.

'Most days. Can the mothers use this hall? It's a simple request. Is your answer yes or no?'

As the vicar said, 'It's a no,' Councillor Arscott's face split into a wide, satisfied grin – and Emmeline realised he was more tiger than bunny.

Back at the Old Rectory, Emmeline slumped in an armchair. There was always another obstacle, she thought. Soon as you stick your head out, sure enough something comes along to knock you down. That was something Neville used to say that was still true.

But Mr Davenport was still beaming. He wasn't downcast at all.

'So?' She couldn't understand why he was so cheerful. Unless he wasn't interested in the plan after all.

'So I knew he'd say that, silly chap.'

She sat up. There was more to this than she had thought.

Mr Davenport went on. 'Councillor Arscott was interested in Nazi Germany a few years ago. Toying with alliances and all sorts.'

Emmeline pulled a face. 'Oof.'

'He wasn't alone in that, but he went further than most. He

arranged visits to Germany and I understand that he personally
met Adolf Hitler in 1936.'

Emmeline wrinkled up her nose. Nothing about Councillor
Arscott would surprise her. 'Yet people still elect him?'

'They do...' He sighed. 'Anyway, don't worry, Mrs Froud.
We have plenty of avenues to explore.'

'Do we?'

It was hard to let go of the idea of that church hall. There
were things that weren't perfect: the Jesus was perhaps too
graphic for one-year-olds, and they'd have to take some of the
more evangelical messages down, but... He shrugged. 'Plenty
might be an overstatement, but we're not stopping now. The
factory are expecting twenty married women workers to start
next January, so for that to happen a nursery needs to be in
place.'

Emmeline gaped at him. Sitting at his desk, Mr Davenport opened a notebook. 'What exactly does the premises
need?'

He hasn't given up, Emmeline realised, and a bolt of pleasure went through her.

'We'll need a kitchen. And a large safe space for playing and
napping.'

'That's it?' Mr Davenport mused, holding his pencil in mid-
air.

'Outdoor space would be wonderful, but unlikely, I
suppose...'

He slap-closed his notebook and raised one handsome
eyebrow at her.

'You should aim high and see how close you get.'

The following day, Emmeline met Dot in the park and they
talked while Matthew, Pat and Hettie drew in the mud with
twigs.

'He's looking for somewhere for us, Dot!' Emmeline said excitedly.

Dot, the most upbeat woman she knew, was still unconvinced. She took off her shoes – her ankles were swollen to twice their usual size – and put her feet up on the bench. Emmeline hoped no one saw. This was terribly unladylike. It was the kind of trivial thing Councillor Arscott would hold against them.

Dot seemed to be on tenterhooks and, suddenly, Emmeline guessed why.

'Any news from Marjorie?'

Dot bowed her head and Emmeline knew that, whatever it was, the news wasn't good. She curled and uncurled her fists in anticipation.

'And?'

'So they've put her in a... care home.'

'What? No...'

Dot nodded grimly.

'And the children?'

'Evacuated to the countryside. I don't know who with.'

'They're young to be without a parent.'

'Much too young,' agreed Dot.

'How long will she be in for?'

Dot's mouth was downturned. She was trying not to cry. 'Until she gets herself better.'

'And how long is that likely to take?'

Dot covered her face with her hands and sighed. 'Who knows?'

They went to the cinema to cheer themselves up, although Emmeline did not cheer up when she realised it was *The Thief of Baghdad* once again. The manager asked hopelessly, 'What can I do?'

'Beggars can't be choosers, I know,' Emmeline said.

She held on to Matthew in the dark and thought how bewildered Della, Deidre and Derek might be. The bed-wetting wasn't likely to stop. Hopefully whoever was looking after them would be sympathetic. There had to be more help, she thought. Marjorie didn't deserve any of this. No woman did. She thought about the clack-clack of her knitting needles and hoped that somehow Marjorie sensed she was thinking of her.

Nothing happened regarding the nursery over the next few days and Emmeline's hopes fell. Mr Davenport was not at home and Emmeline imagined he had dismissed the whole thing. Perhaps he had moved on to something more interesting. Something more of a priority – men's stuff, most likely. Fortunately, a letter from Lydia arrived to distract her. Emmeline had heard that servicemen's letters were censored, and in a funny way Lydia's also came across as though there were chunks missing. It was all half-stories, and information Emmeline didn't know the context for. This time Lydia wrote that she felt left out, but since she didn't want to do what they did, was that really being left out?

Emmeline read it a second time. No, she still didn't understand.

'Miss Picard says I am her cherry.'

Who is Miss Picard? is being her cherry good?

'Valerie reads all the time or listens to the wireless. Boring.'

Valerie? Valerie Hardman? What on earth is Valerie doing at Bumble Cottage? The last Emmeline heard, she was with the woman who ran the hardware shop. Does Mrs Hardman know?

'When she's not at home, she's always out with Paul.'

Paul? Who is Paul now?

'Rex says hello.'

Rex is the dog, I know that.

'Mrs Howard is doing Shakespeare this year. Not even a good one.'

How is she 'doing Shakespeare'?

Emmeline deciphered it the best she could, then wrote back, soothing things, remembering to ask about Margaret-Doll (if she did not, Lydia got annoyed) and telling her of the tiny outfits she had made. She also decided she needed to get to Somerset to see Lydia sooner rather than later. Her daughter was safer in Somerset, but safety was not everything. Something felt out of kilter.

It was a whole ten days after the trip to the Church of Our Lady before Mr Davenport had news. He knocked on Emmeline's bedroom door.

'If you have a moment, Mrs Froud.'

Emmeline made herself presentable, then went downstairs. It was only eight o'clock, but it had been dark for hours and felt much later.

'I may have found somewhere.'

'What? Where?' She could have hugged him.

'Stradsett, it's not far...'

He was looking at her like he would accept a hug. She grabbed his hand instead and shook it again and again. His palm was soft, warm and fitted hers perfectly. They were grinning excitedly at each other and it felt to her that time was standing still. Then he seemed to come out of his trance and asked, 'Do you want to go and see it?'

'Now?' It was so black outside.

'I have to stay in London for a few days, so it's now or next week.'

'I'll get my shoes.'

They were going to see somewhere! He'd found a place! It all seemed inconceivable.

'Should I tell Dot?' she wondered.

'I want to hear what you think first,' he said.

Why are we going to see it if we can't really see it? she was going to ask, but she didn't because she was thrilled at the prospect of this adventure. It was ten minutes' walk away apparently. When she put Matthew in the pram, he grumbled a little but then went back to sleep. Good boy.

Mr Davenport held out his flashlight in front, lighting the way. He said, 'When the war is over and there is light everywhere, we'll miss this darkness.'

'I won't,' she said. She hated not seeing where she was going. She heard him laugh.

They were in front of an old building, again next to a church. He fiddled with a lock and then they were in.

The glow from the torch lit up the room. There were cobwebs hanging from every corner, and something rustled and then whipped away: maybe a bat? She tried not to squeal.

'Needs wiring, I should think,' Mr Davenport said.

There was a drinks bar at one end of the room. They'd need to do something about that too! There was a good-sized kitchen and several lavatories. It was all grimy, with a feel of long-term neglect, but they could also deal with that. A strange noise made her jump and woke Matthew. She picked him up.

'Are there ghosts?'

'Pity the ghosts if there are,' he said. 'They won't last long with toddlers chasing their tails.'

She chuckled.

'Wait,' he said. 'This is the bit I thought you'd like most...'

He was close to her, and she felt his presence all through her body. He flung open the back door and the torch lit up a large outdoor space, protected by a brick wall, an overgrown lawn and bushes and trees.

'Apple trees?'

'And pears. And berries, apparently.'

'The children will love that.'

Matthew clapped his hands, and she laughed. 'Would you like to play here, Matty?'

He nodded his head up and down so vigorously she thought she'd drop him.

She could already see it in her mind's eye: Della collecting pine cones, Derek and Matthew kicking a ball, Deidre running free in her vest and knickers.

We're doing this, Marjorie.

As they made their way back to the Old Rectory, Emmeline was going through all the things that would have to be done. They needed cots and other furniture and the kitchen needed a big clean-up, but it could work – it could be better even than the first hall they had seen. She couldn't wait to get started.

The Old Rectory was in darkness. Mr Davenport didn't say where his wife was and she didn't ask. Holding her breath, she laid the now-sleeping Matthew in the bed and he stayed asleep. Before she crept downstairs, she caught sight of her reflection in the bathroom mirror. A face flushed with excitement looked back at her.

Mr Davenport was in the kitchen, stirring a pan of milk. He'd promised to make cocoa. The kitchen felt hot after being outdoors and they were both buoyant from the achievement. Emmeline sat at the table and tried not to stare at him.

'So!' he said. 'What did you think?'

'It has potential,' she said, aware that this was faint praise.

He sat opposite her and lit a cigarette.

'I have no doubt it will be marvellous when you've done with it.'

Emmeline blushed. She loved and hated compliments. Restless, she got up to check on the milk in the pan and changed the subject.

'What's it like being an MP, Mr Davenport?'

He folded his long legs.

'A responsibility,' he said. 'When I took on the role, I didn't imagine that one day we'd be in a national unity government. I didn't imagine we'd be at war.'

'Who could have predicted it?'

He shrugged. 'It means we can't do all the things we want to do. Being in Parliament is always like this to a certain extent – but I went in with big dreams and now I find us in a fight for our existence.'

For once, Emmeline didn't want to talk about the war. It was like a monster consuming everything in its path. Or worse, it was like a monster inside you – there was no getting away from it.

'And was it something you always wanted to do?'

He met her eyes. 'Politics yes, but being a politician? Not really.'

'How do you mean?' She kept stirring.

'I wanted to be "the man behind the scenes".'

'The puppeteer rather than the puppet?'

He laughed at that. 'I like the way you speak – it's very direct.'

She blushed again.

'I prefer being backstage. But when my father-in-law died,

there were... shall we say "undesirables" on the ballot paper, so I stood, more to keep them out than anything.'

Emmeline nodded. She understood doing something you didn't want to do in order that something worse didn't happen.

'And Mrs Davenport?'

He paused. 'She is ambitious,' he said finally. 'For the country. Always has been. I think that's one reason we matched.'

The cocoa was ready. She poured it into mugs and they sat and drank companionably as the fire crackled. She tried not to imagine life if he were her husband. And if this was her home. And if he were the one she went to bed with...

After he drained his cup, 'Delicious!' he smiled at her, and when he asked, 'What's on your mind?' she was ashamed of the real answer.

'Nursery staff,' she said quickly, her voice husky.

'Ah yes.' Immediately it was as though they were back on more solid ground. 'You need a qualified nurse.'

'I don't think so,' she said confidently. 'I have years of experience looking after little ones – that would be enough.'

'It would be more reassuring if someone had a medical background.'

'I know someone,' she realised suddenly. 'My friend Christine.'

All right, she hadn't asked Christine. She hadn't told her anything yet, but Christine would be for it, she was sure.

'Of course you do,' he said, and his smile was a mix of incredulity and admiration. 'And trainees?'

'What about Mabel?'

'Mabel who?'

'Mabel who works here! She loves children, and you did say you'd probably have to let her go in the future.'

'I did, did I?' He mused. 'You have the memory of a politician!'

Emmeline ignored that. 'And it is *kind of* for the war effort...'

'Absolutely.'

Again, Emmeline had a crazy urge to hug him. Instead, she swallowed. *Be sensible,* she told herself. *This is business. This is politics. It is not affection.*

'I'm still confused about the financing issue,' she said.

'It will be an amalgamation of government, local government and business.'

Emmeline wasn't entirely sure what that meant either, but she nodded. If the finances were taken care of, then she could manage the rest.

'I wish all politicians were like you.'

Now Mr Davenport looked unusually solemn. 'That is high praise.'

'You're welcome,' she said shyly.

'Seriously, I see it as my job to look for solutions and then to help bring them about. You're the impressive one here.'

Again, she blushed, and tried to change the subject.

'And Parliament? It must be fascinating there.'

'I would love to show it to you one day,' he said. 'I think you would...' Their eyes met and he looked at her with – she couldn't find the word – sorrow maybe. But why? 'Like it...'

'I've heard said that everyone should see Parliament once in their life,' Emmeline said quickly, and he smiled, regaining his composure, and said, 'You're so right.'

Once again, that night Emmeline found it difficult to sleep. She tried to keep her excitement funnelled in the direction of the nursery, but it kept spreading into other things. Everything was exhilarating now she had purpose. The thing that had been eluding her for so long had dropped at her feet.

And Mr Davenport. *I like the way you speak. It's very direct* echoed around her mind and she wanted to speak to him again and have him think that again about her. *You're the impressive one.*

And he wanted to take her to Parliament?

Don't think about him. Not like that.

Thank goodness she would be setting up a nursery soon. She desperately needed something to take her mind off the man in the bedroom just down the corridor.

The next morning, Dot pushed the children in the pram to the Hall, while Emmeline wheeled spades, forks and buckets in a wheelbarrow from the Davenports' shed. Dot was amazed. And also tired. After she looked around, inside and out, she said hesitantly, 'It could be wonderful...'

'But?'

'But will mothers want to send their children to us?'

'Why not?' Emmeline said cheerfully. 'After we've sorted it out.'

Emmeline got on her knees in the garden and Matthew, Hettie, Pat and then Dot did too.

'I don't know what I'm doing,' Dot protested.

'Don't do anything,' Emmeline said, because Dot was getting heavy now.

'I want to,' she insisted.

'All right, pull up those weeds,' Emmeline directed. 'We'll have vegetable beds there.' She pointed. 'And a play bit there. It'll be lovely.'

They'd been doing it for an hour or so, and there was a good lot of weeds, when Dot knelt up, wiping her forehead.

'Remember, Emmeline, it's not definitely ours yet.'

Emmeline had pins and needles, so she stood up. She thought, *one day, young women, women like Lydia, Valerie, Francine will have a billion more choices.*

'It will be, though.'

'And if not, your MP will make it so, won't he?'

Your MP, thought Emmeline, embarrassed, yet at the same time it gave her a warm feeling. Mr Davenport had been so helpful. Having a powerful ally made such a difference, and not just for the nursery plans. And then she thought guiltily of Neville. She would write to him, pour all her surplus of love into a letter to her husband. Raised beds were what she was concentrating on. Not extramarital beds.

22

DECEMBER 1940

Lydia

Poor Paul was roped into accompanying Lydia to London. He'd much rather have gone fishing with Valerie. On the train, Lydia read a magazine that Miss Picard recommended, which was mostly about hair-styling, walking in heels and skirt lengths. 'It's our duty to keep spirits up, and that means looking the best you can,' Miss Barbara Johnson, twenty-one, from Putney, suggested. Miss Lettice Fortescue – Lettice? She must be a friend of Potty – said, 'Keeping my clothes and underwear spit-spot means I can fight the Nazis.'

She could see why Miss Picard would approve.

Lydia put the magazine down and asked Paul about his book. Miss Picard said that showing an interest was not just polite, it was *attractive*. Men loved that. Paul went on at length about cubism and Lydia regretted bothering.

In London, Paul put Lydia on another train to Norfolk. Enthusiastically, he waved goodbye, relief in his shoulders. Lydia was going for five days before Christmas. Mummy wouldn't take no for an answer and had connived with Mrs

Howard, making plans over Lydia's head. Somehow, Mummy had even convinced education-mad Mrs Howard that Lydia could miss her last day of term too.

Lydia sometimes worried that she mightn't recognise her mother, but it was never a problem. There she was on the platform at Thorpe station. She was all dancing eyes and wavy hair, a newspaper tucked under her arm and smelling of her customary perfume. She didn't just look neat and well turned out, though; Lydia thought she looked radiant. A lot of women wore patterns or florals, but her mother liked simple, plain lines and solid colours with high-heeled shoes, and they suited her. Miss Picard said that most married women let themselves go. Lydia was proud that her mummy was the exception to the rule.

Lydia also approved of the house where Mummy was living now. It wasn't quite sprawling Bumble Cottage with its animals, books and air of good-quality chaos, but the Old Rectory was quite lovely too. They had both evacuated well, she thought.

Mrs Howard had prepared a box of Somerset treats, including fudge, for her mother and the Davenports.

'This is so generous, Lydia, my goodness!' Mummy started fretting about what she could give in return.

Later that evening, Mummy said she had something to tell Lydia, and Lydia braced herself. She hadn't realised that there might be a motive behind this trip and she feared her mummy was going to beg her to move here. So when her mother told her she was planning to open a nursery, Lydia was surprised then relieved, then confused.

'A nursery? What, like...'

'Small children? Yes.'

In London, her mother didn't work and never had. She took Lydia to school and took her home as she ought. Her parents felt sorry for the women who had to work. *Poor Mrs Hardman, always having to clean.* She knew it also came from a place of *aren't we lucky, we are not like her?* Her daddy used to say mothers should stay at home. He was doubtful that they should have the vote. As far as Lydia was concerned, there had never been any hint that her mummy wanted anything more than to be her mummy.

'This is out of the blue, isn't it?'

'Maybe but I've always been interested in young children, and this way I can be busy even while we're evacuated.'

Lydia scowled. It was bad enough sharing her with Matthew. Imagine sharing her with forty others? But her mother just tucked her hair behind her ear and smiled dreamily. 'It's so exciting, Lydia. I haven't felt like this for years!'

This felt hurtful. *Why aren't I enough for her?* Lydia wondered.

'Why do you need to work?' she asked abruptly.

'I don't need to, I *want* to,' her mother said.

It occurred to her that her mother might be covering something up, so Lydia asked more sympathetically, 'Doesn't Daddy make enough money? For you to live on.'

'Working is not *bad*, Lydia,' her mother responded in a startled tone. 'I don't know why you—'

'I know that!' Lydia interrupted. She wondered what Miss Picard would say. Miss Picard worked too, of course, but she didn't have a husband to support her.

'And running a wartime nursery is a good thing.'

'So it *is* part of the war effort?' Lydia asked.

'Kind of.'

Lydia understood this. It made sense. It wasn't her mother abandoning her family, it was her mother patriotically pulling her weight. It was her mother doing her duty to keep spirits up, only on a different front. Exceptional times called for exceptional measures. It wasn't real life, it was just something she had to do for a while.

. . .

Lydia could tell the Davenports liked her. Adults tended to, she knew that, but she didn't take it for granted. She did her excellent walk around the house, imagining she had stacks of books on her head.

'Neck all right?' Mummy asked.

Lydia told her what she was learning in elocution class and Mummy laughed and said, 'It sounds so old-fashioned' and then, when Lydia scowled, she apologised. 'I didn't have the chance to do anything like that. It's lovely you do!'

'You don't need it,' Lydia said, kissing her mother's cheek, before giving her a very Miss Picard compliment: 'You were born exquisite!'

Lydia and Mummy were invited to join the Davenports for dinner and Lydia realised that this was different to usual and also that her mother was nervous. But in the end, Mr Davenport had to stay late at the House of Commons, so it was just Mrs Davenport, with a housekeeper (with poor posture), who served up and then slipped away. There was a soup – Mrs Davenport complained that it was watery, but it was no worse than any at Bumble Cottage. Then an unnamed meat with carrots and cauliflower that Lydia thought was tasty, and finally apple fritters.

Lydia had excellent table manners; she noticed her mother's relief that she did not slurp her soup, nor did the meat fly off her plate when she cut it. She also knew which subjects to avoid and which not to. She could turn her charm on like a tap.

'Do tell me about yourself, Lydia,' Mrs Davenport said, putting on her glasses to survey her. 'I heard you are at St Boniface school, which I understand is excellent.'

Lydia told her about the importance of a good education. She used Mrs H's phrases and Mrs Davenport nodded approvingly. Then Lydia told her about Rex, a subject she personally found far more interesting.

'He can be nervous of big dogs but he makes friends with

everyone in the end – I would say he's sociable, not like some. He does a funny kind of bark sometimes, but that's—'

'Fascinating,' Mrs Davenport interrupted. 'And your impressions of Somerset?'

'It's jolly,' Lydia said, spearing her carrot. 'Rex thinks there are too many sheep. I have to keep him on the lead in some areas because once, one took fright and—'

'I must go back to Somerset. We went years ago. On our second honeymoon,' Mrs Davenport said. She had diamonds in her ears and a pearl necklace. Lydia noted the rings on her fingers and the jewel – was it a sapphire? She wondered if Mrs Davenport had 'worked very hard'.

'Mind you, I didn't notice where we were half the time, I was so smitten.'

Lydia saw that her mother had gone bright red.

'Where did you and Mr Froud go?' Mrs Davenport continued. A ghost of a smile was sitting on her lips.

Lydia watched her mother's restless hands. She didn't reply straight away.

'We went to Brighton,' her mother said finally – it was like drawing blood. 'I had always wanted to see the pier.'

Once they had gone upstairs and were on their own, her mother became her chatty self again, and was excited about the present she'd arranged for Lydia. At first she told Lydia she should wait until Christmas Day back in Somerset before she unwrapped it, but then she changed her mind: Would Lydia open it now, so that she could see her reaction?

Then Mummy got sad about Lydia having Christmas far from home, for the second year now, and Lydia pretended to be stoical, 'It's not too bad,' when actually she was looking forward to it; there would be Christingle church services, frosty morning dog walks and carol singing and Betsy's family were going to give them Christmas crackers.

Lydia unwrapped the present. It was a miniature wooden bed.

'Margaret-Doll deserves a cosy place to sleep too, doesn't she?'

Mummy said she had found it in an antique shop, but she had sewn the pillows and the blankets herself.

'Look at the little sheet!' she said. 'It's got MF on it.' MF stood for Margaret Froud.

Lydia made all the right noises, but her mother was waiting for her to place Margaret-Doll in it now.

'I left her in Somerset,' she said with her eyes open very wide.

'Never mind,' Mummy said, she was trying not to be disappointed. 'She'll be pleased to have it when you get back!'

23

Emmeline

After Lydia returned to Somerset, Emmeline couldn't help but breathe a tiny sigh of relief. The love she felt for her only daughter was unfathomable, yet Lydia had some strange ideas. Emmeline was also surprised Margaret-Doll hadn't made the trip. In the past, they'd been inseparable.

However, she was relieved that once again Lydia seemed happy and confident – you couldn't fake that, could you? In fact, she was happier and more confident every time she saw her, and the Davenports said that her manners were wonderful. They had heard of Mrs Howard – didn't she used to be a theatre director? She had, and Lydia said that she still did plays, but for the war effort now.

'Wonderful, and you enjoy watching them?'

Lydia had told them she adored them (which was not what she had told Emmeline).

'She'll be helping you out in the nursery too, I imagine,' suggested Mr Reynolds, and Emmeline had smiled but hadn't answered, because it was something she dreamed of, but she sensed Lydia mightn't feel the same.

The nursery would open in the New Year. Both the factory and the hospital were desperate for staff and mothers would make up the shortfall. Christine would be the nursery medical supervisor, which Emmeline and Mr Davenport were pleased about.

However, the loan of the hall came with conditions attached. The council – having done nothing to make the hall habitable – now decided they wanted it as a meeting place for elderly people on Fridays. The ladies couldn't have the loan of the hall unless they agreed to this.

'Is there nowhere we can shunt them off to?'

'Dot!'

'Could you perhaps shut the nursery on Friday?' Mr Davenport suggested. 'Or move to a different location?'

'In summer maybe,' Emmeline pondered. 'Not winter. And I don't think the factory or the hospital would be happy if the mums did just a four-day week.'

They arranged that the toddlers would be there at the same time as the old people and they would just have to work out a way of managing them all. 'How hard can it be?' Emmeline asked, ignoring Dot's anguish. 'If they're anything like my mother-in-law – very hard!' Dot responded.

Then they were told they would have to pack up on Tuesday and Thursday nights too, because the council might want to use the hall then. Emmeline said this was fine – she was still at the stage where she would agree to anything.

One big worry was what to do if there was a bombing, or the Nazis invaded while the children were in nursery care. This was not a far-fetched concern. The Nazis controlled most of Europe now – even the Channel Islands had fallen – and, while the bombing was mostly directed at the cities, they were never entirely accurate and they frequently hit other areas too.

Mr Davenport said an Anderson shelter could probably be built in the garden of the hall. But he also said, 'I'm not sure it's a priority, here, deep in the countryside...'

Emmeline decided they would drill the children on how to react in an emergency. They would practise reacting to a siren, responding to whistles and finding hiding places. It would be a dismal task and wouldn't be of any use in a land invasion, but it made Emmeline feel better to think that they had some kind of plan.

Sometimes, she thought that by living in Norfolk she was taking the coward's way, while other times she thought it was the most responsible option. She thought about the Salts and the Hardmans in London, squirming underground every night, queueing for food or keeping the buses running by day, and she was glad she was away from the city.

She went to the church and thanked God for everything she had, and prayed for the nursery – *please make it good for everyone.* While she was there, she also asked God if He wouldn't mind keeping her mind on her task and her heart pure. Much appreciated.

Emmeline had been working in the hall all morning, painting, cleaning, and she could see her efforts were beginning to pay off. Early afternoon, Mr Davenport popped in and asked her if she would accompany him to an auction house in King's Lynn. An anonymous donor had given him some money to help fit out the nursery. He asked her if Dot wanted to come too and Emmeline said she probably wouldn't. (Heavily pregnant Dot, Hettie and Pat would be a lot.) It was that afternoon.

'Is Mr Reynolds coming?' she asked as they walked out to the car.

'He's doing paperwork for me at the house,' he said. So it *was* just the two of them, and Matthew, of course.

God hopefully didn't think this was a bad thing or impure or not focusing on her task, because it was all for a good cause.

'It was lovely meeting your Lydia,' Mr Davenport said. 'I found her an interesting character.'

Emmeline told him that she expected Lydia would be an excellent grown-up – it was just the bit before that which was tricky. He laughed, then said he didn't know much about children, but weren't they all like that?

In the auction house, he lifted Matthew onto his shoulders.

'Now, Matthew,' he instructed, 'you must stay still otherwise I might end up with two giraffes and a caravan.' Matthew was delighted and kept trying to touch the light fittings.

Mr Davenport bid on, but didn't win, a large table and six tennis racquets. He also bid for and won three picnic tables, a large shelving unit, four blankets, a rocking chair and ten footballs (unused).

'The anonymous donor was generous,' Emmeline said afterwards, eyebrows sky-high.

'Wasn't he?'

'Hmm, you know it's a man?'

He winked. 'Whoever it was has asked for secrecy. I feel compelled to honour his – or her – decision.'

They smiled at each other and Emmeline decided she would go to church the next day as a matter of urgency. Matthew didn't want to come off Mr Davenport's shoulders and rhythmically pummelled his chest with his feet, but Mr Davenport didn't seem to mind. Even that was endearing.

On the drive back, he asked how she found Norfolk life and she told him how making friends had made a difference to her experience.

'I expect you ladies have a lot of fun complaining about the old-fashioned stick-in-the-muds you've been sent to live with!'

'I don't,' she said softly, running her fingers along the gap between the passenger door and the window. 'I am grateful.'

'I was joking,' he said equally gently. 'Yet I am glad to hear that.'

That night, as Emmeline undressed, she saw her own silhouette in the shadows. It was the first time she had seen herself for a long time, and it was the first time in an even longer time that she had cared. Now, she looked closely. She had always been trim. She had bounced back to her pre-pregnancy shape after both children. She was less curvy than she used to be around the hips, perhaps – sugar rationing had probably seen to that – but she still had a high bosom, a flat stomach, slender legs.

She heard Mrs Davenport come home and hurriedly pulled on her nightgown. Imagine if she were caught looking at herself! She was being silly – self-regard and vanity was never impressive; she poured herself into bed and tried to think about all the more important things that demanded her attention.

24

DECEMBER 1940

Emmeline

Neville said it was too dangerous for Emmeline to go back to London, even for Christmas, especially for Christmas.

'We ought to see each other,' Emmeline wrote, although she had mixed feelings. On one hand, she had an obligation: he was her husband. As Dot was fond of reminding her, 'Your Neville is only three hours away, mine is God knows where!' But at the same time, despite her prayers, Emmeline felt she was wheeling towards something dangerous, like walking along a crumbling cliff's edge yet not wanting to stop.

What made it worse was that Neville didn't seem to care.

'No *ought to* about it,' he wrote back, 'but I am willing to come to Norfolk if you feel it's imperative.'

Emmeline didn't like the thought of Neville swanking around the Old Rectory with a disapproving scowl, nor did she want him meeting the Davenports. They wouldn't say that *he* had excellent manners, she was certain of that.

She could imagine Neville telling them his opinions and Mrs Davenport slipping on her glasses and humouring him, and

Mr Davenport feeling sorry for her that she had to spend her whole life with this insufferable bore. It would feel like worlds colliding and she didn't imagine either world would be impressed.

The other thing was, if they were to meet it had to be sooner or later, because once the nursery opened, Emmeline anticipated that it would take up virtually all of her time. For once, Neville was apparently of the same mind, for he wrote that he didn't want to stay at the Old Rectory. He'd splash out and take her and Matthew to a bed and breakfast for three nights.

'That's a waste of money,' she wrote back, but there wasn't an alternative. They compromised on two nights though.

They hadn't anticipated how difficult it would be to find somewhere that would take them, however. The London hotels were full of the unaffected rich and the rest all seemed to have been requisitioned by the military, but eventually Neville found a room in Bury St Edmunds.

Mr and Mrs Davenport, and probably Mr Reynolds too, were staying elsewhere in the countryside.

'We always go to a hotel,' Mrs Davenport told Emmeline. 'But I doubt this year will be as extravagant as usual.'

'There are so many shortages,' Emmeline said sympathetically.

'It's not that,' Mrs Davenport trilled. 'How would it look if we're fiddling while Rome burns?'

Bury St Edmunds wasn't far as the crow flies but Emmeline and Matthew had to get a bus, a train and another bus, and it was all young men in uniform, and when she said she was meeting her husband they assumed he was in the services, and on leave, and it was *that* kind of rendezvous, and she didn't feel able to put them right.

She imagined Neville picking her up and whipping her

round and saying, 'I've missed you so much, beloved, I've been dreaming of being in your arms,' like the husbands did in the films. But it was hard to daydream about something so unlikely. A daydream needed to have a kernel of truth in it to be enjoyable.

She thought of that magazine article Dot had gone on about. *A casualty of the war: long-term relationships.* She had to try to heal this casualty before its condition worsened. Even if she didn't particularly want to.

When she saw Neville greet Matthew, though, she *was* glad they had come. Neville gave him a great bear hug, marvelled at how he'd grown, couldn't believe the size of him!

Mathew begged to be picked up and to be fair to Neville – he always did pick up both children, despite his wonky knees – he picked his son up and wrapped him round him. But Matthew complained.

'Up, up, higher,' he said, as Emmeline squirmed.

'Why's he saying that?' Neville asked.

'He wants to go on your shoulders,' she said quietly.

'Where's he got that idea from?' scowled Neville, but again he did as his son demanded and swung him onto his shoulders, Matthew's feet thumping on his chest, as they had done to Mr Davenport just a few days earlier.

Even in Bury St Edmunds most of the men they saw were in uniform, but Neville didn't care. He kept puffing on his pipe. There was a couple; she couldn't have been more than seventeen and he must have been around nineteen, hardly shaving, and they couldn't keep their hands off each other.

Emmeline smiled indulgently, thinking, *When did Neville and I get so old?*

'Disgusting,' Neville commented. 'Do they think the uniform excuses them?'

'Do you wish you were fighting?' she asked.

'My work at the newspaper is important,' Neville said.

It was, Emmeline knew that, but his job wasn't a reserved occupation. The reason he hadn't been conscripted was because of the state of his legs. He never told people that, though. He let them assume.

'That's not what I asked.'

She was trying to get to know him better, to find the real Neville, the old Neville, but he seemed lost in defensiveness and bluster. She felt like she had to dig him out.

'Do I feel bad that my countrymen are risking their lives for us?'

'I didn't mean it like—'

'Anyway, the answer is no. Fire-watching is dangerous too. I've had a few near-misses, I can tell you.'

Emmeline contemplated the wedding band on her finger. She remembered the excitement of their wedding day. Her mother had been dead two years, her father only one, and here was a man offering to be her shelter and her parachute. Neville complained a lot, but he did so with wit, he was old-fashioned in some ways but rebellious in others – he didn't like to be told what to do but he liked order. He was a mishmash and so was she. He kissed her often and said he dreamed of being a father. He gave her his pay cheque with few provisos. He trusted her, she who barely trusted herself. And he took her to the band-stand in the park and he was a good dancer, until his legs went.

'Do you see the Salts or Mrs Hardman in the house at all?'

'They should have left.'

'But do you see them?' Emmeline couldn't understand why he wouldn't give a straight answer.

'Not much,' he said gruffly. He said he didn't see anyone. He kept his head down and his eyes lower.

Maybe Emmeline was the same. She downplayed the nursery project. Yes, she told him about it, but she didn't tell

him the details and he didn't ask. She got the impression that he
thought it was just a few friends taking care of each other's children and she didn't want to correct him. It wasn't worth the
hassle. In one way that was all it was – he didn't need to know
that she had poured her all into it.

They were too tired the first evening, but on the second they
made love silently, fearfully, as Matthew slept in the corner.

She shut her eyes and thought of someone else. The
strangest thing was, she had the feeling Neville was doing the
same too.

Afterwards, she rolled onto her side, away from him. She
felt tearful suddenly and she couldn't say why. He patted
her hip.

'Bit out of practice, old girl,' he said. 'Sorry.'

25

Emmeline

The nursery would be opening soon and Emmeline and the others were growing nervous. The hall and garden looked better – certainly much tidier – each day. They spent most of their time there, brightening it up, clearing, sweeping, and also fretting. Their young children helped too, in their own sweet ways. Matthew fell into a thorn bush and howled. Hettie disappeared, which gave them a horrendous five minutes, but she was hiding in a cupboard they didn't know about so they decided that was an important find. Anna got her foot stuck in a pot of black paint. Pat collected twigs and put them in rows according to size.

'They're our test pilots,' Dot said about them, and there was a truth in it.

Dot spent most of her time in the rocking chair directing them all. She had backache most days, but she insisted that once the nursery opened, she would be ready for action.

. . .

'I thought I'd find you here,' Mr Davenport said when he came back from his Christmas holiday.

Union Jack flags were strung across the hall, along with some numbers and letters that little Anna had cut out. They had gathered old clothes – for mothers as well as babies – and put them in the shelving unit. The picnic tables fitted beautifully in the garden and the footballs were tried and tested too. Mr Hazell, Marjorie's old hosts, had donated a cabinet and a blackboard as well. 'Don't ask me where they're from,' he had said mysteriously. Christine's hosts had donated lamps and Dot's hosts, the Ingrams, had done the wiring.

'Quite the team effort!' Mr Davenport kept shaking his head incredulously. 'How many are you expecting?'

'Ah,' said Emmeline. 'Not sure yet.'

They hadn't yet had a single mother sign up.

Early the next morning, there was a phone call.

'Mrs FROUD,' Mrs Davenport called. It was 6 a.m.

Emmeline carried Matthew down the stairs and he tried to grab the receiver. Mrs Davenport was only wearing her house robe; Emmeline knew this was another thing she wouldn't like. Indeed, she immediately said, 'Don't give out our number willy-nilly.'

'I apologise,' Emmeline said. She guessed it was something to do with the nursery. Maybe Councillor Arscott had found a way to stop it. Into the receiver she said, 'Mrs Froud speaking.'

There was a silence and then a wretched sob.

'Lydia?'

It wasn't her daughter; it was Mrs Hardman, her neighbour from back in London.

'What is it? Is it Valerie?'

'It's Mrs Salt. And the children.'

'What's happened?'

'Not Francine. But the others. The babies...'

'What on earth happened, Mrs Hardman?'

'They were in the shelter – there was a bomb.' She took a deep breath. Emmeline waited. 'It was a direct hit.'

Emmeline didn't know what to do with herself. Mrs Hardman said she could tell Lydia and Valerie on the telephone, but if Mrs Froud preferred to go there herself... Emmeline said she would. She knew that Mrs Hardman struggled to get time off from the buses.

Mrs Davenport had a cool head in a crisis. 'You will want to be with your daughter,' she said after Emmeline explained the situation. 'Go now, before your nursery opens.'

Emmeline wondered if she might offer to look after Matthew, but she didn't.

'Would it be all right to bring Lydia back here?'

Mrs Davenport's compassionate expression disappeared. 'That's something we would need to discuss...' but then she reconsidered. 'I understand. Please do what you have to do – this is heartbreaking news.'

Mrs Davenport got Mr Reynolds to drive her and Matthew to the station, insisting he would help with the luggage on the stairs. She kissed the air next to Emmeline's cheek.

'This is a blow,' she said. 'Stay strong.'

Her being unusually demonstrative reinforced how tragic it was. How fragile things were.

Even Mr Reynolds was subdued as he took the handle of her case: 'I'm sorry to hear about your friends. This is a terrible war.' And she found herself liking him more.

Only the day before, Emmeline had been thinking how it was possible to pretend the war wasn't even happening. How untouched by or secluded from it she was in Fincham. She had made the mistake of forgetting why she was here – and she was being punished for it. Here was the war, like a dead mouse dragged to her feet by a proud cat. There was no pretending now.

A whole family wiped out? The poor, poor Salts. Poor Mrs Salt. Poor babies.

When a woman on the train asked if she was all right, Emmeline couldn't reply. She would cry if she spoke. The woman produced a puppet from her handbag and proceeded to entertain Matthew with it: Emmeline was so distressed she couldn't even tell the other woman what a help she was.

How could God let this happen, she wondered? And the silly thought popped up that He was annoyed with her and her longing for a man she shouldn't be longing for. She told herself to stop being so ridiculous. *She* was not the centre of the universe, she was not how God made His decisions.

As she watched out of the train window and tried to take it in, one sentence kept coming to her in bold, capital letters:

THIS WAS WHY WE LEFT

This was why – she had become so immersed in her new life, in her many tasks, yet she had let herself forget the simple reason for the evacuation: escape from the danger. Neville had been proven right again, God bless him. He hadn't been pernickety or fearful or overly anxious. He hadn't been intent on getting her away to serve his own interests, Emmeline could see that now. If they had stayed, they would have been in that shelter last night. It was not wise to think of the young Salt children yet, but Emmeline's thoughts kept racing towards them. She had to acknowledge them, she had to incorporate their loss into her being somehow.

She wondered why she was in such a hurry to get to Somerset. Might it have been better to wait a few days, to take in the dreadful information first? No, she needed to clutch her daughter close. It was a primitive, maternal urge when everything around was falling apart.

By mid-morning Emmeline and Matthew were standing in front of Lydia and Valerie in Bumble Cottage, and Emmeline was wringing her hands. She had practised what she would say on the fraught walk from Chard railway station and she delivered it exactly as she had planned:

'Girls, I have terrible news.'

26

Lydia

Until that day, Lydia hadn't known babies could die. She had thought death happened only to old people. *You've got it wrong,* she wanted to say. Maybe Mrs Salt had perished, maybe at a push Maisie Salt might have, but not the chubby small boys who couldn't walk on their own or even tell you they were thirsty.

All? All four? Mrs Salt. Maisie. Jacob. And little Joe. Was her mummy sure? Mightn't they still be waiting to be rescued?

Lydia collapsed onto the carpet and, for a short while, she let go of her posture and her spine completely. Matthew kept trying to pat her shoulder and she pushed him away. Mummy was still talking and it was like explosions in the background and then it dawned on Lydia that she was expecting her to go and live in Norfolk with her now.

'You liked it, didn't you?' Now Mummy was an insect humming in the garden, a stinging one. 'And the Davenports loved you.'

Lydia shook herself back into the living room. *Concentrate.*
'It is a beautiful house,' she admitted.

'You'd be all right sharing with me – and Matthew?'

'I wouldn't have my own room?'

Mummy looked pained. 'I don't know.'

'Could I bring the dog?'

Now even more pained.

'I don't...'

'Mummy, I think I should stay here,' Lydia said.

She couldn't see why this news – catastrophic as it was –
would bring about such a change in her life.

Her mother looked exasperated. 'But I think you should be
with me.' Kneeling down at Lydia's side, she whispered, 'We
should be together.'

'That's what Mrs Salt said,' Lydia responded bitterly, and
watched as her mother whipped backwards as though she'd
been hit. Lydia said, anyhow, she needed to support Valerie –
Valerie wasn't strong – and she saw this worked on Mummy.

'It is special that you girls look after each other.' Her eyes
were red from crying. 'Like sisters. I am so glad you have that.'

Poor Francine. Who did she have now?

After Mummy and Matthew had left, Lydia told Rex what
had happened and he snuggled into her like a good boy. She
could never leave him. Ever. No one loved him like she did. Not
Paul, Valerie nor Mrs Howard. She wished she hadn't got rid of
Margaret-Doll. That little face and those eyes that blinked
when you shook her would have been a comfort now.

Lydia didn't know what to do with the feelings and the
memories bursting inside her. And she also didn't know what to
do with that ugly bud of relief that was glad that she was still
alive. She didn't want to die, she had so many plans.

Mrs Howard told her, 'Stiff upper lip,' in her no-nonsense
tone, but she also made her cocoa and squeezed her arm whenever she went past.

Lydia wanted to send Francine something to show that she cared. Once again, she wished she hadn't thrown Margaret-Doll away – Francine had always admired her so. Mummy had said she ought to write a card. Mrs Howard called it 'expressing your condolences', but it all came out so babyish or artificial that Lydia decided it would be best to send nothing at all.

Over the next few days, Lydia felt changed. She felt as though she was grown up while all the other children at St Boniface school were childish, concerned only with irrelevancies. Listening to them bleat on about algebra problems made her impatient. Hearing them argue over which seat was whose made her think they were pathetic. For the first time, she even felt apart from Betsy and Flora. She was mired in tragedy – a wartime tragedy – while they worried over the elastic of their knickers or multiplication.

The shock of the Salts' family demise accompanied her everywhere and was on her mind constantly. It was with her at playtime, at breakfast, at bedtime and in lessons. It was like a shadow that she couldn't escape. She couldn't think of it, yet she couldn't *not* think of it. She wished Francine were here so she could comfort her, but she wondered if Francine mightn't now hate her given that Lydia still had an adoring mother and father, a little brother and a special dog, and even Valerie and Mrs Howard and Paul, while Francine had no one.

Mrs Howard insisted Lydia went to school – nothing must stand between a girl and her learning – and Lydia didn't have the power to resist, but although she attended in body, in her mind she was not there. Her marks, already poor, fell further. She turned up late, refused to listen, cared only about Rex.

Valerie, who, like Lydia, had known the Salt family since she was a baby and loved them dearly was also shattered. But

Valerie's way of dealing with it was curling up like a comma, escaping into her books in the library or her silly radio shows. Mrs Howard seemed to approve of Valerie's way of grieving. Lydia's sullen bewilderment she seemed to find less palatable.

27

Emmeline

'I was so sorry to hear about your neighbour,' Mr Davenport said when Emmeline next saw him, back at the Old Rectory some days later. There was no let-up in the bombing of London and every bit of news was more sobering than the last.

Emmeline meant to say something but instead she let out a sob.

'She was my friend...' she mumbled.

'There, there, Mrs Froud,' he said softly.

'I'm all right!' Emmeline pulled herself together quickly. It was just Mr Davenport's face, his voice – it did something to her. If Neville's expressions and manners irritated her, Mr Davenport's had the opposite effect. She suddenly wanted to hold his hands. She blew her nose loudly into her handkerchief. She was repulsive, but she didn't care. In fact, it was probably for the best if he found her disgusting.

'How was your Lydia?' he asked, his expression full, not of revulsion, but of concern.

How was Lydia? She certainly wasn't the girl Emmeline had put on the train fifteen months earlier. She was like that child's big sister. She was dog-crazy, which was a new development, and she had a faraway look in her eyes. How had she taken the news? As well as could be expected. It was easier to connect with Valerie, who – always the more straightforward – had immediately burst into tears.

'I don't know.'

'And how are *you* coping?' he added.

'I don't know the answer to that either,' she admitted. 'Devastated. Shocked. Sad.'

He smelled wonderful, she thought, after the horror of everything, after delivering the news in Somerset, after the funerals in London. His scent was something erotic. And she was a bad, bad person for noticing, especially now.

It was a grey-skied and chilly Sunday morning. Even the bare trees outside the window looked sorry for themselves. Mr Davenport lit the kitchen fire and then poured them both a sherry. Although she felt she shouldn't, she felt unable to resist. She even smoked one of his cigarettes.

She told him about the heartbreaking funerals in the cemetery in London, and the tiny coffins. He listened carefully. He told her about a great friend he had lost in the early days of the war and how it inspired him to do more. And she told him, yes, if anything, the experience had made her more impassioned to do something – both to provide a place of safety for children and to help the war effort. No, she could not single-handedly win the war, but they were not single-handed, they were many-handed, and if they all pulled together then they would win. And *that* was more important than ever. That was all she knew. His eyes were gentle on hers and he nodded in agreement.

Mrs Davenport swished in, and Emmeline felt torn between annoyance and relief at the interruption. Pulling a face at the sight of the rather dishevelled Emmeline, she said, 'I'll put the kettle on.' Then she turned to her husband: 'Darling, there are constituents in *real* need to attend to.' Emmeline was just apologising when Mrs Davenport noticed the sherry glasses. At first, she seemed to freeze before she picked them up and emptied them into the sink. Then she smoothed her hair back and dismissed her husband, 'I'll keep an eye on Mrs Froud from here.'

They didn't manage to open the nursery on the second of January, but they did get it ready for the fifth.

'Do you think anyone will come?' Dot wondered. 'We can't have gone to all this bother just for Hettie, Pat, Anna and Matthew.'

'It would be wonderful if Della, Deidre and Derek could come,' Emmeline said, but on this subject, as usual, Dot didn't respond. Emmeline didn't voice these private thoughts often precisely because they rarely got a reaction. Still, she increasingly felt as though the nursery was somehow in their honour.

Emmeline put a sign on the door: NURSERY. ENQUIRE WITHIN. And she put notices on a few trees too. But it rained and the ink spilled and *enquire within* didn't make sense on a tree trunk anyway.

The Davenports insisted that they invite a journalist friend along to the nursery opening. And the journalist wanted to put a ribbon across the nursery door and to take a photograph of Mr Davenport snipping it.

'It's a little over-the-top, isn't it?' said Emmeline, who never liked a fanfare, but Dot clapped her hands and Christine and Mabel chorused, 'Super idea!'

'We don't have any scissors,' said Emmeline irritably, even though she had been using some just an hour earlier to cut some index cards, but with a flourish, the journalist produced a pair.

Mr Davenport snipped and after four or five goes, the ribbon split in two and he announced, 'I now pronounce this wartime nursery officially open!' and the journalist clicked his camera again.

Emmeline was used to seeing a relaxed Mr Davenport at home, but now, out in the world, she couldn't help seeing how different he looked: suave, debonair, like Cary Grant. It didn't help that Dot was cooing over him to the other women.

'Let's take a photograph of you with the nursery manager,' said the journalist.

Mabel pushed Emmeline forward. 'That's you.'

'All of us.' Emmeline called out, 'Come into the picture! It's a group effort. Christine... Dot? Mabel?'

But the journalist wanted only the two of them. It *had* to be the two of them: Mrs Froud in her apron and Mr Davenport in his suit – 'London mothers and country politicians', 'MP opens wartime nursery!' muttered the journalist, perhaps thinking of likely headlines as he ordered them around.

'Closer together, please, I could drive a truck between you...'

They shuffled nearer each other. Emmeline could feel Mr Davenport's arm graze hers and it made her feel foolishly hot. Blushing, she bit her lip and apologised.

'Closer than that...' instructed the journalist.

'Good grief,' Emmeline said, which made Mr Davenport chuckle. And then it was done and they could go inside and show the journalist what they'd made of the place. The other women were thrilled – they loved a bit of pomp and circumstance – but Emmeline wished everyone would go away.

'Hasn't he got a war to report on?' she asked under her breath.

'Women in the workforce *is* a war story, isn't it?' Mr Davenport said encouragingly. 'Chin up, it's all a means to an end.'

He winked, and Emmeline felt she might dissolve. For days,

she had been trying to convince herself she did NOT desire him, she was just being friendly, it was just gratitude, she was just overawed. That afternoon, it was difficult to label it anything other than what Dot's magazines might call lust.

28

Emmeline

The eventual headline was *Wartime Nurseries Lift Off* and it was a lovely feel-good story in a sea of bad news, and also an advertisement that they hadn't had to pay for. Emmeline and Mr Davenport looked jolly in the photograph, although Emmeline regretted the state of her hair. She had just taken off her hat and it looked like it. She touched Mr Davenport's face on the page with her thumb and tried to imagine what she would think about him if she didn't know him. She would think he looked a pleasant person, she supposed. Sincere. Engaging. If she was someone who didn't know either of them, she might have thought he was married to her, the woman he was standing so close to—

Guiltily, Emmeline turned to the article. She couldn't help noticing that the phrasing was *all* about the help for the war, rather than helping mothers or children, but she didn't mind that any more. How could she? The mothers and babies would benefit. She had got what she wanted; what did it matter that others had got what they wanted too?

She wondered what Mrs Salt would have said about it all. Probably something like, 'Today's news is tomorrow's fish and chips papers,' or 'Are there no hairbrushes in Norfolk, Mrs Froud?'

There was a line in it that said: 'Enabling young mums to do their bit.'

'Less of the young,' said Dot, laughing, when she read it.

'That was my favourite part!' Emmeline laughed too.

Most importantly, the day the newspaper article was published the nursery was inundated with applications. Mothers knocked on the door, sent letters through the post or tackled her in the street.

'We're going to need more staff!' Dot said.

Mabel was on standby, as was another mother from London, Mrs Hodges, and a grandmother, Mrs Pound. Both agreed to come in every day if needed. When they'd first proposed it, it hadn't seemed likely they'd need extra help. It was overwhelming and wonderful. At times, Emmeline felt she had to pinch herself to know that it wasn't a dream.

On 6 January 1941, the first children came. There were bicycles outside for the women to borrow to go straight to the factory if they wanted. The women who were working in the hospital would walk because it was only five minutes away. The cyclist mothers went off squealing and giggling, like children themselves, although Christine, Dot and Emmeline didn't have time to wave them off – their hands were full.

They made porridge and put the children in highchairs to feed them. They had to take turns because there weren't enough highchairs. The noise was tremendous. And Emmeline thought of Marjorie and imagined what she might have thought of it all.

'More highchairs,' called Emmeline over the racket, 'put

that on our list.' They had a list of things still needed and it was already over three pages long. 'More bibs, please. And spoons...'

Then there was the dance of burping, and winding, and nappy-changing. Anna, Hettie, Pat and even Matthew, who were familiar with the hall, helped settle in the new ones. They helped them pull up their socks and showed the bigger ones where the loos were.

After the rush another woman came in with two small children, bringing their total to their maximum: ten.

'I don't have a job though.' The woman sounded and looked exhausted. Emmeline thought of Marjorie. 'I sleep standing up sometimes...'

'We can have volunteers here, or in there, or' – Emmeline leaned forward and whispered – 'you can go home and sleep.'

'I won't have to pay?'

'Can you contribute to food and the nappies?'

She nodded eagerly, a changed woman. 'I'll come back before lunch,' she said.

'Very well,' Emmeline said. This was exactly what they were for. 'Go and rest.'

As they packed up that evening, Dot tapped Emmeline on the hand.

'Ever felt like a pawn?'

Emmeline's heart sank. She guessed this was connected to the newspaper article, but what was she supposed to do?

'How do you mean?'

'They're playing us. Your Mr and Mrs Davenport aren't interested in our nursery, they just want votes for their party.'

This hurt. And Emmeline didn't feel it was true either.

'It doesn't matter what their motivations are. Our interests converge. I get to take the load off mothers and they get more popular. We're all supporting the war effort. Win-win.'

But Dot was shaking her head.

'You never win against people like that.'

Emmeline thought for a bit, then decided. 'I don't need to win,' she said. 'We're on the same side.'

This time, Dot rolled her eyes. 'If you say so.'

One child shouted, 'arrow' at them every morning, with increasing frustration.

'What is he saying?' Emmeline queried. Was it local slang?

Only Mabel could decipher it: 'It's hello!' She was another one who was proving herself invaluable. A lot of the children didn't speak, though. Emmeline tried to remember when Lydia's first word, 'Dadda', and Matthew's, 'Mama', had been. At about eight or nine months, maybe? Some of these toddlers were just overawed. And then there were the children who didn't stop speaking!

'My mummy has a baby in her tummy and it better be a girl this time otherwise Daddy is going to make a baby with someone else.'

Another child said, 'My mummy likes American soldiers.'

'We all like the American—'

'No, Granny says she *really* does.'

None of the children had any discretion, it seemed.

And the nappies! Emmeline had never changed so many in her life – the hall smelled of Dettol.

'Better than the alternative!' Dot laughed.

Matthew was having a lovely time. He got under the adults' feet and played with the other toddlers and drank his milk and wandered around holding his tin bus. It was hard to watch him with so much else going on, but whenever Emmeline did, it made her smile. For a sociable child like him, this place was heaven.

'We need coat hooks,' she told Dot, who was in charge of

'the list' that day. At the moment, the children came in and threw their outdoor clothes in a pile. And no one had names on their coats.

By the end of the first week, Emmeline felt excited at the thought of telling Mr Davenport about her success. What would he say to her? Once, in a film, she had seen a man so pleased with his wife that he bought her *all* the flowers in the flower shop. But Mr Davenport was away in London. It wasn't just voting in Parliament, although there was a lot of that; there were committees, meetings, negotiations. There was a war to win. Looking after children wasn't important compared to that, she reminded herself. People were dying in this Godforsaken war. The world did not revolve around her. She remembered Councillor Arscott's harsh words for her 'vanity project' – she must be careful to remember what this was all *for*.

She channelled her feelings into a long letter to Neville. The tragedy of the Salts was a reminder of how risky life in London was right now. Neville was a good man to be defending the capital – she only wished he would tell her more about it. She prayed by her bed and on Sunday in church. It was easier to control her wayward imagination when Mr Davenport wasn't there, she told herself, even though it didn't feel it.

29

Emmeline

Far from being a disaster, 'Old People Friday' (not its official name) came to be everyone's favourite day of the week. The elderly attendees like Mrs Carter, Mrs Dolby and Mrs Jones didn't just walk to the hall, they skipped.

'Where are the babies?' they demanded. 'I need a cuddle.'

They sat with the toddlers in their arms, read to them or played peek-a-boo.

'A tonic,' they said. 'The best medicine.'

Even the old men, especially Mr Carter and Mr Harris, liked the children. One old man who, according to his daughter, never usually did anything except sit and doze now got on the floor to build houses out of playing cards. (He did struggle to get up, but they managed in the end.) Another brought in a box of wooden bricks that his son used to play with. Most Fridays, by the end of the afternoon Emmeline had a tear in her eye.

Monday was for delousing, prayers and singing/Bible. Unfortunately, or fortunately depending on your perspective, delousing took up most of the morning. To get them through it, they had a competition – who had the child with the most lice in a single head? The numbers were kept on a chart in the back room.

Matthew, sadly, was all too often in the top five. Lice loved him!

Emmeline told Lydia this when she wrote and Lydia replied, 'What is the matter with him?' And then just as Emmeline was worrying that Lydia was not growing any more compassionate, she wrote sweetly that Emmeline was the best mummy in the whole world.

On Wednesdays, they did gardening/tending to vegetables, whatever the weather. Thursdays and Tuesdays at the nursery were singing, dressing up, playing. Friday was also cod-liver-oil-and-orange-juice day.

One thing Emmeline worried about was the war games. Children, children who hardly spoke, who could barely feed themselves, were shooting and cowering and killing.

'Should we stop them?' she asked the other women.

'It's normal for them to imitate what they hear,' Christine explained.

'It's imaginative play. Didn't you do it?' Mabel said.

'Not like that!' Emmeline said.

Nevertheless, they decided to keep war-talk to the minimum, at least in the nursery, if they could. Which was hard, because war-talk was *everywhere*.

Emmeline couldn't say the nursery ran smoothly. There was the time they ran out of porridge and Mabel had to chase all over town to find some more. There was the day there was no electricity. There was the day a cat got in a back window, causing havoc. And every day there was Little Alice – ten months old – who refused to be put down for a nap.

'What should I do?' Christine despaired. 'Every time I put her down, she howls like there has been a murder.'

It was a good thing they didn't have close neighbours. Emmeline could only imagine the complaints if they did!

'Hold her, I guess,' Emmeline suggested. She had never had this problem with Lydia or Matthew. They'd both started crawling away from her as soon as they possibly could. 'She'll get used to us.'

The terrible day Christine heard her brother was killed in Egypt, they didn't get a lot done through the tears. Or the day Mrs Lucas heard her father-in-law had stepped on a mine in Italy, and came to the nursery in shock. Dot came into her own that morning, making her sweet tea in the kitchen and listening to her grief.

If Emmeline had once felt that the war was far away, she felt that no longer. It was everywhere, everyone was being affected. *How long can we hold on for?* she wondered. But they were open! They provided a sanctuary for children – which in turn provided peace of mind for their mothers. And their mothers worked so hard at the factory and the hospital. Emmeline couldn't have been prouder of all of them.

Look what we can do! she told herself. Becoming a mother didn't have to mean the end – it could be the beginning. She hoped some of this would rub off on Lydia one day. She wanted Lydia to believe that she could be anything she wanted to be.

It wasn't only the mothers' achievements she was proud of. Within weeks, some little ones were potty trained. The three-year-olds were picking out letters or writing their names. One-year-old Herbert took his first steps. Two-year-old Molly could tie a bow in her hair and would help you with your shoelaces if necessary. Dot said they should get Molly into government: 'She'd tell Churchill what to do.'

One evening, when Emmeline's feet were killing her and she

was dreaming of going straight to bed, Mrs Davenport called her downstairs.

'Might we borrow you for five minutes?'

'I'll just put Matthew down,' Emmeline said, glad of an excuse for a moment to consider what she was wanted for. These days, after racing around all day long, both she and Matthew slept like logs.

When she came into the drawing room, Mr Reynolds was pouring himself a drink and Mr Davenport looked as mystified as she felt. They had not seen each other for a while, he was busy in Parliament and she with the nursery, and she knew that was for the best. She would not jeopardise her stay in the house, Matthew's well-being or the nursery – and it would jeopardise all of that – for a silly crush.

She hoped it wasn't about another newspaper article. Although she understood their purpose, since Dot's comments they made her feel used.

'So, darling,' Mrs Davenport addressed her husband as he fiddled with his cigarette case, 'some of your letter-writers have gone insane.'

Emmeline looked over at the desk where she saw there were the usual towers of letters, although possibly the stacks were higher than usual.

'What, again?' he said. 'Is it about the badgers?'

'No, not the badgers.' She paused dramatically. 'About the wartime nursery.'

Emmeline's heart was racing.

'I give you: Exhibit A.' Mrs Davenport picked up a letter from the top of the pile and held it away to read, glasses on: '"It's immoral. It's disgusting. It's a disgrace and you are tarnish."' She looked around witheringly. 'I think they mean "tarnished..." and by association, unless they—'

'I get the picture,' cut in Mr Davenport, taking puffs on his cigarette. 'Are they all like that?'

'Not all. But most.'

She dished out the papers to each of them.

'Oh!' Emmeline sat back down with one:

'Mothers stay home. This is sinful. There's a place in hell for women who abandon their babies.'

Emmeline's hands were trembling as she argued: 'But they're not abandoning their children... That's the whole point.'

It got worse. 'She-devils!' one said. 'Witches. The steak' – they had spelled it wrong but it was too horrifying to laugh – 'is too good for them.'

'What about the nasty ones?' Mr Davenport joked, before noticing Emmeline's tearful countenance and becoming concerned.

'Oh dear, Mrs Froud, you're not used to this...'

'I could *never* get used to this.' Emmeline had never been so shocked in her life. Was this the general public? These nasty people walked among them? They were like a pack of howling wolves. She had never been exposed to such ill-feeling before, and certainly never been the target of it.

'It's a concerted attack – many of them use the same language. This one' – he dangled the offending letter – 'is not even from Norfolk. They're writing from Leeds, for goodness' sake. Writing from Leeds to Norfolk to complain about a wartime nursery. We must be doing something right,' he added defiantly.

'I think so,' said Mr Reynolds unexpectedly. 'Quite the zeitgeist.'

'Less German please,' Mrs Davenport said in a surprisingly jokey tone and he clapped his hand over his mouth. They were very friendly with each other, thought Emmeline, she hadn't realised.

'How about this one?' Mr Reynolds read it out. 'You politicians are all the same: I will knife you in the heart.'

'Heart-warming,' Mr Davenport said sardonically.

'For goodness' sake,' Emmeline cried out. This was *abominable*. Nothing had prepared her for this.

'Do you want to reply?' Mrs Davenport said, serious again. 'I think we should.'

'Not to that one.' He gestured to the vile one in Mr Reynolds' hand. 'We'll put out a standard response. We'll emphasise that it is voluntary. No mother is forced to put her child in nursery.'

'They'll say it's a slippery slope.'

'They're deliberately misinterpreting what we're doing,' piped up Emmeline, still in shock at the violence.

'Absolutely.' Mr Davenport leaned back in his chair and crossed his arms. 'For these people, there's no slope that is not slippery and descending into the flames of eternal damnation.'

Emmeline let out a nervous laugh, but the others didn't.

'Don't engage on their level,' Mrs Davenport advised. 'All you have to say is: *I support the wartime nurseries because of the war effort.* That's all.'

Emmeline looked between them. She thought, *but it's not just that, is it?* but she didn't want to say. She glanced at her aching feet. There wasn't a part of them that didn't hurt.

'Right,' said Mr Davenport to his wife. 'I'll write it now, and if you could look over it later, we'll send it out tomorrow?'

He looked sympathetically at Emmeline. 'Don't worry, Mrs Froud. You have our full support.'

30

Emmeline

The nursery had been open for four weeks, the children were learning and Emmeline was learning too. The importance of regular nap times, quiet zones, imagination areas and keeping children busy. The importance of tissues after explosive nose-bleeds. The importance of teaching children *appropriate* language.

'Why won't you play with Hettie?' she asked sweet Freddie one morning.

'Because she's a bloody pain in the arse,' he replied.

'Freddie!'

Emmeline had been bitten twice, once on the arm, once on the cheek, and had been forgotten about in a game of hide-and-seek. She had burned her hand on the kettle, tripped over the shoes in the hallway, lost three jumpers and four pairs of socks. Christine had insisted she saw the doctor about her feet and now wore a rather more practical pair of shoes than she liked or was used to. The heels on these had only two inches rather than her favoured four. Neville, who had surprisingly strong opinions on women's fashions, would not approve.

Emmeline thought they should celebrate surviving the month, but Dot wasn't in the mood: 'I'm so uncomfortable.'

She was holding Alice, who increasingly let herself be put down for twenty-minute periods but no longer than that. Dot rarely complained, so Emmeline peered at her and saw that her friend looked more tired than usual.

'Should we get you to the hospital?'

It was reassuring that the hospital was so close.

Dot laughed, then winced.

'Hettie and Pat were late, so this one will be too,' she said. She had done her calculations; 'I'm only thirty-five weeks and Hettie came at forty-two. Bloody reluctant to see the world, she was. Still is.'

They fed the little ones, then there was winding and changing, playing, organising... It was delousing Monday and, for once, Matthew was blessedly lice-free. They had two new toddlers – Harold and Ivy – energetic twins, with a grateful mother who had brought jars of marmalade for Emmeline and the staff.

Emmeline was thinking about a tea break when Dot leaned over the table, closed her eyes and let out a groan.

'Mabel,' called Emmeline in alarm. 'Christine!'

Both were with the bigger ones in the garden. Mrs Hodges was rocking one of the babies, and she shook her head with a look that said, 'This isn't in my job description.'

Emmeline led Dot into the kitchen. 'I'll get help, Dot,' she reassured her friend.

Dot had put Alice down, and for once the little girl was not crying but sitting on a mat looking around her, astonished. Dot had got down on all fours and was making a sound that Emmeline could only call meowing.

'Lady in labour back here,' Emmeline called into the

garden. *Lady in labour?* She didn't know where she got that expression from. 'CHRISTINE! Dot needs you now!'

She didn't know if she could be heard over the cacophony of noise. The children were singing: 'Row, row, row your boat...' with actions.

'It can't be this quick, Dot!' Emmeline told her. 'Let's get you to the hospital.'

'Gently down the stream,' the children bellowed.

'I want to push,' Dot said through gritted teeth.

'Ho no,' said Emmeline. 'You can't do that here, Dot.'

Matthew sauntered into the kitchen, holding his bus. 'I need a wee, Mummy.' He paused, surveying the situation. 'What's Aunty Dot doing?

'Merrily, merrily, merrily, merrily.'

'I'm pushing,' Dot growled, her face red and eyes petrified. Under her skirt, she worked at her underwear, and flung a great pair of off-white pants into the air. They caught on the lid of a saucepan.

'Not now,' insisted Emmeline, but the baby was not waiting.

'Life is but a dream.'

That baby was waiting for no one. Dot's elbows were on the floor now, her hands were fisted balls, her rump up in the air. There was nothing Emmeline could do. Dot let out an ear-splitting, full-throated howl.

Finally, Emmeline gathered her wits about her. She grabbed a teacloth and dashed over to her friend, just as the baby made its own sweet way headlong into the world.

Two days later, they *were* in the newspapers again: *Nursery's newest baby delivered by staff on the premises!*

There was a grainy photo of Dot and Emmeline and baby Errol, named after Dot's favourite actor, taken at the hospital about four hours after his hasty entrance in the world.

'I thought Pete said no to calling him Errol!'

Dot chuckled. 'He's not here though, is he?'

'It's hardly his fault!' Emmeline said, still feeling elated. The whole experience was incredible. As for 'delivered by staff', it wasn't quite true – Errol had largely delivered himself.

'No, but it does mean I get to name my baby what I want.' Dot smirked. She insisted she'd be back at work just as soon as she was back on her feet, and Errol would be the youngest – and cutest – member of the wartime nursery.

31

Lydia

The way the light came through the stained-glass window in the corridor of St Boniface school, it was as though it was singling Miss Picard out. Lydia was dazzled.

At first, Miss Picard reprimanded Lydia – she said she had heard of her recent poor attendance, her lackadaisical demeanour – and then she mimicked Lydia's downcast expression.

'How can you expect admirers with a face like a bad weekend, Miss Froud?'

'Wet weekend,' corrected Lydia.

'Exactly – what is the matter with you?'

By then Lydia could hold in her distress no longer, and she burst into loud hot sobs. Miss Picard steered her into the staffroom and insisted on firing questions.

'Is it a love affair gone wrong, chérie?'

'No!' Lydia said, affronted. Miss Picard was wonderful, but she had never seemed able to distinguish between children's and adults' issues: Lydia was eleven, not twenty-one.

'Then quoi?' Miss Picard asked as if there was no other thing that could be a cause of such distress.

Lydia told her about the Salts and how she couldn't believe it and it was unfair and... and poor Francine and poor Maisie and poor babies and... She sobbed.

Miss Picard smelled of spicy perfume. Her skirt was short, and Lydia couldn't help being mesmerised by the sight of her stockinged knees. People always remarked on her mummy's shapely legs, but these were ridiculous.

'Don't fret, darling, this sadness will only add to your allure. You will use this, you will recover, and you will make me proud.'

Lydia sniffed. 'And I miss my dad, too. He's still in London.'

In danger, she wanted to add, in case Miss Picard didn't realise.

Miss Picard actually put her arm round Lydia, even though this was against her own policy.

'Is he a good man?' she asked urgently.

'Ye-es?' said Lydia, not sure where this was going or how it was relevant.

'I thought so,' Miss Picard said, nodding vigorously.

Miss Picard thought Lydia should go to finishing school. It didn't have to be in Switzerland, although the best ones were. Otherwise, she didn't see how even the most charming young lady – such as Lydia – would be able to attract the most eligible bachelors.

Lydia worried. 'But I do my deportment exercises every day,' she moaned. 'And there is a war on...'

'And you are truly exceptional, chérie,' Miss Picard reassured her, her arm on Lydia's sleeve. She always had impeccable nails too. 'But there are battles ahead...'

'You mean like Italy or Japan?'

Miss Picard laughed her tinkly laugh. 'I mean for you – on the home front.'

. . .

The next day, Mrs Howard asked Lydia how she was feeling.
She wondered if there was anything she could do for Lydia to
cheer her up. Lydia had been waiting for Mrs H to ask, since
she had already asked Valerie. (Of course, Valerie had requested
something quite dull.)

'I would quite like a mirror in my bedroom,' Lydia
suggested.

'A mirror?' Mrs Howard repeated, incredulously.

'I need it for electrocution class.'

'Elect— oh, elocution. I see,' Mrs Howard said coolly. She
folded her arms and pressed her chest to her neck. Lydia
waited. There would be more, there always was. A few seconds
later, Mrs Howard delivered: 'Much as I am pleased you have
finally found yourself an interest, Lydia, I hope you concentrate
on your more cerebral subjects too.'

Lydia, who did not know what she was talking about, smiled
her prettiest smile. Mrs H irritated her lately. She had two types
of conversation: inquisition or lecture; and Lydia enjoyed
neither. This was a lecture, Lydia decided, so she made her face
look obliging and let the preaching wash over her.

'Lydia?'

'Certainly!' Lydia agreed.

A mirror was produced a few days later. It was smaller than
Lydia had hoped for, but it would have to do. As she handed it
over, Mrs Howard seemed in two minds. 'It's important not to
put emphasis on one's appearance, Lydia,' she said. 'How one
looks is the luck of the draw – how one *acts* is the important
thing.'

'Absolutely, Mrs Howard,' Lydia said. She found her own
tear-stained face the most fascinating thing in the world. Others
might pore over maps, or obsess over art, Valerie and Paul might

be bewitched by poorly scripted radio shows – but Lydia's face in the mirror was succour to her. She could occupy herself with it for hours. Every bump, every flaw, every lash, all were under her scrutiny.

She was going to win all the battles.

32

APRIL 1941

Emmeline

Lydia was having a wonderful life, she reassured her mother. She loved Bumble Cottage (although she sometimes lamented the fact that it wasn't tidier. The volunteer boxes were *everywhere*). The Davenports had managed to retain their full-time housekeeper, hadn't they? Emmeline thought this was a bizarre observation for a small girl, but she explained, 'The rules for Members of Parliament are sometimes different.'

It was Easter and Lydia once again resisted coming to see her mother in Norfolk. She didn't outright refuse but suggested the St Boniface schedule wouldn't allow it or that the travel was too time-consuming.

Emmeline understood that these were excuses, and it hurt. She wanted to show off the nursery and she wanted to show off her daughter. She missed her dreadfully. The nursery was brilliant at keeping her occupied, but Lydia's absence was a dull ache that wouldn't go away.

Lydia wrote that she had suggested Mrs H put on *Cinderella* that year. Emmeline thought calling Mrs Howard

Mrs H was overfamiliar but she didn't want to expend precious goodwill correcting her on this. Mrs H was thinking about it, but Lydia did not expect her to think for long. Mrs H doesn't like love stories, Lydia wrote with exclamation marks. Emmeline thought this another interesting observation, but although she asked for more information, Lydia didn't elaborate, preferring to go on about Rex or the joys of her electrification class.

Emmeline worried that there might be a mother-shaped hole in Lydia's life, but nothing in Lydia's letters ever overtly suggested there was. Had Mrs H replaced Emmeline in Lydia's heart? Emmeline didn't think so; nevertheless, she read every letter very carefully, looking for clues. And if she had, wondered Emmeline, what would she be able to do about it from all these miles away anyway?

Emmeline loved the variety of ways in which the children arrived at nursery. Some toddled in carefully and hung up their coats, just so. They looked cautiously around them and then made their way over to the toy box or to a favourite friend. Others tore in like little whirling dervishes, scattering and clattering around. Others were tearful, full of sleep and clutching at their mothers. Some were already playing 'let's pretend'. One little girl liked to come in as a cat – woe betide if you didn't call her Tabby! A little boy loved pretending to be a cowboy and galloped around on his horse (a broom) for hours.

The mothers approached the nursery in very different ways too. Some slung a leg over their bike saddles without a backward glance. Some hugged their children for so long, Emmeline itched to peel them apart. Some wanted information – who, what, why, where, when? – and others wanted to *give* information – Eric had a bad night, Brian has not done a number two for three days. Emmeline's heart warmed to them all.

There were so many applications for nursery places, Emmeline thought they might have to put in a limit. Most of the mothers went up to the old bicycle factory up the road. Emmeline still didn't know exactly what went on there, but she understood it was a shadow factory – which meant it was top-secret war work. Others went to work at the hospital, not only in nursing but also administration.

And some went back to bed. And, as far as Emmeline was concerned, why not? If that was what they needed.

One morning, three-year-old Billy stormed into the nursery and refused to take off his coat or hat. Billy's dad was missing in action, so everyone was mostly sympathetic. His mum was at the end of her tether and was grateful to have a few hours of respite.

Christine gave Emmeline a look: 'This one could do with some fresh air today.'

Mabel said, 'Like dogs. They're always worse when it's windy.'

There wasn't a situation Mabel couldn't find an old wives' tale for.

They were just serving up porridge when Mr Davenport and Mr Reynolds walked in. Emmeline hadn't seen Mr Davenport for a few weeks since, despite the relentless bombings, he had been staying in London. She liked that he took his work so seriously, but it did worry her and, although she wouldn't say anything, she wished he would stay somewhere safer. Ever since the nursery had opened, she had been keen to show him the amazing children and how well it was being managed. The fact that she felt a lift in her heart when she saw him was beside the point.

Mr Davenport was one of those people who know instinctively how to talk to children. She shouldn't have been surprised – he was always sweet with Matthew and he was famously good at speaking to voters – but still, it was quite something to see him in action. He didn't talk down to the little ones, neither did he use a baby voice, but he was interested, and the children sensed that was the case and responded in kind.

'Look at me,' said Herbert, doing a skip.

'Look at me,' insisted Hettie and did a little dance.

'Listen to me,' said Claire, who hadn't previously talked. She burst into song: 'All things bright and beautiful.'

'You smell,' shouted Matthew, before Mabel whisked him away.

Emmeline took Mr Davenport's arm and steered him and Mr Reynolds into the kitchen.

'And here are some of the children eating breakfast!' she announced proudly, just as Billy threw his porridge at her. The porridge landed on her head, while the plate clattered on the floor, spinning round before coming to a full stop at Mr Reynolds' polished shoes. She felt this heavy warm sludge on her head start to run down her ear and cheek.

Mr Reynolds looked appalled. Mr Davenport looked like he was trying not to laugh.

'I see he's not a fan of porridge,' he said. 'I can't say it's my favourite either.'

'Christine, please take over,' Emmeline called before dashing out of the room, clutching her head. The impact had actually hurt, although that was nothing compared to the indignity.

In the small bathroom, the children were lining up with Mabel.

'Porridge!' Cecily called out.

'You look like oats!' said Matthew – her own Matthew! – 'Oat Mummy!'

'Thank you,' Emmeline said dryly, bending to survey herself in the only mirror, which was one foot off the ground. She had never looked more ridiculous.

. . .

She had to pull and comb and scrub to get the porridge out of her hair. And the soaking made her blouse wet and see-through. Her cheeks flamed as she relived the incident. She changed her top – it was a smart idea of Dot's to have spares of everything, not just for the children but for the adults too.

Nearly half an hour had passed before she felt ready to charm the visitors again, after that humiliating start.

'Another unpredictable day! Aren't they just darlings?' she came out saying, but neither Mr Davenport nor Mr Reynolds were anywhere to be seen.

'They left,' Christine told her. 'But not before we worked out some of the kids have bed bugs.'

It never rains but it pours, thought Emmeline. 'Great.' She sighed. 'Did uh... Mr Davenport leave a message?'

'I think they were just glad to get out of here.'

Mr Davenport wasn't at home that evening either – good – although Mrs Davenport and Mr Reynolds were. They were drinking, heads close together, in the drawing room, and, as Emmeline tried to creep past with Matthew, they called her in.

'Did you get all that stuff out of your hair?' a very stubbly Mr Reynolds asked.

Emmeline smiled weakly. 'Yes, thank you.'

'I thought it was going to be there forever.'

'It was a trying day—'

'There, there,' consoled Mrs Davenport. 'Get some rest.'

That was kind. However, as Emmeline hurried up the stairs, she heard them tittering. 'We shall fight them over porridge...' And her cheeks flamed again.

It wasn't until another week later that Mr Davenport returned to the nursery, and Emmeline was glad that this time he was on his own.

'Is it safe?' he asked, peering round the doorframe. Emmeline's heart leapt, even though she knew it shouldn't. He had such a lovely smile.

'Safer than London.'

'I'll take my chances with the bombs rather than a one-year-old with a bowl of porridge. What a weapon!'

She laughed. She had got over it now: there wasn't much alternative. She took him to the kitchen, where a vast copper saucepan was bubbling.

'Mm, what's cooking in there?'

'Nappies.'

He jumped back.

'I have to clean it out later today too – it's a mucky job. You can help if you like.'

Now he grimaced; and then explained why he'd come.

'I need to advise the committee on how you are getting on. I spoke to some of the parents – they are pleased. The factory is pleased. The babies look content. I'll be reporting back that it's a triumph—'

Emmeline interrupted him.

'Have you had any more correspondence?'

She couldn't help thinking about that terrible threat: *I will knife you in the heart*. What kind of person even thought this, never mind wrote it down, put it in an envelope and sent it?

'Not nearly so much as before,' he said. 'Please don't worry, Mrs Froud. Now, back to this – approximately eighty wartime nurseries have opened nationwide: As far as I'm concerned, this is the flagship, though.'

It was ridiculous, but Emmeline felt tears prick her eyes. She didn't need endorsements from him, she was confident enough to know they had created something special and valuable, but it was still lovely to hear. Eighty nurseries! She was part of something very impressive.

'It's hard to believe you've achieved all this in such short space of time.'

Emmeline found it hard to believe too. She smiled at him and this time, when he met her eyes, she felt hot from head to toe. *Think of God*, she thought. *His eyes were everywhere. Failing that, think of Neville. He had a bad word to say about everyone.*

'It's important to keep busy.'

He didn't look at her when he said, 'What do you think will happen if you don't?'

She shrugged, but she had gone red again.

The nursery adventures continued. No matter how down Emmeline was, or how bad the news from London, as soon as she walked into the hall and saw all the children she cheered up. She couldn't not. Those expectant faces, ready and willing to laugh and play and dance and learn.

And she loved helping the women too. Mrs Pratt walked forty minutes to bring her son to nursery and Mrs Collins cycled with her two in a basket on the front of her bike; she was going back to work in the hospital – 'I'm so excited. I thought that part of my life was over.' Another mother was proud to be the hospital's first female porter.

Emmeline had worried about coping without Dot but actually it wasn't too bad. Mabel, Christine and Mrs Hodges made a formidable team and Dot and Emmeline had disagreed over some nursery policies as well. One area of contention was hand-washing (Dot thought a quick rinse would suffice), another was education. Dot thought children should have a good time – Emmeline thought they should have a good time AND do some learning. Emmeline had instituted a reading corner and many families had donated books.

'Why books? They can't read!' Dot had scoffed.

Soon they had stacks of *Janet and Peter*. Beatrix Potter. *The Wind in the Willows. Alice's Adventures in Wonderland.*

'We've got so many!' Dot remained unimpressed. 'Is it because everyone hates them?'

Each of the staff had their strengths. Mabel was entertaining. Christine was reassuring with a thermometer and good at talking to parents. And Dot *definitely* brought the fun. With Dot at home with baby Errol though, Emmeline managed to sneak in some more learning camouflaged as fun. For example, they sang the rainbow song and other rhymes and no one seemed to notice that they were gaining knowledge about colours and months.

One afternoon, Mabel called her into the kitchen: 'I think you need to hear this.'

Emmeline, who was carrying a howling Iris Whitlock, and Tommy Collins, who was feeling sick, hurried in.

'I'm a bit wrapped up at the moment...'

Mabel, who was usually slow to panic, said, 'Never mind that, listen to the news...' and now Emmeline heard fear in her voice.

The Palace of Westminster has been attacked.

'Parliament?' whispered Emmeline. *Where Mr Davenport spends most of his working days?*

'Sounds like it, doesn't it?' said Mabel. She was pale, tinged with green and her teeth were chattering.

The Commons Chamber was hit by bombs and the roof of Westminster Hall was set on fire. The fire service said that it would be impossible to save both, so it was decided to concentrate on saving the Hall.

'What about the people?' whispered Emmeline as the news moved on to Churchill's latest speech. 'Was anyone hurt?'

'They didn't say,' Mabel whispered.

Emmeline had prayed that Mr Davenport would be around less so she might stop thinking about him, but she certainly hadn't meant anything like this. She stood still, as if a single movement might make the difference between life and death. She didn't know what to do.

'Go and see if there's any news at the house,' Mabel urged. 'Or I can go.'

Emmeline was trembling. She thought of the Salts buried underground. Not Mr Davenport as well, he was far too alive for that. And he had so much to do – and it wasn't possible, was it? They would have said.

'It'll be fine—'

'I know you want to be at the Old Rectory,' Mabel said firmly. 'Go. We'll manage here.'

Emmeline took one of the bicycles, and rode like the wind. She rarely cycled, because of Matthew, and she would have taken pleasure from it, only her emotions were whirling, out of control. My God, he *would* be all right, wouldn't he? The report didn't say anyone had been killed. But that meant nothing. Families had to be contacted first. Details would come out later. As she pedalled, her mind went through all different scenarios. She even went over what she would say in her head if Mrs Davenport answered the door.

She didn't get as far as the house; she saw him walking along the road.

'You!' She was laughing, stupidly, insanely. She jumped off the bike and let it collapse with a clunk to her side. She wanted to grab hold of him, shake him or screech, 'You're alive!'

He looked pleased, but then he looked concerned. 'Is anything wrong? The nursery? Where's Matthew?'

'No, I... I was just worried,' she said. She knew she had to calm down. She was making a fool of herself, but she had been so scared. 'I heard there was another attack. At Westminster.'

He covered his face with his hands briefly, then shook his head, smiling at her.

'Ah. Well, not many people know it, but we don't meet there any more.'

'I didn't know that.'

'No, I'm sorry...'

His expression was astonishingly tender now, and he looked like he wanted to hold her. Perhaps in a more private place he would have, Emmeline thought. It was *good* they were not in a private place. She doubted she had the requisite self-control. She would have to pray more.

'Thank you,' he said softly, 'for your concern. I understand there were no casualties.'

'I was just being overly dramatic,' she said. 'Silly me!' She picked up the bike and held it between them like a barrier to stop herself from clutching him.

'Thank you for caring,' he said quietly.

Emmeline gulped. He knew how she felt, she realised. He knew even better than she did. She stared at the ground, wishing it would swallow her up. Only now she remembered that she was wearing her unflattering shoes, her hair was askew and a child had scribbled hearts on her arm. What a fright she must look!

'I care...' she said. 'About everybody.'

She couldn't read his expression any more, but she hoped that was enough to hide her feelings. Every part of her was shaking, but it was not fear any more – it was more than that. She cycled slowly back to the nursery, relief on her shoulders, but feeling more longing to touch him than she had ever felt before.

33

MAY 1941

Lydia

The first thing Daddy said when he came to Somerset was: 'Don't say I never come!'

In the twenty months Lydia had been in Somerset, her mother had been six times. But Lydia was sympathetic to her father, visits or not. He worked very hard in his job, and he looked so forlorn. She threw her arms round him. He was wearing his Sunday best. Unfortunately, it made him look like an undertaker, but she saw he had made an effort and it made her heart swell. When she took him to Bumble Cottage, she waited for his expression to change – and it did.

'Wha...? So *this* is your place? I had no idea!' He wandered around the house looking shell-shocked, and she was glad Mrs H was out at her volunteer group. If he thought the house was posh, then he would struggle to deal with *her*: she was poshness personified. He liked Rex though, said he'd had a dog as a boy: 'Buster.'

'I didn't know that,' Lydia said.

'There's a lot you don't know,' he said cryptically.

'Tell me!' Lydia chirruped but he just shook his head.

She made tea and he said it was just how he liked it, and no, he wasn't hungry, he'd had a sandwich on the train.

'You're in your element,' he said. He seemed awkward, even nervous of her. She thanked him. She didn't know what he meant, but she supposed it was something scienc-y.

'The Blitz might be nearly over, but London will still be dangerous, Lydia. You should stay away. Our family are making enough sacrifices as it is – we shouldn't make any more.'

Lydia put her hand over his.

'I have no intention of coming back,' she told him. The word 'ever' teetered on the tip of her tongue. She decided to keep it from him. That was between her and Rex. He looked worried again, tugging at his stiff shirt collar.

'That's not what I mea—'

Lydia was charmed. 'You have nothing to worry about, Daddy,' she reassured him. 'I am very happy with my evacuation.'

34

Emmeline

Dot was back to work – accompanied by five-month-old Errol – and she and Emmeline were preparing breakfast for the early birds, the children whose mothers worked the first shifts at the factory, with Matthew, Hettie and Pat playing tea parties at their feet, when more news came on the wireless. This time, it was announced that the British government were confident that Nazi Germany had *failed* on their bombing attack. That didn't mean they wouldn't try something else, but for now – it appeared – the Blitz was over.

Emmeline could feel her shoulders lighten immediately. The menace from the skies had been neutralised. She sank down at the table and buried her face in her hands. A sob came out.

'Oh God. At last.'

No more needless deaths? no more night-time bombings? It was hard to imagine.

Dot had a different perspective: 'It doesn't mean the war is over.'

'No, but...'

'And a lot of our children will leave.'

'Leave?' Emmeline squeaked as she realised her friend was being serious. 'To go where?'

'Back to London.'

Back to London? London had been an uninhabitable place in Emmeline's mind for so long that the idea of people going back there – even without a Blitz – seemed dazzling. She wasn't ready, no one was ready! The cities were in ruins – and Dot was right, it wasn't like the war had finished. And Neville insisted that everyone should stay put until the war was won.

'Will you go back, Dot?' she asked.

'Not me!' Dot responded cheerfully. Her home had been destroyed last September. She often talked about how if they'd been in it at the time they would have been buried alive. 'Nowhere to go. They've promised to rebuild, but it could take years.'

'What about Christine? Or Mabel?'

'They're here for the long haul, I imagine.'

Dot was right, though. Plenty of the women came in to tell them their children would be leaving. By the time the third mother told her she and her children were returning to London, Emmeline had stopped being surprised.

Emmeline tried not to have favourites, but secretly she thought Kitty Andrews was one of the best children there (apart from Matthew, of course) and her mother, Mrs Andrews, was always prompt at the end of the day, and not too early at the start.

'Have you somewhere to go?'

'My in-laws want me back with them,' Mrs Andrews said.

'But you could stay here in Norfolk?' Emmeline tentatively suggested.

'I like it here, but there's no place like home, is there?'

'Absolutely,' said Emmeline, her heart sinking. *Home sweet home*, she thought. But was it really so sweet?

By the end of the day, it was clear that about ten of the thirty children would be leaving them. It wasn't an exodus, but it wasn't nothing.

'We're a *wartime* nursery,' she complained to Dot. 'Not a Blitz-time nursery. I think they're making a mistake. Anything could happen!' *Think of the Salts*, she thought. They had thought they were safe...

A few days later, Emmeline saw Councillor Arscott in the post office. It had happened before, and usually he ignored her and she busied herself with envelopes and stamps, but today the councillor made a beeline for her.

'You'll be closing the nursery down then,' he said, and it wasn't a question.

'As long as there are mothers who need care for their children, we'll stay open.'

The postmistress was weighing a parcel, yet she looked up with a sympathetic smile. Emmeline recognised her as difficult-Billy's grandmother.

'I thought it was for evacuee mothers and children?' Councillor Arscott continued.

'Not just them.'

'I thought it was for mothers doing war work?'

'They *are* working,' she said through gritted teeth.

He eyed her slyly. 'There are other reasons you should close it down.'

Emmeline stepped back from him. His lips were shiny and when he spoke bits of spittle flew.

'I beg your pardon?'

He smirked at her now with that little rabbity face and then he said, 'Wouldn't it be a shame if you were caught in a scandal?'

The postmistress looked up with a startled expression that probably reflected Emmeline's own.

'I don't know what you mean,' Emmeline retorted. She told herself: *He can't read my mind.* Whatever scandalous feelings she might have, no one in the world knew them – not Dot, not Lydia, not Neville, and certainly not Councillor Arscott.

'Children need good morals.' Councillor Arscott tipped his hat at her. 'Good day, *Mrs* Froud.'

Emmeline felt a crawling, nervous sensation all over her skin. What was he trying to say?

'You've got very good morals so far as I can see,' the postmistress said comfortingly. 'Don't give him a second thought.'

35

Lydia

Now the Blitz was over, Valerie's mother, Mrs Hardman, was coming to Somerset to take Valerie back home to London. Lydia could have hugged the woman. She felt confident her own position in Somerset was secure – her father had made sure of that, and Mrs H had confirmed it, telling Lydia that she was free to spend the duration of the war in Somerset if that was her preference. Lydia was looking forward to having Bumble Cottage back to herself again. To not have to see Paul and Valerie chuckling over the wireless or earnestly dissecting books by the fire as though the characters in it were real or important.

Lydia hated always feeling left out. Those two even went fishing together and were so silent and so still on the riverbank that, the one time she joined them, Lydia had felt like singing or dancing – anything to get a reaction. Together, they were a couple of oddbods, which was strange because separately, they were almost normal.

When Mrs Hardman arrived, she seemed even more nervy than Lydia had remembered. Valerie was excruciatingly formal with her mother too, which made Lydia feel sorry for the woman. When Lydia saw her mummy, the first few minutes were taken up with hugs and kissing, poking and admiring. Valerie and her mother didn't even touch.

'It's much safer now, isn't it?' she prompted Mrs Hardman, hoping to convey that they were on the same side. 'London, I mean.'

'It is.' Mrs Hardman shot her a grateful look.

'And the education there is just as good as here,' Lydia added, because that was the sort of thing grown-ups said.

Valerie scowled at her.

After a picnic in the garden, Mrs Hardman and Valerie went for a walk and Lydia tried to make Paul laugh. He was in a rotten mood. Mrs H called him 'monosyllabic', but Lydia wasn't sure what it meant, so she called him 'grumpy pants'. Paul shook his head like these things – all things – were beneath him. When the Hardmans eventually came back, Valerie went upstairs to pack, but it transpired that Mrs Hardman had changed her mind. There followed some terse discussions and then a conclusion: Valerie was going to stay, after all. Lydia realised they expected her to greet this news as if it was brilliant.

'You're staying? Marvellous!' She was actually wondering why Mrs Hardman was such a pushover.

Paul hugged Valerie, and Lydia didn't like that either. There was no need.

'Everyone prefers Bumble Cottage to London,' Lydia said once Mrs Hardman had left, no doubt doing her downtrodden walk all the way back to the railway station.

'Francine didn't,' Valerie reminded her.

'I suppose.'

And look what happened to her, thought Lydia. She'd ended up God knows where without anyone who loved her.

. . .

Mrs Howard had decided that Lydia should attend the state school rather than St Boniface in September. She seemed to anticipate Lydia being upset about this move, but the truth was Lydia didn't mind, because Miss Picard too had announced that she was leaving. And without Miss Picard, what was the point of school anyway?

Everyone had thought Miss Picard was having a love affair with the art teacher, Dr Wolf. He was not young, and his substantial hair was grey, but it was universally agreed that he was dashingly handsome, so when Miss Picard announced she was marrying, everyone naturally assumed it was him.

'Good grief,' Miss Picard said, laughing with her hand over her mouth (if someone caught sight of teeth or tonsils, she'd be mortified). 'Do you not know me at all?'

Miss Picard's girls stared at each other. Flora's lips were set in a startled grimace – she had been a big spreader of the Dr Wolf wedding theory.

'I am marrying a man of business. A man who will take care of me.'

'You won't leave us though, will you?' Elsa Morgan asked. It wasn't only Lydia who was obsessed with her etiquette teacher; Miss Picard had a fan club.

'I have to, girls,' she explained. 'For me, marriage is the pinnacle, the goal. Joyful as it's been to mentor you, this is my *raison d'être*. The happy-ever-after. And I daresay it should be for you, too.'

She pulled Lydia aside.

'Your roots may be less strong, but your trunk is most forte!' she said. (She often mixed French with English.) 'Keep practising your walking, your speaking – the war will last a little longer, but life goes on and you must be ready for it.'

Blinking up at her, Lydia promised that she would be.

36

Emmeline

Although some families had left Norfolk as soon as the Blitz was over, the nursery didn't feel too empty or too quiet for long because other children joined, including many from the town.

'We didn't know if we locals were allowed!'

'Course you're allowed!' declared Emmeline warmly.

Mrs Barker worked at the post office. Mrs Davis who used to be a seamstress was going to help make military uniforms.

'We thought this place was just for London families?'

'Everyone's welcome,' Emmeline said. She wondered if Councillor Arscott had deliberately encouraged townspeople to think they were not. Anyway, the numbers went up quickly now. More women arrived to take the place of those who'd gone – especially at the factory and the hospital – and so there were more children who needed to be looked after.

Emmeline was looking to make improvements. That was the way her mind worked: She did not rest on her laurels. She was constantly thinking, what can we do better? She was learning so much about running a nursery– but she was also learning about herself. She had discovered she was a grafter; an innovator. That she liked lifting people up. One day, she told herself, all mothers would have the choice. This was her goal. By the time Lydia had children, it would be her right.

There were other things to learn. Stanley Burton had pulled up a stool and found the chocolate iron tablets, on the top shelf of the cupboard. He hadn't eaten them – *thank goodness* – but he *had* sucked the chocolate off all of them…

That was when they put a lock on the kitchen door.

The nursery was increasingly spartan. As the war went on and on and the shortages kicked in, they had less stuff. Anything aluminium had been collected for the effort. The cushions and the dressing-up box likewise. The toilet paper was squares of newspaper and the food was increasingly tasteless. Yet every morning the children toddled in the door like they were going to a party. When they caught a glimpse of their friends, they raced to hug each other, some of them falling over in their enthusiasm.

'Friendship is a wonderful thing,' said Dot one morning, nudging Emmeline, as Bertha and Mimi reunited at the doors as though they'd been apart for years.

'You never greet me like that,' Emmeline grumbled, but Dot laughed.

'That's because as soon as you arrive, you give me work to do!'

When Emmeline had first arrived in Norfolk, she'd had only Matthew to take care of. Now she had more than she could count. It was exhausting, it was bewildering. It was wonderful.

Mr Davenport was at home a lot more nowadays. When Emmeline saw his coat and hat hanging off the hook, her guilty heart sang at the thought that he was in the house. When she saw him in the kitchen or on the stairs, they did a silly dance around each other, determined not to brush by each other and even though they never touched, Emmeline felt a sizzling, bubbly feeling she had never known before. Did he sense it? she wondered – sometimes she wondered how he could *not* sense it.

Thank goodness for Matthew. If she were alone with Mr Davenport, who knew what she would be tempted to do! (She could admit this to herself, but no one else.) She couldn't help thinking of Councillor Arscott's cold eyes on her in the post office. *A scandal?* He was just speculating, she supposed. Hoping to catch a transgression even though there had been none. He wasn't a mind-reader. And anyway, there was no scandal! You couldn't get in trouble for your thoughts, however wicked those thoughts were. Every Sunday, Emmeline went to church and prayed for more strength. Nothing must happen between her and Mr Davenport. Not even nearly. Never – for a thousand reasons – not least because the nursery depended on it.

37

Emmeline

The local Women's Institute were donating some funds to the war nursery and they invited Emmeline and Dot for lunch. Dot, who hated any kind of formal 'do', said she'd stay back at the nursery but that Emmeline should try and win the raffle. Matthew would stay away too, because what small child enjoys a sit-down lunch? Emmeline was looking forward to it though. On that morning, she opened the nursery and did the breakfasts. It was a cod-liver oil and orange juice day – a messy day. Late morning, she changed her clothes in the back room. Dot whistled when she saw her outfit and declared she looked a treat and Mabel shouted that she was beautiful! (Mabel reminded Emmeline of Lydia sometimes, with her free-flowing compliments.)

Emmeline took the bus to the next town. She could hardly believe it: *Emmeline Froud from Stepney East invited out to a fancy lunch!*

Lunch was a small chop and a baby potato. There was a fug of strong perfume in the air that Emmeline tried to ignore. A lady came round with raffle tickets – barely a day went by without a raffle for 'our boys' – and she bought five. She half-hoped she might win the third prize – a doll, which she would give to Lydia – but the thought of drawing attention to herself here made her anxious.

The woman on her left was a mother of six and the woman on her right ran a volunteer shop. When Emmeline said she was from the nursery, the shop volunteer said, 'Bravo.' And the mother of six said, 'I had a nanny when my children were small. Marvellous woman: she read stories every night and even today my eleven-year-old son loves reading.'

'Not all women can afford a Nanny ,' Emmeline said, but she said it politely.

The mother said, 'Of course,' and then turned to talk to the shop volunteer on her other side.

'Who is our guest today?' the shop volunteer leaned forward to ask.

'Our MP.'

'Not Mr Davenport?'

'That's him!'

Emmeline was shocked and pleased. Looking around her, everyone else seemed content at the prospect, too. She felt like saying, 'I know him!' but of course she didn't.

Mr Davenport arrived, and he was dressed formally, in his dark suit and tie with his white shirt. But his manner wasn't formal; he was correct and polite, but also relaxed and open. He was probably the same height as Neville, Emmeline realised, but they had little else in common.

'I want to talk about all the tiny things you do that make a difference. Every stitch, every letter, every coin in every tin is supporting our fight against the Nazis.'

The women were spellbound. They put down their forks and they laid down their spoons. The mother of six next to her was muttering, 'Hear, hear,' under her breath; the shop volunteer was nodding and readying herself to clap.

He is as good as Churchill, thought Emmeline proudly.

'When it is over, and it will be over, and we will win, you should be so proud of yourselves for your contribution. I know you won't slap your backs, or rest on your laurels, but I hope each of you, in your heart, knows that you did it.'

The applause was loud. Afterwards, Mr Davenport came to each table and shook hands with each person on it, and she waited and waited for her turn and, when he arrived, he winked at her.

'Would you like a lift later on, Mrs Froud?' he asked, skipping the pleasantries.

'I can take the bus,' Emmeline said, embarrassed to be singled out, yet also delighted.

'It's no bother,' he said. 'I'll find you after the raffle.'

Her hands were shaking as she went to powder her nose. In the privacy of the Ladies, the verdict on his speech was as positive as had been the reception in the hall, and the verdict on him even more resounding.

One woman said, 'He's an absolute dish.'

'Happily married though,' said another.

'As am I!' the first lady corrected. 'One may look without buying.'

They both laughed.

Emmeline didn't win the raffle although the women both sides of her did. And then there were more speeches and it was time to go and the hand-shaking continued out into the street. Emmeline wondered if Mr Davenport would be embarrassed about her, but he didn't seem to be; he introduced her to everyone as 'Mrs Froud, an evacuee mother, all the way from London.'

'We know who Mrs Froud is!' one man responded. 'She's

the lady who gets things done!' He pumped Emmeline's hand up and down, as did his wife.

'You've created a tremendous place,' the woman said. 'I work at the hospital, and we couldn't do without the nursery mothers.'

Even as they got in Mr Davenport's car, the couple were still complimenting her. It was lovely, and she was grateful, but she also felt tired out.

'Don't you find it exhausting?' she asked. 'All this socialising!' She thought it was easier to talk to four-year-olds than forty-year-olds.

'I enjoy the local things,' he said. 'It's Westminster that's more difficult.'

'In what way?'

'The decision-making. The lives lost to save lives,' he said, and his mouth was tight. He had driven about a mile before he asked, 'You've not seen the Norfolk coast before?'

'I haven't.' She smiled. 'Before I came, I thought I'd be in a little gift shop selling sticks of rock.'

'Instead, you've galvanised an entire town.'

She couldn't stop smiling as she looked out of the window. Never in a million years could she have imagined that the evacuation would lead to this.

The beach was closed off, of course it was. They were turned away at a roadblock.

It was an intimidation of barbed wire and 'polite' notices. DO NOT ENTER, TURN BACK NOW. Piles of sandbags and tyres.

'Ah,' Mr Davenport said. 'I should have known.'

'It doesn't matter,' she said – and the truth was, it didn't. She was enjoying the change of scenery. She was also enjoying being out with him. He was so attentive to her, even in public, and it was sweet he wished to show her the sea. His leg was close to hers now. She couldn't help admiring his hand on the gearstick, his face in profile. Gosh, but he was an exceptional man. She couldn't understand why he wanted to spend his precious time off with her.

He pulled up in a small shady area under a canopy of trees. He was telling her about the fuel allowance but it was hard to concentrate on his words. What would she do if he kissed her?

Of course he had no intention of doing such a thing!

But what if he did?

A few nights back, when she had come downstairs late, she saw he had fallen asleep in his armchair. He looked so vulnerable suddenly, his head to the side, one hand over his heart, the other hanging down towards the floor where his papers were piled up. She hadn't known whether to wake him or not – it was not her business – but she had put a blanket over him and he had half-smiled in his sleep.

He was saying that he believed new laws would be passed to make cars safer.

'I see,' she said. Safety in cars was the last thing on her mind – unless it meant safety from married men in cars. He felt something too, she was certain it wasn't just her. His breath seemed louder and faster than normal, as though he was nervous, and she imagined hers was the same.

When he took her hand in his it felt perfectly natural, and she didn't have the willpower to say no.

'Next week, I will have been in Norfolk for one year,' she said brightly.

'What a year it's been!' His fingers stroked the back of her hand, her knuckles. She could hardly breathe.

'It's been the strangest year of my life,' she said. How long could she pretend he wasn't touching her for?

'Mrs Froud,' he said suddenly, and his face was close to hers.

So much desire was building up inside her. Her attraction

to him was stronger than anything, stronger than her nerves, stronger than her willpower.

'Yes?' Her voice was high-pitched.

He leaned over to her and then his lips were on hers and she was powerless to do anything but respond. He was kissing her, and she was kissing him, and she had never felt anything like this before – not in her entire life.

'We mustn't,' she murmured, yet still she let her lips kiss him. This was nothing like she had been imagining, nothing like her daydreams, it was better, far better, it was heavenly...

But perhaps all the praying *had* worked because, just then, real life pushed her back to earth with a bump. In her mind's eye, she saw Mrs Davenport, Neville, Lydia, Councillor Arscott – all revolted at her, all glaring at her as though she were a head-louse. She pulled back sharply. Wiped her mouth with a sleeve, held up her hand.

'We mustn't...'

'Mustn't what?' he mumbled, and kissed her again. This time he kissed her neck, oh, and her throat as well. She thought she might yelp with the terrible pleasure. She had never felt this way before – for anyone – and the fact that he seemed to feel it too only multiplied her ardour.

'Must not kiss,' she whispered. *Do not enter. Turn back now.*

'Understood.'

He was unbuttoning her blouse, and his hands were over her breasts, and she couldn't stop responding, she couldn't. She wanted to see where this would go. Now he had one hand on her skirt and he was pushing up the hem, goodness gracious, and she found the sight of her own stockinged thigh, with his beautiful hand caressing it, mesmerising.

But...

'We can't,' she murmured.

'You must know I find you irresistible. And I think you feel the same.'

No. She was so hot and bothered, her desire obliterated the future, it wiped out everything, but she had more self-control than that. Think of the *scandal*...

'But you're married.'

He looked at her with those beautiful eyes – ever so slightly crossed, those long eyelashes she loved.

'And so are you,' he said quietly.

'And – I think...' She was out of breath. 'I think Councillor Arscott might have guessed. And he'll use it against us – against the nursery.'

'He can't prove anything.'

'No...'

He licked his lips. 'Is that what's stopping you?'

'I can't hurt *her*,' she said. Neville didn't figure as much in this as he should; she didn't know why. But Mrs Davenport did – Mrs Davenport had opened her home to her. It felt like the paper dolls they cut out at nursery sometimes – each one of them was interlinked.

He rubbed his eyes, then looked at her again. 'What if I told you she's in love with someone else?'

Emmeline startled. 'Who?'

He shrugged. He put his hands on the steering wheel but, instead of starting the car up, he put his head down.

'You know who.'

'I don't.'

But suddenly she did. Of course she did. Mr Reynolds, who was always there, even when Mr Davenport was not. Mr Reynolds, who was always standing close by her and...

'She wants to be with him but it's complicated.'

'Even so...' she stuttered, 'I still can't... It would still be wrong.'

He nodded slowly, shifted back and straightened his tie and it felt like an ending. She wanted to say, 'No, wait, I didn't mean it. Kiss me again,' but she didn't.

'I understand. That's one of the reasons I like you – because you are a good person.'

'Because I won't have a thing with you?'

'Yes.'

And then a car drew up alongside them. A man in a uniform, a woman in a dress. They looked none too pleased to discover other people in their private place.

'Please take me back.'

He started the car engine.

She felt a wave of disappointment. She wanted to do the right thing, but didn't he want to fight for her some more? It was confusing, yes, but shouldn't they discuss their feelings? They drove in silence. She got him to drop her at the nursery because it felt wrong to go back to the house, his house, his wife's house! After the highs of the day, she felt like crying.

She should have let him seduce her and be damned. It would be worth the scandal, it would be worth anything, just to be in his arms for five more minutes. She couldn't stop thinking about it. When he touched her, the attention and wonder on his face was so erotic. No one had ever looked at her like that before. Not Neville, and there had been no one else.

Or maybe she wished nothing had happened at all. She felt like she was on a see-saw of emotions. One moment she felt she was right to resist, the next, she felt she should have thrown herself in, to lead a life without passion was a waste of a life, especially now in wartime when everyone was doing it, since nothing was guaranteed.

Back in the nursery, the children were putting on a concert, and Dot was helping them rehearse.

When Emmeline came in, Dot scowled. 'You took your time, Mrs Froud!'

Emmeline couldn't think what to say. She hated herself. She hated secrets.

'You didn't win anything then?' Dot continued obliviously.

'No.'

'Don't look so sad.' Dot threaded her arm through Emmeline's. 'There'll be another time.'

The children were lined up in their hand-me-down sweaters and their home-haircuts and Emmeline suddenly wanted to cry at their innocence. Dot was pleased with herself. She had taught them a new song 'The Farmer Wants a Wife'.

'*E I E I O! The farmer wants a wife.*' They chorused. It was unbearably wholesome.

'*The farmer wants a dog.*'

The farmer wants a mistress, Emmeline thought to herself. *The mistress wants a good talking-to.*

Emmeline felt devastated. She knew one thing – she couldn't live at the Old Rectory any more.

38

JULY 1941

Emmeline

Matthew cried all the way to Thorpe railway station and halfway back to London.

'No go! Bombs!' he shouted, and Emmeline regretted that she had made him rather too cautious. Or was it Neville's fault? She wasn't sure.

'Not any more, darling. All gone!'

(All gone had been his first words – not about bombs but about porridge.)

Emmeline needed a break. She needed to re-connect with her home and her life in London. She had let herself drift away from all that tethered her and she was in danger of being lost at sea. She couldn't be in the same house as Mr Davenport, not now.

The old couple in heavy coats opposite had given them uncertain glances when they got on, especially with Matthew howling, but now they offered him blackberries and the elderly man said he could scribble over his crossword if he liked.

'I never manage it any more,' he said sadly.

Matthew drew something over it that he announced was a cat and the elderly man was pleased.

The flat at 67 Romberg Road looked the same as ever from the front. Her home that wasn't a home any more. The Salts' place upstairs was empty – Emmeline didn't know where poor Francine had ended up.

While Emmeline had been far from here, it had been simple to pretend to herself – even if she hadn't been doing it intentionally – that life here was carrying on just as usual. That her dear upstairs neighbour was still singing or putting on lipstick or worrying about something she'd heard on the wireless, and the children were still squabbling and making up. Now though, there was no pretending.

Those poor innocent children. Maisie who loved tap dancing. Jacob tooting his toy recorder, and baby Joe, just starting out, too young even to have discovered what he liked or didn't. She had buried herself in other people's children rather than think about them. But now she remembered – Maisie singing 'London's Burning' and getting shushed. Baby Joe enjoying a cuddle. Jacob delighted at his bottle.

Whose enemy had they been?

The bed was made, just as she'd left it. Everything was clean, but there was a stale smell of absence. It hadn't been aired recently. Neville wasn't staying here, she suddenly realised. It might be that he came and collected the post – there were a few envelopes stacked up tidily – and then went elsewhere. But where? He couldn't be fire-watching every night, could he?

The quiet was strange. Mrs Hardman was not in her basement flat either. She must be on the buses, or out with friends. If Emmeline was struggling to maintain her old values about the sanctity of marriage despite the pressures of the war, she suspected Mrs Hardman was less conflicted. And why shouldn't she be? Emmeline scolded herself; unlike her, Mrs Hardman was a widow – a single woman – in these tumultuous times. Who she chose to spend her time with was not anyone's concern.

Matthew needed lunch and to see his father. Emmeline needed to see Neville too, before she decided on her next steps. Marriages got torn apart by war, unless you worked at them. She remembered Dot telling her this what felt like a long time ago. Only Dot had been gleeful about the idea of marriage casualties, and Emmeline was not. She had to give her marriage a chance.

At the reception area to Neville's office, a woman was napping, draped over the desk. Emmeline coughed, hoping she would wake. It seemed like ages before the woman opened her eyes.

'Um, I'm here to see Mr Neville Froud?'

'Do you have an appointment?'

'No, but I'm his wife.'

The woman couldn't be less interested. Yawning, she directed Emmeline and Matthew to a room full of typewriting girls and a few men at desks towards the back.

As Emmeline walked down the aisle towards Neville, the person next to him nudged him. He looked up and the expression on his face was thunderous. He was aghast that she was there. Then, remembering he was in public, Neville jumped up, switching the look on his face to a delighted one. 'Emmeline!?'

He looked around him. 'This is my wife. And this is my son,' he said to his colleagues. Some stood up and said, 'Hello there,' or 'Nice day for it!', but not all of them showed an interest. That woman over there, fingers curled round a telephone wire, didn't. That man in the corner with the fine moustache and the hat pulled low didn't. The pale young woman at the back of the room didn't even look up from her typing.

'Why didn't you tell me you were coming?' Neville said.

Maybe to them, he sounded gregarious and full of bonhomie but Emmeline could only hear the reproach.

She felt like crying. She had wanted him to be what she hoped he would be. For him to push all thoughts of Mr Davenport aside. But Neville couldn't eclipse Mr Davenport. He wasn't big enough or strong enough or bright enough. He was only her husband. He wasn't the sun.

'Is everything all right?'

'I thought I'd be spontaneous,' she said, and he gave her a bleak look.

Out in the street, Neville lit himself a cigarette and then one for her. 'You've got to go back to Norfolk.'

Emmeline bristled. There was no *got to* about this, she thought. She wanted to go back for the nursery, but if she went back, there was no way she would be able to resist her host any longer. Her whole being was crying out to get closer to him. She could barely think about anything else. Not even with Neville right in front of her. Mr Davenport had mesmerised her. She was a bad person. No matter how much she prayed, both in church and at home, all she wanted was for him to lie on top of her and— Neville didn't realise it, but their marriage depended on how he behaved now.

'You've built such a lot there,' he said.

This was kind. This was supportive, but it didn't sound like her Neville.

'They're developing new bombs, you've not heard of them – the V1s and the V2s.'

'I *have* heard of them...'

What did he think? That she'd become a country bumpkin? Emmeline was proud that she was probably more aware of what was going on in the world than she had ever been before.

'We can't have Matthew here.'

'No bombs, Daddy!' said Matthew.

Emmeline tried to put her annoyance at that to one side, but it was quickly replaced with another one.

'Where've you been staying, Neville? You've not been home.'

'I'm always at work or fire-watching.'

'Still?' Emmeline's heart ached.

He blew out smoke rings, wispy, insubstantial things. 'No rest for the wicked.'

'You don't seem pleased to see us.'

'I am!' he insisted. He was lying. But what right did she have to complain? They were both lying.

He tried to kiss her cheek, but she dodged away. 'Only, it would have been safer if I came up to see you there. Or in Somerset perhaps. What about Lydia?'

'Lydia is fine,' she said haughtily. 'I'll be at the flat tonight. If you want to come by...'

He pulled a face. 'It's difficult.'

'So it seems.'

Maybe she shouldn't have, but once Matthew was asleep that evening she used the spare key and went into the Salts' flat. It was mostly cleared away, apart from a few boxes, but she found some shoes and mittens with a string attached so you couldn't lose them. And a children's book, *The Princess and the Pea*. Inside it said, 'This Book Belongs to Francine Salt'. In the kitchen, she found two snow globes that didn't snow and a toy car with a tyre missing. What loss. What stupid, pointless, cruel loss. She wanted to scream; all the emotions were knotty inside her. And the only person she wanted to talk to about it with, she couldn't. And then she had an idea.

'I'm so glad you're back,' Mr Davenport said in a low voice that seemed to connect directly to her heart. It was the next afternoon and Mrs Davenport and Mr Reynolds were in the drawing room, only five steps away. They had a new typewriter and were arguing over the ribbon.

'I was afraid I'd frightened you away.'

'Frightened!' yelped Matthew. He usually ignored adult conversations but he had an ear for things that were private.

'Shhh,' Emmeline told Matthew. 'We're moving out,' she said to Mr Davenport.

Mr Davenport passed his hand over his forehead and it seemed a gesture of infinite woe. He looked like a Greek statue. Why did he have to be so impossibly lovely?

'Not back to London? You're not giving up the nursery?'

'I'm not. We'll be nearby. The nursery will stay open.'

He kept swallowing like his throat was dry. 'And will I be able to see you?'

'No,' she said, yet her voice was quivering. 'You won't see us again.'

She thought of Councillor Arscott and his veiled threats. The nursery wouldn't survive a scandal. *She* wouldn't survive a scandal. And although she reckoned the Right Honourable Mr Davenport could talk himself out of most things, she didn't think he'd survive a scandal, either. His seat wasn't that safe.

He nodded gravely. 'I understand.'

Stop me, Emmeline thought. Her heart was breaking. *Tell me you want me again.* She would do anything just once, a goodbye once, a kiss, a proper kiss, all of it, she wouldn't pull away this time, she was almost willing his hands upon her— but then Mr Reynolds bounded out the drawing room, holding a file.

'Mrs Davenport told me you were off?' he said to her breezily. 'What a shame.' And then he turned to Mr Davenport: 'Can you sign these papers?'

. . .

The Hazells' house was just as she remembered, a tiny two-up two-down, in a row of similar houses that used to house farm workers. Emmeline had sent a telegram from London and Mrs Hazell had met them at the station. 'Of course, we'll have you and Matthew. It will be our pleasure.' Unbelievable kindness. It was near to the nursery – an important consideration. Plus, of course, it was away from Mr Davenport – the most important consideration of all, but the one she could not tell anyone.

The Hazells told her the hours when she could use the kitchen and the washing and the bath. Mrs Hazell was now working at the old bicycle factory: 'Can't tell you what exactly, but...' She was so proud of herself. 'I haven't worked out of the home for thirty years, but it's for the war effort.'

'You've gone over and above the call of duty,' Emmeline said sincerely.

'You spent too long with politicians; you even talk like them now,' she countered. Everyone laughed, including Emmeline.

Every morning the Hazells left for work even before she did, and even though Emmeline's days at the nursery were twelve hours or more, she was often the first one home too. Mrs Hazell usually stumbled in, exhausted and her hands filthy, but satisfied with her job. Mr Hazell also worked in a factory and in his free time did something with pigeons. He also liked going to the pub after work.

They didn't ask questions at first, but a few days after she had moved in Mr Hazell gruffly said he was just wondering if that MP fella was ever unkind to her or – he paused – anything like that.

'Nothing like that,' she said.

'Good. I've never heard any rumours about him – he seems a well-meaning chap, but you never know. People take advantage.'

Emmeline remembered once telling Mrs Hardman that single women were vulnerable. Mrs Hardman hadn't taken it particularly well, she recalled. She wondered what Mr Hazell would have done if she said he HAD done something 'like that'.

'I love having someone to fuss over,' Mrs Hazell said, clearly delighted to be hosting again. They were still sad about the Marjorie incident – as was Emmeline – but told her that the children, the three D's, were now definitely out of care as a family member had stepped forward and taken them on.

'That's good!' Emmeline brightened. 'And Marjorie herself?'

They said they didn't know, but Emmeline felt that they were hiding something and pushed for more. Mrs Hazell looked at her husband.

'Could be better.'

'Where is she now?'

'In a home.'

Emmeline nodded. Dot had told her this. 'That's not too bad, is it?'

Mrs Hazell looked towards her husband again like she was waiting for his approval. He nodded slowly, so she continued. 'For imbeciles.'

Marjorie! Emmeline covered her mouth in shock. That poor, dear girl.

39

SEPTEMBER 1941

Lydia

At her new high school, Lydia effortlessly made friends and boys chased her around the playground. Someone asked if her previous school had been strict.

'Strict?' Lydia considered the question. She had not noticed if it was. If it was, it had nothing to do with her. Lydia did her own thing. If there were rules she liked, she kept to them, and if she did not like them, she did not.

At the new school, there were several children from her old school in London. About half of the evacuees had gone back, but the other half had stayed. Another child asked her if she was Valerie's sister.

'Do we look like sisters?!'

Lydia wasn't insulted – the girl obviously didn't mean it as an insult – but she could easily have been. Valerie was quick-witted and she no longer looked washed out, but she was no Miss Picard's 'chérie'. You wouldn't say *she* was pretty as a picture.

Despite sharing a house, Lydia and Valerie didn't spend a

lot of time together. Valerie was usually stationed in the library, listening to shows on the wireless. Lydia thought she could be attractive if she tried, but she didn't. If anything, she tried the opposite. Valerie also had no interest in material things. You could dangle some gold-plated candlesticks in front of her and her eyes wouldn't light up; she wouldn't care about the price or the metal, although she would probably ask about its history.

Lydia's mother wrote that she'd moved. Not back to London, nor to Somerset, but to live with another family in Norfolk. Only ten minutes' walk from the first house.

'This is much better,' she wrote, but Lydia didn't think it was. 'The house is cosier.'

Cosier was never a good sign!

'You must visit,' her mother wrote. 'There isn't much space, but, for many reasons, life is simpler here.'

Nothing made sense. Why her lovely mummy would have moved from a life of ease in a beautiful building with sophisticated people to what sounded like a shabby little place was mystifying. In what way was it 'simpler'?

Lydia's worst suspicions about her mother's move were fulfilled when she eventually went to stay. The Hazells were generous, certainly, but their house was poky as a sardine tin, square as a sugar cube, and smelled damp. She could possibly have forgiven these things, but it also had nothing exquisite in it, nothing at all.

She had to sleep on the floor of her mother's room, which was also shared with Mattthew. Didn't it feel like a terrible step backwards to her, too? But her mother – a bit like Valerie – didn't seem affected by her surroundings at home. The only surroundings she was interested in was the nursery. Lydia realised, that was all she cared about now.

The Hazells didn't have running water or a bath where Lydia could float for hours, but a tin bucket like they used to have in London.

'Can't we visit the Davenports?' Lydia asked one day while her mother was combing her wet hair.

Her mother didn't say anything for a while and then answered, 'They're busy – you know, he's an MP, and she works hard. They're often in London.'

'I liked Mrs Davenport,' Lydia said, thinking of the way the woman's diamond earrings had twinkled over her supper.

'I know you did.'

The next day, Lydia was persuaded to go to see her mother's workplace and she found this unimpressive too. Perhaps if you weren't used to the luxury of Bumble Cottage you might be inspired by the utilitarian hall converted into a nursery, but Lydia wasn't. And the children were exhausting! Relentless. It was like being around a thousand Matthews. Worse than Matthew – she would swear half these children were out of their minds. One little girl followed her around, saying, 'Why are you here?' and a snotty boy was shouting, 'Bloody hell,' and the babies were crying.

'What does Daddy think of this place?' she asked when the toddlers went for their nap and there was some semblance of peace. She could only imagine what Miss Picard would say: 'Quelle horreur!' probably.

'He's not interested.'

'Nor am I.' Lydia snorted, glad she and her father were on the same page.

Her mum didn't say anything, but her lips turned down.

The next day, when her mummy got up early – she opened the nursery at seven! – Lydia said she felt ill. Mummy was irritated at first and then when Lydia persisted she was concerned

– some children at the nursery had ringworm, could it be that? Lydia scowled; did she have to be so gross? Mummy didn't know what to do, so Lydia told her she just wanted to go back to sleep and Mummy agreed to pop home at lunchtime.

After she had been at the high school for a while, and was no longer 'the new girl', Lydia asked if anyone wanted to play her favourite game of 'I'm getting married in the morning!' and there was a whole host of volunteers.

This time, Lydia wasn't the only bride. There were loads of candidates, and one boy took on the role of vicar and turned it into his show. And there were wedding night jokes that made Lydia scowl. And then a teacher found out and decided it was inappropriate. Lydia couldn't understand it. Miss Picard would have loved it!

'It's just a game,' she argued furiously.

Mrs Howard was 'invited' in to the school for a conversation about impropriety.

'It's a storm in a teacup,' she concluded as they marched home (Mrs Howard did not merely walk). 'I don't see what's wrong with acting, do you?'

'No!' Lydia was relieved, but she should have guessed it would be all right – Mrs Howard had always preferred her and Valerie to just 'get on with it'.

'You are so sensible in some ways and daft as a brush in others,' she said, ruffling Lydia's hair.

Paul, who was at home for a tennis tournament, laughed at her – not for the inappropriate game but for getting found out – and then begged Valerie to go fishing with him.

40

OCTOBER 1941

Emmeline

Lydia's last visit hadn't been their most successful. At the Hazells' house, she hadn't held back in grumbling about having to sleep in the same bedroom as Emmeline and Matthew.

'We're at war, Lydia, some people don't have the luxury of a home at all.'

Emmeline had taken three days off from the nursery, but Dot had struggled to cope without her and begged her to come in. Emmeline hadn't expected Lydia to be *that* uninterested in the nursery either. Didn't she used to play with Matthew? Didn't she used to rock baby Joe and play with Jacob Salt? Maybe not. Maybe it was Valerie and Francine who did all that. Maybe Lydia just used to borrow Emmeline's make-up.

The children adored Lydia and ran up to her, wanting her attention, but that made it worse.

'I thought you liked children,' Emmeline said finally, exasperated.

'Animals are much better.'

. . .

That autumn the days were long and balmy. At the nursery
they had missed the opportunity to have a summer fete and now
they didn't know whether to put on an autumn fayre. People
were having such a rotten time, it might seem obscene to have
fun – but was it actually important? Emmeline asked the Old
People Friday crowd – they were a reliable source of wisdom for
her – and they got very animated at the idea, so she and the staff
decided to go ahead. They had an apple-bobbing stall, a hook-a-
duck stall, a tombola and a second-hand book stall. They had
teas and coffees and served alcohol at the bar.

She invited the Davenports, but only as a formality, and she
felt certain they wouldn't turn up. She should have known
better. They were consummate politicians after all.

It was the first time Emmeline had seen either of them for
the last five weeks or so. Just as she was taking in the sight of Mr
Davenport guessing the weight of a cake, Mrs Davenport strode
over to her like she had a raging bee in her bonnet.

Oh God, thought Emmeline. *It's all going to come out.*

Councillor Arscott was there too and she could see him
staring over at them curiously. 'Did we do something wrong,
Mrs Froud?'

'Not at all,' Emmeline said, mortified. She knew she was the
one who had done something wrong.

'It was just, you left in such a hurry.'

'The opportunity at the Hazells came up, so I took it. I apologise if it felt abrupt – I didn't mean it to.'

Mrs Davenport peered at her. 'The nursery looks smart. We
still get more correspondence about it than any other subject.'

Emmeline was unsure how to respond. Was that good or
bad? But Mrs Davenport had moved on to a new subject and
Councillor Arscott had moved out of earshot too.

'How is young Matthew?' she asked briskly.

'Settled in, thank—'

'And Lydia?'

'Very well.'

There was a shout and a cheer. Mr Davenport had correctly guessed the weight of the cake.

Mr Hazell had set up some stocks and there was a plan to throw sponges at the person in them. There'd been lots of jokes about who'd go in them, but few volunteers. In the end, Emmeline stepped forward.

'Let's get it over with!' she laughed.

She was about to get in position when Mr Davenport appeared, rolling up his shirt-sleeves.

'Allow me,' he said.

It was so strange to have him there in front of her, especially since for the past few weeks, she'd thought of little else. Sometimes, she imagined he was making love to her, not the half-hearted congress she and Neville engaged in to keep their marriage a marriage, but full-blown, cinematic lovemaking. After a suitable amount of resistance, she would let him see her naked. She would kiss every part of him. Sometimes, these imaginings were so vivid that for a moment she would think they were real. Now, she flushed as these images flashed before her. *My Goodness, what would people think of her if they knew?!*

'No,' she said. 'I don't think that's appropriate.'

'Throwing sponges at your MP? I think it would be a big draw for the crowd.'

As they were debating it, several men who were observing shouted encouragingly.

'I'll pay a guinea.'

'I'll give three!'

'You see!' Mr Davenport winked at Emmeline and then got in position in the stocks. It was undignified and Emmeline was relieved she didn't have to. And the customers rolled up their sleeves and commenced throwing the sponges. The children missed wildly, as Emmeline had guessed they would, leaving Mr Davenport largely unscathed. But then the grandfathers demanded a go.

'Should I let them?' Emmeline pondered.

'Of course,' Mr Davenport said through gritted teeth. 'It's for the war effort, isn't it?'

Thwack. They threw the sponge straight into his face. Emmeline couldn't bear to see it. She thought some of them were being far too aggressive about it. Neville would have been too, she supposed, if he had the chance to pelt a Member of Parliament! By the time they'd finished, Mr Davenport was wringing wet from head to toe. His white shirt had gone see-through. Impossible not to stare at his— no. He was lucky not to have a black eye; some throws were not only accurate but vigorous. Emmeline had never seen Councillor Arscott so happy.

Dot rushed to put a blanket round Mr Davenport. Emmeline wished she had thought of it. He was shivering, but he was laughing too.

'It's nothing more than I deserve, is it?' he said, flicking back his wet hair and giving Emmeline a hopeless smile.

Emmeline gulped. This was *impossible*.

41

1943

Emmeline

The war rumbled on. And yes, they got used to it. People will get used to almost anything if they have to. Norwich was attacked again and one of the children, Tony Hutton, lost his grandfather there. The bombings were called the 'Baedecker raids' because Hitler was targeting areas of cultural interest. Emmeline had nightmares about the factory getting hit.

At its peak, the nursery had fifty children and a waiting list. Emmeline didn't know exactly how many children were on it – Dot guarded it closely – but it was rare for a child on the waiting list to get a place because, once one had a place, children tended to stay until they went to school.

They took local and evacuated children up to four years old. They took children of mothers who worked, of mothers who didn't. Of mothers with one child and mothers with nine (yes, nine!). They took children of mothers on the edge of a nervous breakdown and mothers who were giddy with the joys of motherhood. One time, Emmeline got the children to chalk a picture of their mothers and found that thirty-eight had black hair, two had red hair and several had none.

Delousing Monday went from weekly to once every two weeks and then once every three weeks. The current record-holder was Joan Carpenter with fifty-six blighters. Matthew was in third place with his twenty-six. Dot had never caught them, Emmeline had had them three times, and poor Mabel was rarely without them. Dot claimed lice didn't like clean hair, but Emmeline said, 'That's just an old wives' tale.'

'And?' said Dot defensively. 'Nothing wrong with old wives!'

There were accidents – one child nearly fell out of the window and another scaled the table. You needed eyes in the back of your head. Christine was a big believer in a good airing so, when the sun shone, she liked the children to be outside. Little Josephine Locke got too much sun and her mother was furious. It took her a long time to convince her to bring Josephine back again.

Dot instituted the idea of an accident book and then accidentally spilled tea over it.

Matthew had outgrown the nursery and in September, joined Firside Primary. When Emmeline took him in for his first day at school, she found she knew half the children there – they were nursery babies. She also knew the teacher, Mrs Whittle, whose son was at the nursery. Matthew was looking forward to big school. He was capable and resourceful, a sociable boy. He would fit in, she hoped.

Once she left him, Emmeline had a moment to take stock. They'd been in Norfolk for four years and it was all Matthew knew. Living out of a suitcase, living apart from her husband and daughter, would never ever have been the plan. But the fact was, they were both thriving. She'd always hate those who'd started this terrible war yet, for her, the reality was it hadn't been too terrible. The evacuation had not only taken her to a place of safety, but it had also taken her to a place of purpose. But now, she wondered if those days might be coming to an end.

Lydia didn't want to meet in London, had no interest in her old life in the city, but nor did she particularly want Emmeline in Somerset: 'You'll only feel bad about the nursery.' She came up to Norfolk every few months. Emmeline knew it was duty, rather than pleasure.

The Hazells were good to her, even if Lydia was less than complimentary about their house and their food. Not to their faces – she had pleasant manners – but privately to Emmeline. 'How do you all live like this?' she would ask.

Not only was Lydia growing up, she was growing away from Emmeline, too. Everyone said that was normal and to be expected. Christine said, 'You can't keep them at the nursery stage forever.'

Dot said, 'You're closer to her than any other mother and daughter I know,' and Mabel said, 'Birds of a feather flock together,' whatever that meant.

Lydia was interested in her looks, so Emmeline took her to the hairdresser's in Fincham and paid a small fortune for her to have a wash and set. For fun, Dot drew a thick pencil line up her legs for stockings. Dot would have loved a daughter who was interested in her appearance, but Hettie and Pat were both tomboys. Emmeline said, Hettie reminded her of Valerie, always with her nose in a book. Lydia agreed but said, 'Valerie is different now,' although she couldn't explain how.

Lydia's other big love, of course, was dogs and Emmeline found they couldn't cross the village without her introducing herself to every one they met. She knew every dog-walker. Whereas Lydia could be judgemental about just about anything

– food, furniture, hairstyles – when it came to dogs, she was pure of heart and did not discriminate. She loved them all, great or small.

'When the war is over, we'll get a dog, shall we?!' Emmeline suggested.

Matthew hollered appreciatively, but Lydia just shrugged. A shiver went down Emmeline's spine.

'Do you not think the war will ever be over?' she asked, her voice shaky; but she realised she had chosen the wrong bit to focus on. She hadn't appreciated that war or no war, Lydia was still not planning on coming back to her.

Emmeline saw Neville maybe twice in those two years, although he never stayed overnight at the Hazells' and there were awkward times when they struggled to find anything to talk about. She would have talked about the nursery, but he found that boring, although if she didn't talk about the nursery he didn't understand what she did with her time. When she suggested seeing him in London, he said he was working, or that it was too dangerous.

'The doodlebugs!' he sighed. 'We can't risk it.'

'Neville! We're husband and wife.'

'Which is why I've sworn to honour and protect you.'

Emmeline didn't think the vows meant that they should never be in the same city at the same time, but she knew she couldn't change his mind. She didn't know how they'd spend the night together again. It had been so long. She prayed for answers. Maybe he was just nervous. Once the war was over, they'd simply have to get on with it.

Mabel had a boyfriend now. Jimmy was in the army and when he was on leave he came to the nursery. He was good with little ones and liked a sing-song. He taught them, 'Hi de hi de hi de ho', from the song 'Minnie the Moocher', and everyone laughed at the children singing back to him, except Emmeline when she found out what the song was about.

More Americans came to Norfolk. The factory girls were enthused – and not just the younger ones. Dot went out *a lot* and Emmeline thought about poor Peter, fighting for his country. She also thought her friend was taking advantage of her hosts, the Ingrams – sometimes she wasn't home until after midnight! – but she'd never say that.

Dot didn't say what she did on her nights out, but one time Emmeline saw a mark on her neck – a love-bite? And she once heard Dot saying, 'What's good for the goose is good for the gander' to Christine. In a way it was a relief that Dot didn't confide in her. Emmeline knew she'd struggle with hearing it. Dot probably thought it would be because she didn't approve, but it was more complex than that. How could Emmeline be disapproving when she'd almost done the same? How could she not be jealous when she *should* have done the same?

Emmeline tried to ignore her conflicting feelings about Mr Davenport. When she wasn't chasing after the children, she immersed herself in the newspapers. She paid particular attention to what was going on in the House of Commons. She liked to think of him influencing Churchill's speeches.

She thought of passing him on the stairs of the Old Rectory. She thought of him reading his letters. She thought of him opening the door to them that long-ago first day...

Did she regret turning him down?

Yes and no.

It was important to do the right thing. But doing the right thing was sad and lonely too. She couldn't let herself think of him kissing her. Her telling him to stop. Him stopping. Then starting again.

She sometimes wished he'd never kissed her and then they

could have continued living at the Old Rectory, gliding past each other, gazing at each other longingly, dreaming of a different life. Other times, she loved that he had kissed her. But her conscience was clear and her marriage was intact. She had beaten the odds and of that she was proud.

42

Lydia

Lydia had always known she was a pretty little thing, but she didn't realise until she was thirteen what a potent thing that was. And then it became her superpower. She who had never been the best at anything was the best at looking pretty. And pretty, she realised, got you things.

Paul didn't fully enter Lydia's consciousness for a long time. She knew Francine had liked him, because he gave her piggy-backs and played chase, but Lydia didn't want piggybacks or to play chase, so they'd had less to do with each other. And she knew Valerie liked him because they were always going off to the pond together or squashed up in the library, his feet on her lap or his head on her shoulder. But Lydia found him boastful: *School is so easy – why are you so bad at maths, Lydia?* Or *Tennis is so cool – why don't you play?* She was also busy with boys at school.

And then early one morning Lydia and Rex were bumbling along happily when she saw Paul coming out of the hut where the two land girls were staying. The land girls were bonny and strong and 'not Lydia's type'. They wore baggy trousers and blouses with grass stains and their arms were scratched from thorns.

The thing was: Paul didn't just come out of the hut, Paul and the land girl kissed in the doorway. It had the quality of a photograph, like they were framed by the doorframe, and it was a proper kiss too. *She is old!* was Lydia's immediate thought. Both land girls were three years older than Paul. About the same age difference as between her and Paul, in fact.

She wondered what he had that drove everyone wild. This secret – was it a secret? – made her feel odd. Were they *in love*? Would they get *married*? She might have discussed it with Valerie, but she and Valerie didn't talk much. Valerie liked listening to *It's That Man Again* on the wireless, or talking about her father, who saved two small girls in a fire before he died. Lydia didn't know what to say to that, or even if she should say anything. She thought about writing to her mother – by contrast, Mummy was brilliant to talk to and could always make you feel better – but it wasn't something you could put in a letter and she wasn't due another visit for a while.

After a few days, she asked the land girl about it. The land girl blushed and the blush told Lydia everything.

'Don't be daft,' she protested. 'He's much too young for me.'

Lydia kept her eyes on her and knew that she was lying. She was glacial. Sucking in her teeth like she'd seen the milkman do, she stroked Rex, buying herself time.

'Don't say anything. Mrs Howard would kill me,' the girl broke finally.

Lydia negotiated two pairs of stockings and four hairgrips for her silence. She was pleased with this, but that wasn't the most remarkable thing about the episode. The remarkable thing was how differently it made her look at Paul.

43

JULY 1944

Emmeline

They had been saying it wistfully for a while, but by 1944 the war was definitely, finally, indisputably, turning in their favour. The Nazis had developed their terrible weapons, but nothing could erase the fact that, with the might of the Russians, Americans, Canadians, Australians and everyone else, the pushback was under way.

In Norfolk, the wartime nursery was booming. The staff were content. The little children were flourishing. The parents felt reassured, and Emmeline was getting on too. Finally, she had managed to almost entirely bury her feelings for Mr Davenport. She could never entirely get away from him, being a public figure as he was, so she heard when he stood up in Parliament and when he gave a speech. She would hear his name muttered in the queues at the post office or catch a glimpse of him in the newspapers, and she had a narrow escape at the bank one time, but she had managed not to see, hear – much less touch – him in two whole years. He no longer occupied her every waking thought.

Dot always said the days were long, but the years went by quickly, and Emmeline found this to be true. Mabel and Jimmy got engaged. Christine's husband came back. Dot and her Peter were in love, again.

And how were Emmeline and Neville? Fine, thank you! They saw each other twice a year and it was more than enough – whereas Emmeline saw Lydia maybe four times a year and that was never enough.

Emmeline was especially proud of the nursery garden; whose heart couldn't fail to be lightened by the sight of the magnolia tree in bloom in the early spring? There was a swing, where the children lined up for their turn. (There had been a near-broken-nose incident when Deborah Holman had run into the swing just after Ian Byford had given it an almighty shove, but nothing since then.)

Babies grew up and more babies came. Mums came and went too, and, if the new ones seemed less capable than some of the mothers before them, Emmeline was mostly sympathetic. Many of the mums had been chopped out of their communities, forced away from their families and put up here – safer yes, but sadder in many ways. No grandmother, no mother-in-law, no aunties. How would they know what to do about cradle cap? How would they know when to worry about that cut or that lethargy? Or if their children's speech development was normal, or if they were behind? And some of them didn't have time to worry; they were living hand to mouth, day to day, after a telegram reporting a husband missing in action or stuck in a prison camp or, God forbid, downed somewhere over France. They didn't have time to worry, so Emmeline worried for them. Emmeline believed in taking care of them, and she spent many evenings comforting mothers and letting them know they were doing a great job in trying circumstances.

Sometimes, she wondered if it was too much – the mothers working in the factory and then having to take care of their children as well. Wasn't that a load too heavy? Was she *contributing* to that load by encouraging it? But when she spoke to the women, they were as one on the issue: work gave them a sense of achievement, they were proud of their efforts, they were glad of the money, and they were grateful their children were looked after, safe and entertained.

Emmeline hoped that after the war their contribution would not only be noted, but continued. They had such limited resources and yet they had created something magical. She was glad Matthew had spent his younger days in the nursery and, when she thought of Lydia, she found it sad that she had spent her own early years in the flat at Romberg Road; although she knew Lydia didn't see it like that – Lydia thought Matthew was the one who had it hard.

She still thought of Marjorie and her three children, often.

And she thought of her dear friend Mrs Salt and her lost children.

And then a letter came from the council. Four pages long and it took her two reads to get to the gist of it. The gist of it was: They weren't going to be funded any more. Signed, of course, Yours faithfully, Councillor Arscott.

'What?' yelped Emmeline. 'They can't be serious!'

She grabbed her coat, told Dot she had to go out on an urgent errand, grabbed one of the bicycles and flew down the street on it. Then she had to stop the bicycle to lower the saddle. Why were young women so tall? And then away she went.

She got to the council building within half an hour. A few friends stopped to chat to her, but when she explained she was on important business they waved her on.

'Good luck, Mrs Froud!'

It made her think of how things had changed since she first came here knowing no one, but she didn't have time to reminisce. There was no sign of the receptionist this time, or indeed anyone, so Emmeline rapped on the door that she knew was his.

There he was, her old nemesis, Councillor Arscott, hunched over a desk, his round glasses glistening and his nostrilly nose twitching. She thought of Rudolph Hess. She thought of Ebenezer Scrooge. He was somewhere between the two. Well, she wasn't going to be Tiny Tim today.

'Ah, Mrs Froud,' he said as though he'd been expecting her to turn up. Everything about him made her angry.

'What's this mean then?' Emmeline waved the letter at him, then read out snatches of it. "*The factory is going back to normal pre-war production, so...*" The war isn't even over yet!'

'What can I say? We are winding down the wartime nurseries.'

'Our purpose – our *raison d'être* – goes beyond that...'

'Not for us it doesn't,' Councillor Arscott said, and sucked in his teeth. 'Wartime nurseries equal wartime only. That was the remit. We didn't have nurseries before, so...'

'So?' Emmeline realised she still hadn't caught her breath. She remembered him saying, 'Why not get a nanny?' Supercilious twerp!

He stood up. 'Mrs Froud, we gave you a reprieve back in 1941 when the Blitz came to an end. Please don't come asking for another, because I'm afraid we won't be half so tolerant of you and your ilk a second time round.'

'M-my ilk?' Emmeline stuttered.

'Mothers,' he said, pointing his finger at her and jabbing it with each word, 'should not be cycling across the countryside...'

'I beg your pardon!' Emmeline shouted.

'Mothers should be in the home.'

Little bits of spit sprayed over his paperwork.

'Mothers will be anywhere that's needed, thank you, Councillor Arscott,' Emmeline said, turning on her heel.

.   .   .

Emmeline didn't go back to the nursery. She couldn't. She was in a state of abject fury. She leapt on the bicycle. Everything had been rolling along so nicely. And they were doing a good thing at the nursery, they really were. The children were acquiring new skills every day. She loved seeing them go from nappy to toilet trained. She loved seeing them go from speechless to conversational. From crawling to skipping. From being afraid to say boo to a goose to leaping at you from behind a curtain. No one was *forced* to put their children in their nursery. Not a single person was and no one ever should be – it merely gave mothers a choice.

She couldn't bear to think of the women's faces when they heard this news. Half of them were working at the factory and many would want to stay on *whatever* was produced once the war ended, a quarter were at the hospital, and the other quarter needed a bloody good rest – but that wasn't the point. They provided a service. A great service.

She racked her brains as she pedalled. Lydia would be happy if the nursery closed down, and Neville would be, too. And that made it worse. She didn't have many people on her side. She would have to galvanise the few she had. She couldn't even bear to tell her dear Dot because Dot would be devastated. And Mabel, Christine and Mrs Hodges. Their fates rested on her shoulders.

Emmeline hadn't been to the Old Rectory for three years and as she approached, she was shocked how different it was to the Hazells' tiny, terraced house. About five of their house could fit in here. She got off the bicycle and propped it against the wall.

Please let *him* answer, she thought as she knocked on the door. Not Mrs Davenport. Nor Mr Reynolds. She did not want to be patronised today. The gods of wartime nurseries must

have been looking down on her for once, because it *was* Mr
Davenport who stood there.

'Mrs Froud!' he said and he sounded delighted to see her.
'How *are* you?'

'Not good.' Emmeline was not in the mood for small talk.
'The council want to close us down. They're going back on our
agreement.'

'Come in,' he said at once. 'Let's talk this over.'

She had worked up a sweat on the way and had she thought
about it, she wouldn't have wanted him to see her in this state,
but there was no turning back now. Stepping over the threshold,
she realised how rare it was to be in this house without
Matthew for a shield.

He fussed around her while she took off her coat. 'It's been
an awfully long time – too long,' he exclaimed.

The contrast between his enthusiasm and Neville's cold
manner was stark, but then Mr Davenport was an actor – that
was what politicians were. Actors in search of an audience. His
shirt-sleeves were rolled up, and he was wearing braces and the
baggier trousers that were popular now. Once again Emmeline
thought that, if you didn't know him, you would never guess he
was an MP. He looked more like the inspirational teacher in an
America movie.

Emmeline reminded herself that Mrs Davenport and Mr
Reynolds were probably nearby going through papers in the
drawing room, chortling at all the letter-writers and their obses-
sions. And if they weren't here, she mustn't be sucked in. She
mustn't be charmed. This was business.

He led her through to the drawing room, which still
contained his desk with the leather top and the inkwell that
Matthew had once managed to stick his fingers in. The typewriter was on another desk, its ribbons out, like blue entrails
after a bloody fight.

'Take a seat. Let me get you a drink.'

'Why aren't you in Parliament?' she asked brusquely.

'Oh.' He was surprised at her abruptness. 'Actually, I've been rather ill.'

'I hadn't heard,' she said, then regretted it because it might sound like she had been following his whereabouts. She had, but she didn't want him to know that. An illness had not been reported. 'I'm sorry.' She sat down in the armchair where she used to sit, suddenly weary.

'I made it!' He flexed his muscles as a joke. 'Apparently, I gave everyone a fright – but I don't remember much of it.'

Emmeline felt ashamed – ashamed that she didn't know, and ashamed that she was storming around, making demands. Now that she knew, it seemed obvious. His face was thinner than before, his eyes tired, with blue-ish bags beneath them.

'I shouldn't have bothered you.'

'Not at all, I'm ready to be bothered. I need to be bothered.'

Emmeline passed him the letter from the council and told him about her conversation with Councillor Arscott.

He sat at his desk, then sighed as he raced through the letter. Then he looked up at her apologetically. 'I wonder if this is more about getting back at me. He was incandescent when I exposed his links to Nazi Germany. I wonder if you and the nursery are just caught in the crossfire.' Emmeline had wondered the same. He brought his hands together, the tips of his fingers softly touching.

'Can you help?' she asked.

'First of all, don't panic,' he said.

'Too late for that,' she admitted.

He smiled. 'For a start, the war isn't over yet. I don't see how he has any grounds for this.'

'It's not just the war,' she explained, although part of her was annoyed. *Haven't I explained this hundreds of times?* 'The nursery will still be a lifeline for many mums even after the war ends. And it is for the children. And for me, too.' She realised she was being honest with herself about that, possibly, for the first time. She whispered, 'I think I might have gone quite mad without it.'

It *had* saved her. And if it had been in existence earlier, it might have saved poor Marjorie, too.

'I understand that.'

'I know we always framed it as part of the wartime nurseries scheme, but I always hoped the nursery would be for peacetime, too.'

Emmeline knew she needed to calm down. Being aggravated wasn't helping. She took deep breaths and looked around her. As usual, the room was full of newspapers, boxes and notes.

'I am sorry to intrude,' she said finally. 'What were you working on?'

'Top-secret stuff,' he said with a wink.

'Ah, the badgers are back again.'

He laughed and then in a low voice added, 'It's so good to see you, Mrs Froud.'

He promised he'd raise an objection at the next full council meeting. And then he warned her: 'I'm not the council though – I'm in national government. I can't make or overturn local decisions.'

'But your voice has more power than ours.'

'I don't know about that.'

'Don't be so humble,' she countered irritably and he laughed again. The sound of it went right to the core of her. She couldn't be irritated with him for long.

He asked after Matthew and Lydia and she said, suddenly focusing her disgruntlement elsewhere, 'Lydia doesn't visit enough.'

'That must be hard,' he said. The simplicity of this statement moved her.

'How is Mr Froud?' he asked then. Was it her imagination or did his voice sound croaky?

'He is... Mr Froud,' she said nonsensically. *My husband. For better or for worse.*

She heard the door and Mr Reynolds and Mrs Davenport walked in and you couldn't not think that, of the three, *they* were the pair and Mr Davenport was the odd man out here.

'Dear Mrs Froud!' Mrs Davenport said, kissing the air next to her. 'A sight for sore eyes!' She was more perfumed than ever, and she looked different, lovelier somehow. Emmeline felt like an ugly sister and she couldn't wait to get away.

'How is the dog?' Emmeline wrote to Lydia that evening. 'Give him a big kiss from me, and one for yourself, my love.' She hummed and hawed about mentioning the threat to the nursery, as she knew it was not Lydia's favourite subject – not by a long shot. But Lydia had to understand: Emmeline wasn't just doing it for the mothers from London, she wasn't just doing it for the mothers in Norfolk. It was vital that *all* mothers had more opportunities. One day, she was sure, Lydia would thank her for it.

44

Lydia

Lydia had a boyfriend pretty much continuously. Her mother had met her father at a young age, so it wasn't absurd. Her daddy rarely wrote but one time she got a letter from him saying, 'I hope you're not running around with boys.' She ignored it. When boys asked her to be their girl, she said yes, and then they walked with her, carried her bag or brought her presents. She couldn't seem to help it.

One boy – Saul Clarkson – was a favourite. He bought her daffodils. Some were wilting by the time she received them and he apologised. When she went to his house, she saw it was old but in a bad way, and shabby, and suddenly Lydia didn't see a future in their relationship. She told him that and his eyes filled with tears. He was still the only one who she let kiss her on the lips, but she was clear that they weren't boyfriend and girlfriend any more.

Had she stayed in London, she wouldn't have known people like Mrs Howard in Bumble Cottage. She wouldn't have known people like Flora, who had a piano in the living room and a cello in the hall. She wouldn't have known people like Betsy, who had an actual tennis court in the garden.

But she knew them now – and a little knowledge can be a dangerous thing. Although Saul Clarkson might have been the sweetest boy in the world, he wasn't enough for her. If she married a boy like Saul, she would never have a Rolls-Royce, big dogs loping around a big garden, or a choice of fancy clothes. And no one could tell her those weren't important.

An old friend, Leonard, turned suitor. He bought her tickets for the cinema, and cake, and on Valentine's Day he gave her a necklace with a locket.

'We could put a picture of you and me in it?'

'We could...' responded Lydia doubtfully.

Then there was Harry. He was in the year below her, so he would have been unsuitable, except that he was tall, and hairy – everyone called him 'mature' – and he lived in the town and his father was a doctor and he was going to be a doctor, too.

'You can take me out if you are?'

He looked appalled. He scratched his spots and made one of them bleed. She had gone too far – she had a habit of doing this.

'I'm joking!' she said quickly, and relief filled his face like a child given chocolate.

45

Emmeline

Three weeks after Emmeline had gone back to the Old Rectory, there was a full meeting of the council. Mr Davenport was going to contest their stopping the funding for the wartime nurseries.

Emmeline was wearing an old but smart dress with a thin belt and matching hat, and Dot looked lovely with her hair curled and a pleated skirt and blouse. Christine, Mabel and Mrs Hodges were holding the fort at the nursery.

Mr Davenport was in a three-piece suit, with a pocket watch at his waistcoat. Emmeline tried not to notice how debonair he looked. Would he ever not have that effect on her? He was out of her league, she thought, and then told herself off for being ridiculous. They were both married – leagues were irrelevant.

They met in the large echoey entrance hall that smelled faintly of luncheon meat.

'We're third on the agenda,' Mr Davenport explained. 'So

we'll have to sit through' – he looked through his notes – 'a proposal for a new roundabout and an item about fences.'

'Will you say the war is not over yet?' Dot asked urgently. 'I mean, that's the obvious point to make, isn't it?' She was fretting.

'That will be one of our arguments,' he said.

'And the others?' Emmeline asked, but Dot interrupted her. 'Do you get nervous, Mr Davenport? Giving speeches?'

'Not if I know I'm right,' he said.

'You *are* right,' Dot and Emmeline said at the same time, then they all laughed.

Dot and Emmeline trooped upstairs to the gallery overlooking the chamber.

'Remember we used to spend five days a week in the cinema?' Dot grinned.

Emmeline grabbed her hand and squeezed. 'We've come a long way, haven't we?'

'You hated *The Thief of Baghdad* so much!'

'And I never got to see the end of *Rebecca*!'

Before long, it was Item 3. The Chairman invited Councillor Arscott to speak. He stood, stooped over like a man double his age. His clothes were ill-fitting and his manner pompous. He was so unlikeable that for a moment, Emmeline felt sorry for him – but when she whispered that to Dot, Dot slapped her hand on the rail and hissed, 'No!'

'We want to shut down the wartime nurseries, we believe we will save money.'

Emmeline found she had no sympathy for him anymore. And then Mr Davenport took the stand.

'We object.'

Mr Arscott folded his arms, a supercilious grin spread all over his face.

'The war is over.'

'The war is *not* over. And I put it to you that the nurseries should not shut even when it is.'

Emmeline leaned back in her chair, relieved that someone this eloquent, this at ease in the world, was on their side. Her thoughts took her back to the kiss again and she shook her head: one moment of recklessness, that's all. She had almost made it through the war unblemished. She mustn't bother with all that now.

It struck her how ludicrous it would sound if she told anyone. *He kissed you years ago and you're still harping on about it? Get over yourself, woman.*

What would she tell Lydia if she were in her position? *Grow up*, probably!

'These are not *only* wartime nurseries...' Mr Davenport was saying.

Exactly, Emmeline thought. She had been saying this for years.

'Why should they continue? Important reasons.'

That's right, thought Emmeline, nodding along.

'He's great,' Dot whispered. 'Well done.'

Full of pride, Emmeline squeezed her hand.

'I want to talk about the state the London children were in when they came to the countryside.'

Emmeline snapped her head upwards.

'Riddled with lice – you may have seen them with their shaved heads. This was not a fashion choice. And you may have heard about the sickness – there was a lot of vomiting, due to poor diets – and their poor teeth...'

Emmeline felt herself redden. *What is he saying about them?* She took her hand from Dot to clutch her handbag. She couldn't even look at her friend any more. At no point had Mr Davenport indicated he would ever say any of this.

'Nearly all of them had bed bugs. I hate to say it, but they were filthy. And violent. And the language used by some of them... Words I can't bring myself to repeat here today.'

Emmeline could not believe her ears. *Is he on our side or not?*

She glared at him in open-mouthed horror, but he wasn't looking at the gallery but was gazing around at the councillors in the hall.

'These wartime nurseries are part of a national strategy, a strategy to pull our country together and push our people forward. If we can save a few children from a life of low expectation, deprivation and poor outcomes, then it's worth spending a few pennies now.'

No wonder Churchill never took his advice. He was a disaster!

'These children are essential to the rebuilding of our country – so do we say no, or do we say yes?'

Some people were already clapping a yes. Mr Davenport lowered his hands like a conductor, telling them to stop.

'Money spent on our children – our future – is *never* wasted.'

Emmeline couldn't bear to look at him. The absolute *weasel*.

She couldn't imagine what Dot was thinking. Betrayal, that was it. Mr Davenport was a traitor. Neville had been right all along: MPs were all a load of cheats, cowards, self-interested so and so's.

How dare he? Everything he'd seen or she'd told him in confidence was being used against her. Fleas. Nits. Sickness. Swear words. She hadn't had the faintest idea that this was what he thought of them – of her. She had thought he liked her. Well, maybe he did; but clearly, he had never *respected* her.

They were still clapping like seals down in the chamber. And then hands were raised.

'So you are suggesting keeping the nursery running after the war is a *moral obligation*?' spat Councillor Arscott.

'Exactly that,' Mr Davenport said smoothly, and she loathed him then, almost as much as she loathed Councillor Arscott. 'Keeping the nurseries going is the moral thing to do. And let me also tell you, investment now is a big investment in our country's future.'

'That sounds like something the people in the opposition party would say.' Councillor Arscott said.

'So what if it is?' Mr Davenport said smoothly. 'It's important to do what is right rather than follow tribal allegiances.'

Now he had the audacity to look up at her and wink. Emmeline froze.

'Thank you, the Right Honourable Mr Davenport MP for King's Lynn,' the Chairman said. 'And we'll take a break here.'

Emmeline pushed her way out of the balcony section, leaving Dot behind. She raced down the stairs and there he was, pulling on his coat and hat in the foyer. He beamed at her.

'We have time for a quick cigarette, Mrs Froud.'

'I don't believe it!'

'I'm sure they'll give us a few minutes.'

'Not that. I mean – what a thing to say!'

He looked up at her. She saw he was surprised. Genuinely. But that was no excuse.

'All that stuff – about nits and sickness and bed bugs and no manners.'

'Ah!' So the penny had finally dropped. Good. He gestured for them to move to the side of the room for more privacy. 'I only said that to win them over,' he said quietly. 'That's the goal here, isn't it? To keep the nursery going?'

'I don't want to win them over if that's what you think.'

'Let's see what they have to say... I have a feeling it's going to go our way.'

Our way?!

'I don't want to. I don't want to win like this.'

'You've focused on the mothers for long enough, Mrs Froud. Let's focus on the children too.'

'How little you think of us evacuees... filthy, louse-ridden, mothers with low morals. Vomit. On your doorstep.'

The brim of his hat obscured his expression at first. Then he took off his hat and she saw he looked puzzled. 'I didn't mention my doorstep. Or low morals.'

'That's what you meant though.'

'I didn't. I had to say *something* to convince the men in the council, Mrs Froud, this is politics. I thought you understood.'

'Was that your opinion of me?'

'Never. If anything, your morals are far too high.'

He looked her in the eye but this time she would not melt, she would not be diverted. She was too furious to respond. He sighed and put his cigarette tin back in his pocket.

'Let's go back in and see what they decide before you lecture me.'

Emmeline couldn't stop thinking about what he had said. It put everything in a different light. The way he had sat Matthew on the stool and cut his hair. She had thought it was tender. In fact, he was laughing at her. He probably told his colleagues all about the little family from London accompanied by their funny little insects! He had made jokes about Billy and the porridge, but now he was using it all as ammunition against her. The feral London children. He probably laughed about them with his friend, Churchill. The jibe about the teeth – did Dot hear that? The snipe about the bed bugs.

For years she had wished she didn't find him so irresistible, but now, for the first time she realised she was able to resist him. She had found out his real thoughts about her – and they were far from what she had thought they were.

Back in the chamber, the Chairman was talking.

'Thank you. We'll put it to a vote. All those in favour of closing down the wartime nurseries, please raise your hands.'

Councillor Arscott gleefully raised his, but when he looked around and saw that his hand alone was up, his mouth fell open.

'That is one vote FOR the motion, thank you,' the Chairman said. 'And all those against closing the wartime nurseries, please raise your hands.'

Eleven hands were raised. There were big smiles at such a conclusive result, although Emmeline's mouth was set in a grimace. On one hand, they'd won. On the other, she felt she would like to punch everyone in that room, starting with Mr Davenport. How could he?

Mr Arscott's head was so low, it was almost on the desk.

'We have no objections,' the Chairman continued. 'So the funding of the nursery will not stop until the war is over, when we will review the situation.'

'What's it all mean?' Dot clamoured next to her. 'Why don't they just speak normal English?'

'It means we keep going,' Emmeline said flatly.

Dot whooped and shouted, 'Yes!', but Emmeline couldn't even get up from her seat. She was still mortified. She had never been so humiliated in her life – and that was Mr Davenport's fault.

46

Emmeline

Dot, Christine and Mabel were mortally grateful to Mr Davenport, which drove Emmeline up the wall. They talked about him like he should be sainted.

Emmeline decided that they would have won without him. In fact, she was certain she could have done a better job than he had. On and on her friends went. Now they were wondering if they should bake him a pound cake to show him their appreciation.

'Emmeline will know if he prefers sweet or savoury.'

'No, Emmeline does not know,' Emmeline snapped. 'And there's no need to get him anything anyway. He was just doing his job.'

'He went over and above,' insisted Dot, a phrase that invariably made Emmeline snort.

'You do realise what he said about us? Flea-ridden, nits, filthy.'

'I've been called a lot worse,' said Dot cheerfully.

'He didn't mean it like that,' chipped in Mabel. 'My Jimmy says he was just "wooing the crowd".'

The way she said 'My Jimmy' before every opinion she expressed was another thing that infuriated Emmeline (especially because she was fully aware that this was something she used to do with Neville).

'Then he's a fake and a phoney,' insisted Emmeline.

'That's what Churchill does. My Jimmy says—'

'And so is he.' Emmeline couldn't stop herself.

'My Jimmy is a fake and a phoney?'

Everyone dissolved into giggles.

'No, Churchill is,' said Emmeline, her anger falling away at the ridiculousness of the discussion. 'Bake Davenport a cake if you like. I want nothing to do with it.'

'We'll write him a card and we'll put all our names in it except yours,' suggested Dot facetiously.

'I don't care what you do,' Emmeline told them.

Emmeline knew Mr Davenport wouldn't be able to resist coming by, fresh with success. She'd give him an inch and he'd take a mile.

And two weeks later, he did. He came in carrying three dolls that she recognised as the type Lydia had once had. Hard face, soft bodies; these were expensive ones from America. Sweet Margaret-Doll. Whatever had happened to her? He handed them over to the women and they were all, 'Yes sir, yes sir, three bags full,' while Emmeline scowled in the background. If they were an apology, they did not go far enough.

'I suppose you feel like you own us now that you've saved us,' she said sneeringly.

'Not at all,' he said, and then whispered, 'Mrs Froud, can we talk?'

Some children came running over just then, though, and he handed out the dolls, as the children squealed.

'They cost a fortune,' Dot said approvingly.

'Buying everyone's favours,' Emmeline muttered. Part of her anger was at herself for being taken in by him. She'd fantasised about him for years – and in the end, he was just another horrid man.

'You're always welcome, Mr Davenport,' Dot went on. 'If you and your wife have a child, do bring them along. We've not done 'mates rates' before but for you we'd make an exception.'

This made him cough. 'Thank you, I'll keep that in mind.'

Emmeline flushed. *Why does Dot have to be like this?*

'Any nieces, nephews... illegitimate heirs? Same too. We'll do a family-package.'

Mr Davenport laughed. Emmeline didn't.

'Stop hounding him,' she said.

Once he'd left, Dot shook her head. 'What's up with you? You said he was only ever kind to you and Matty.'

'He was.'

'You'd think he was Al Capone the way you treated him just now.'

'I didn't like what he said about us.'

Dot guffawed. 'He got us the funding though, didn't he?'

Emmeline realised the best thing to do would be to have nothing to do with him again. But it was hard to resist his visits; he always came in with bags of toys or a treat for the staff. He seemed to think they were his pet project.

'So I thought I might bring in an old train track I have, and a gauge train, if you have the space.'

'If you like,' Emmeline said, then stalked off. She didn't want anything from him ever again, but she also knew some of the children – most of them in fact – would be thrilled.

She sensed he was enjoying the push and pull of their interactions – but she wasn't. She was still furious.

On Old People's Friday, he sat with the elderly attendees and talked about the old days and won all them over too. Another time, he came in with a sack of small clothes for the littlest ones. Then another time with old papers for drawing on.

'He's like Father Christmas.' Mabel swooned. 'Even my Jimmy says he'll vote for him next time.'

'That's probably why he does it,' Emmeline interjected.

Mabel considered, then pulled a face. 'I like him.'

Emmeline had kept the newspaper articles. The one at the house about London and the one about the opening of the nursery. She looked at them again. It was all about image for him. Or he and Councillor Arscott were in some kind of game, a rivalry, and they didn't care who got hurt. He didn't care about the nursery – wartime or otherwise – he just wanted to get one over his old enemy.

Yet, when Mr Davenport didn't visit the nursery for a while, she missed him. He didn't come for the next six weeks, and she was raging with herself and worried that he was ill again. Perhaps he was dying. Then she would never get to tell him what she thought.

That Spring, the magnolia tree in the garden looked beautiful. The babies napped beneath it in their prams. The children spent hours outdoors. Hopscotch was a favourite, along with skipping, kicking a ball, or, even though Matthew was no longer there to instigate it, firing at each other with pretend guns or throwing themselves onto hand grenades.

The owner of the factory came to the nursery with a small glass trophy.

'We couldn't have kept going without you,' he said.

Misty-eyed, Emmeline accepted the award. At the bottom was an engraving: COMMENDATION OF SUPPORT FOR INDUSTRY WORKERS.

Soon they would be reverting to the production of bicycles.

'You'll still need the mothers to help though, won't you?' Emmeline said confidently.

The owner blustered. 'Certainly,' he said. 'If there are any jobs left after the men.'

Dot had another madcap idea: the children should do country dancing. She had been given a book on it. Once Emmeline had read that it was the ideal way to encourage coordination, physical exercise, stamina and social skills, she agreed too. On one condition: she wouldn't have to be involved. She had given up that sort of thing when Neville's knees went – and she didn't miss it.

They set it for Friday afternoons, after lunch once the old people had gone home. Fridays were always a little wilder than the norm.

First, Dot, Christine and Mabel learned dances from terrible diagrams in the book. Then they tried to apply them in real life. But the children wouldn't follow the instructions and got tangled up with each other. Josephine fell over and Ian refused to hold hands with anyone but Nessa. One child wet himself – a big puddle on the floor – yet kicked up a fuss about being taken away to be changed. It was chaos but a success.

It was during the third country dancing session that Mr Davenport next came to visit, this time with a box of crayons. Emmeline didn't know how long she could keep being annoyed with him, yet she wasn't ready to forgive him either.

'I thought you'd forgotten us,' she said sullenly. Gosh, she was so petty, she hated herself.

'I was in France,' he explained. 'Peace negotiations.'

She looked at him. As excuses went, this was pretty brilliant. Nevertheless, he hardly needed to give her excuses as to why he hadn't been. He didn't owe them.

'I wish I had known. I thought you were poorly again.'

'What would you have done? Come and stuck the boot in?'

She was going to protest, but he was twinkly-eyed, teasing her, and she couldn't help laughing too.

The country dancers set off and immediately it was disorder. They were supposed to form two lines and join hands in the air to create an arch, but they seemed to have created four, so there were arches everywhere but who knew what half of them were doing? There was a lot of giggling.

'Have you not showed them how it should be done?' Mr Davenport asked Emmeline.

'No, because I don't know how it should be done either!' she admitted.

'I see,' he said, and then he held out his arm. 'Mrs Froud?'

She backed away immediately. 'Not me...'

'Come, for the children's sake.'

The children had noticed, and clapped and squealed. 'Mrs Froud, MRS FROUD! Dance!'

Dot was behind it. 'Come on,' she shouted. 'Dance with us!'

It would draw more attention if she made a fuss. Emmeline took Mr Davenport's arm and let him lead her to the front of the hall. Some of the mothers who had arrived early for pick-up stopped talking to watch. Emmeline swallowed. This was NOT what she wanted.

He put his hand on her waist and she felt so embarrassed. She was now bright red.

'Ladies and gentlemen, children,' Mr Davenport announced. '*This* is how we country-dance.'

Emmeline could hear Dot explaining to some of the mothers: 'It's the MP, Mr Davenport.'

'My husband voted for him. I voted for the other one.'

Mr Davenport twirled her one way and then the next, instructing her as they went along. And then he whispered to her: 'I did what I thought was best. It was politics, nothing more. I'm so sorry if it upset you.'

And then he continued: 'Left, right, left, right, that's it. Now right, left, right...!'

Emmeline was speechless. She concentrated on her feet. They looked tiny compared to his, but she still didn't want to step on him.

'The thought that it hurt you distresses me greatly.' And then in a louder voice he said, 'And turn round. You've got it.'

The children, mothers and the rest of the staff were clapping them.

'See, Mrs Froud, you're a natural,' Mabel yelled.

She was hot-cheeked. Still moving the way he wanted her to move. She tried to remember the children and their mothers in the hall. She tried not to think about the way he looked at her. The way he was holding her. The way it made her feel.

She heard one of them say, 'I'll *definitely* vote for him next time.'

Emmeline escaped to the Ladies. There was no getting away from it; her longing for Mr Davenport was back and more powerful than ever. Try as she might to go over the ridiculous things he said at the council meeting – and they were ridiculous – she couldn't make them stick, she couldn't turn him into the enemy.

He did what he thought would save the nursery – and he was right.

If she ever told Dot how much she craved Mr Davenport, Dot would laugh. She wouldn't be horrified though. She was attuned to baser instincts. And that was horrifying too, because Emmeline did not want to be that way. 'Just kiss him,' Dot would probably say.

There were newspaper articles on how the war had 'lowered inhibitions'. How people were throwing away their morals and making wicked decisions. They were full of passionate nights under the stars: the attitude was 'what does it matter if nobody knows?' and 'we could be dead tomorrow'.

If she told Mabel or Christine, they would suggest restraint: 'You're a married woman, Mrs Froud. And he's a married man!'

Or perhaps, even if they weren't a conscience, they'd be practical – 'Where can it go?' 'It will all end in tears'.

She wouldn't do anything, of course she wouldn't – she was a 34-year-old married mother of two! – but she had never battled with herself so much. It was her own private war.

Think. Concentrate. Not on him but your own family.

What if people found out how she felt? Neville would be shocked. It was clear he did not think there was life in this old dog. But worse than that, there was Lydia. Lydia would be furious, if not heartbroken. Lydia might never forgive her.

Nothing could happen. Ever. And perhaps he didn't want it to anyway; he was probably just toying with her, courting her vote.

As she splashed her face with cold water, she sighed to herself. She was as lovesick as a teenager, a stupid old lady who should know better, way past the age for silly crushes. She would write to Neville tonight. A good letter home would focus the mind. She would not make more of a fool of herself, she would not.

Perhaps if Neville paid her more attention – in *that* way (in any way!) – she wouldn't be left feeling like this. She felt consumed by desire, as though nothing else of her existed apart from the longing she felt for him. How did she ever function before she met him? How would she ever function again?

She hid out in the Ladies for ages, yet he was still there when she re-emerged. That wasn't the plan. She wished he'd gone already.

'I was waiting to say goodbye,' he said. His eyes were full of concern.

That she couldn't do what she wanted to do with him made her curt.

'You needn't have,' she said shortly.

'Would you come outside with me a moment?' he said. She pulled a face, but followed him out nevertheless.

It wasn't possible that he didn't know how much she desired him. Desire had turned her into a monster.

'I'm sorry,' he said. 'That I upset you.'

'I know you are.'

'It did work, though.'

'And if it hadn't?'

'I would have funded it out of my own pocket,' he said.

'What? Why?'

'Two reasons. One, it works. I see it works.'

'And the second?'

'To make you happy,' he whispered. 'Since I met you, that's all I've ever wanted to do.'

It felt like the most erotic phrase of her entire life. She swallowed. She turned to go back inside. She had to get away from him.

47

Lydia

Lydia never knew what to do with herself when she visited her mummy in Norfolk. In Somerset she was busy, walking with a poker-straight back with the Bible balanced on her head, or with boyfriends and admirers – or dogs. She was helping out at the nearby Smarts' kennels. She cleared up after dogs, stroked them, played with them, and most days took one or other to the vets. And if people thought Lydia was dog-crazy, she had nothing on the Smarts – the Smarts lived and breathed dog. 'They won't live long, so you have to give them one hundred per cent,' was Mrs Smart's philosophy. She didn't need to say it, though – it was clear that this informed everything she and her husband did at the kennels.

If Mrs H had taught Lydia the joys of wealth and Miss Picard the joys of having sex appeal, then it was the dogs who taught her about enjoying the moment.

In Norfolk, she was just following her mother around like Rex did with her. She didn't tell Mummy, but the nursery reminded her of the hall she had been evacuated from. It wasn't the only reason that it made her feel strange, but it was a factor.

'What do you hope to do after the war, Lydia?' Mummy asked, surprising her. This was a question the teachers and Mrs H liked asking, not her mummy, who was usually sweetness and light and 'whatever will be, will be'.

'I don't know yet.'

'There's work in the nursery if ever you...'

'Me? Small children?' said Lydia, but what she meant was – *why are you still holding out this hope?*

'You'd be excellent.' Mummy was determined not to be ruffled. 'It's just like looking after dogs.'

Lydia snorted. 'The nursery won't still be running,' she scoffed, but her mother was being deadly serious.

'I hope it will be – and more. It's so important, darling. We have the children of factory workers and health workers. And do you know, there are parents moving into this area for the nursery because they know we provide such good care!'

Her mother wiped her hands on her apron, her face full of pride.

None of this interested Lydia. Not one bit.

'Maybe,' she said. Her mother looked ecstatic, so Lydia realised she needed to rein her in a little. She had NO intention of working in a nursery – in Norfolk, in Somerset, in London or anywhere. 'Just until I get married.'

Her mother looked puzzled. 'And then what will you do?'

'I'll look after my husband,' Lydia said quickly. 'And my dogs. What's wrong with that?'

'Nothing wrong with that,' Mummy said quickly. 'If that's what you want – and if you can afford it.'

'If I choose the right husband, I will be able to,' Lydia told her.

Sometimes, when her mother gaped at her like that, mouth open, it reminded her of one of Paul's freshly caught fish.

48

MAY 1945

Emmeline

All good things come to an end – and bad things too. Six years after war broke out, the Nazis were defeated. And so Emmeline's stay in the country came to a close.

The Hazells walked her and Matthew to the railway station. Emmeline tried not to be too emotional, but this couple had opened their home to them. They had shared their lives, their food, their home with strangers. They were quiet, unassuming and generous. When she thought about it, it made her heart full.

Emmeline had kept busy. So busy. She had run a goodbye party for the children and a handover party for the staff and had given them school photos and play reports. So very busy.

She had not seen Mr Davenport, not since their country dancing. She hoped that, now the war was over, he would no longer dominate her thoughts. She felt that once she was back in London, the last few years would take on the quality of a dream. Moving forward, they would not and could not stay in touch. He wouldn't want to either, she was sure of that.

. . .

Neville had rented a flat for them in West Hampstead.

'It's nearer my work,' he said, and he also said that he thought she could do with a change from Romberg Road.

'A step up,' he called it, although she saw it was more of a sideways step.

It was a three-bed flat, so there was room for Lydia to come back – when she was ready – but in the meantime Neville, Emmeline and Matthew occupied one room each.

'Just for a while, so we can get used to each other again,' Emmeline told herself. The first night, she and Neville sat side by side on the sofa, which was still in its polystyrene cover, careful not to impinge on each other. When the lack of affection between them upset her, Emmeline reminded herself to be patient and not to give up. It was going to take a while before they rekindled their relationship, she was prepared for that.

'So?'

'I'm going to open a nursery here in London some day.'

She liked saying it out loud. She liked hearing the words. Christine was managing the nursery in Norfolk. Mabel was staying on until her baby was born. They still had Mrs Hodges. Some of the mums worked in the bicycle factory now, some in the hospital, and some didn't work at all.

Neville had lit a cigar. 'No one's going to want a nursery any more, Em!'

'What do you mean?'

'War's over. Wartime nurseries are finished.'

Neville always spoke with utmost certainty. It was something she used to like about him.

'It's time to let it go,' he went on. 'How would you finance it anyway? Without government grants?'

Neville didn't know what work they'd done or how wonderful it was. She'd managed to bring up their child in an unfamiliar place. She'd managed to have a job *and* keep Matthew with her all day long. She had led a life of independence and purpose and she had enabled the women around her to do the same. The women at the factory, the women at the hospital, the women who needed a rest, they were able to do those things – because of her. She could have said all this to Neville, but he didn't want to talk about it.

Those first few days back together were difficult. She and Neville really were like strangers. Worse than strangers, because at least with strangers you don't have high hopes. With strangers, you didn't once promise to love them and obey them, and you didn't put all your dreams into them.

Neville. Her husband. Before Emmeline went to sleep, cold cream on her face, rollers in her hair, she tried to remember the good times. She remembered a young Neville writing her a sweet note. Like Lydia, he was affectionate on paper. She pictured a Firework Night, holding hands. She remembered a first kiss outside an underground station, their reflection in a rainbow-coloured puddle. But the Emmeline in those memories didn't feel like her anymore. She was a different person back then too – it wasn't just him. And these memories felt old. There was nothing more recent she could hang on to. She could hear him snoring in the room next door. Was he oblivious to the gulf between them or did he know and was merely covering it up too?

She scanned the weekly magazines for stories about people who had repaired relationships torn apart by the war and, yes, there were some. But they were generally about men who came back changed after seeing their best friend die next to them, or men who had changed after losing an arm or a leg or worse. No one talked about what happened when the *woman* had changed. When the woman had built a business, started seeing a whole new world, maybe fallen for someone, and then had to come back down to earth again.

'Will you make fruit cake again?' he asked her one time in the kitchen. Was it an olive branch, she wondered?

'If you like...' she said coquettishly.

She imagined he came from behind her and tucked her head under his chin. But he was already halfway out the room when he replied: 'Up to you.'

How did you get it back again? The love, the romance, the touching – what did you do to put a marriage back on track?

There was advice on submitting, dolling yourself up, or making yourself smaller or quieter, but she did not want to do those things. And anyway, where was the relationship advice for men? Where were the articles telling men they should listen more or help more in the home?

'Look what I achieved!' she wanted to say to him. She didn't expect accolades or awards, just acknowledgement from the man who was supposed to love her whatever.

After a while, she got used to the flat and started to think she could do something with it. And over the next few weeks they continued their discussions about the nursery, but Neville's position never wavered. He was a stubborn old goat, another of the things that had once attracted her to him. 'He sticks to his guns,' she had told her aunt in Coventry admiringly. Funny how aggravating she found it now.

'Women will go back home. There's the marriage bar for a start – married women are legally prohibited from some jobs. Look at Mrs Hardman. No more buses for her.'

'She doesn't have small children.'

'Exactly!' he said triumphantly, which didn't make sense, but he didn't seem to notice or care. He was on a roll now. 'There's no *need* for nurseries,' he added. 'The mothers will be at home again.'

It was exasperating. 'Surely not all of them?' Trying to make him see her point of view was exhausting.

'Most of them!'

But Emmeline *could* see a need and she couldn't understand how he couldn't see it too. It wasn't just their need. It was *her* need. She needed to do something. And she was a stubborn old goat too.

She didn't often let herself look at the newspaper articles from Norfolk that she had kept. She didn't want Neville to catch her daydreaming. When she did allow herself though, she thought how excited she looked. She was once a person full of fire and ambition. It made her sad, and jealous of what might have been. It never helped her to see it, yet she couldn't bring herself to throw the papers away.

Many times she thought about getting back in touch with Mr Davenport, but what would he say? What would he do? He had desired her once, more than desired her, she was sure of it. But now the war was over, no one said, 'we could be dead tomorrow' anymore. Being reckless was over. Being measured was back and he probably didn't feel the same way about her now.

49

MAY 1945

Lydia

Valerie Hardman was going to London for job interviews. The day before she went, she said she thought a walk with Lydia and Rex might help calm her nerves.

'You're going to miss the victory parties!' Lydia said, horrified. Valerie was never a party person. She had missed many, supposedly because of her tummy aches and nausea, although Lydia thought it was probably her bad skin that kept her away. When she did come, she slid away into the kitchen and helped serve drinks, or sat in a corner. But still, this was the party of the century, and everyone knew it was the event at which Paul Howard and Valerie Hardman were destined finally to get together.

'I have to get on with my future career,' Valerie said. She was so earnest, Lydia often had the urge to tell her to let down her hair – or take off her glasses, they were thick as jam jars – but if she did, Valerie would think she was the silly one.

They walked across the fields, their usual path, and it was bursting into summer. Daffodils, tulips, lavender, everywhere,

irrepressible. It was like it wasn't just them, nature too was cele-
brating the end of the war. They had nearly finished their
circuit when Lydia noticed a handsome-looking man making his
way towards them. Lydia did her usual winning smile, but he
ignored her. He had eyes only for Valerie. She realised he was
one of those few men who were somehow inoculated against
her charms and that touched a nerve. Valerie was plain, her lack
of effort around her appearance was deliberate; it seemed
ridiculous that this was another man who was not interested in
her. Another man who would choose Valerie over her. She
stormed after Rex.

And then once he'd gone off and Valerie was left gazing
after him, she explained that he had been very sweet to her
once. *What a weird thing to say.*

'Was he a boyfriend?'

Lydia had jabbed and jabbed until Valerie had been
pricked.

Even so, Lydia could still hardly believe it when Valerie
said, 'He did save me in a way...'

*If Valerie had feelings for this good-looking man, shouldn't
Paul be made aware?* It wasn't fair to keep such information
from him, Lydia told herself. Telling him was only doing the
right thing. Though there was something more too, something
buried in a tiny box at the bottom of Lydia's heart. She didn't
like Paul and Valerie's closeness – she never had. Valerie should
have been closer to her. Paul should have been closer to her. She
did not want to be the perpetual gooseberry.

Paul was always teasing Lydia about Leonard or Saul or
Harry, and so the next time he did, Lydia snapped back, 'What
about Valerie? You never tease her. She's the one who's got all
the fellas on the go!'

Paul went quiet and his face seemed to shift into darkness.
She didn't know what to say next. She hadn't expected such a
strong reaction.

'How do you mean?' he demanded. 'What boys?'

'Men, really.' Lydia giggled, picturing the man from their walk.

Paul chuckled too; he wasn't taking this seriously yet. He was going out fishing, or at least she guessed he was – he had all his outdoor equipment and a sketchbook and pencils, which he kept dropping on the floor.

'Like who?'

'Just people... don't believe she's all innocent like she makes out,' Lydia said. Let him wonder. Being vague was more compelling. Miss Picard would have applauded that.

Lydia invariably enjoyed a party; they always came with a raft of compliments and new beaus. Often, boys would request a dance or to walk her home or to take her address. The victory party was going to be brilliant. She had a variety of offers of boys to go with and she had already been asked so many times to save a dance she'd be able to pick and choose.

Two parties had been organised, one for the little children and one for the adults, but the teenagers were having their own unofficial do as well. That day in town, everyone was in such a good mood. Such a weight had been lifted. Even those poor people who had lost a husband or a son, or those who were still waiting for news, even they managed a smile. The war was over. Real life could resume. Finally! And yet the change that was coming – whatever it was – made Lydia feel unstable and a little concerned. Nevertheless, she was determined to have a good time.

Mrs H poured her a sherry and they toasted. 'Here's to peace... At long bloody last!'

Some people said it was the best night of their lives. There were bands and piano-playing and sudden bursting into song. People who didn't swear were swearing, people who didn't drink were drinking, people who didn't dance were dancing, and Lydia let Leonard smooch her and, when he put his tongue in her mouth, she didn't recoil but let him for three, maybe four seconds before she pushed him back – 'That's quite enough, Leonard!'

And then Saul walked her home and she let him kiss her, too. After all, it was Victory Day...

'Knock, knock?'

The following morning, Lydia stood in the doorway of Paul's room, like she sometimes used to, but she felt shy about it suddenly. He was still in bed. Hastily, he pulled up the blanket to cover himself, but she still glimpsed his pale chest, the hairs that led to that special place. His sketchbook was on the floor – more pictures of fish.

'Did you enjoy the parties?' Lydia had looked for Paul, but there were so many people that she couldn't find him. There was a rumour that he had tried to kiss a girl – not Valerie – but Lydia thought it unlikely.

'Not much...' he said.

'Sorry to hear that,' she said, and she was, but she also wasn't. She made to leave.

'Thank you,' he called from his bed.

'For what?'

'For telling me the truth.'

'I'm your friend,' she said. 'It's what friends do.'

It wasn't long before Paul left for university and Valerie moved away to work in Bristol. They didn't stay in touch, they weren't talking any more. Lydia hadn't expected that. She felt guilty, though she told herself it wasn't her fault. Valerie should have been honest with Paul, she thought, and Paul should have been honest with Valerie.

Lydia was staying on at her Somerset school. She had two more years to go. Once again, she would be the only evacuee at Bumble Cottage.

'You're not an evacuee any more though, are you?' Mummy said snippily when she told her that.

'There doesn't have to be a war for there to be evacuations.'

'What are you evacuating from, then?'

Lydia declined to reply.

50

OCTOBER 1945

Emmeline

Emmeline wasn't ready to give up on her dreams. She went to a training workshop in London for nursery staff. It was disorientating being in a classroom again, like putting your foot down after a long game of 'off-ground touch'. But she loved the sense that she was learning something, and she loved meeting the other women there. They were so wise and so stoical. Endlessly they discussed how to continue the nurseries now that, since the war had ended, there was far less government help.

She told Neville where she'd gone and he snorted. 'Matthew and I not good enough for you?'

'It's not that,' said Emmeline, but she didn't argue with him. There was no point.

A few weeks later, she heard about another workshop. She could stay at home and be the wife and mother Neville wanted her to be, or she could plough onwards. She didn't want to upset her family, that was never her intention, but she felt she had to have a scrap or crumb of something that was uniquely hers!

She booked a place.

'Do you know *why* we're making these leaps forward in child development theory?' the speaker began. Emmeline put her hand up, but lowered it when she realised it was a rhetorical question. Instructors loved those, she remembered.

'It's the evacuation. It has shown us so many differences in child development. It would take years to do the experiments – in fact, we wouldn't be allowed to do them!'

The whole morning was excellent. They talked about primary carers, attachment and consistency. These were ideas Emmeline understood somewhere deep in the core of her, but had never heard discussed and certainly had never put words to. After the session she had a head full of theories. It was incredible to have people take what they did in the nurseries seriously. It had never happened before. Such things fascinated her.

She felt she couldn't let all these ideas go to waste. She had to keep going, regardless of what Neville thought.

Neville did not speak to her for five days after the workshop and the atmosphere in the home was horrible. Nevertheless, it was worth it, Emmeline thought. She signed up for another.

Emmeline hoped Lydia would be so impressed with the new flat in London that she'd agree to come back to live, but when she finally visited, the autumn the war was over, she didn't make a single remark on it. Not the pale curtains with the songbird pattern that Emmeline had hemmed and hung so carefully, nor the glass lampshades she had selected. Nor the rug in the hallway that was her pride and joy.

After they had caught up on all Lydia's news: Rex, the kennels, school, Mrs H, Valerie – in that order – Emmeline told her about the nursery she hoped to open one day.

'I don't get it. You ran a wartime nursery and the war is over. What's the point of setting one up now?'

'The point is that mothers benefit from having somewhere

that will look after their children if they need or want,' Emmeline explained. She had it down to a few words now.

Lydia screwed up her pretty face and peered into her cup like she was divining fortunes. 'Why have children if you're not going to look after them?'

Lydia agrees with Neville then?

'They *do* look after them, darling, just not all the time.'

Was it the time Lydia had spent away from her that had filled her head with values that were the antithesis of Emmeline's own? Or would she have turned out like this anyway? Emmeline had no idea.

'They *should* look after them all the time,' Lydia continued.

Emmeline was reminded of a phrase of Dot's: 'The best parents are those who haven't had kids.'

'So you're saying if you have children, you'll never leave them with anyone else?' Emmeline asked pointedly.

'I won't send them to a nursery,' Lydia said defiantly.

Goodness, she was as bad as Councillor Arscott. Emmeline had always known she had a fight on her hands with the nursery idea, but she hadn't realised that this time the opposition would come from her own family.

51

FEBRUARY 1946

Emmeline

It was Erroll's birthday and Dot called Emmeline from the telephone box in the street. Emmeline could picture her there exactly, the glass windows steamed up with smoke.

'Five!?I can't believe it! Where have the years gone?'

'Come and see!'

'It's too soon,' Emmeline whispered. 'Neville won't like it if I keep disappearing back to Norfolk every five minutes.'

It never failed to astonish her that she had to include Neville in her calculations again after so many years of freedom. She didn't tell Dot that she was already in Neville's bad books, what with the workshops she was doing and the time she was now spending at the library. She tried to keep it secret from him but she also didn't like to lie.

'I'll have to come to you then,' Dot said.

True to her word, she rolled up early one Saturday morning, stockings wrinkling round her ankles, but twirling in her new coat and hat.

'You look lovely!' cooed Emmeline.

'It's not too much?' Dot asked; her outfits were the only thing she ever expressed doubts about.

'It's not,' said Emmeline, then gasped: 'Where's Errol?'

'I left him back. The older ones look after him, so— Oh, Emmeline, you look as fantastic as ever!'

Dot made Emmeline feel better about everything. All the frustration she had inside her, that things weren't happening fast enough, that her family weren't supportive enough, seemed to drip away. At least she had her old friend.

'How are you getting on with Pete?'

'Great!' Dot said. 'As long as he makes himself useful.'

She was more interested in talking about the Americans who were still on the nearby airbase.

'They're not going anywhere.' She raised her eyebrows pointedly, but Emmeline chose to take no notice. 'How about you and Neville? Still love's young dream?' she went on.

Emmeline tried to find her voice – she would have liked to share her marital woes with her friend – but she couldn't. She thought of their separate bedrooms and it made her feel ashamed. They might as well be in separate countries.

'We're getting to know each other again. Like millions of couples who were apart in the war, I suppose.'

Her friend squeezed her. 'You always do the right thing. You're like the angel on my shoulder.'

Emmeline couldn't speak. She wondered if being an angel on Dot's shoulder was such a good thing. It clearly had done nothing to hold Dot back – and had done nothing for herself either.

Neither Emmeline nor Dot were good at keeping still, so they went for a walk along the Thames, past the bombed-out buildings and the construction work. Dot kept marvelling at it all.

'I sometimes forget how bad they had it here,' she said, shaking her head. 'What a time it was.'

Later, when they ducked into a tea room and had ordered teacakes, Dot said, 'We've never been together without the children!'

'It's weird, isn't it? I keep expecting to be interrupted with "I want a wee" or "my tooth has fallen out!"'

'And that's just Mabel and Christine,' quipped Dot.

They reminisced over the day Christine burned the hot-cross buns. The time Freddie sucked the chocolate off the iron tablets. The lice contests. Old People Friday.

'And what about when you did country dancing with your Davenport?' Dot continued. 'It was like watching Scarlett O'Hara and Rhett Butler.'

Emmeline swallowed, hoping both that Dot would stop and that she would go on.

'He had such a thing for you! Did you never...'

'No,' insisted Emmeline. If anyone found out about how close they'd come, even her dear Dot, she would die of mortification.

'He did! Talk about smitten! He couldn't take his eyes off you.'

The subject made Emmeline's head ache.

'I'm married and so is he, so...'

'Didn't you hear? They've split up.'

'What?'

'Rumour has it that Mrs Davenport was in love with someone else all this time.'

Emmeline's mouth fell open. At the time she had believed it was true that Mrs Davenport's affections were directed elsewhere, but since then she had started to think and fear that this was exactly what a man looking to have relations with someone not his wife would say.

'How do you know this?'

'Everyone knows!' Dot continued casually. 'It won't take

him long to find a replacement though, I'm sure. He's a decent chap – for a politician.'

Tears filled Emmeline's eyes. She wanted to know more, she wanted to know everything! But at the same time, she couldn't bear it.

'Remember we spent an entire month watching films?' she said, changing the subject.

'Pete can't believe that I know all the actresses and actors. I told him – if you had watched each of them twenty times, you'd remember them too.'

Neville wouldn't care, Emmeline thought, but she chuckled anyway.

'You should go on that wireless show – *The Brains Trust* – as one of the experts!'

It was a beautiful day, cold, but the sky was light blue with swirling clouds, so they finished their tea and walked some more, and then Dot said in a little voice, 'I don't suppose you want to go and see Marjorie?'

She was moving her tongue around the gaps from her missing teeth, which she did when she was nervous.

Emmeline was delighted. 'Marjorie is here? In London?'

'Uh-huh.'

'Of course I want to!'

Emmeline couldn't believe this. She also couldn't believe Dot hadn't suggested it before.

'She's at home?' she asked.

'Not quite. And Emmeline...' Dot warned. 'She is different from how you remember her.'

'Aren't we all?' Emmeline said brightly.

They bought marzipan on the way. And then they saw a wool shop and Dot suggested getting something from there too.

'She still knits?'

'Beautifully,' Dot said emphatically, and Emmeline grinned: *it can't be all that bad.* 'They have special needles.'

Three stops on the tube, some more walking, and then they were at a grey building partially hidden behind a high wall. There were sturdy gates and doors, and the building had iron bars at the windows, and they had to sign in and be checked. There was a guard at the door and Emmeline let him rummage through her handbag, although her cheeks turned hot as the invasion of her privacy. The corridors reminded her of the nursery before they'd made it homely. She kept a chirpy expression on her face. She didn't want to seem threatening. She didn't want to look uncomfortable, either. She wanted to look like she was perfectly at home here even though she wasn't.

She remembered Mrs Salt once telling her about a distant relative in an asylum – she had turned it into a horror story: The stink of disinfectant. The howling. She couldn't sleep for weeks afterwards. Emmeline's parents, also used to talk in hushed tones about a place called Bedlam. Surely things had got better since then, though? It was the 1940s. It wasn't just child-care theory that had advanced in the war. They understood all sorts about human psychology now.

They were in a long ward of many beds – so many beds, a bit like the cot room at the nursery. Dot didn't hesitate, so Emmeline tried not to either. But she felt shy walking past some of the beds where people were moaning or groaning or sleeping or talking to themselves.

'Jesus loves you,' shouted a man and she started saying, 'Thank you, He loves you—' but Dot shoved her arm and hissed, 'Shhh.'

She led Emmeline over to a big lady sitting up against the headboard of a bed. She was knitting a large colourful rectangle. Her tongue was out in concentration. Her hair was wild and straggly and her eyes vacant. Emmeline's heart fell.

'I've brought someone to see you, my love,' Dot said in a

tone gentler than Emmeline had ever heard her use, even all those years working with small children.

Marjorie didn't look up.

Dot perched on the side of the bed. 'It's Mrs Froud. You remember her. Matthew's mummy? Norfolk? Pretty lady? You said she always looked stylish.'

Still nothing.

'She ran the nursery I told you about. It was a wonderful place.'

Dot took some marzipan out of the paper bag and popped it in Marjorie's mouth like she was slotting money in a slot machine. Dot offered a piece to Emmeline, but Emmeline shook her head – she couldn't eat – so, shrugging, Dot ate it herself.

Emmeline wanted to cry. *What did they do to you?*

They sat and watched their old friend knit. It was something – maybe the one thing – she hadn't lost; she was still an exceptional knitter. They stayed only for a few minutes more, but to Emmeline it felt like an eternity.

'Marjorie's children are thriving,' Dot said as they sat side by side, this time on the bus. Emmeline was struggling to make sense of what she'd just experienced. She scowled out of the window, at the puddles in the streets.

She remembered sweet Della, scrambling upright in her arms. Derek, who liked to play everything. Eager-to-please Deidre with her tiny pigtails.

'Do they visit their mum?'

'The family decided that it was best not to. But they have good lives, Emmeline. You must believe it.'

The bus stopped so suddenly that the women had to grab the poles to stop themselves from going flying.

'Poor Marjorie. She could have been saved.'

'You don't know that,' Dot said.

. . .

Once Dot had got back on the train to Norfolk, Emmeline felt washed out, and by the time she got home, she felt even worse. The flat was a mess. In the kitchen, the washing-up was piling up and nothing had been put away. She had only been out eight hours, nine at most. It was as though Neville had been deliberately incompetent. As she went past his bedroom, she saw the clothes that had been worn were on the floor and the clean laundry she had done for him had been tipped up and mixed in with them.

She felt heartbroken for that sweet attractive woman in the pea-green coat who had always reminded her of her own daughter.

And she thought, *what would Neville have done with me if I had a funny turn?*

Neville looked up from the depths of his newspaper with a weird expression.

'So?'

Don't rise to it – whatever it is.

'What?' she enquired as sweetly as she could.

'What did you two *ladies* get up to today?'

She wouldn't ask why he said ladies in that way, she would simply tell him. She began with Marjorie and what had happened.

He held up his palm. 'You went to an asylum?'

'Yes...'

'I don't want to know about your lunatic friends.' He shifted in his seat. 'It's depressing.'

Emmeline wanted to cry. 'She's not a lunatic.' And if they weren't to talk about depressing things, she wasn't sure what they would talk about.

'You always want to talk about the Salts too, don't you? But there's no point, you only get upset.'

He was at least trying to communicate with her, she told herself. He couldn't help it if the words came out wrong. They reminded her of clothes that had gone through the mangle and come out stretchy and malformed but were, essentially, the same.

She looked at his feet in slippers and his soft pink hands. At the shiny bald ring at the back of his head – another thing not to be mentioned. From the front he had great hair. Only she and God (and extremely tall people) were party to this secret. He placed his newspaper down on the table next to him and picked up his teacup even though it was empty. She was surprised to see that his fingers were trembling.

'What about you and her?'

'What?'

'That Dot. You still yabbering on about the nursery plan?'

Actually, no, she thought.

'You talk about her a lot – are you...? Did you... have a relationship?'

'Good grief, Neville!' Emmeline didn't know if she should laugh or cry. 'Where on earth has that come from?'

'It's not unheard of,' he said, but you could tell he'd realised his mistake instantly. 'It's not that unusual. You don't have to go all Queen Victoria on me.'

Queen Victoria? Whatever next?

'Dot is my great friend,' she said, her voice aquiver. She felt stung and the more she thought about it, the worse it was. 'Not a lover! And I find that insinuation upsetting, that you would slur our friendship in that way. Or think I would—'

'All right,' he said tersely. 'I get the picture.'

'Did *you*?' she snapped.

'What?'

'Have another woman? Is that what this is about?'

He walked out of the room.

So Operation 'Get-Close-to-Neville' was on the back

burner once again. Because really, who wanted to get close to that? She sniffed back tears. She wouldn't cry over him, she wouldn't. At that moment, she hated him, and she hated herself even more for being with him.

Two weeks later, on another Saturday, Emmeline was tidying and cleaning and missing her old life. Was she the only fool nostalgic for the purpose the war had given her? Was she the only one who dreamed of people who she shouldn't be dreaming of?

There was a newspaper under the sideboard cabinet and she tugged at it. It looked like it had been hidden there, or at least put there deliberately. Inside, there was a note:

Neville

We need to go back to how things were. Please, only talk to me about work and nothing else. It's for the best, you know it too. If you can't manage that, I will leave the company. I am not changing my mind this time.

I will always hold you in the highest regard and think back on our time together with fondness.

Brian

There hadn't been another woman. He'd told the truth about that.

But there had been *someone*.

And then, Emmeline realised why he had accused her of being in love with Dot. And she understood it had nothing to do with her. And everything to do with him. It was that man in the corner with the fine moustache and the hat pulled low who wouldn't meet her eye, she thought. Call it a woman's intuition, call it what you like, but she was certain that he was the Brian here. He and Neville had been in love. She knew it.

How dare Neville tell her what to do? How dare he try to make her feel guilty? It was unconscionable. But Emmeline decided she wouldn't bring it up with him. Instead, she would carry on in her own sweet way. And after all, here it was. There was no reason to hold herself back any more.

52

SEPTEMBER 1947

Lydia

Lydia stayed in contact with Betsy and Flora from St Boniface, or rather Betsy and Flora stayed in contact with her. When they got together, they laughed over their worship of Miss Picard.

'I would have done anything for her!'

'I wonder if she was in love with the man she married or if she married for money?'

'Wha-at?' asked Lydia astonished. 'Miss Picard wasn't like that!'

'Oh, she was!' her two friends laughed. 'She was exactly like that.'

When Lydia was with them, it felt like the years dissolved and their differences disappeared, but gradually she realised that this was an illusion; beneath their shared history, and beyond the veneer of politeness, in reality their lives did not overlap and they were going down different paths.

Betsy was going to finishing school. Flora had a job in her family's business, but would give it up just as soon as her George Mountfitchet popped the question.

They cooed over photographs of George as if he were a kitten, but what Lydia didn't say was that she would like one just like him, and that she thought it wasn't fair that it came so easily to Flora.

Two years since the war had ended and Lydia was still helping out at the kennels and still living in her same room at Bumble Cottage. She didn't pay rent, but since Mrs H never asked for any, she didn't feel rent was warranted. She felt certain she didn't impose or impact on Mrs H. Valerie had left and still visited often, but Lydia made sure she kept out of her way. Lydia still thought of the Salts – no one else mentioned them, but the loss was inside of her; it was like something that should have been whole had been hollowed out. She regretted not writing to Francine Salt. She didn't quite understand why she didn't, and only knew that, as time went on, it became more and more impossible.

'I'd like to go to finishing school,' Lydia told Mrs H shortly after meeting up with her old pals.

'It costs hundreds of pounds, Lydia, I'm not sure your parents could afford that!'

That told her.

If she couldn't go to finishing school, and if Mrs H tired of her living here rent-free, her only option was to return to London. Lydia couldn't put into words how badly she felt about it. It wouldn't even be her childhood home she'd be going back to, but a strange flat in another dismal road with rubbish on the kerb and overcooked meat smells. Her mother was still obsessed with other people's babies even though the war was over. Lydia would be expected to be among them and be a part of it and in the city at large she would just be another customer in the pie shop, another heel getting stuck in the drains, another search for another uncomfortable seat on the tube.

All she wanted was a George Mountfitchet to keep her in the style she had become accustomed to. Why was this so complicated? And then, a few days after the disappointing finishing school conversation, the thing Lydia had been dreading, happened.

Mrs H said, 'Now your exams are over, isn't it time you stood on your own two feet?'

In other words, Mrs H wanted Lydia to leave.

Lydia was getting sent back to the city – how would she ever meet a Prince Charming with a pretty country pile there? What would she do about Rex? No one would love that dear dog like she did.

'I'm not sure Mummy has the room. And she's busy with the nursery...'

Mrs H sighed like she'd anticipated this. 'And Daddy?'

'Daddy is Daddy,' Lydia said. No one expected anything of him.

Mrs H's face was sympathetic. 'I suppose you could work at the kennels full-time now. The Smarts might be able to house you, too.'

'All right, I'll ask,' said Lydia, breathing a sigh of relief at this near miss. Rather that than London. Rather *anything* than London.

Lodging with the Smarts was nothing like living at Bumble Cottage. Lydia's bedroom was in the loft and there was no electricity up there. It was candlelight or torches. But it was cheap, Rex could come with her and she loved the dogs. It was an excellent arrangement, but it was temporary as far as Lydia was concerned. It was like a holiday, only she didn't know what her real life looked like. Or rather, she knew what it looked like, but she wasn't sure how to get to it. She was such a long way from husbands and children, but Lydia knew about distance, she knew about travel. She knew a situation could change in the blink of an eye.

In theory, finding a husband shouldn't have been hard.
Lydia had a traffic-stopping face coupled with an impressive,
much-admired figure, and she did have admirers queueing up to
take her out. But the ones who queued were lower class, like she
was. Men of wealth were more elusive than she'd imagined.
And single men of means looking for a wife seemed to exist only
in fairy tales.

Lydia hadn't been away from Bumble Cottage for long when
she arranged to meet Valerie at a tea room in Bristol. The last
she'd heard was that Valerie and Paul weren't talking, so, when
Valerie said she and Paul had 'got together' just before he left to
pursue his art in America, Lydia was surprised; and then she
found that she didn't like it. It wasn't just that she felt excluded.
It was also the feeling that Valerie had something she didn't
have and maybe also that she didn't deserve. Valerie didn't even
want a boyfriend – she was a career girl through and through;
Lydia was the one who had always played the 'I'm getting
married in the morning!' game', the one who dreamed of
walking down the aisle.

53

Emmeline

Emmeline had learned about the Hampstead Nurseries on one of her workshops: they were the flagship for childcare. They were the place where all the new developments in nurseries were coming from. Everyone wanted to know how they did it. This time, Emmeline wanted everything to be right when she opened her nursery. Last time, everything had to be quick because it was an emergency situation. Urgency had taken priority. This time, she would do it at her own pace.

Mrs Friedman, who showed her around, was wearing tight trousers and had short dark hair and was that a German accent? Neville would have a fit. But Emmeline did approve as they went from room to room, their heels clacking in time on the tiled floor.

'Now the war is over, we expect a baby boom.'

'Yes, but newspapers say there'll be no call for nurseries,' Emmeline said. 'They're saying mothers won't want to use them anymore.' Not just the newspapers, that was Neville's line, too.

'Officially there won't be. They'll pretend. But' – Mrs

Friedman tapped her thin nose – 'we know better, don't we? We know that good safe places for children will never go out of fashion.'

Outside, small children were playing:

> *Oranges and Lemons, said the bells of St*
> *Clements.*
> *I owe you five farthings, said the bells of St*
> *Martins.*

Emmeline remembered the Salt children singing that in the shelter and a lump formed in her throat.

'I'm hoping to open one near where I live,' she said.

'Good. I can give you some addresses of locations you might find suitable,' Mrs Friedman said. 'We have to remake the country. It's a chance to improve. The men will want it to stay the same, hey – the same discrimination, the same *domination*. If we want conditions for women and children to improve, we'll have to do it for ourselves. Do you see what I mean?'

Emmeline thought that was slightly unfair – some men were forward-thinking (the Right Honourable Mr Davenport) and some women were backward-thinking. Nevertheless, Mrs Friedman's passion for nurseries was unmistakable.

'What do most of the mothers do for work?' Emmeline asked.

'Mothers *and* fathers,' Mrs Friedman corrected her. 'I have no idea.'

'But?'

'I am aware of psychiatrists, launderette workers, a nurse, a dancer, a postmistress, a baker.'

'When we did it, the only way we could get the authorities to agree was if the majority of women were involved in the war effort,' Emmeline said.

'Times change.' Mrs Friedman almost smiled at her.

Emmeline felt excited, but wary. 'My biggest problem this time is financing,' she said.

'Get a loan,' Mrs Friedman said.

'It's as easy as that?'

'Go and find out...'

54

MAY 1948

Lydia

Each time Lydia went to her parents' flat in London she wanted to despair.

'I wouldn't say we're comfortable,' Mummy said once, looking around the horrid little place with satisfaction, 'but we're getting there.'

It was about the size of the library at Bumble Cottage. The walls were thin, the furniture was flimsy and the garden was tiny. Yet, her parents were pathetically proud of it all. They often insinuated they were a cut above everyone else because of Dad's job at the paper. Well, they weren't, not enough. Mrs Howard had ashtrays worth more than anything at Lydia's parents' home.

Over Mummy's cauliflower cheese, she said, 'Daddy, you'll walk me down the aisle, won't you?'

Her parents' mouths fell open in unison.

'I didn't even know you were courting!' Her mother's voice was high-pitched with surprise.

Her dad was shaking his head incredulously.

'I'm not!' Lydia explained. 'I was just anticipating the future.'

'There must be someone?' pressed her mother. 'Or else why would you ask? Tell us, Lydia!'

Lydia realised she'd made a mistake.

'There isn't. You'll be the first to know, I promise.'

Sometimes Lydia wondered if she was being punished for some of the incidents in her past that still caused her shame. There were a few – especially her burying of Margaret-Doll. And the letters she never wrote to Francine. She *had* written them in her head – such tender language, heart-felt condolences– but she had never managed to get them down on paper. Could Francine forgive her betrayal?

She remembered that Francine once told her she thought she'd started the war – 'The whole war? How could it possibly be your fault, Francine?!' she'd said. Francine had been by the fireplace, half giggling, half deadly serious. 'By having bad thoughts.' It had made Lydia laugh at the time. 'No one's that powerful, Francine – specially not you!' she'd replied.

Now she got it. It was silly and superstitious, but still... She sometimes felt like that, too. Like, if a bad thing happens it's just what you deserved. Other times, though, Lydia's thoughts swung to the opposite extreme: she *wasn't* asking for much, was she? Her future husband didn't even have to be that wealthy. She wasn't talking duke or bishop. Not even Lord or Sir. She wasn't like Valerie – she didn't want to change the world at all. She wasn't like her mother – she didn't want to change the world through nurseries. Her desires were much smaller than anyone else's, she didn't want to change the world. Her goals should have been more achievable – and yet they were much harder to attain.

She would make a good wife, she knew that with utmost

certainty. And it wouldn't be take-take-take, she would deliver –
she would run a comfortable household, she would have as
many babies as he wanted. She would line up every evening,
pretty as a picture, with a glass of whisky for him. In fact, he
would be getting the better part of the deal, Lydia decided. Not
her. Him. Whoever he was. She just had to find him.

55

FEBRUARY 1949

Emmeline

It was a risk to borrow money from the bank. Of course it was. But there was no way round it; Emmeline had little money as collateral. She went through a financial plan with a young man in the bank who looked too young to be holding down a job.

She was giving it her best shot. Emmeline didn't know if anyone would want to send their children to nursery nowadays, or if Lydia and Neville were right and in peacetime, mothers would choose not to work.

Mrs Friedman assured her that the Hampstead Nurseries would send her their 'overflow' children. And Emmeline had found a cheap space to rent not a long walk from her flat, with a sympathetic landlord. It would be all theirs, which meant they wouldn't have to pack away every night or share with retirees on Fridays. A full-time nursery – what she'd dreamed of.

As Emmeline worked to get the venue ready, her mind went back to clearing the hall during the war. The way the ladies had pulled together. She missed them, but nevertheless there was something satisfying about doing it by herself. If ever she felt too tired, or despondent, she just thought about Mrs Salt and her lost children, or poor Marjorie, and that gave her the kick to continue.

Last time round, she'd had Mr Davenport's help too, of course. All these years later, she still thought about him much more than she ought – well, she oughtn't be thinking about him at all. His friendly face. The way he listened. The way he enthused. Those kisses that had set her on fire. His touch that she couldn't get enough of. Yet it was just ten minutes of passion – twenty minutes at most. It seemed absurd that some people lived in relationships like that full-time. She was almost glad she didn't. She would never get anything done! Late afternoon, she would leave and race to do all the chores at home, the washing, the ironing, the getting dinner ready. Matthew came home from school by himself and let himself in, which Neville disapproved of, but Matthew insisted it was fine. Neville didn't like anything she did, but Emmeline didn't care anymore. She had a way of looking at him nowadays, that silenced him. If she doubted herself, and the affect her ambition was having on her family, she just thought of that note from Brian. Neville was not the doting husband he liked to present himself as.

Initially she couldn't decide what to call the nursery. (She hated making this decision by herself.) In Norfolk, their nursery was the first and the only one, so there was no need to call it anything but 'the nursery'. Here, however, there were several such establishments so, if only to avoid confusion, they needed to be distinct from one another.

Mrs Friedman suggested something from a nursery rhyme. Miss Muffet who sat on a tuffet and then was frightened by a spider. Humpty Dumpty who couldn't be put back together. Unlucky Jack, the friend of Jill, who had cracked his skull. Emmeline settled on Bo-Peep because, while Bo-Peep had obviously lost the sheep in her care, they had found their way back eventually and the rhyme ended on a rare positive note.

But then Emmeline thought Bo-Peep was too flowery. Instead she would name it after the street it was on – Frognal Lane. She could have pictures of frogs everywhere! Children loved a cute frog. But then she reconsidered again. There was a Frognal Lane school and a Frognal Lane doctors there already and she wanted to make the nursery more personal to her. She wondered what Mr Davenport would suggest. He might remind her why she felt strongly about nurseries. Then the answer was obvious. The answer was knitting with her back against a headboard:

MARJORIE'S NURSERY

She put the plaque up on the wall next to the door. Some people assumed Marjorie was a friend who had died in the war and Emmeline didn't correct them. In a way, she had.

One morning when she was in Marjorie's Nursery alone, painting the dado rails in what would be the playroom, to her delight Dot appeared, peering round the door, getting white paint on her fingers.

'Any room for any more?'

Emmeline threw her arms round her best friend.

'What on earth are you doing here?'

'We're moving back to London,' Dot said with a laugh.

'What? All of you?'

'All of us!' she said. 'There's not enough work in Norfolk. Needs must...'

'I can't believe it,' Emmeline felt tearful. Out of everyone, Dot was her favourite person to work with. 'And you really want a job here?'

'Absolutely.' Dot patted her stomach. 'And can this one have the first space?'

Emmeline blinked at her friend's belly, which she hadn't noticed was round. She didn't ask whose baby it was. Some things were best not to know.

'Congratulations!' Emmeline squealed and hugged her friend again. She felt certain it was going to work out, after all.

Emmeline employed three more staff members as well as Dot, none of them much older than Lydia: Bess, who'd been in London throughout the war and was fazed by nothing; Ellie, whose father had died in the Normandy Landings; and Bella, who had a daughter herself. They would take young children from nine months to four years – and also older children before and after school.

And there were plenty of children. Mothers and toddlers queued up to join and some mothers said they had heard Emmeline had run an excellent nursery in Norfolk.

'It's really happening,' Emmeline said incredulously to Dot as they ran around making porridge, gathering coats and boots and overseeing the finger painting.

'Well, of course, it is!' said Dot. 'I didn't doubt it for a moment...'

Two days after they'd opened, there was a cacophony of shouting in the street so loud, it reminded Emmeline of D-Day. Out of the window, she saw crowds gathered just outside. This was always a busy part of town, but there were definitely more people than usual – and all were looking towards the nursery. Mothers and children mostly, but these weren't interested in coming in and instead were trying to block others from entering.

As Emmeline looked more carefully, she realised that while they gave an impression of being many, there were probably only twenty objectors or so. The oldest must have been about seventy, the youngest were babies in prams. They had posters on sticks. WE DON'T WANT A NURSERY HERE.

'One, two, three, four,' the crowd chanted, 'we don't want nurseries anymore!'

'Good grief,' muttered Emmeline as she edged away from the window.

'You are amoral,' one woman, who must have spotted her peeking at them, screeched.

'Don't worry about it,' Dot said dismissively. 'Bunch of crazies with too much time on their hands.'

'Wonder if my Neville is out there?' Emmeline tried to joke. She didn't say 'wonder if my Lydia is' – her daughter's stance was the more hurtful.

'Mothers should be with their babies,' the screeching continued.

'Mothers should be able to feed their babies,' Emmeline muttered to herself. She remembered Mr Davenport saying when there was opposition: *we must be doing something right.* The noise got louder, and inside the nursery, some of the little ones took fright. Incensed, Emmeline shouted out of the window, 'Leave us alone.'

Bess wanted to ignore them. 'Weak people trying to feel good about themselves.' she said. Emmeline tried but it got to her. In Norfolk, apart from the obviously deranged threat to stab Mr Davenport, it seemed it was mostly elderly people who wrote those letters of complaint. The Davenports and Mr Reynolds agreed that it was harmless stuff – people were distressed about the war and the nursery was a convenient outlet for their discontent. But here, it was young women, with children. And it was peacetime! And they weren't sending letters, they had actually turned up to protest.

'How can they be so against something that would ulti-mately benefit them?' Emmeline mused, astonished.

Dot shrugged. 'They don't see it that way, that's how.'

'They're like the anti-suffragettes or the witch-hunters. Women are entitled to help in bringing up their families. There's nothing wrong with it.'

'You'll not change their minds, they have to change their minds themselves.'

Emmeline realised she had got more passionate about the nurseries over the years and that she should perhaps be aware of different opinions. She should listen. She should try and see it from their point of view – otherwise she'd be just as bad as them.

They disappeared but came back to protest the next morning when she opened up and the day after that. She invited them in and – credit to her – one woman eventually agreed. Tentatively, she stepped in and stared around, 'Oh, it's nicer than I expected,' she began, but then remembering her position, she corrected herself. 'One, two, three, four...' she began chanting.

'You don't want the nurseries anymore,' interrupted Emmeline coolly. 'Yes, I understand that.'

'But the point is – however *nice* you make it,' the woman said 'nice' as though it were a terrible word, 'children should be at home!'

'And if they can't be?' Emmeline stood firmer than ever. She had listened to their argument, she told herself, and still found it stupid.

'If they can't be... I don't know.'

The woman scuttled off. The next morning, as Emmeline cautiously opened up, no protestors came, nor the day after that. It wasn't until a week passed that Emmeline felt she could breathe a sigh of relief. They had gone. She had won and she and Dot – who in this pregnancy had the hugest of appetites – celebrated over a slice of bread pudding.

A few days later, the owner of Bugs Bunny Nursery (why

hadn't she thought of that name?!) in the next town called her up in tears; they'd moved on to hers. Emmeline told her to stand her ground, they would move on to someone or something else soon – which they did.

Dear Mr Davenport, she thought frequently, way too frequently, *if you could see me now!*

56

Lydia

Lydia was walking along the main road from the station to the kennels when a car pulled up alongside her. She kept her head down and marched on, but the driver sounded the horn and then wound down the window.

'Lydia! LY-DI-AH!' he shouted. She didn't know him, but she did recognise the woman in the passenger seat with the coal-black hair and the impossibly red lipsticked lips.

'Miss Picard!' She suddenly wanted to cry. She had loved this woman. 'Is it really you?'

'Mrs Picard-Richardson,' the woman corrected. 'I noticed you on the platform, just as charmante as ever.'

They told her to get in the car and they'd give her a lift. She didn't need a lift, but she clambered into the back seat. She was delighted to see her old... what was she? Her mentor? Her older-sister figure? Her husband was a heavyset man with several chins. His grey suit was dark under his arms.

Mrs Picard-Richardson twisted around to asked her what she was doing.

'Well, I was walking home.'

But she was another one. 'Noo, I mean, what are you doing with your life, chérie?'

'I work at the kennels,' Lydia explained. The way people focused on her occupation would never not annoy her. She saw Mrs Picard-Richardson and the man meet each other's eyes.

'Darling, you'll love this,' Mrs Picard-Richardson said, pressing a flyer into Lydia's hand.

Lydia glanced at it: *Miss Weston-super-Mare, 1949*

'I don't watch this kind of thing.'

'Not *watch* – you should enter it.'

This time Lydia looked at the flyer properly.

'Weston-super-Mare? I don't even know where that is.'

'It's only up the road,' Mrs Picard-Richardson said.

'About twelve kilometres from here,' her husband added.

They were like a double act. *What's it to do with you?* she wondered. Nevertheless, she examined the paper again. Something about it *did* appeal.

'What do you get if you win?'

He had a laugh like a donkey. How had Miss Picard ended up with him?

'Read it.' Then he laughed again. 'A pretty girl like you can read, can't she?'

That was just rude! 'A trophy. And seven guineas? I can make more than that dog-walking!'

'It's not just that,' Mrs Picard-Richardson said, her voice tinged with the same impatience as when she was speaking to some of the less exquisite girls at St Boniface. 'You win that, you go to Morecambe!'

'Why would I want to go to Morecambe?' Lydia was enjoying the interaction now. It certainly made a change. Mrs Picard-Richardson was as wonderful as ever, and it was not impossible to ignore her ass of a husband.

The man mimicked her. '*Why would I want to go to More-*

cambe?! Because if you win the beauty pageant at Morecambe, the world's your oyster.'

'You could be,' continued Mrs Picard-Richardson in a hushed, reverential tone, 'Miss Great Britain!'

Lydia considered. This was a diversion from her man-meeting plan and yet it was not in opposition to it. In fact, it seemed quite complementary. A parallel road perhaps.

'How much if I win Morecambe?'

They both chortled, his chins wobbled. 'Hundreds of pounds!'

Now they were talking.

'And Miss Great Britain?'

Mrs Picard-Richardson looked at her husband, who had stopped laughing. He put his hand on his wife's knee. 'Let's not get ahead of ourselves...' he said.

57

Emmeline

Marjorie's was stricter than the wartime nursery and there was less garden space for running around, but it was a happy place. Emmeline put an advert in the local paper calling it a 'home from home'. People donated some toys, although it was often the things you wouldn't expect that became most popular with the children: a tyre, a fireman's helmet, a washing-up liquid bottle.

They were near a factory that built aircraft parts; a lot of the children had parents who worked there, and not just their mothers: Mr Maynard had three children and his wife had died from cancer on VE Day. Mrs Lees had run away and Mr Lees was left bringing up Shirley Lees by himself.

Neville hated that Emmeline was out all day, but the era of his having a claim to anything when it came to her had gone. He was out all day too – he still worked at the newspaper office. Still mooning over his colleague Brian quite possibly. She never told him what she knew, preferring to keep it to herself, but she would never forget it. He didn't ask her what was wrong. He didn't want to know.

Lydia was preoccupied, not with dogs this time but with spending weekends in various seaside resorts.

'But Lydia, do you have the money for this gallivanting?'

'It's fine!' Lydia always said. She was another one who papered over cracks.

As for Matthew, sweet Matthew just got on with everything.

On Fridays, Marjorie's closed early. Emmeline waved off the children and their parents, and then the staff, and then Dot, who was finding pregnancy harder this time. She enjoyed the hour or so on her own, putting everything away, thinking about the week ahead, her mind often on some new child development practice she'd read about.

She heard someone at the door. The parents often forgot a hat or bootees, a bottle or a book.

She opened the door smiling, but it wasn't a parent.

'Mrs Froud? Dot told me you'd be here.'

Mr Davenport was smiling apologetically, holding his hat, mackintosh over his arm, leaning towards her.

Emmeline couldn't find any words. It had been years, but he looked the same. Silver around the edges of his hairline, the same broad encompassing smile. The slightly wonky eyes. The most handsome man in the world. His appeal hadn't worn off – to her, at least.

'I remembered you once said you'd like to see my workplace.'

'Parliament?' she replied, and her voice was shrill.

'No other,' he said.

'That was' – she counted back and was incredulous – 'nearly five years ago.'

He laughed. 'A promise is a promise.'

Emmeline laughed too. She couldn't help it. It was like he was a ghost come back to haunt her. A matinee idol in the cinema. The politician swooping in to save them. He was all things, and he was back again. Spending time with him was probably dangerous to her equilibrium. Although, what equilibrium? she thought. Ever since she'd found that note to Neville, she'd had none. And this was an opportunity she couldn't miss out on. *Parliament!* This was a once-in-a-lifetime chance. And part of her was wondering – was it true what Dot had told her? That he wasn't with his wife anymore?

She had to sign in at a desk: 'Guest of Mr Davenport'; and that phrase made her feel elated, but then there was a bag check, which reminded her of visiting Marjorie at the asylum.

'Can't be too careful,' the guard said as he rummaged through her things. It reminded her also of Mrs Davenport's concerns the first-ever time they met.

There has been no security protocol, nothing.

One purse, three dummies, a letter from Lydia, a bar of American chocolate for Matthew from one of the nursery parents, handkerchiefs, old tissue, a broken lipstick, a new lipstick in a box, four crayons, one unsharpened pencil, a shopping list, a creased photo cut from a newspaper from a long time ago.

The guard didn't so much as raise an eyebrow. He just told her where she should go next.

In the gallery overlooking the chamber, it was all men, and it seemed they were mostly journalists. She was glad she had smart hair and high heels today. She didn't look like she worked in a nursery, people often said that, and she didn't look terribly out of place here either. People might think she too was a professional.

It was Prime Minister's Questions and there were long speeches. There were even longer responses. Here too, it was mostly men and it was only men who spoke. The few women there put up their hands, but the speaker never selected them to speak. Everything was couched in impenetrable language, 'The Honourable Gentleman, I put it to you.' She remembered Lydia used to say, 'She's swallowed a dictionary,' about Valerie. Everyone in the House of Commons must have been feasting on them.

'Now you know how I spend my days.'

Emmeline and Mr Davenport were out on the bank of the Thames, watching the boats meander past.

'I think I'd prefer having porridge thrown at my head,' Emmeline smiled wryly.

'It's not dissimilar.' He grinned. 'Sometimes it's a madhouse in there.'

They laughed.

'How many children do you have at Marjorie's now? I like the name, by the way – after your friend?'

She didn't know anyone who had a memory like him.

'Thank you. Yes – and we have forty children, and a rota of ten staff.'

'Incredible.'

'It's a lot of work but I love it.'

He bit his lip. 'I'm glad it worked out for you.'

Had it worked out for her, she wondered? Marjorie's had been built on debt; the nursery's existence was more precarious maybe than it looked. Her beloved daughter still lived away, with no intention of coming home, and her husband was a closet homosexual. She didn't say any of that, but instead smiled at him. He did have a few wrinkles now, she realised, at the edges of his eyes and his lips – but then, she did too.

Meeting him became a habit, the best kind of habit. On Friday afternoons, Mr Davenport would come to Marjorie's Nursery and pick her up and take her out. If he was early, he came inside and helped chuck toy cars and crayons into boxes or wipe clean the blackboard. One time he brought in all the sheets and nappies from the line because it looked like rain. Occasionally, if he was running late, he would call and they would meet at the Lyons Corner House instead. They found they had a billion subjects to discuss (and a few to avoid).

Neville was not talking to her – or Emmeline was not talking to him; she didn't exactly know who had started it. That's not to say the atmosphere in the West Hampstead flat was rotten, but there was no affection.

Can I go on like this forever? she wondered. Sometimes, she thought she could. The nursery dominated her days, her children were safe and now that Mr Davenport was back, if only on the periphery of her life, she felt a contentment she hadn't felt for years. So what if her marriage wasn't perfect? As long as she could keep these precious tea-shop afternoons, she could cope with anything.

58

Lydia

Valerie initiated their get-togethers. Lydia was never sure why – they didn't have much in common. She considered telling Valerie about Mrs Picard-Richardson, but they'd never met; and she would have told her about the beauty pageant when they next went out together, but decided at the last minute that Valerie probably wouldn't approve.

In the Ladies of the tea-rooms, Lydia mouthed in the mirror: 'My name is Lydia Froud and I live in Taunton. My measurements are 32-22-32. I love dogs and...' she was going to say winning – but Mrs Picard-Richardson had insisted, 'Do not try to be funny' – so Lydia changed her mind: 'Babies. I believe babies should be with their mums at all times.'

She wouldn't tell Valerie or anyone until *after* she won and then she would say:

'Didn't you hear? I am Miss Weston-super-Mare and I'm going to Morecambe!'

She couldn't imagine Valerie's face if she told her that. She couldn't imagine Paul's face. She couldn't imagine Mrs

Howard's face. The only person she wanted to talk to about it was Francine Salt – she could imagine Francine's cheeky grin.

Back at the table, Valerie was reading the menu, probably looking for spelling mistakes. If Lydia had transformed herself into a dishy girl since the war, Valerie had gone the other way; she looked like a headmistress. No, actually she looked like Mrs H. She was only twenty-one – why did she want to look as middle-aged as possible? It was like she had found childhood so uncomfortable that she was prematurely playing at adulthood.

Valerie's yearning for Paul irritated Lydia, too. *Just tell him*, Lydia thought, exasperated, but Valerie didn't chase clarity in matters of romance, but preferred to wander lonely as a middle-aged cloud instead.

Sometimes, Lydia thought what a good wife she would have made Paul. She would have gladly made him tea while he painted or washed his tennis-whites. She would have hosted his arty-parties. They could have kept dogs and she would have looked after Mrs H. In fact, it seemed so obviously idyllic, it was hard to understand why this was not happening. But Paul was in America now and, anyway, Valerie – wireless-obsessed Val with her frumpy glasses and her unstylish hair – had always been his first choice.

At the kennels, Lydia mostly wore trousers and boots. On her days off, she wore skirts and blouses. This was not good enough for the contest. For that, Lydia needed a bathing suit.

'I'll get you one,' Solly – her latest beau – said. 'My treat.'

A few days after her meeting with Valerie, she and Solly went into town and Solly said he'd wait outside the shop and smoke a cigar. She told the shop girl she wanted the prettiest bathing costume they had and when the girl made a funny face, like, *who are you to make demands?!*, she told her what it was for, and the girl squealed and fetched the manager. Then that manager fetched *her* manager, so there were three of them waiting outside the changing room at the back of the shop. They gave her three costumes to try, all in a new stretchy fabric. Lydia pulled the nicest one on over her underwear and then slipped on a pair of heels. It was chilly in the shop, but she was too excited to care

She pushed back the curtain and, although these were strangers and she was half-naked, she said, 'Ta-da!'

They clapped her.

'Really? Is this the one?' Lydia didn't usually lack decisiveness, but for once she was quite over-awed.

'That's the one,' the manager's manager said. 'Give us a twirl.'

'Ooh!' said the manager. 'That's Miss Weston-super-Mare, that is.'

'You must win,' the girl squealed.

'I'll do my best,' Lydia promised.

'And if you do' – the other manager gripped her arm so tightly she feared it might bruise – 'tell everyone where you got your costume.'

She had forgotten Solly was outside. When she eventually went out, he grunted, 'I'm not doing this again.'

59

SEPTEMBER 1949

Emmeline

Emmeline and Mr Davenport had been meeting up for the last few months. Only twice had they missed each other; once when he had a work trip to Malta and once when Matthew had suspected chicken pox and had the week off school.

Summer was slowly graduating to autumn. The sky had changed from blue to grey. She had gone from short-sleeved dresses to cardigans and coats. Whatever she wore, Mr Davenport looked at her approvingly. Although he came into the nursery to help Emmeline pack up sometimes, he never came while the children were still there, and she was glad. She was sure that if she saw him interacting with the children with that kind, easy way he had, she might fall in love with him, and she couldn't have that.

Dot had baby number four, Audrey – a beautiful name for a beautiful girl. Maybe if Dot hadn't been busy with pregnancy, labour and her new baby she'd have noticed a change in Emmeline's disposition. Maybe not. Emmeline tried very hard not to be changed, even though she sometimes wondered if it was crazy happiness rather than blood that ran through her nowadays.

Matthew had been selected for his school rugby team and was doing well at his studies. Lydia had visited once and was as loving but as determined to stay in the West Country as ever, and Emmeline and Neville were still not speaking: if she had something important to relay to him, she wrote it on scraps of newspaper over the tales of crimes and wife-beaters and prison sentences.

She and Mr Davenport had a regular table at the Lyons Corner House, a leather booth with soft lighting, and even a regular waitress, with big cheeks and a Scottish accent. Mr Davenport was as charming with the staff, as ever. They had two hours together and they were strict about keeping to this.

On maybe their third or fourth meeting, Mr Davenport had asked her if she would call him by his first name: Lawrence.

Biting her lip, she had agreed. 'And you may call me Emmeline.'

'I have always loved that name,' he had said. 'After the great suffragette, I presume?'

'No, sadly. After the midwife who delivered me. I was a breech birth – apparently she earned her money that night...'

That had made him laugh. 'You? A difficult birth? I don't believe it.'

She loved hearing him say Emmeline almost as much as she loved saying the word Lawrence.

On this particular afternoon, Mr Davenport – Lawrence – was jittery and immediately Emmeline feared that he was going to tell her they couldn't meet again. She knew she couldn't bear it if he said that. Everything would fall apart. She wouldn't be able to do without him a second time. Yet when she asked him if there was anything wrong, he said nothing and she decided she would not ask him again. If he didn't want to talk, she wouldn't push him. It was work, she told himself, the party, or maybe badgers again.

They had their tea. They had their cakes.

It had been a busy week at Marjorie's. Potato printing, fancy dress contests, getting ready for harvest festival. Maurice fell off the picnic table in the garden (what was he doing on there?) but was fine, Sheila Appleby chipped her front tooth running into the sink. They had fifteen applications to start in January.

Sometimes, the children pulled up chairs and put blankets over the top, forming a protected, cosy den. This was how Emmeline felt with Lawrence, as if she were in a den away from the rabble of politics and disapproving husbands... With him she felt more herself than anywhere else.

And then he said, 'You'll have heard Mrs Davenport and I are divorcing?'

Emmeline didn't know how much she should let on she knew. She had never been quite sure if it was true.

'I heard something, but...'

She felt for him. The end of a marriage, for a man like him, must be a humiliation. He folded his napkin, his eyes lowered.

'How do you feel about it?' she asked.

'I worked for her father for many years. It was a political match – it should have stayed that way.'

'I see.' Emmeline's heart was racing. *Why is he telling me this?*

'I'm also standing down at the next election.'

This was a day of shocks. Covering her mouth, Emmeline spoke through her fingers: 'Why?'

'There will be other ways to effect change. And I daresay I'll be better at those.'

'For example?'

At last, he grinned at her. 'You haven't lost your curiosity,

Emmeline! I'll write for the newspapers. I'll go and give speeches. They already call me 'nursery man' and mothers-friend.'

'I don't think they mean it as a compliment.'

'I don't care how they mean it.' He shrugged. 'Anyway, there's a pension.' He kept his eyes on her at all times. 'And I happen to know someone who runs an excellent nursery.'

Now she let herself smile.

'Maybe she could find me a job teaching country dancing or' – he continued – 'boiling nappies?'

'Or cutting hair?' she suggested playfully.

The way his beautiful lips turned up! 'Exactly. She could even put me in the stocks for a small fee.'

They both laughed.

'Is this what you want though? To leave Parliament?'

'Parliament was never my dream. It was Mrs Davenport who should have stood, not me. She was the ambitious one. I haven't the appetite any more. Also...' He rubbed his eyes. 'It's been hellish. I'm not the only one who feels that way. A lot of us have run out of steam – and that's okay. There's a whole load of brilliant people ready to navigate the country post-war. It doesn't have to be me.'

Emmeline couldn't imagine anyone better to navigate the country post-war than him, but she admired him all the more for acknowledging his fatigue.

'I always wanted to know... were you the anonymous donor at the auction?'

'That would be telling.' He grinned. But then added that he regretted that he was outbid on the tennis racquets, and winked.

'Big changes ahead,' she said.

'Yes.'

The waitress came over to collect their plates. She lingered to chat about the weather and how busy they were and her long hours and... *please,* thought Emmeline, *leave us alone.* They only had such a short time. Neville and Matthew expected her home and Lawrence usually had evening sessions at the House of Commons to go to. She tried to cover her impatience. Perhaps he too was not as relaxed as he seemed, since as soon as the waitress turned away, he spoke urgently.

'We were right not to get entangled back then,' he said.

Entangled didn't seem the right word, but she agreed. They had nothing to be guilty about. Scandal averted. She had not been a scarlet woman.

Was this all he wanted to say, though, that he was glad nothing had happened between them? Emmeline's sadness at this told her that she wanted him to declare himself, she really did, and yet he simply paid the bill, helped her on with her coat and hat and said nothing.

Outside, the roar of buses and lorries felt like a shock after the calm of the tea rooms. He hailed a cab and one pulled up much too quickly. As she was getting in, desperate at all the things left unsaid, he spoke quickly.

'I want to be with you.' He chuckled self-consciously. 'You don't have to decide anything now, there's no hurry. But you should know.'

She couldn't believe what she was hearing. It was more, so much more than she had ever dreamed of him saying. She shook her head in puzzlement. *Am I imagining this?* She felt like one of the women in the films she and Dot had watched over and over again. Things like this didn't happen to ordinary women like her.

'Emmeline,' he whispered as he closed the cab door for her, 'I love you.'

60

Lydia

The Miss Weston-super-Mare Contest was to be held at the Grand Hotel on the seafront, but Lydia didn't know where it was, and neither did any of the people she asked in the street. Leonard had driven her there that morning and had optimistically booked a double room for that night in the names of Mr and Mrs Smith.

'I'm not sharing,' she kept telling him, but he said, 'Two singles were too expensive,' and 'I *have* driven you all this way, Lydia!'

Some pretty girls were walking along purposefully and she instructed Leonard to follow them – without looking creepy – and she had guessed right; at the end of the road, they went into a hotel. Leonard parked up and she was relieved that, while his car was not the most expensive model there, it was not the cheapest either.

In the foyer, the girls – her competitors – were signing in. Most of the contestants were with their mothers, some with friends, some with boyfriends, and Lydia evaluated each one of them quickly:

Prettier than her.

Less pretty than her.

The organisers handed her a paper full of long words – she seemed to have to sign her life away – she didn't bother to read it. They couldn't make you do stuff, could they, even if you'd signed a contract? You could just disappear if needs be. She skimmed over 'No smoking in the public areas' and 'ABSO-LUTELY no alcohol to be consumed on the premises'. Expectations were that the winner would do nothing to harm the reputation of Weston-super-Mare.

Lydia snorted. That was vague.

Since the fateful day when she and Miss Picard – no, Mrs Picard-Richardson – were reunited, her old mentor had been full of encouragement. She and her husband had told Lydia they'd be her agents if she liked: Find her contests, modelling jobs, anything she needed...

'I'm not sure,' Lydia had said. Mrs Picard-Richardson always gave her a feeling of getting more than she had bargained for.

'Think about it.'

'I will.'

She didn't say to Mrs Picard-Richardson, *you said you'd never work again* – because that would be impertinent.

Getting ready for the contest, Lydia felt not unlike a dog. Ears, skin, fur, weight, all had to be checked.

They would do a whole circuit around the outdoor swimming pool.

'Slowly, ladies!' they were advised by a shaggy-haired man in a suit holding a clipboard as they did their practise-walk. He said if they felt it was too slow, it was probably the right speed. This struck Lydia as poor advice.

Lydia raised her hand. 'Do we actually get into the pool?'

Everyone laughed. (The answer was no.)

The audience filed in and sat in deckchairs around each side of the pool. They looked like normal people mostly. Men in hats and suits, women in hats and sundresses. Lydia did not immediately see any eligible bachelors, but you never knew. Mrs Picard-Richardson had been adamant she might find someone here.

There was a wireless personality there – Valerie probably would have known him; he was an old man from *The Brains Trust*, apparently, and in his shorts and socks with sandals he looked like a mad professor. There was another elderly chap, this one from a dancing show, and a woman who looked a bit like Mrs Howard. These were the judges.

Lydia's lip curled. Her fate to be decided by these three unattractive old people? That didn't seem right.

High heels on a slippery surface was an accident waiting to happen, but Lydia was confident that, thanks to Mrs Picard-Richardson's classes at St Boniface, she was one of the best walkers there. If this was what it depended on, then she'd be a shoe-in. Lydia laughed at her own joke. She would have told the woman next to her, but she was busy complaining about the advisor.

'He pinched my bum!' she whispered, outraged.

Lydia felt concerned. The man had not come anywhere near her. Did this mean she was not in the running?

Then the advisor handed her a number to put on her wrist and, for a second, Lydia was a little girl again with a name tag on a train to anywhere and for a moment, she couldn't breathe. The girl next to her said, 'Miss Froud, it's your turn.'

She could do this: chin up, smile. She knew this better than anyone: Smile and get selected.

The word *du jour* was *bombshell;* they were bombshells this, bombshells that. 'Not just a pretty face,' was the other line of the day. It wasn't enough to be pretty, you had to be a good person as well or at least pretend you were. Once she'd done the precarious circuit of the pool, Lydia wanted to fling her arms round the compère with relief.

'This is Lydia Froud from Taunton. She's 32-22-32 and look at those pins.'

She'd hoped the compere would ask her how she stayed in shape. They'd asked the contestant before that and her dry answer of soup and crackers had received just a smattering of applause. Lydia would say that she worked at a kennels and was always running around with distressed dogs; surely that would win people over?

But he didn't ask her that. She got, 'What is your favourite thing to do?' instead.

Lydia paused. Don't try to be funny, she reminded herself. And try to appear a good person.

'I love to fish,' Lydia finally decided.

'To fish?' he repeated, taken aback. Everyone seemed surprised.

'Yes!' she said. 'In the local lakes. I've caught pike and mullet before.'

He collected himself, tugged his tie, clicked his jaw. 'She's not just a pretty face! She's a fisherman.'

She came third.

She should have said she liked crocheting.

Leonard kept saying, 'Third is amazing, Lydia,' and 'Your first contest too!' and he didn't mind driving her home since the hotel offered him a full refund. Lydia didn't think it was amazing. She wasn't going to Morecambe and she wasn't going to be Miss Great Britain.

But when she told Mrs Picard-Richardson, she said, 'Didn't I tell you!' and 'Next time, you'll win, I'm sure, chérie.'

61

Emmeline

It was quite possibly the longest week of Emmeline's life. She could not wait until tea next Friday – it was impossible – and yet wait she had to. Wait and think and sizzle and dream.

At the nursery, she clapped her hands for attention and then forgot what she was about to say. She called Bella, Mabel and Ellie, Mrs Hodges. She did a load of washing and then, instead of hanging out the clean clothes, she dumped them back in the dirty water again.

Bess said, 'What's the matter, Mrs Froud? You're worse than the children!'

Emmeline felt like she was going crazy. Every waking hour – possibly every sleeping hour too – was consumed by the conversation they had had the week before.

She couldn't remember it as exactly as she would have liked, but she knew his love had been there, love had been flowing between them, in his eyes, in his hands and when he pressed his lips against her cheek goodbye. Did he say he wanted to marry her? No, he had not said that, Emmeline, be serious. Did he say he wanted to be with her? Yes, he had, he really had.

In the past, she would have talked to Mrs Salt. She would quite like to have talked to her other old neighbour, Mrs Hardman, but Mrs Hardman had the wrong idea of her. She'd *let* her have the wrong idea of her for so long she didn't think she could turn that round now. She knew what Dot would say if she told her. It would be what she'd been saying for the last ten years and no doubt would involve geese and ganders and what was good enough for them.

That week, Emmeline watched Neville in a way she hadn't done for years. If he brought up a cup of tea, if he kissed her on the lips, if he told her he loved her, she resolved, then maybe she would stay with him. He was being tested and he didn't know it. She was being unfair – but then again, he was failing every test. And she knew that perhaps she would have stayed with him, she would have tried harder, if it hadn't been for that note. She had always – no, that wasn't quite right – *sometimes* suspected something wasn't right between them. That note, a simple love/farewell letter, had confirmed it.

A woman she could compete with – if she were the competing type.

Not a man.

Perhaps if she left, it would work out for the best for Neville too, she told herself, although she did not really believe it.

Other than Mr and Mrs Davenport, she didn't know anyone who was divorced. She didn't think she even knew anyone who was separated. But then let her be a trailblazer, she told herself. As she had been, unexpectedly, with the wartime nurseries, so she would be in this. If that's what it took.

She would meet Mr Davenport and make a plan.

'Neville,' she said sharply that Thursday evening. No more writing on newspapers. She wanted to be sure this message was received. 'I have to go out tomorrow, I will be late.'

He made no sign that he'd heard.

'I said, I will be late.'

'What do you want me to do about it?' he grumbled.

If she left, *when* she left, Neville would not be broken-hearted. He might be shocked, angry, ashamed, but somewhere along the way they had lost sight of each other.

Mr Davenport saw her. Mr Davenport, who had championed her dreams even when he thought they were daft, even when they were tiny wishes. Even when they were against his interests.

Think what she and he could achieve together!

If Neville found out about it, he would have her out on the streets before she could draw a breath, she didn't doubt it. If Neville was an unemotional husband, he would be a vengeful ex-husband, this she knew to the core of her.

She would have to be careful.

That was all right, Emmeline was always careful.

On Friday morning, Emmeline made herself look as attractive as she could. She knew she looked more alive than ever, now that everything was a possibility.

At the nursery, she whirred around, unstoppable, singing rhymes, painting rainbows, even as Dot cautioned her that finances were looking bleak. Her life had not ended with the end of the war. Far from it. This was just the start of her dreams coming true.

62

Lydia

'I think you should enter the pageant at Saunton Sands next,' Mrs Picard-Richardson said. 'There's no reason you couldn't be the next Miss Saunton Sands!'

'I thought you had to be from the town, or at least nearby!' Lydia said.

Mrs Picard-Richardson was aghast at such ignorance. 'Maybe once, not anymore. Anyway, it's not far.'

'It's miles away!'

'Alors!' said Mrs Picard-Richardson said, which is what she always said when she'd had enough of a conversation.

Competing had been fun, but ultimately it had not been fruitful. She had neither met any fascinating men nor been placed first. She had failed at both her objectives and Lydia was not a girl who was inclined to pursue failure.

'I don't really get it,' Lydia sighed.

'What?'

'Any of it. The walking around the pool, the bathing suit, the questions...'

It had all felt odd. Old-fashioned, although Lydia didn't think they held beauty pageants in the old days. Maybe they did.

'People just want to forget the war.' Mrs Picard-Richardson always explained things as though she had explained them one hundred times before.

'Yes, but...'

'What better way to forget the war than to look at beautiful young ladies?'

Lydia thought of Rex pawing her awake, or tucking his nose under her arm in the morning. Those *were* two better ways, at least.

'Maybe, it's just me,' she pondered.

'It's your duty, Lydia!'

Lydia wasn't a pushover, she really wasn't. But the idea that it was her patriotic duty to walk around swimming pools in a bathing costume at the weekends had a certain appeal too.

Lydia didn't tell Leonard about the next contest, but instead went by herself on the train. It was Miss Lyme Regis and the winner of this would go on not to Miss Morecambe but to Miss Southern Counties.

Perhaps because Leonard wasn't there, mithering on about hotel rooms or his petrol coupons, she felt freer to chat to the other contestants: a secretary, a nurse, a primary school teacher.

'Kennel worker? You like dogs?'

'Of course.'

'You don't *look* like you do!'

Cheeky mare. 'What does someone who likes dogs look like?' Lydia countered.

The girl – the secretary – surveyed her with her pale eyes. 'Not like you.'

She didn't get placed at Lyme Regis. Not even top four. Mrs Picard-Richardson said it was a fix, it had to be.

Third time lucky in Woolacombe. Saul drove her and Rex. Although he had offered, Saul was annoyed that Rex came and made the car seat hairy *and* that he had to hold the dog while she got ready backstage.

She wondered what her parents would think about the revealing nature of her bathing suit. She realised she didn't know what they would think about much. She was more able to predict what Mrs H would say: 'Is this viable, Lydia? As a long-term venture?' Or even Valerie, 'I heard a show on the wireless about it; it looks interesting...' (when Valerie said *interesting* she meant – *it's not my cup of tea*).

'You're not from here around here, are you?' one of the girls cut into her thoughts.

'Yes,' said Lydia. 'I came here during the war.'

That was the good thing about being evacuated. You belonged *everywhere*. And a lot of people felt sorry for you.

This time the question she had to answer on stage was: 'What do you do?'

'I work in a nursery,' she lied. She knew so much about nurseries, she was sure she could pass as an expert.

'Flowers. You grow plants?'

Lydia grimaced, but decided not to show him up by correcting him.

'That's it!'

'Show me your hands,' he said, and, mystified, she obliged. He held her hand up to the light. 'By Jove, she's got green fingers!'

The crowd loved that.

She came fourth.

'Fourth is not bad, Lydia,' Saul said comfortingly in the car. He would say that – he was keen to get his hand down her top again.

'Fourth.' She shook her head despairingly. It just wasn't good enough. No one remembers fourth. She had no sash, no crown, no prize money. No rich man had noticed her to sweep her off her feet. And the summer was nearly over. She held Rex as he sniffed out of the window.

'I'll only be plainer next year.'

Saul laughed. 'Impossible!'

'How about a kiss?' he said when she got out of the car and his tone was already entitled, defensive. 'It was a long drive!'

'Next time,' she promised.

Lydia still wrote to Paul. He would want to hear about Rex. She didn't dash off frequent letters like she did to her mother, though; she wanted to be enigmatic. She told about the beauty contests although she didn't tell him she'd come fourth. Let him think she won them all. She couldn't predict what he'd say either, but it seemed an easy way of reminding him how pretty she was.

'That's so unexpected,' Paul replied. 'At first I thought you meant you entered the dog!'

In the next letter, he said, 'I do remember you walking around with my copy of *Great Lakes to Fish In* on your head. I was annoyed.'

'My posture is excellent, thanks to your *Great Lakes to Fish In*.'

'It is,' he wrote. And 'I never met anyone who enunciates how now brown cow as clearly as you do.'

More men should be funny like Paul, she thought.

The beauty pageants in London seemed a lot sleazier. They were held in clubs in Soho with flickering red lights outside. The seaside ones were more genteel. Wearing a swimsuit by a swimming pool made sense; wearing a swimsuit with a fluffy tail in a men's club in Soho didn't.

Even in a genteel fading seaside resort, though, sometimes Lydia would stare out at a sea of suits and feel like a pig hanging in a butcher's shop with sawdust under her trotters. She could hear people critiquing her as she strutted around. Some thought she was too skinny, some she was too fat, and some something too indecent to dwell on.

Whenever she regretted competing, she thought back to going to the theatre for the first time with Mrs H. She had never seen a live performance before and she couldn't believe how close the actors were. It was *Toad of Toad Hall* and she had felt for the people playing trees. She thought they had sad eyes. Then they'd seen *The Tempest* and the man who played Caliban had worn less than her. They'd seen *Pygmalion* and the girl who played Eliza had made a fool of herself.

Part of life *is* making a fool of yourself, she thought – and if everyone is making a fool of themselves, is it even making a fool of yourself?

The pageants were simply theatre of a different kind, theatre without the boring dialogues and the spitting old men, Lydia rationalised. She remembered the man who had played Prospero. At the stage door, he'd asked her if she'd be a sprite in *A Midsummer Night's Dream*. All Mrs H's productions would have been improved if they'd dropped the pretence at high culture and admitted what they wanted to see – pretty girls wandering around in swimsuits.

Plus, the contests fitted in with her work at the kennels. And fitted in with her dreams. Nevertheless, it still grated on Lydia that she had never taken first place.

The last pageant of the season was held in Minehead. Lydia took the train on her own. She didn't like it, but her beaus told her they were busy.

'It's now or never,' she thought, but she came fourth again.

This time, Mrs Picard-Richardson was there and she was full of praise. Lydia would win next year, she would, she absolutely would. Lydia had hoped for a lift back, but Mrs Picard-Richardson was busy talking with her friends, so she sloped away to the railway station.

Lydia didn't usually bother with newspapers. They made you frown, and frowns were bad for wrinkles. Nevertheless, today she picked up the copy that someone had left on the bench. She usually went straight to the agony aunts, but this time she paused on the front page; there was a photograph of a man she thought she recognised. For a moment she didn't know how – and then she placed him. The family Mummy had been evacuated to before the Hazells. Classy people. The Davenports, that was it. He was a Member of Parliament, so he was often in the newspapers. She had loved the chandeliers in the drawing room.

> *The MP for King's Lynn, Lawrence Davenport, was walking away from Parliament, alone, when he was pounced upon and stabbed in the heart. Police apprehended the perpetrator. It is understood that perpetrator had sent several threats to at least five members of Parliament and had been waiting for the opportunity to strike. Despite valiant efforts by the public and emergency services, Lawrence Davenport MP died on the spot. The MP leaves behind his heartbroken wife, Lady Rosemary Davenport.*

Mummy will be upset, thought Lydia. She would call her when she got home.

63

Emmeline

Lawrence didn't come to the nursery, so Emmeline packed up by herself, and with a spring in her step and hope in her heart, she went to the tea room to meet him. It was hard to stop herself smiling inanely at everyone she saw – she had been looking forward to this ever since they parted last week.

He would grin that gorgeous grin he had, and they would talk about all the things they would do today, and the next day and the next. They would talk about their lives together, how would they practically do this... this being together. She could picture the future so clearly, it might have been on the billboards of Piccadilly Circus. Could see herself coming home from work, greeting each other, her leading him up to Bedlington.

Gosh, she was so in love. Blissfully, utterly, infinitely in love.

He wasn't there but he had been late once before. There had been a sudden downpour and for once he had failed to hail a taxi. He came in blown about, wonderfully dishevelled. She really should have told him she loved him then.

Ten minutes. Then twenty.

I'll order for us both, she decided. And even though she was beginning to have worries, she liked that she knew what he'd most likely choose. He would like a slice of that Bakewell, she thought. She got some bread pudding for herself. But she didn't feel like eating on her own, so she just picked and nibbled. And waited.

There was no hurry, she knew. Tonight, maybe they would go to a restaurant, or even a hotel. People did that, she'd heard, you didn't even have to stay the night, you could stay just for a few hours! She couldn't wait to get to their lovemaking, the love-making that was so long overdue and so dreamed of.

Maybe they hadn't arranged to meet this week? Could it have been next week instead?

Maybe he'd changed his mind? She doubted this, but she was in a search of explanations. She gave him two hours. Still nothing.

The tea rooms had revolving doors, which she usually enjoyed but today as she stared fixedly at them they seemed designed to trap or confuse her. Men who resembled him in some way rotated in; it wasn't until they were in the café itself that their differences became apparent.

Could he have gone to another Lyons for some reason?

She gave him an extra hour, so a total of three, and when still there was nothing, she went back to the West Hampstead flat that still didn't feel like home, disheartened and on the brink of tears.

There would be some simple explanation. 'Am I forgiven?' he would ask beseechingly, and she might jump into his arms, 'Always.' They would kiss and perhaps they would be in such a hurry to make love they would do it standing up like they do in films, or else they might leave a trail of clothes, like breadcrumbs in a forest, to bed.

Neville was proud of the telephone they had had fitted

recently. He thought it was a shame more people didn't have telephones in the war, but Emmeline thought, if they did, would she have got all those lovely letters from Lydia?

That evening, Lydia called.

And now Emmeline knew.

Lawrence Davenport would never be hers.

64

OCTOBER 1949

Emmeline

The funeral was as terrible as she'd expected, but it was also terrible in a way she hadn't anticipated – it felt like it had nothing to do with him. It felt like something imposed upon him. And all Emmeline wanted to do was tell him about it and have him tell her his thoughts and for them to laugh about it together. How ridiculous it all seemed.

The great man, Prime Minister Winston Churchill, was in the Church of Our Lady in Shouldham. He made a speech about Mr Davenport: a great Member of Parliament, a conscientious man, fair-minded, working hard for his constituents and his country... future ahead of him, violently taken, forces of evil, etc. It was all true, but Emmeline couldn't take it in – she didn't want to hear it.

Councillor Arscott was also there, with some other local dignitaries. Thankfully, he did not speak. They sat at opposite ends of the same pew, he looked straight past her, his nostrils quivering. Imagine what Mr Davenport would say about that! The vicar who led the service was the one who wouldn't let them have his church hall for a nursery. Now he was talking about Mr Davenport's humanity.

'A rising tide lifts all boats,' he said.

Well, your boat wasn't lifted very far, thought Emmeline bitterly.

She pictured Lawrence waving her off in the taxi – the last time she would ever see him. If she had spent the night with him then... Maybe they would have made love all night and then some more in the morning. If she had said yes to him, they would have had that time together to make up for all the time they didn't have.

Maybe she could have changed the course of those few days. Maybe, had he been with her, the madman might have alighted on someone else. Mr Davenport would tell her, 'dreadful news,' and they would be sobered by it – but they would be together. They would still have a future.

Around her, people were quietly weeping, but Emmeline hadn't cried, wouldn't let herself cry. She was stony-faced, angry.

On the wireless, they had said Mr Davenport wouldn't have had a moment to escape, nor a minute to think. He wouldn't have known what was happening and he died at the scene, pretty much instantly. Emmeline suspected this was an invented story, one concocted to soothe. She played out what she thought had happened over and over in her mind. He would have been smiling at the thought of some joke in the chamber, he would have been enjoying the balmy air... Would he have suspected the man who came up to him, who drew closer and closer until...? Surely he would have realised what it was? He must have been terrified.

Apparently, the perpetrator had been targeting several politicians for years. It was 'bad luck' that was the day he decided to act on his threats, and it was bad luck that Mr Davenport had been there, minding his own business.

Bad luck seemed an incredible phrase for it.

The perpetrator would be put in prison: 'Throw away the key,' everyone was saying, but what good would that do? Lawrence Davenport was dead. Nothing would bring him back.

It felt like they had wasted all that time – not just from the day he declared himself in the car and she had resisted, no, from a time long before that day. If she hadn't resisted, they might have had years and years together.

Bad luck?

And now she was grieving in secret and it was agony. Mrs Davenport was gracious, even beautiful, in black, wearing a hat with netting over her face – a kind of bride in reverse – and Emmeline couldn't let on to her. Mrs Davenport was never alone. Mr Reynolds did not leave her side. Emmeline even heard her say to someone that she 'didn't know what she'd do without him' and that Mr Reynolds had 'saved her life'. It gave Emmeline shivers, but she couldn't untangle why. Mrs Davenport gave a short speech. 'You know the MP yet not many people know the other Lawrence Davenport. He was a deeply loving man, a partner, and' – she surveyed the room, was she looking for Emmeline? No, she wasn't, she was an interloper here, a nobody – 'a great friend.'

Even while his coffin sat there in the church, there was a buzz about what was going to happen to his parliamentary seat. It made Emmeline feel worse that Mr Davenport's death was being touted as the end of a political dynasty when for her it was much more than that: it was the loss of the man she loved and it was just about the most heartbreaking thing in the world.

The day Lydia had told her, she had come off the telephone and Neville had glared and said, 'You look like you've seen a ghost.'

She must have looked seriously grotesque for him to comment.

Steady, Emmeline. She held on to the back of a chair, tried to force a smile.

'You really are white as a sheet.'

'Too much powder,' she lied.

'Hmm,' he said with narrowed eyes.

She had to get out. The flat felt too small to contain the enormity of this. Grabbing her coat, she raced outside, Neville's 'What about tea?' ringing in her ears. She walked and walked. She didn't know where she was going, only that she had to keep moving. If she stopped for a moment, she would break.

A few days later, testing herself, she told Neville: 'Remember the family I stayed with in Norfolk? The man was murdered in the street.'

Neville said he already knew.

She said she might go to the funeral. Day return. She managed to say it without crying. He said, 'I suspected you might.'

Everyone was invited back to the Old Rectory, but Emmeline didn't want to go. She didn't want to be in that house without him. There were so many memories there: talking together over cocoa in the kitchen, watching him smoking a cigarette in the drawing room. And they could have had so much more...

A young man in military uniform sought her out and offered her a lift to Thorpe station. He seemed to know who she was, but she didn't recognise him. Maybe they had met at the house at some point, or at the fated council meeting?

They exchanged respectful comments in a murmur – *what a terrible thing to happen, what is the world coming to* – as he started up the car. Then they were silent for the rest of the journey, which Emmeline appreciated. She wondered if she would ever take in the magnitude of what had happened. The love of her life was dead. And she had never told him she loved him.

They reached the station and the man parked up and turned to her.

'I'm in a bit of a quandary actually, Mrs Froud.'

'How so?' She wasn't really interested in the young man or his quandaries.

'What's Mrs Davenport's first name?'

'Rosemary – Rosie. Why?'

'Does she have a second name, or another given name that you know?'

'Not that I'm aware of.'

'So the thing is... I was the first person there that day. I was walking just yards behind him. And he was calling for someone, not Rosemary, but another name.'

Emmeline felt cold. Her entire body tensed. *Don't ask right away*, she said. *Be calm.*

'What name?'

He had a curious, yet gentle expression on his face, as he turned to her and said, 'He was calling for Emmeline, my Emmeline. Those were his last words.'

Emmeline's heart was now in her stomach. *Bad luck*, she thought to herself. *Bad, bad luck.*

'Mrs Froud?'

Emmeline knew she had to speak sooner or later. She picked up her handbag and rested it on her knees. 'I think not. Was there... anything else?'

The man shook his head and she got out the car. As she was about to walk away, he called to her. 'Don't worry, I won't tell anyone,' and then he drove away.

65

JANUARY 1950

Lydia

Lydia hadn't seen her mother for nearly six months. There had been one reason after another and, perhaps for the first time, Lydia had grown to properly miss her. No one supported her like Mummy did. There were letters and now weekly phone calls, but none of it made up for the sight of Mummy's pretty face spilling over with affection. Lydia missed that.

Lydia still hadn't told Mummy about the contests because, despite Mrs Picard-Richardson's encouragement, she wasn't sure if she'd do them next summer. And she was busy with the dogs and Mummy was busy with Marjorie's Nursery.

'It is all fine,' Mummy said, although she often added hesitantly, 'Financially, there are worries but I pray it will work itself out...'

'Can't Daddy help?' Lydia would never admit it, but she felt slightly disappointed by her father recently. She had always been a daddy's girl, but since the end of the war it was hard not to see that he didn't support her mother much. Mummy seemed to carry everything on her own – and he wasn't even grateful.

'No need!' Mummy said lightly. 'Now tell me all about you, my sweet girl!'

The real reason Lydia didn't tell her mummy about the beauty pageants was that she feared she wouldn't approve.

It was New Year's Day and Lydia was pacing up and down the railway platform at Chard. Some lads whistled at her and she rolled her eyes. It was cold, the ground was frosty, and her hands were tinged with blue because she had left her gloves at the kennels.

And then she was here.

'Mummy!'

They clasped each other and both burst into tears.

'You smell like Mummy!' Lydia – who was never usually emotional – said.

'And you smell like dogs, Lydia!' Her mummy laughed. And then she pulled away. 'Let me look at you.'

And they held each other at arm's-length and her mummy was smiling at her, but Lydia's heart sank. Her mummy, who used to be the shiniest, prettiest woman in the whole world, had aged. This was not just a case of six months of growing older, it looked like years and years had been added to her. Mummy was crying, as she often did, but it was not just that making her look pitiable; she looked shrunken or shrivelled, like your fingers after too long in the bath.

'Did...' Lydia didn't quite know where to start, but she wanted to know *everything*. 'Was the journey all right?'

'Fine, darling. And some lovely people on the train shared their lemon cordial with me.'

Why does she look so utterly decimated?

'Is Matthew well?'

'Very.'

'How about Daddy?'

'You know Daddy!'

They walked towards the high street, past Woods Hardware store and the post office. Her mummy had only the lightest of bags. Her shoes were flat – she used to live in impractical heels, even for nursery work – and her legs were mottled like corned beef. It wasn't her fault; it was still hard to get stockings. But it couldn't just be rationing and the war that had done this to her. She looked like she'd given up on herself. Mrs Picard-Richardson would have been mortified – or, more likely, triumphant at being proved right.

Back at Lydia's attic room, Mummy collapsed onto the bed, disappearing into the pillows. Lydia brought her tea and hovered and asked what she wanted to do, and Mummy apologised; she hadn't thought that far ahead. Lydia stared. Who was this woman inhabiting a worn-out version of her mother? Out of desperation, she asked, 'My hair is knotty, would you brush it for me?'

At this, her mother nodded delightedly. So they sat for hours, like they used to, Lydia on the floor with her hair in her mother's hands; only this time, every so often, Lydia's mother put down her brush and wiped away silent tears.

66

Emmeline

How had she ever thought she would have a happy-ever-after with Mr Davenport? What madness had overtaken her – and him? The soldier's words had confirmed what she knew – he *did* love her; they were just too slow to do anything about it.

Dot often asked Emmeline if there was anything wrong, but Emmeline couldn't tell her about her and Mr Davenport's secret meetings and the depths of her grief. Fortunately – or unfortunately – there were plenty of other things that were wrong that she *could* talk about.

Emmeline worked at Marjorie's six days a week. Unlike with the wartime nursery in Norfolk, she charged. She had to. They were thinking of lowering the age of acceptance from nine months to six months. Part of her thought that was too young, but another part thought that the sooner the mothers who wanted to were back working, the better society would be.

She kept her eye on child development practice all over the world and attended workshops. Marjorie's Nurseries had more play time and more toys than the wartime nursery. They did counting and the alphabet and singing and catch. The inside space was large and airy and to some extent made up for the small yard that was their only outside space. They got tiny chairs and set them up in a massive circle in the mornings for an assembly.

The children were adorable and kept her busy. A suspected case of polio, thank God, turned out to be nothing. There was a bee sting on the chin and someone fell off a see-saw. There were bric-a-brac sales, bad smells and a lot of country dancing.

In the mornings, she walked Matthew to his school and then raced to the nursery. He came to the nursery at lunchtime by himself and after school. He played cards or marbles, mostly. She might have missed Lydia's childhood, but she wasn't going to miss Matthew's. Not a single minute of it.

Matthew had lost his Norfolk accent and one day he asked if he had ever lived anywhere else than here.

'Yes, darling!' Emmeline said, mystified. Did he really not remember? 'In East London and then in Norfolk.'

'Did we never live in Somerset?'

'No, that's Lydia.'

'Did you lose a someone special in the war?' he asked her another time, after a long day of play-fighting Nazis in the street.

'Not only in the war,' she said, thinking of her Mr Davenport. And then she told him about Marjorie and the Salts and he was so moved that for once he put his arm around her. 'That must have been so hard.'

'We just got on with it,' she said.

Dot had arranged a work experience girl. Emmeline went down to meet her.

The girl had a polka-dot bow in her hair, like the ones Lydia used to wear. Emmeline thought her face looked familiar, but couldn't quite place her.

Smiling, Dot pushed the girl forward.

'Hello, Mrs Froud!' she said politely, holding out a slender hand to shake. 'I'm Deidre.' And Dot could contain herself no longer; she sang out, 'It's Marjorie's girl. Remember?'

You could have knocked Emmeline down with a feather. Deidre was thirteen now and she wanted to work with children. She was small and thin, but not frail; she had a determined face and bright eyes and when she saw the babies, her face lit up.

After Emmeline had got over the surprise, she asked Deidre about her brothers and sisters. 'Derek wants to join the navy,' Deidre said, 'and Della wants to be a nurse. Are you crying?'

Emmeline didn't want to let go of the girl's hand, even to wipe away her tears. She was over the moon to meet her.

'Come on, let me show you around.'

67

Emmeline

Emmeline found out that Lydia was competing in beauty pageants from her old neighbour Jean Hardman. Who had found out from Leonard's mother, who, in turn, had found out from Leonard's fiancée, Barbara.

'Why didn't you tell me, Lydia?' Emmeline asked on the telephone. She tried not to sound as exasperated as she felt. If she did, Lydia might hang up on her – she'd done that before when Emmeline had asked the wrong thing. Emmeline wasn't sure what annoyed her most – the way she'd found out or what she'd found out – but she *was* cross.

'It's nothing really,' Lydia said. 'It's just a hobby.'

'I'd love to see you...' what was the word? 'compete.'

'You'd never understand.'

'I do understand,' insisted Emmeline, although she wasn't sure what Lydia meant. What was there to understand? – Lydia was entering contests. And?

'Let me know when the next one is and I'll come,' she said, and Lydia harumphed.

The next one was in Minehead. Emmeline met her in Taunton and they took the train together, and Lydia talked about how she wanted to have a marriage like her parents'.

Everything is not what it seems, Lydia.

Emmeline listened as Lydia went on about the boys and admirers who she had no intention of walking out with because they weren't half so nice as Daddy.

She watched as her daughter strutted out on to the platform. Emmeline didn't realise her legs had got so long. How had that happened? This was a girl who only ate sweet things. She was waving at everyone like they were there exclusively for her.

'Teeth and eyes!' a glamorous woman next to her was muttering to herself. 'Chest out! That's it.'

She remembered Lydia playing her getting-married-in-the-morning game. Her little girl had grown up a beauty and, although Emmeline didn't prize these things as much as some, it still gave her joy.

Lydia came third.

She looked shocked, then elated, then ever so grateful. Emmeline wanted to leap onto the stage and hug her.

'Well done!' she shouted, and then covered her mouth with her hand, hoping people would think it had come from someone else.

'I don't believe it!' Lydia kept saying as she was presented with her sash. 'Thank you so much!'

She was led over to the compère, who shook her hand, then kissed her cheek. She kept covering the O of surprise her mouth made. And wavering and tittering and beaming.

Waiting outside the back door, among the rubbish bins, Emmeline felt dowdier than ever. She'd had her hair set the day before and had thought it looked reasonable, but now it seemed unfashionable. She hadn't realised until she saw how different the young women were from her. She was from the older generation, that was for sure. How could she not have understood that? She came from the make-do-and-mend generation – these were the make-up-and-go.

'Congratulations!' Emmeline cried out when Lydia appeared. 'You were a—'

'Don't!' With shock, Emmeline realised that Lydia was furious. 'Third! Again! Unbelievable. What do I have to do to get first?'

'I thought you'd be pleased,' Emmeline said meekly.

'Whoever is pleased with third place? And did you see the woman who came first?'

'Uh-huh.' It wasn't possible to miss the girl who came first. She had perched on a golden throne, shaken hands with everyone, had been given bouquets of flowers, then posed for endless photographs.

'Gap-kneed, bad skin and a big nose.'

She had been perfectly pleasant-looking, Emmeline thought, but did not dare say.

'It's luck of the draw, isn't it?' she said comfortingly instead. 'You're ALL beautiful!'

'Hmmm.'

Despite her suitcase and her towering heels, Lydia marched towards the station and Emmeline struggled to keep up with her.

'Dogs,' she said.

'Pardon?'

'I've got to get back to them. Dammit. I'm glad Daddy didn't see me lose – he would have been disappointed.'

It was funny how Lydia's image of Neville was so different from Emmeline's.

'I don't think he would,' Emmeline ventured.
'He would!' insisted Lydia.

68

Emmeline

The books didn't add up. They hadn't been adding up for a while, Dot had been warning her, but financially, Dot was a pessimist and Emmeline was always hoping something would happen to turn things round. Nothing had, and now they were in trouble.

The cost of running a nursery without council or government funding was too much. The burden now fell on the parents and the majority of parents could barely afford it. Some of them were weeks behind. How Emmeline would have loved to say, 'Look, you don't have to pay!' – she struggled to sign off the demands that Dot wrote to send to late payers – but she had rent and staff and insurance and a gazillion other things to cover.

Lydia's old friend Valerie Hardman got in touch on a crackly telephone line from Bristol. After the reintroductions and catching up on everyone's news, she said: 'I'm thinking about doing a feature on the wartime nurseries.'

Although she always asked Lydia what Valerie was up to, Lydia never wanted to talk about her, so Emmeline had never properly understood her job. 'A feature?'

Valerie explained she was working for a wireless station and they wanted to shine a light on interesting stories.

'And I thought of you... I hope you don't mind.'

Dot would tell her: publicity is good. 'The more people who know about us, the more chance there is of a business or sponsorship opportunity.'

Valerie wanted Emmeline to talk about supporters – 'Who couldn't you have done without? Who made the biggest difference to you? – that sort of thing.'

Emmeline curled the telephone wire in her fingers. Leaning against the hall wall, she thought of her main supporter, Mr Davenport, and the plans they had made together.

She had lost so much, but then the whole world had too. The world didn't even know it, but they lost all the good things he would have brought. He had been tremendous, but he had still had so much more to do.

And he'd lost out, too. He'd had so much vim and vigour in him. *Remember him in the stocks, laughing at the flying sponges. Remember him in his wet shirt, shaking his head like a puppy. Look at him distracting Matthew so he could shave his head.*

Look at him showing her around the nursery garden that first night, the spotlight on his face. Their few stolen afternoons together over tea and buns. Not enough of them. In the future, the unspent hours, days and years they should have had together. They needed more time. It wasn't fair.

'Mrs Froud?' Valerie was asking. 'Are you still there?'

'I'm sorry, Valerie, I can't do it. Not right now,' Emmeline said, choking back a sob.

'I understand,' Valerie said softly.

She was always a sweet-natured girl.

69

Lydia

The summer of 1951 was going to be the breakout one, Lydia
had decided. She dyed her hair. When Mummy saw it, she
shrieked, 'It's white, Lydia!'

'They call it platinum blonde.'

The dye had turned her hair distinctly straw-like, but she
had to get noticed somehow. She didn't want to look stale.
There were a couple of women on the regular circuit who never
got placed and they were a bit like old wallpaper that had
bubbled.

'Tell me to stop before I get to that stage!' she told new
friend and fellow competitor, Bertha, and Bertha promised she
would. Bertha declared Lydia had a few more seasons left in
her yet.

When she visited home, Lydia didn't know what to say to
Matthew. She found herself tongue-tied around him. He hadn't
been separated from Mummy for years, and although she was
glad about how things had turned out, maybe she felt jealous of

him. Lydia thought he was a mummy's boy, although her mummy said, 'He isn't, he's his own person.'

'The lady doth protest too much,' Lydia said. (Sometimes Mrs H's sayings came in handy.)

She and Matthew hadn't lived together since he was one. He was now nearly twelve and had grown tall and strong. Mummy said that he was clever, although Lydia took that with a pinch of salt, because no doubt she told everyone the same about her.

When Lydia told Matthew she had once come third, he said, 'First the worst, second the best, third the one with the hairy chest.'

'First *is* the best, stupid.'

'Not that you'd know.'

Mummy helped with her nails and choosing her clothes. Her heart obviously wasn't in the pageants, but she did it for Lydia and Lydia liked that she did. This year was the year. She'd either get through to Miss England or she would try to find herself another way out.

There were a couple of women at the kennels who were unmarried and had let themselves go, and Lydia did not want that. Some of the boys who had been her most ardent suitors were drifting off now; she had neither the means nor the motivation to keep them interested.

Even Leonard had stopped ferrying her around.

'I love seeing you – and Rex, Lydia.' Leonard, of all her boyfriends, most loved a wet nose and floppy ears. 'But I'm engaged to Barbara now...'

'So what?' she retorted.

Leonard was so shocked he couldn't speak at first. And then he said, 'So uh, she won't be pleased if I take you out any more. I am sorry.'

You will be, thought Lydia bitterly. She realised she would have to take the train on her own yet again with everybody else – *the general public!* – and it made her feel downcast. She should be driven around in a car.

'You could always learn to drive yourself,' suggested her mummy.

Lydia laughed. 'Mo-ther! No!'

70

Lydia

A week before the Bognor Regis contest, the girls were invited to a special dinner. Lydia accepted: it was a chance to survey the opposition. Clara Cooke was only sixteen, with a baby face. Rebecca Lewis looked a bit like a glamorous version of Francine. Martha Fowler was tall yet wore heels and was a bit intimidating. Lydia guessed the judges wouldn't like that. There was a 'type', of course there was. The judges' favourites were usually the curvy – but not too curvy – girls who were between five foot three and five.

They put each girl next to an important someone in the community and Lydia's neighbour was a man named Mr Raymond. He spilled over his chair and had a marmalade moustache as thick as a broom. Lydia was sure she recognised him and tried to remember where from.

She didn't know many men who had fought in the war, but the ones she did know didn't talk about it. Mr Raymond did though. Mr Raymond told her that during the war he was in France, he was in Germany. He was *everywhere*.

The girl on the other side lost interest in his tales of heroism, but Lydia didn't. Mrs Picard-Richardson would have called him a gift horse: 'Don't look him in the bouche, chérie.'

It was when Mr Raymond said he'd like to take her out some time that Lydia remembered. He was the director of one of Mrs H's plays. He'd taken her out in his car years ago. Which put his claim to have practically single-handedly defeated the Nazis in a different light. Nevertheless, he was very complimentary, so Lydia said she could possibly be persuaded.

She talked it over with Mrs Picard-Richardson, who made approving noises.

'Chérie, he could be useful to you.'

Useful. She felt there was something ugly about the word, but Lydia told herself not to be ridiculous. The last thing Mrs Picard-Richardson was, was ugly.

It occurred to her that it was Mrs Picard-Richardson not, as you might expect, Mrs H, who was the person who had filled the mother-shaped hole in her life in Somerset. It was a strange realisation.

The next day, Mr Raymond and Lydia went out to dinner and then on to a bar. He was generous but each compliment and each drink felt like a next step with no return.

'You're going to win, I'll see to it.'

'How can you see to it?' she said, pulling at one of her ringlets. She held her hair in front of her eyes. The white was incredible; it gave her a harsher look, which she preferred.

He was a heavyset man, twice the size of her and twice her age. He liked boxing. He plucked a paper from his dark briefcase. Lydia read where his fat thumb was pointing. It took her a moment to get it, but there it was in black and white.

'You're not actually a judge?'

'I am!' he said and winked.

'Goodness,' she said, this was a lot to take in.

The paper also said he owned a film company.

'Do you?' she asked.

'I don't talk about it.'

'I don't want to be an actress,' Lydia said, and he looked genuinely relieved.

'What do you want to be?'

'A wife,' she said. 'And mother.'

He liked that answer. 'Sweet child,' he said. 'Traditional girl in an' – he rubbed his palms – 'extremely *modern* body.'

Lydia wasn't totally revolted. She was not a squeamish girl and prided herself that she wasn't; some days, she cleared up after thirty dogs!

'Can I take you out?' he asked.

'You're taking me out now, aren't you?!' teased Lydia.

'I want to do it again,' he said. 'And again. And again.'

That was three agains, thought Lydia. Not bad.

'Are *you* married?' she said. It would do well not to look too keen.

'What would you say if I was?'

'I'd say no.'

'I am not married. And I am in the market for a wife.'

They smiled at each other. They had reached a mutual understanding. This was going swimmingly, thought Lydia. Other women were fools for settling for less.

He kept plying her with gin and she couldn't understand why. They had all the agains ahead of them. But she wanted them to have a lovely evening and it seemed important to him. She wanted to have something good to report to Mrs Picard-Richardson and to her family for once but the excitement she felt disappeared somewhere between rounds.

'That's enough for me!' She had a distant memory of one of Mrs H's longer lectures on moderation.

She was half drunk. She was incapable. He had a room nearby. He took advantage of her.

Lydia had no idea how she got back. One moment she was throwing up in an unfamiliar bathroom, the next she was turning the key to her hotel room, turning and turning it before it released, and then finally falling in. Bertha was fast asleep. Maybe Lydia shouldn't have woken her up the night before a contest, but she couldn't help herself.

'I had a terrible night.'

'You'll be all right, doll,' Bertha said without lifting her head from the pillow. She had told Lydia she was nineteen. Her paperwork revealed that she was twenty-two.

'It was *really* bad,' Lydia said. She couldn't believe it. Without opening her eyes, Bertha lifted up her bedcover so Lydia could climb in.

Lydia sighed and went to her own bed. She didn't sleep and Bertha's snoring didn't help.

'You look wrecked,' Bertha said in the morning. Every morning, she touched her toes fifty times and then did: '*I must, I must improve my bust.*' She even did finger exercises. '*Exercises, exercises, I must do my exercises.*'

Lydia thought wistfully of Mrs Howard: 'The best form of exercise is a good book.'

Lydia begged Mrs Picard-Richardson to meet her before the pageant but she refused. Why wouldn't she? Did she know something had happened?

'Please!' Lydia couldn't understand Mrs Picard-Richardson's intransigence. Wasn't she her Chérie? 'Otherwise, I won't enter the pageant...'

This worked. When Mrs Picard-Richardson came and met Lydia in the hotel foyer, she covered her own mouth and led her away from the crowds. 'You look dreadful.'

'Last night...' Lydia began. 'Something awful— that man... He's—' The words stuck – not in her throat, they didn't get that far – in her brain, or perhaps her heart. One day, she knew, she would bury what happened to her. She would hide it away like she once hid Margaret-Doll, but she wasn't ready to do that yet.

Mrs Picard-Richardson placed her index finger to her pouting lips in a look she used to do in the classroom.

'What?' said Lydia. She didn't care about impertinence. She suddenly felt very like a girl from London again and ready for a fight.

'I don't want to know about last night,' Mrs Picard-Richardson said finally.

'But—'

'Just get out there and win some prize money, chérie,' she demanded then she turned on her high heels and left, her back straight and her head like she had a tower of books on it.

Like Lydia, Bertha had also been evacuated and had close ties with her second family. Both Bertha's 'mum' and her 'other mum' were in the audience today. Mum was crying. Other Mum was unwrapping cress sandwiches. Lydia wished she'd let her mummy come today. She wanted to see her sweet, concerned face. There was no one else like her. But Mummy would be at Marjorie's nursery as usual, looking after all those other people's children. She pictured the children, from the stories her mummy told her. This one who liked dancing to Glenn Miller, this one who smacked everything with a wooden spoon, this one who never wore shoes... It all felt a world away from here.

Lydia knew she wasn't going to win today. She wasn't even going to get placed.

Squinting into the sea of faces, she saw Mrs Picard-Richardson, her sweaty husband, and the terrible Mr Raymond, all together, all friends. She no longer wanted to be picked. And she would never speak to any of them again. She had only one mother – only one person who loved her unconditionally – and from now on, she would never forget that.

For the next few nights, Lydia kept waking up gasping, as though something black had descended on her. One time, she woke thinking Rex was whimpering, yet as she crawled over to his basket to console him, she realised Rex was peacefully sleeping, it was she who was making the distressed noises. She felt pinned down, like a wall had collapsed onto her. She felt foolish too, naïve, like she was the one who had made the wall collapse. In the daytime, too, certain things could trigger an association: gin. The word 'modern'. A black briefcase with a copper clasp. Anything to do with Bognor Regis.

And then two weeks later and it had turned from a bad memory into an actual situation.

Her monthlies were late.

From the outset, Lydia knew she wouldn't tell him. She could not. She thought about telling her mother, but although she knew Emmeline would rush in and take care of her, she didn't *want* Emmeline to rush in and take care of her. She pretended to herself it was because Mummy would be too busy with the nursery but the prospect of disappointing her was too painful.

She tried to get in contact with Leonard – hadn't he always

loved her? But he did this overwrought sigh: 'Please, Lydia. I thought you understood.' The *please* especially annoyed her. 'I don't want to break Barbara's heart.'

What's so special about Barbara? Lydia fumed inwardly. Why did Barbara get all the care and attention when she got none?

She tried to rekindle things with Saul, but he had moved to Manchester for work.

'You can visit me here,' he offered, but she had never liked him that much, so she didn't.

She tried to contact Harry, for hadn't Harry had the softest spot for her, ever?

'Lydia Howard, is it?' his mother said her name like it was a swear word.

'Not quite, I'm Lydia Froud,' corrected Lydia. There was a pause.

'I don't think he wants to see you.'

About three weeks after that, while Lydia was still mulling over what to do, Mrs Smart came out to the kennels to tell her that Mrs H was poorly and it was possibly a stroke.

'I'll go to Bumble Cottage after work,' Lydia promised.

'Paul's there,' Mrs Smart added, and it felt outrageous that this piece of information should be an afterthought when it should always be front and centre stage.

'Already?' Lydia asked. Her voice was high-pitched and one of the dogs growled. What did this mean? Things must be bad with Mrs Howard – or had he got fed up with tinkering around on the other side of the world?

And that was when she started thinking.

She did still have options.

She thought of that long-ago September morning in 1939

when they were first evacuated. Valerie had a beautiful suitcase, but Valerie never really cared for beautiful things. Valerie lived in her head – it was Lydia who lived in the real world. Lydia had managed to get that suitcase AND keep the lovely fruit cake that had been offered in exchange. These things weren't impossible. You *could* have your cake and eat it...

71

Lydia

That day, Lydia two-stepped up to her attic room. She had a chance to get out of here. It wasn't that she hated the place, but it was long past time to move on.

'Are you taking Rex?' asked Mrs Smart, daft Mrs Smart.

'Not this time,' Lydia said. She took care over her outfit, eventually choosing the one that had got her second place in the last contest. It was difficult to cycle in heels and a slim-fitting skirt, but it had a helpful slit at her thigh and a bit of resolve can get you a long way.

Paul answered the door at Bumble Cottage. If he was surprised to see her, it didn't show. His hair was longer than it used to be, but other than that he had hardly changed. He was wearing a shirt and tight trousers. Lydia didn't pay much attention to men's clothes, but his clothes were fashionable rather than classic. He looked a tonic.

He kissed her on the cheek, and she thought to herself, 'Ah, this is New York style.'

'How is she?' Lydia asked in a voice that, even to her, sounded too syrupy.

'She's doing better than she was.'

'How about you?'

'I'm managing,' he said and bared his teeth. 'You look different, Lydia.'

'The years do that to you apparently,' she said, and regretted it instantly. Paul had never been a fan of Teasing-Lydia – she'd do better with Concerned-Lydia.

'Can I see Mrs Howard? I've been so worried.'

He told her to go through.

Paul wasn't Mr Purity like he liked to make out. He'd been having it off with that land girl behind everyone's back, after all.

There were two obstacles, as far as Lydia could see. One was Valerie – and the second was timing.

Things had to move quickly, otherwise it wasn't going to work.

As she chatted with poor Mrs H, and held her hand, and held a glass to her dry lips, she looked out of the window towards the barn. He was in there. Her solution was in there. All those years playing 'I'm getting married in the morning!' was in there.

Whereas Paul had swung the Bumble Cottage door wide open, he opened the barn door only slightly.

'What's wrong? Is Mum all right?'

'She's fine. The doctor has arrived, he's pleased with her progress. I came to see you.'

Back at the kennels, she had decided honesty was the best policy. She would tell Paul her situation and see what he thought. She would put forward her idea. What a partner she would be! Devoted. Houseproud. Dog-loving. And he could take it or leave it. But now she had seen him, Lydia wasn't convinced that the truth was the best approach. Paul had got more handsome, more desirable, more successful than ever. His art was selling like hot cakes in America, and in Britain too. She knew people said he could have anyone. Now, she could believe it. Why would he choose the girl he saw as his little sister?

There had to be a way around this.

She looked at his paintings instead of staring at him. She would never understand why he chose fish over dogs.

'Dogs are better,' she said. She had to say something.

He said, 'Dogs are overly sentimental.'

'You say it as though it's a bad thing.'

'It is – in art.'

Although she hadn't come here to argue the point, she couldn't let this go. 'They're not, Paul. Everyone would like a picture of a cute Dalmatian, especially a puppy!'

Rather than a lobster, she didn't say.

He shrugged. The conversation wasn't interesting him. 'The art world says otherwise.'

Paul wasn't pleased when Lydia started undressing. The skirt came off with an easy swoosh. The blouse was more complicated.

'What *are* you doing?' he asked, brows drawing together in alarm.

'Paul,' she said sweetly. This was going to be more difficult than she had thought. But she was mired in this now, entrenched in her position; she had to keep going forward. She stood in her corset, best knickers, stockings and suspenders, still in her heels. She had stood in less in front of crowds of people; that didn't embarrass her – what did was his reaction. She walked over to him and tried to kiss him.

'Paul, I've always been in love with you.'

He looked shocked as he unwrapped her arms from round his waist and held his hands up.

'Woah,' he said.

'Woah, what?'

'Woah, I need time to think,' he said. 'I'm flattered, Lydia.' But he didn't seem flattered, he looked petrified. 'But this has come completely out of the blue.'

'Not to me it hasn't.'

Things had to move quickly.

They kissed. But he still demurred.

'I don't think it's right, Lydia. You're family.'

'It is right, Paul,' she insisted through gritted teeth.

Again, he retreated. He was a cold fish, colder than the bloody fish he painted. She bet he wasn't like this with Valerie. She bet he wasn't like this with the land girl. He wore a belt rather than braces, and she pulled at the buckle ineffectually – the little metal bit wouldn't come out its place – but then it did. It was time to call in the big guns. The clock was ticking.

'Let's just lie down, side by side.'

She put her fingers and mouth everywhere, and then resistance was futile. He was implicated.

Seven weeks later, they told Mrs H, who was unsteady but was getting better.

'Confounding expectations,' Mrs Howard said proudly, and Lydia thought for a moment that she already knew about her and Paul, but then realised she was talking about her own health. She had defied her prognosis.

'Now what's up with you two? You're not looking after more strays, Lydia?'

She smiled indulgently at them both, and then, before Lydia or Paul said anything, her expression changed and Lydia realised she had put two and two together. Lydia didn't ever know how she worked it out, but she did. Mrs Howard had always talked about her strong instincts, honed in the theatre world.

'We're getting married, Mum,' Paul said.

'Who are?'

That cut, Lydia thought, and it was on purpose.

'Me and Lydia.'

'Lydia and I,' corrected Mrs Howard.

'Lydia and you?' quipped Paul. 'That's unexpected.'

'Not as unexpected as you and Lydia, dear,' Mrs H said. There were icicles dripping off every word.

They sat in the living room quietly, as at a funeral, and Lydia remembered the day she'd been told that the Salts had been killed. Her mother had wanted to take her away then, she remembered. She was glad she'd stayed.

When Lydia had told Paul she 'might be' in the family way, four weeks after they'd made love in the barn, he'd slid to the floor with his face in his hands while she'd stared at him impassively. Had his legs really given way or was he just acting? She didn't know.

'It mightn't be that bad,' she told him. 'Or it might be a mistake, it could be nothing, we can wait and see.'

But he had wiped his eyes and said, 'sorry,' and 'very sorry,' and 'what was he thinking?' and 'what did she want to do?' and 'Christ, I don't believe this.'

She didn't like the way he swore. She knew he liked to be rebellious – or, what was the phrase? Avant-garde? But still. It took him about three hours to come round to the idea, but he did come round, as she knew he would – despite his bohemian appearance, despite his creative profession, at heart he was a nice, middle-class boy with a strong moral compass.

Before midnight, she, Lydia Froud, was engaged to Paul Howard.

'Have you asked *her* parents for their permission?' Mrs Howard asked now. It was hard to tell whether she was pleased or not. Not, suspected Lydia, but that wasn't a happy thought, so she blotted it out. Rex had come over with them, so she tickled his head, and here was one person, at least, who looked at her adoringly. (Lydia knew he was not a person really, but still, he was more than a pet.)

'Not yet.'

'That's not respectful, Paul,' Mrs H scolded him.

'We're going to London soon,' he said. He sounded nervous. 'We wanted to do it face to face.'

'Do it quickly, please. There's a reason there's an order to these things. And you can put an announcement in the paper. I will help with the wording if you need. And, Paul...'

She gestured to him to come closer. He went to her side and she whispered something in his ear. Lydia couldn't hear what was said but she could guess, she could definitely guess, and when she heard the reply – 'No, not yet' – she was convinced she had guessed right. Valerie, of course, had wriggled her way in there somewhere.

When Paul came away his face was red, and Paul didn't usually go red, even after he'd played a lot of tennis.

'What did she say then?' Lydia asked pertly.

He shook his head. 'Nothing.'

Of course it was something. Or someone.

72

Emmeline

When Lydia came to look around Valerie's nursery, she was wrapped up in a big coat, even though it was warm. Emmeline thought she looked peaky. She looked different, too, but then maybe that was because the last time she'd seen her daughter was competing at a beauty pageant with a face full of foundation and rouge. She worried something had happened, but Lydia was wreathed in smiles and kisses.

She had brought a friend with her, although he ambled in a good few minutes after Lydia. He'd been having a cigarette outside, apparently. He was very good-looking. Emmeline had a vague recollection of meeting the friend before, but she wasn't sure until Lydia introduced him.

'Paul Howard. You remember, Mummy!'

Ah, the boy from the house where Lydia had been evacuated. Tennis player, painter, fisherman. Wealthy children have a myriad of hobbies.

Lydia had brought them a Victoria sponge in a tin.

A first time for everything!

'Did you make this?' Emmeline asked, peeling off the lid cautiously. She half-expected something terrible to jump out. One of the children at the nursery had recently brought in a frog. Another kept a spider family in a matchbox.

'Of course,' Lydia said, 'I love baking!' She said it more to Paul than her mother. Emmeline didn't say anything. She remembered claiming similar herself back in the day. Lydia set the cake on the table; it had become a little battered on the journey from Somerset.

A few children were crying. Colin was smacking Michael Terry over the head. Dot swept over and grabbed Colin, but Michael was howling. Emmeline picked him up and carried him on her hip, jiggling him a little as she went. His mother was an eminent scientist and was concerned because he was only learning one language. Things were different now from when they ran the wartime nursery, Emmeline and Dot often marvelled. Back then, the women would have left their children with anyone – now, the mothers wanted to know their children would be excelling and improving.

She wondered why Paul-the-friend was here. An interest in childcare? As he surveyed the scene around him, all the colour drained from his face. She remembered when Lydia first visited the wartime nursery and was an absolute pain. Paul, however, seemed like a fish out of water. He almost looked scared.

'Do you want a hold?' she said, offering the little one to Lydia. She turned up her nose. 'The children will have their nap soon.' Emmeline smiled reassuringly. 'It will get quieter then.'

But the noise was terrible now.

'It's like being on a plane,' Paul observed.

She thought that was possibly the strangest and least apt comparison ever, but of course she had never actually been on a plane.

'Do you like flying?' she asked.

He shook his head. 'Hate it.'

She took them into the back room, where Bess was folding clothes. Dot raised her eyebrows at the sight of Lydia and Ellie was smirking. Emmeline knew her staff thought Lydia was spoilt, but out of respect for her, they wouldn't say it. Secretly, she agreed Lydia was a little spoilt, but she didn't know a way back.

Emmeline had never told anyone about Mr Davenport. Maybe she would have told Lydia if Lydia had ever expressed the slightest bit of curiosity, but she did not. No, she would never tell her daughter – what good would it do? Her daughter believed in her parents' marriage the way other people believed in the tooth fairy.

Nowadays, Emmeline almost wondered if her desire – not only for him but in general – had ever really existed. It was like a mythological creature. She faintly recalled her lust for Mr Davenport in her early weeks at the Old Rectory, which had nearly left her banging her head in frustration, and the kisses that had her panting for more, but it felt so remote to her now, it felt as though it happened to someone else, not her.

For different reasons, she and Neville had put all that behind them, and now she no longer felt sad that he didn't want her 'in that way', but relieved. She had work to do! However, Emmeline wanted Lydia – and Matthew too one day, of course – to enjoy passionate marriages, relationships full of love and desire; but she suspected Lydia did not prioritise that highly. Lydia wanted a good match. A wealthy man. Status over sex. Comfort over kisses. And that was her right.

· · ·

Emmeline hadn't had a chance or the money to sort out the nursery kitchen or the office. She looked at her surroundings through Lydia's eyes and saw how shabby they were. On one wall, a calendar was stuck up haphazardly. There were lists everywhere. Notes on every surface.

Do not give Billy milk.

Why does Colin have spots?

Where are Emily's mittens?

Is Len left-handed?

Cath Doctor visit tomorrow at 2.

'What are you two here for anyway?' she asked brightly after Mrs Hodges had excused herself.

'Paul has people to see in London and I decided to come along.'

'Will you stay? Matthew can sleep on the sofa and—'

'It's fine, Mummy.' Lydia took hold of Paul's hand, then cleared her throat. 'We'll be over to see you and Daddy tomorrow afternoon if that's all right...'

She said it so quickly that Emmeline wasn't quite sure she'd heard the 'we' or if it was an 'I' who would be over tomorrow. Paul, staring at the calendar with a blank expression, gave nothing away.

'Of course,' Emmeline said. 'We' – she made the 'we' clear, even if she had no idea what Neville thought about anything – 'will be delighted.'

Tomorrow then, she thought. *Whatever it is, will come out tomorrow.*

'Thank you for coming,' she said.

'My pleasure,' said Lydia. 'I wanted to show Paul around. And I'm proud of my mummy, building all this from scratch.'

Spoilt or not, this girl could melt Emmeline's heart in an instant.

Lydia

Lydia kept hold of Paul's hand as they walked away from Marjorie's, partly to keep him from running. He had clearly taken a turn, and she realised bringing him here mightn't have been such a bright idea after all. She had thought it might bring him round to the idea of babies – she hadn't considered that it might have the opposite effect.

'Our child won't come here,' she said. 'I don't believe in nurseries.'

'How do you mean?' he snapped. 'Do you think we just imagined the whole visit?'

'Ha.'

Paul could be irritating at times. He was very literal, for example. He often pretended he didn't understand her when she was sure he did.

'I mean, I don't see the point of them.'

'That's different then, isn't it, from believing in them?'

Why did he have to be so pedantic? It was like talking to Valerie sometimes. Circling a point, never getting to it.

'I'll stay at home with our babies.'

'Babies?' he repeated in a strangled voice.

Lydia thought of Margaret-Doll and how dearly she had loved her. The hard face and the soft yielding body. Little Margaret-Doll who she used to tuck under her arm like an umbrella and went nowhere without. Plough on, she thought. Ploughing on had never failed her.

'Most of the mothers here work! You wouldn't want me to, would you?'

'I thought you liked your job at the kennels,' Paul said.

'I do. For now. Obviously not once the baby is born!'

'All right,' he said docilely. 'Whatever.'

Sometimes Paul reminded her of the meekest dogs in the kennels. The ones that had been rescued from people who kicked and abused them. But who had kicked him? It was infuriating.

Paul had only come to London to meet his agents and his customers. He liked being in the city, though; she saw him watching everything with a thirsty curiosity. He had that in common with her daddy, she thought. He had recently acquired a camera and he would take photographs, sometimes of the most ridiculous things. She wanted him to take photographs of her – she had come third in a beauty pageant! – didn't she look prettier than most women? But he was more interested in photographing water running down a drainpipe or a stop sign or a taxi's back tyre.

Back at the hotel, she thought they might make love – after all, there was no fear of pregnancy now and the doctor she had seen in Somerset had said it was safe. Yes, she had asked. But Paul winced at the idea and said that he had to go out for meetings.

'Can't I come?' she pouted.

He pulled up his scarf over his mouth.

'Not this time, honey,' he said. Honey. It was an Americanism she liked, but she didn't like him saying no to her.

He said he'd be back later, yet she wasn't sure he would. This wasn't how it was meant to be, was it? Even though it was only 5 p.m., she put on her pretty, short nightie – bought with him in mind – and got into bed.

Once she was alone again, she certainly didn't feel like a princess any more.

74

Emmeline

'Lydia's coming here tomorrow,' Emmeline told Neville as she rushed around, tidying up.

'What does she want?' Neville asked, which wasn't agreeable, but Emmeline was curious about that too. 'Is she coming back to live in London?'

'I doubt it,' Emmeline said, although she would always hope it.

'Probably wants money for another dog.'

As far as Neville was concerned, Lydia lived an uncomplicated country life surrounded by dogs at the kennels. Emmeline was certain that it was a lot more complex than that, but she realised she didn't really know what it was either. She felt like she only ever got to see one side of her daughter and that it was all the other sides that were infinitely more interesting.

She got out the cushions she had been saving for best and a fresh tablecloth. There was talk about do-it-yourself on the wireless. Emmeline had some ideas for wallpaper. Neville said, 'What? Do you think this is an MP's house?' And she bristled.

He loved taking pot shots at her but she wouldn't let the hurt show. Mr Davenport was still her secret, a beautiful heart-breaking secret, but it was all hers. She let herself unwrap and examine it but only late at night.

'No, it's just important to make an effort.'

She listened to all the wireless shows – it had started because it gave her something to talk about with the young women at work, but now she enjoyed them. The ones that little Valerie Hardman made were jolly good. *The Woman on the Clapham Omnibus* was memorable and there was a particularly affecting series about thanking the people who'd done you a good turn.

Emmeline baked all Saturday morning. Usually on a Saturday she did the ordering for the nursery, and accounts and reports, but a visit from Lydia was rarer than a comet, she would get back to them. Emmeline was working on cutting their operation back by using cheaper products at Marjorie's, but Dot wanted her to come up with other ways to save money, too.

She sent Matthew to the shop – twice, because she forgot to tell him to get baking powder the first time.

'All this fuss?' he grunted. At twelve, he was at the age where he grunted more than he spoke.

'She's your sister!' she scolded. Sometimes – often – her family refused to behave in the way families ought to behave, and she found it painful. Then she thought about Mr Davenport, Mrs Salt and Marjorie and pulled herself together. What happened to them was heartbreaking. A son who moaned about errands and a husband with a habit of making digs at her wasn't the end of the world.

She had stopped being resentful of all the time she and Lawrence Davenport never got to have. What was the point of that? She was always learning from the children at the nursery and their short memories and the way that, for them, time was not linear but a series of unrelated incidents. She learned to be grateful instead for the stolen moments she and Lawrence had had together. There had been a depth of feeling. There had been an awakening. It had been short but oh, it was so very sweet.

When Lydia and Paul came to the house that afternoon, Emmeline tried to figure out what was going on. Her daughter looked fuller in the face, that was it. But that didn't have to signify anything. She was wearing a dress for once, a cardigan and high-heeled shoes with exposed toes.

Paul was only marginally more comfortable than he had been yesterday. Neville had heard of him and his art – he was better-known than Emmeline had realised. She supposed he was quite down-to-earth for such a famous person.

'Dad, why don't you show Paul into the parlour?'

'What parlour?' Neville snapped.

Emmeline stared at them. *What is going on?*

'The front room,' Lydia said, blushing. 'We'll stay in the kitchen.'

Neville scoffed. 'There's nothing in there.'

But Lydia persisted. 'Da-ad, Paul wants a word with you in private.'

Paul looked as if he'd like to curl himself into a ball. Emmeline was going to say, 'What's he got to say that he can't say in front of all of us?' but she stopped herself as she realised.

She watched Neville and Paul walk slowly into the other room like they were following a coffin. She wanted to say to Lydia, 'What on earth have you done?' but she couldn't. She felt like she didn't know her daughter well enough.

75

Lydia

As they walked to the railway station, Lydia kept saying, 'That went well' as though if she said it enough times it would come true.

Daddy had looked shell-shocked when he came out of the front room/parlour but he didn't say anything to Mummy, he just pinged his braces, then picked up the newspaper and went back to where he'd left off. Mummy had looked bewildered, but Lydia kissed her and said, 'Daddy will explain. We have to get back.'

Once they got back to Somerset, Paul escaped straight to his barn. He didn't do emotions, either, which he blamed on boarding school.

But you're not there now, Lydia thought.

She didn't know where she should go. Officially, she still lived in the attic room at the Smarts', but she missed her old room at Bumble Cottage and didn't she belong in the house? Especially now she and Paul were engaged.

She followed him to the barn – she didn't know what else to do – and watched him painting. She felt like this was a way to get to know him better. He coloured the whole canvas straight away, slopping on paint as if in a hurry. Only later came the fine strokes and the care and the detail. But if he didn't like something, he just obliterated it, he didn't mess around trying to improve it.

'I like that bit there,' Lydia said helpfully.

It was a posy. He was trying to branch out from fish, but neither his buyers nor his agent wanted him to. It was torment for him, but he persisted, doing double the work. Some fish for his regular customers, some flowers for his self-esteem.

'Can you not watch? It puts me off,' he said after a short while.

She thought, I'm your future wife, but she knew he wouldn't like that. 'I think it's beautiful!'

'I just don't like people seeing my unfinished work.'

'We've known each other all our lives, Paul – I've seen the unfinished you a thousand times.'

He rolled his eyes.

She picked up her suitcase again. It occurred to her that it was one of the only things she had left from her old life. Everything about her, from her platinum hair to her high-heeled shoes, had changed remarkably – beyond recognition even, a complete reinvention – but not this suitcase. She thought again about Margaret-Doll, buried not far from here, and it made her feel emotional.

'I'll go back to the Smarts' then, if you're working tonight.'

He gave her a chaste kiss on the cheek, promised he'd see her in a day or two. He was much quieter than Lydia remembered. Where was the rambunctious boy, always bashing things or yelling? She tried not to be disappointed by it. He's an artist, she told herself. They're known for needing a lot of time alone.

Look at – she couldn't think of a living famous artist to compare him to – Michelangelo.

But Paul wasn't alone. He went out drinking with his friends and he made phone calls in the evening, and one time she thought she heard Valerie's voice.

The next few weeks felt like a dream to Lydia, almost as if they weren't really happening. She couldn't help thinking – *is this my life?*

She did go back to Bumble Cottage: she had thought about moving into Valerie's old room – since she wasn't an evacuee any more, she would shortly be the woman of the house – but she realised her room was the bigger and brighter one. One day, she might share Paul's. One day, they would have Mrs H's.

This was better than living at the Smarts' – she would walk there and back for work – and Rex was happy wherever she was. She had thought this would be the last summer of the beauty pageants, but no, she was liberated from that – or, rather, the baby growing inside her had liberated her from all that.

Every morning, without fail, her first waking thought was *where am I?*, which was strange because it hadn't been like that when she first came here.

Mrs H wasn't in the best of health and Lydia did her best to get people in to look after her.

'Where's Valerie?' Mrs H asked a lot.

'Working,' Lydia explained. 'Don't worry, I'm here.'

The question of Valerie was on Lydia's mind a lot, too. Was Valerie still pining for Paul? Lydia feared this, and felt her old friend needed to be set straight.

'Paul, you've got to tell her soon.'

'Tell her what?'

'That we're... you know...'

'I'll tell her when I see her,' Paul said.

He was exasperating.

'And when will that be?'

'At the exhibition?' he suggested. He was putting on an exhibition at a prestigious gallery in London; it was to be his introduction into the UK art scene. Many people were invited to the launch, including Valerie.

Lydia tsked but she understood why Paul didn't want to be alone with Valerie when he broke the news. He was hoping other people would shield him from her reaction – he could be cowardly.

His artworks were wrapped and wrapped again in newspapers until they had doubled in size, rather like the way Lydia felt she was going. The packages made her think of fish and chips. (She was also hungry constantly.)

The packages arrived in London before they did and, by the time they got to the gallery, the artworks had been unpacked and mostly hung on the walls.

'They're magnificent,' she breathed. She knew Paul didn't particularly value her views yet he liked her to be encouraging. When she once asked, 'Can't you paint me?' he became furious and said, 'Why do you always ask me that?' even though it was the first and would be the last time she'd ever said it.

Paul and his agent were watching a group of young staff debating where to hang the last pictures that had been flown in from New York. Lydia watched them. It was going to be a long day. Paul's agent was very kind to Lydia and she liked him enormously, until Paul said dismissively, 'He's like that to everyone. He's a charmer, it's his job.'

Paul said he didn't have strong feelings about where the pictures should hang or which one was to take pride of place or which one should go across from that window because of the lovely light, but he had told Lydia that some of the curators had no idea.

She sidled over to him. 'Are you worried about seeing Valerie?'

'No.'

Sometimes, she thought he lied about everything.

Lydia had wanted to be there when Valerie arrived – she told herself it was because they were once as close as sisters but she knew it was really because she wanted to keep a watchful eye over all hers and Paul's interactions. But she had already spent three hours at the gallery, shadowing Paul's every move, and he was growing more irritable with her by the second.

She went outside and drank some water in the dying sunshine. Now she was expecting, she was thirstier than she used to be. Then she had to go to the Ladies again. She was weeing more than she used to as well. She wasn't sure if she was imagining it. She had no one to ask about such private things – everyone would disapprove at one or other aspect of how she'd ended up here. Even Betsy and Flora. *Especially* Betsy and Flora. Bertha. Mrs Picard-Richardson. Francine. Valerie... No one would have a good word to say.

She was still in the cubicle fixing her suspenders when she heard two women gossiping at the sinks.

'Is the woman following him everywhere his fiancée?'

'He won't settle down, that one.'

'He's like his father.'

Lydia held up her head and came out, with exuberant 'Excuse mes!,' and made her way back into the exhibition. There were security guards, cloakroom attendants and pretty girls loading up trays of alcohol. And then she saw them: Paul, with Valerie. And it felt like everything stopped. They were hugging in the middle of the room and they looked natural together, like they had been hugging all their lives, and it made her heart sink.

She wished Valerie had never come to Bumble Cottage. It was all better before then, best when it was just Francine, her and Paul. He used to give her piggybacks around the garden, pull at the bows in her hair: *last one's a rotten egg.* She used to give him her Brussels sprouts, her lettuce, her puddings. It was simple, until Valerie came and he stopped giving her his time.

76

Emmeline

A few days after Lydia and Paul's visit, when Emmeline was still trying to make sense of it all, Dot greeted her in a miserable voice from behind the copper saucepans in the nursery kitchen.

'What is it?'

Dot wasn't pregnant again, was she?

'I'll tell you later.'

'Tell me now,' Emmeline insisted. They had twenty minutes before the 'invasion' of the early birds. They could talk while they prepared the activities for the day. She planned to do shadow puppets in the back room. Emmeline could only ever do dogs or crocodiles although some of the other girls could invent wonderful, magical creatures.

'I think we've got six months left, eight months at most,' Dot said.

'What?' said Emmeline. While she was aware the accounts weren't brilliant, she hadn't realised it was that bad.

'The nursery,' clarified Dot. 'We don't have enough money

to go on. We have to pay the girls, we have to pay ourselves – we have to buy food... We can't just keep borrowing, Emmeline.'

'We can,' Emmeline's voice was wobbling.

'We can't,' Dot said firmly.

Emmeline sat down. She couldn't imagine her life without the nursery. She could lose herself in the children. When she was in their worlds, their beautiful, wonderous worlds, she felt no pain, no loss. Everything felt right at Marjorie's – she had that rare certainty that she was in the right place, right time, with the right people. But apparently not with the right accounts.

Being with the children was probably the only time when Emmeline was not in mourning. She had got through her grief because she had the nursery. She had chubby-legged children with elastic-band wrists, and curly hair and learning to toddle and learning to say thank you and learning to write their name, every single day.

And now, it looked like she wouldn't have that for much longer.

'There are no more government or council grants we can apply for?'

'I've applied for them all. Women and children just aren't a priority.'

She remembered Councillor Arscott saying that a long time ago. Not in wartime, and not in peacetime either.

'There must be something,' Emmeline said guiltily. She had promised she would find ways to save money, yet she hadn't done so.

'There isn't.'

'We've *always* found something...'

Dot shrugged. 'The only thing...' she began slowly.

'What, Dot?' Emmeline said.

'No, it's—'

'If you have an idea, tell me!' Emmeline squealed, since she had nothing, no idea at all.

'You wouldn't go and see Mrs Davenport, would you?' She's an MP now. And she talks a lot about women's issues.'

'No. No way!'

'She remarried, you know,' Dot said quietly.

How did Dot always know these things?

Emmeline pulled a face. 'I'm still not going.'

The Old Rectory had been tidied up a little around the front, and there was a swanky silver car in the drive, but other than that Emmeline couldn't see that much had changed. She had asked Matthew and Neville if they wanted to come up to Norfolk for a trip, but there was football to shout about and Neville thought it was pointless anyway, so she had come alone. Dot would have come, but she was needed at the nursery, still poring over the books, looking for an extra number or a decimal point that would make the difference.

Going cap in hand to his widow? Would Mr Davenport have wanted her to do it, she wondered? He might have said, 'It is just...politics,' and 'Follow your dreams, Mrs Froud!'

Or he might not.

A housekeeper invited her into the drawing room, where Mrs Davenport – now Mrs Reynolds – was expecting her. This was very different from before, yet the room looked much the same too, although perhaps it was slightly more organised – the papers were in stacks and the blankets were neatly folded over the chairs.

Mrs Reynolds welcomed her, then invited her to sit. She was as confident and certain as ever, and she put on her glasses to concentrate. Emmeline couldn't tell if she was pleased to see her or not. She never could work out what was on her mind.

Mrs Reynolds had stood in the by-election precipitated by

Mr Davenport's death. Emmeline had read about it in the news-papers. 'It was always an ambition of mine,' she was quoted as saying. 'Perhaps I should have stood years ago – but things were different for women then.'

Emmeline laid out the case for nurseries, as she had in this room once before. Mr Reynolds, now with full black beard like a Russian or a philosopher, came in but nodded at her to continue. Emmeline explained how the nurseries needed either national or local government help.

'Enabling mothers to work – if they wish to do so – is vital,' she agreed when Emmeline had finished. She spoke like she was making a speech to a large crowd. 'We *need* affordable nurs-eries – and you're right, Mrs Froud, the government does need to contribute. This is something I'm going to advocate.'

'That's amazing,' Emmeline said. She was truly touched. Mrs Davenport – no, Mrs Reynolds – still believed in the nurs-eries; she might even have believed in them all along.

'Thank you for coming.'

Mrs Reynolds got up and Emmeline realised the meeting was over. She hadn't got to ask for what she needed yet.

'There is... I mean... the problem is, until that day when our nurseries are funded, we need help. Perhaps' – Emmeline hated herself now. Hated asking for anything. Knew that Mrs Reynolds would always see her as someone who did all the taking and never gave. Why wouldn't she? That was how it had been with them all along – 'you could make a contribution now?'

Mrs Reynolds was smooth as glass. 'Everything I have is invested in my campaigns, I'm afraid.' She took off her glasses and blinked like an owl. 'I do support the nurseries though, and you have my word, I will see what I can do.'

Realising that further resistance was probably futile, Emme-line shook the woman's hand, her heart feeling tight.

'Thank you.'

Mrs Reynolds escorted her to the doorstep where Matthew had once thrown up and where Mr Davenport had welcomed them, telling them everything would be all right. And there, she met Emmeline's eyes. 'I know my ex-husband was in love with you,' she said in a much lower voice. 'I can see why.'

Before Emmeline could say anything else, the door had closed.

77

DECEMBER 1951

Lydia

Lydia and Paul married in the church where Paul's parents had married. It was a family tradition.

'Don't let that put you off,' Paul said.

She didn't know if he was being funny or not.

'And one day, our baby will marry there, too,' Lydia told him, cupping the curve of her stomach. It wasn't quite a bump, it was a mound maybe, but she watched it constantly, like it was a volcano about to erupt.

Mummy and Daddy came. They scrubbed up well. Matthew came too, sullen and long-limbed. Lydia had said, 'Does he have to?' and Mummy had looked astonished and just said, 'Lydia!', which meant he did.

Lydia had said she was surprised her mother would take a day off from other people's babies and her mother had looked so hurt that she wished she hadn't said that. What was wrong with her? She found herself saying nasty things a lot.

'Of course I'll come, of course!' Mummy had kept saying over and over. 'You're my daughter. I love you.'

'I know, Mummy,' Lydia had said, 'I didn't mean it, it was just nerves.'

And her mother had kissed her and said, 'You have *nothing* to be nervous about – after all, you love him and he loves you.'

Lydia crossed her fingers – one of those things was true. The other, she was working on.

Her wedding gown was just about the most expensive item of clothing she'd ever had. And then it cost more to have it let out again. Lydia told the dressmaker that the bump made a great shelf, but the dressmaker hadn't laughed and Lydia had hastily said that she had always had 'terrible wind'.

Paul wore his shell-shocked expression throughout the service and Lydia wished he would at least close his mouth, or flatten his wild hair. He looked like someone had knocked water over his canvases. Rex, however, was the most fantastic best man/pageboy she could have asked for. If people thought she and Paul had nothing in common, they had no idea how much they both doted on the dog – even if they couldn't agree on his name. (Paul still thought calling him T.Rex was droll.)

After the church, they went back to Bumble Cottage so that Mrs H, who was largely chair-bound, could join in the celebrations. Lydia found herself creeping around, listening to other people's conversations while she fiddled with a button or put ice in another drink.

'I knew he was in love with an evacuee, but I didn't know it was that one,' someone said, or did Lydia imagine that? She thought she heard things all the time. It was just like with her memories – she became less sure if she'd experienced them or just imagined them. Everything seemed unlikely. Had she really dug a hole in the garden and buried Margaret-Doll?

'Valerie is a bigwig in wireless now...'

'Can you be a bigwig in wireless?'

The people talking both laughed, the laughs of people who haven't hesitated to avail themselves of the free champagne.

'What does this one do, then?'

'She works with animals apparently.'

'She'll be able to tame Paul then!'

'No one tames a Howard. Mind you, she looks like she would win a wrestling contest.'

'Is it a shotgun wedding then?'

'That or she lost her figure quickly.'

'Shhh.'

They realised she was there, listening.

'Wonderful day!' the women said, unperturbed, raising their glasses. 'Congratulations!'

One of Paul's friends was a professional photographer and had agreed to take their photographs. Paul had arranged this – you would have thought he'd organised the entire day, the fuss he made about it. The photographer set up his tripod in the garden and got under the blanket, one arm up in the air like the hand of a clock, and she thought, *why is he taking so long?*

Her smile was making her face ache; every part of her was stretching, her clothes over her belly, her skin, her lips – her fingers were almost too fat for the wedding ring. After the baby was born, she would pop back, slack, like the elastic in a game of cat's cradle.

'I'll stay if you want,' Mummy whispered. Why did she always look so concerned? 'Let me know if you need me.'

'I don't, Mummy,' Lydia told her proudly. 'I'm a married woman now!'

How she loved saying that! *A married woman!*

She was wiped out. Paul was going to stay up late with his friends, but she was so tired, she whistled for Rex and went up to bed – in the room she had lived in since she was nine years old.

78

Emmeline

They were going to send out the letter in two months and they would give the parents two months' notice after that. Emmeline had retyped it several times, determined to get it just right. All the staff had signed it. Regrets. Apologies. No options. The nursery was going to have to close.

Many of the mothers would have to give up their jobs and stay at home. Others might be able to find a place at another nursery, but there would be competition for those and they might be more expensive because of the higher demand – and they didn't have Emmeline's generous rates. Longer-term, the outcome for most would probably be having to make a choice between career or family, with nary the opportunity for both.

Emmeline and Dot were doing the last jobs in the kitchen before going home. It had been another eventful day; Little Billy Touson who played drums had poked his drumstick into Ruby Waite's eye. Fortunately, no real damage was done, but it created quite the disturbance. They had been putting on a concert, which in Emmeline's mind was their last hurrah. The children were singing 'Teddy Bears' Picnic'.

Dot put on the wireless. Emmeline didn't mind it at work so much these days. It could be quite cheery, compared to the horror of the war years, at least.

And in the news today, the Right Honourable Mrs Reynolds, the MP of King's Lynn, has crossed the floor of the House to join the opposition. We can see them congratulating her.

'What's happening?' breathed Emmeline.

Dot shrugged.

And do we know why she has moved? the commentator asked.

Apparently the MP has been interested in nurseries for some time – ever since the first wartime nurseries came into being – and she is impatient with the lack of progress on the issue. If you remember, she was married to the late Lawrence Davenport MP, who played an instrumental role in setting up the scheme. It seems she has carried that interest on and is keen on forcing the Government to act. And here she is speaking now.

Mrs Reynolds' voice rang out:

I truly believe women should be supported in bringing up their children – funding nurseries creates opportunities and benefits not only those most deprived but everyone. I saw that first-hand during the war. I propose a motion that the government provides support to childcare providers by taking on some of the financial costs.

Dot and Emmeline looked at each other, eyebrows raised.

And then another person spoke:

Is it the taxpayer's responsibility to support feckless women to take time off from their parenting duties?

Mrs Reynolds did a big pantomime laugh.

That's not what this is. This policy is to enable those parents – mostly mothers – who want to continue to contribute economically to the nation to be freer to make their way.

And now, said the commentator, *something that will be a lot more interesting to the majority of our listeners than nurseries: the cricket scores.*

Dot clicked off the wireless.

'She talks the talk,' she said. 'But can she walk the walk?'

'Too late to save us, whatever she does,' mused Emmeline. 'Far too late.'

'We've still got a few months!' Dot reminded her, heartily. 'Anything could happen!' But Emmeline knew that her friend believed it was over too. She'd seen the job adverts that Dot had circled, in the newspaper, for cleaners and shop assistants. 'Must have experience,' they all said. Dot would struggle to find a different kind of work – but then so probably would she.

As they locked up, Dot slung her arm round Emmeline. 'We did try,' she said. 'You can't say we didn't give it a good go.'

'It's not over yet!'

Now it was Emmeline's turn to remind Dot.

Emmeline walked home slowly; she was never in a hurry to get back to the flat. There was clearance work and building work everywhere. The country was rebuilding – while she herself was dismantling.

She felt hollowed out from it all. To lose one nursery was unfortunate, to lose two was agony, and her grief at Mr Davenport's death was again back with her in full force. It did that nowadays: she would be bumbling along thinking everything was all right, then it would hit her in the solar plexus. Mr Davenport had thought she could do anything. *She* had thought she could do anything. But it was as though without him there to believe in her, like Tinkerbell without the applause, some kind of magic spell had broken.

What was the point of anything? She had tried. She had tried and failed. Everything she did turned to dust. And now she would have to spend the next few months trying to find new nurseries for some of the children or consoling those parents for whom a new nursery would be out of their reach.

She took a diversion across a park where young mothers pushed prams or sat on benches in the late afternoon sun. It reminded her of when she and Dot had just met each other in Norfolk and the beginning of their grand plans.

The wartime nurseries had been a success, she reminded herself. The peacetime nurseries had been a success too – for a while. And if they'd had more funding, they would have been a success for a long while to come. Perhaps forever. But no one wanted to spend money on women and children. As priorities went, they remained pretty low.

Emmeline felt privileged that in her nursery work she was often the recipient of a child's first word. Dot and the others had a theory that the first word was an indicator of a child's personality. It was just a joke, but now when Emmeline thought about it – *More. War. Cat. Kiss. Cake. Mama. Love You. Goodbye. All Gone* – it seemed to be the story of her life.

She smiled at the young women in the park, but they were caught up in each other and their children and didn't notice her. She wanted to go over and say, 'The years go by so fast!' But she knew it would mean nothing to them, not when their days went so slowly.

One of the mothers picked up her son from his pram and held him up in the air so he was looking down at her face. He was laughing a little two-tooth laugh. How she missed the Matthew and Lydia from back then. How she missed so much— But she couldn't live like that, she must keep in the here and now.

When she got back, Neville said he'd just warmed up the soup: 'Do you want to dish up?'

Marjorie's had less than four months left. What could possibly change in that time? Surely, they had come to the end of the road. As Emmeline spooned up the liquid, the carrots and the parsnips, she was assailed by memories – the Norfolk nursery's opening day, the children arriving, the gratitude of the mothers, the stocks at the autumn fayre, country dancing – and she could feel the tears coming again.

'Thank you for the soup, Neville.' Unlike him, she wouldn't point out that it needed salt.

Neville looked up. 'Don't say I don't do anything for you.'

'Don't,' she told him. 'Just hold me. Just for one minute. Please.'

He grimaced, but he rested his cigarette on the ashtray, got up, came round the table and put his arms round her as she had asked.

'What's all this about then, eh?' he said.

And she sobbed.

79

MARCH 1952

Lydia

Lydia packed everything she'd need in the hospital into the suitcase Valerie had given her, so long ago now. On top, she put the beautiful blanket that a friend of her mother – a friend she had never heard of – had knitted.

When she went into labour, Paul, who could not drive – who claimed he'd never needed to in New York! – suggested she got the bus to the hospital. She could have drawn her nails down his face, she was that furious with him. And she was frightened. She aspired to be like the dog-mothers who took themselves off and delivered their pups themselves, but she had a feeling this wouldn't be her.

'I'll sort something out,' he said quickly. He'd gone white.

'It's too late,' she said bitterly. Wasn't this typical of him?

He went out and when he eventually came back, he was with a friend who said he could drive them in his work vehicle. It was a vegetable van. Her husband had got a vegetable van to take her to hospital, for heaven's sake!

She arrived stinking of cabbage. She was only a little

dilated, but the doctor who examined her said they'd keep her in and watch her progress. When she reported back to Paul, he said, 'I don't know what any of that means,' even though she'd given him a book on childbirth. She sensed this lack of understanding was a deliberate choice on his part. He liked being ignorant about certain things.

He said he'd go off to find the canteen.

'You've only just had your lunch.'

'For later,' he said indignantly, 'you said best to be prepared!'

She missed her mummy. She'd promised, 'I'll come as soon as you want me,' but Lydia didn't want to have to ask. She wanted her here, by the bedside, now. She kept thinking of her mummy's sweet face when she'd given Lydia her Christmas present, full of excited anticipation – 'Margaret-Doll deserves a cosy place to sleep too' – and it made her want to cry.

While her husband was on the prowl for food, a different nurse arrived and Lydia was relieved because, unlike some of them, she seemed to know what she was doing. Her hair was in a fashionable bowl cut and she had pretty shoes on with her starched apron. She studied Lydia's notes, then looked up in surprise: 'You're one of the evacuees?'

'That's right.'

'And you decided to stay on in the West Country?'

'Yes,' Lydia said proudly. She had adopted this land, she supposed, and she thought – although others disagreed – that was even more special than being born to it.

'I knew an evacuee girl once. I don't suppose...'

Lydia sighed to herself, but she knew that it would be a bad idea to get on the wrong side of this nurse.

'What was her name?' she asked dutifully.

'Valerie Hardman.'

Lydia might have guessed. Over the past few weeks, it felt like Valerie was haunting her. It was the little things. Lydia might be enjoying a lovely show on the wireless about puppies and then at the end it would say, 'and this was produced by Miss Valerie Hardman.' Or she found things of Valerie's left in Bumble Cottage – a once-white vest, a tortoiseshell hairclip.

'I know her. We were evacuated together.'

The nurse looked shocked. Although she had asked, she didn't seem to have expected that.

'How is she? She was such a lovely girl. My heart went out to her.'

Lydia thought, *I'm lying here with my feet in stirrups, and you want to talk about my husband's ex-girlfriend?* It felt like there was no escape. She wanted to get up and walk out of there – no, *she* wanted to stay – she just wanted this nurse to disappear.

'She's fine,' she said coolly.

Perhaps the nurse heard the frostiness in her tone, or realised that this was an inappropriate conversation, because she busied herself with the equipment and the checks. Soon, they were making other, more fitting conversation like 'do you have names?' instead.

The pain was building. Lydia chewed her lip as waves of agony washed over her. She didn't know if she was going to survive this. Why didn't people say how dreadful childbirth was? The book on childbirth that she'd given Paul had clearly glossed over it for some reason. How did people do this more than once? Why hadn't Mummy warned her?

Knowing Paul was pacing on the other side of the door, like the husbands did in films, didn't help. Only after the midwife told him he could go home – 'Have a rest, you'll need it!' – and she was sure he'd left the building did her labour start to progress more rapidly.

'You're doing well,' the nurse said. Lydia gripped her hand

and didn't yell. She wanted the nurse to be pleased. If she saw Valerie again, she wanted the woman to be able to report that 'Lydia was ever so brave'.

The agony continued and the nurse, who by now Lydia adored, finished her shift and skipped off home, and a different nurse came. By this point, Lydia was beyond caring if she knew Valerie or if she thought Lydia was brave or not. As she gripped the new nurse's hand, the unfortunate replacement yelped, 'Not so tight!'

But Lydia couldn't help it. And then the awful, the magnificent, splitting-into-two sensation. The baby was coming out, the baby was coming!

'I can't!' she shrieked.

'You can!' the nurse insisted.

And the sudden release, the sweet evacuation from her body. There it was, slippery as an eel. She had spent so long staring at Paul's bloody fish paintings that she was almost surprised it was human.

It was a tiny little girl, shaped like a sweet, and she was everything.

Paul came to visit the next morning. He was shy, and undone, somehow. His hair was wet and his eyes were red. He was too nervous to pick the baby up; he just stood above the cot, peering down at her.

Lydia tried twisting her wedding ring round her finger. It still hardly budged, but surely it would soon. She was looking forward to her body becoming her own again.

'Are you happy, Paul?'

'Very,' he said, but he wouldn't meet her eye.

Another nurse came over and stared at the clipboard at the end of Lydia's bed. 'Congratulations,' she said 'The baby is a very healthy weight, considering she's so early.'

'Hear that, Paul,' Lydia said without missing a beat. 'She's a healthy weight.'

'Your mother is here,' Paul said.

'How did she...?'

'I called her,' he said guiltily. 'I'm sorry.'

Mummy crept into the room slowly, as though uncertain how she'd be received, but Lydia held out her arms and she dashed into them. Mummy told her how brave she was, and how serene the baby was, and Lydia's heart was full.

'She's a healthy weight, Mummy,' Lydia said.

Everything was going to be all right now.

'What are you naming her?' her mother asked.

'We haven't decided—' Paul began.

'I have!' interrupted Lydia and he gave her a dark look, which she ignored, and moved away.

'Don't laugh,' Lydia warned.

Mummy looked nervous. 'Why would I? What is it?'

'Margaret!' she said, and if Mummy thought it was funny Lydia naming her baby after her one and only doll, she didn't say it.

Paul just stood there in the shadows, blinking slowly, the corners of his mouth turned down.

Lydia had a recurring dream where Paul unearthed Margaret-Doll from the bottom of the garden and screeched at her, 'Look at how you treat those you love.'

She would wake up to find him snoring lightly – obliviously – beside her. It was doubtful that he thought that about her – he didn't think much beyond his paintings, his fishing and his tennis.

And the wireless; he always made a beeline for that.

Apart from the dreams, though, Lydia loved her life in Bumble Cottage. Mrs H was still poorly, and they had a lot of people coming in to see to her, but the housekeeper took care of them and Lydia managed to avoid most of it. Her world was mostly just her and the baby. Paul wasn't the most devoted husband, but these were the compromises you had to make. He'd agreed to a second child in theory – certainly no more – and in return she was the most supportive wife you could ask for. She made sure Margaret didn't bother him and she didn't ask him to do much for them. Sometimes he volunteered to push the pram around the garden and once he even brushed her fine baby hair.

Over the next months, Paul's career continued on its upward trajectory (a fact that surprised Lydia, seeing as he seemed to do very little to make that happen). In some quarters, Lydia became held up as an exemplar of how a wife should conduct herself. She espoused 'traditional, old-fashioned' values. The wife at home supporting the world-renowned artist. What her nursery-obsessed mother thought about that, she didn't say.

Lydia, with Margaret on her hip, was even featured in a magazine article, 'The artist and his muse – the Ex-beauty queen and the King of Paint'. And although Lydia thought it a nonsense – Paul's muses were more likely mackerel or plaice than her – she carefully cut out the article and put it in a scrapbook for Margaret to enjoy one day.

It's ours, all ours, she would often think, looking around Bumble Cottage with satisfaction. She had everything she had set her sights on.

80

MAY 1952

Emmeline

Emmeline spent the weekend in Somerset with her daughter and son-in-law and her adorable baby granddaughter. Neville stayed back in London with Matthew. Paul might be a cold fish – no pun intended – but he was unfailingly polite and when she came to see Lydia – this was her third visit since the baby – he never made Emmeline feel that she was intruding. She liked him and it felt like he might like her.

She was careful with Lydia and with Margaret. She wasn't quite walking on eggshells but she was trying not to be overbearing. She did not see herself as an expert, but Lydia thought she saw herself in that way.

'How's the nursery?' Lydia asked.

'We're closing it down,' Emmeline announced with a mouthful of scone. Lydia felt strongly about baking, cream and jam and the correct order of things, although sometimes Emmeline felt that it was a role she was playing rather than a serious interest.

'I don't believe it!'

Emmeline was holding Margaret. The beautiful swirl of golden hair sometimes reminded her of Marjorie's children and sometimes of the Salt children. Margaret – '*do not call her Maggie!*'– was such a special little thing and Lydia was a more wonderful mother than Emmeline could have imagined.

She had heard about this, this bolt of love for one's grandchildren, but she had never given it much thought. Here it was, and it was amazing.

Margaret didn't make the loss of the nursery any less heartbreaking, but she was a good distraction. It sometimes seemed to Emmeline that life was a series of distractions to help you overcome one tragedy and the next. She still occasionally went to church, but although she enjoyed it, it never quite gave her the relief she sought. Mr Davenport did not deserve to die like that. This was what she knew.

'It's true. We can't afford to run it any more. We get no help, nothing, and if we put the prices up, the parents will leave. Most of them are already stretched financially.'

'After all your work? You made it such a beautiful place!'

The compliment, given spontaneously, warmed Emmeline through, until Lydia made her next point: 'I don't see how you can't just put some more money in.'

'We're not rich, Lydia!'

Sometimes, Emmeline wondered about the world her daughter had inhabited for the last fifteen years. Lydia had no idea about scrimping and saving. She had been plucked out of a normal existence to live in luxury. Didn't she realise that most people's lives were not like that?

'I know that, but can't you get more loans?'

'We're still paying one back.' Emmeline sighed. 'It's all arranged. The letters have been sent out. There's just one month left and then goodbye, Marjorie's,' she said, the brutality of her words hiding her hurt.

Some of the mothers had cried. Mrs Frost, who'd lost her

own mother recently, had sat in storytime corner with her head in her hands: 'What am I going to do?' God-fearing Mrs Everett had sworn, and Mr Maynard, Maureen's widowed father, had punched the palm of his hand. Mrs Williams, who had three children – twins and a baby – said she'd have to drop out of university. And practical Mrs Keller who did something in a bank said, 'Can't we pay you more or something?'

Emmeline explained that they would have to charge a lot more just to break even and most families wouldn't be able to afford it. She and Dot had looked into everything. They had begged the council; they had written to their MPs. Running a nursery was expensive, there were corners that just couldn't be cut.

Still, when Margaret gazed into Emmeline's eyes, Emmeline no longer felt as lost as she had. At least she had her children and grandchildren. Marjorie and Mrs Salt were always with her, tucked in her heart, a bittersweet reminder to be grateful for what she had.

Lydia got up and rummaged in her handbag.

'I'll sort it.'

'Don't be daft!' Emmeline snapped, and Margaret blinked in surprise, her little face falling – she was about to cry.

'There, there, Margaret, Nanny didn't mean to frighten you.'

Undeterred, Lydia was writing a cheque.

'Will that be enough?' With a flourish, she held up the slip of paper, with the handwriting that Emmeline knew intimately from all the years of her letters. She squinted at it over Margaret's shoulder.

'No! You can't.'

'You're doing a great job,' Lydia said. 'And this is just to tide you over. One day, you'll get support from other places, won't you? Isn't that what all the discussions in Parliament are about?'

'But—'

'I want to.' Lydia shrugged as though that decided it.

'You don't agree with it, you've never liked it... you were always against it!'

'I know,' Lydia said. 'I still am. But that doesn't mean I want it to fail. Not after all the love and work you've put in.'

Emmeline couldn't believe it. She briefly wondered what Mr Davenport would say to this. He'd smile at her: *take it, that's politics*. She tried not to dwell on Mr Davenport and what might have been anymore. It was too painful. She had made her life with Neville and it wasn't a bad life after all. Forgiveness and tolerance kept them together. An understanding of what they were and what they were not. They both adored their granddaughter, they both found Paul and his profession a little odd and they had started talking again. It had happened so gradually that Emmeline almost didn't notice it. And now, she and Neville shared private jokes about Paul's fish: 'Cod you believe it?' 'Meet me at your Plaice'. Neville had declared himself the champion after his: 'Tunaver, close your eyes when you kiss me,' which even Emmeline had to admit was pretty good.

Perhaps Emmeline should have remembered that Neville had a sense of humour, but for a long time he hadn't been interested in making her laugh. And now he was. But sometimes certain ideas, special words, took her back to a moment in time when her life was going down a very different path – passion, intellectual stimulation, the company of a soulmate... She pulled herself together. Her daughter was offering her, and the nursery, a way out. She couldn't accept it, though. Or could she?

'Who do I make it payable to? Marjorie's Nursery?'

'You'd do that for us?' Emmeline asked with tears in her eyes. It was like being granted a wish by a genie – this would keep them from going under for the next four or five years.

'Yes, because I know it will make you happy.' Lydia leaned towards her mother. 'Who else would I do it for? All these years, you thought I just wanted to marry a wealthy man for fun? You think I didn't want to take care of my family? I'm a rich, married lady now and *I* get to choose what I spend our money on. And I choose you. That's what it's all about really, isn't it?'

Emmeline faltered, suddenly unsure of everything she thought she knew. Perhaps she had never truly understood her girl. Lydia had been an enigma to her, perhaps from even before the evacuation. But Emmeline had loved her. They had loved each other – whether they understood each other or not – and now Lydia had grown up. She was different from how Emmeline had expected her to turn out – and that was okay. Your children didn't have to have the same outlook on life as you – in fact, perhaps it was important they didn't. Growing up in a different generation is a powerful thing – almost as powerful as genetics – and now there was a cheque on the table that would be a lifeline for the nursery and for so many parents and children.

Lydia would experience this difference in outlook with Margaret one day, Emmeline didn't doubt it. But for now, the only thing that mattered was that Lydia cared about her family as much as Emmeline did – and she wanted to show it in the very best way she could.

'Are you sure?'

'Absolutely.'

'And Paul?'

'You're family, Mummy, he loves you.'

'Thank you!' It was all she could say. Words would never be enough.

'You're welcome.' Lydia winked at her. 'Oh, and you said you'd never seen the end of *Rebecca*?' She shoved a slick paperback at her. 'You can read it now.'

As she flicked through the pages, the words blurred. She could hold back the tears no longer. She vaguely remembered recounting the story to Lydia of the poor trapped bird in the cinema and thinking Lydia did not appear to be listening. It seemed that, as a parent, this was another thing she had got wrong: she had underestimated her daughter. She sobbed, resolving never ever to do that again.

'Hand over my baby, Mummy, and you can celebrate with another scone,' Lydia said.

Emmeline wasn't ready to celebrate the saving of the nursery just yet – there was plenty of planning to do and Dot would have to re-examine the accounts – letters to parents would have to be sent, apologies would have to be given, but in the meantime she kissed the top of her granddaughter's head, gave her back to her adoring mother and then kissed her too. Never had she felt so lucky.

81

TWO YEARS LATER

Emmeline

Emmeline was driving Neville home from the doctors' surgery on Frognal Lane. She'd recently acquired a sit-up-and-beg Ford Prefect car. It was head-turning, even more so when people clocked that it was a lady behind the wheel.

Neville's cyst was benign. *A wonderful word*, thought Emmeline. So the pair were in much better spirits than when they had set out first thing that morning.

'Thank you for taking me,' he said.

'You're welcome.'

There hadn't been a question that she wouldn't, although Neville liked to pretend there was. She doubted he would have made the appointment or taken time off work if it were the other way round, but she didn't concern herself too much with these questions. They only led to uncomfortable truths – and what was the point?

'What time will you be back?' he asked.

Every day the nursery shut at six, she cleared up for forty-five minutes and – now that she had the wonderful car – it took only ten minutes to get home. Yet still he asked.

'About seven.'

'What will we have for dinner?' he wondered. Since he'd stopped working at the newspaper, and now that sugar was off the ration, he talked a lot about food and ate a lot too. At one point, Emmeline had wondered if it wasn't a cyst but a sweet that had lodged its way inside him.

'Chops. You could boil some potatoes.'

'I'll wait until you get back,' he said.

Of course you will, she thought.

When she dropped him off, he hesitated at the passenger door like there was something else.

'There are carrots, too,' Emmeline reminded him.

'Thank you,' he said again.

'You already said that.'

'I mean it, though – for everything.'

Emmeline sensed, although he'd never say it directly, that he was thanking her for not leaving them.

'I'd better go...'

'Get your Skate on,' he said, before winking at her several times. 'That's one I've been saving for Paul...'

She was smiling as she drove the ten minutes to work with the windows down. It was a beautiful day. The birds were singing to each other from their different perches. Flowers brightened the grass verges. The park was filling up with people determined to wring some fun from the upturn in the temperature. Men were loosening their ties. Women were gathering up their skirts. It was everything you could want from a summer day in London.

After lunch, they would take the children to the park. They did this most days now; walked up to the park, set up base, counted insects and ran around. It was something Marjorie's Nursery had a reputation for: 'Marjorie's toddlers' sleep through the night because of all that fresh air' 'Marjorie's toddlers' know the difference between a moth and a butterfly, a finch and a sparrow'.

Emmeline remembered those weeks with Matthew when they'd just arrived in Norfolk and were outdoors from morning to night and although at the time they were hard, she saw now that they had helped shape her and him. She was grateful that they had got the chance to live somewhere else. To see a different way of life and to lead a different life, too. It had made her bolder, more adventurous. Mr Davenport would never have wanted her to shrink or hide away: although, for a short time after his death, she had, she felt she was back to herself again.

Emmeline expected a cheery 'Good morning, Mrs Froud,' from the staff as well as the toddlers. As she arrived that morning, some of the children came over to show her their latest favourite things: a shell, a book, a piece of putty. Afterwards, she went to her office, opened the official-looking letters and looked at the accounts. Nowadays, that was a far less scary task than it used to be. And nowadays, she mostly felt pride rather than despair.

Deidre was at the door, holding baby Nessa, who had joined last month. Nessa's mother was a florist and often brought them spares. Today there were vases of roses on the windowsills.

'She won't let me put her down,' Deidre said.

'I knew a baby like that once,' reminisced Emmeline. It had taken Alice three months to settle in. She wondered what Alice would be like now, fourteen years later. Quite possibly creating havoc wherever she went.

'I'll hold her for a bit.'

Relinquishing Nessa, Deidre shook her arms, relieved. Nessa – like Alice – was weightier than she looked.

'There, there, little one...'

They also had a child at the nursery with a penchant for throwing porridge, which reminded Emmeline of the exploits of Billy. Every year, his mother wrote to Emmeline with photos. Billy was now a strapping lad who loved rules and was excited about going into the army – the only similarity to the old Billy was his love of cricket. He was a champion bowler, apparently.

Sometimes, a toddler just needed the comfort of being cradled by an older woman. Emmeline knew this. And sometimes, a toddler could be an enormous comfort to an older woman. Emmeline knew this too. It was how she had grieved.

'Lydia called,' Deidre said.

Emmeline's face softened at news of her daughter.

'She wants to know how Neville's appointment went.'

'Okay.'

'And she asked if you could look after Margaret and Dennis next weekend?'

If Emmeline had worried that her wealthy grandchildren would look down on their working-class grandparents, they didn't appear to – not yet anyway. And if she had worried that her daughter would restrict grandparent time, she was wrong about that as well.

'Squidgy Nanny,' Margaret insisted on calling her – Emmeline wasn't quite sure why – Neville was 'Funny Grandad' while Matthew was 'Uncy Matts'.

Apparently, Mrs Howard was Granny H.

'Absolutely!' Emmeline grinned down at Nessa as she finally – *finally!* – closed her eyes. 'I'll call her as soon as I've got a free hand...'

Her staff ran a tight ship. The women were different from the inexperienced mothers who had banded together during the war, although their boundless energy sometimes reminded her of Mabel, who ran her own nursery in Suffolk nowadays and had two small children of her own.

They had managed to acquire six second-hand tricycles. It was an effort to lug them to the park, but worth it once they were there to see the children triumphantly spin the pedals and propel themselves forwards. To the surprise of the other staff, and the children, and perhaps to herself, Emmeline got on one of them. With her feet on the pedals, her knees were nearly up to her cheeks and everyone howled with laughter. It was hard work, harder than it looked, but she made it all the way to the trees and then back. The children and staff cheered.

It's good to surprise yourself, she thought.

One of the children yelled, 'Well done, Mummy – I mean Mrs Froud!'

Emmeline had not been able to be the mother she wanted to be to her own children. She hadn't got to do the day-to-day parenting that she loved. Lydia's separation from her had broken her heart.

But there were positives. Lydia claimed that she had thrived and while Emmeline would not have chosen it, she had made the most of her time in Norfolk and now in London. She was privileged to be a mother-figure to hundreds of small children, and now as she looked at the line of little ones waiting for their turn on the trikes, she thought she couldn't ask for much more than that.

82

Lydia

One Saturday morning, the Howards pulled up outside the West Hampstead flat and as usual, for a half-second, Lydia thought they had come to the wrong place. And then she remembered: this was where her parents lived now. It was small compared to the flat in Romberg Road and it was *very* small compared to Bumble Cottage, but she was glad to be here.

Rex was with the Smarts, Dennis was asleep, but Margaret had been awake the last twenty minutes and asking, 'When will we be there?' so often she thought Paul might explode. He wasn't in the best of moods.

'I remember saying that on the train to Somerset,' she reminisced as he parked outside the flat. He didn't say anything – he probably knew the story of her evacuation better than anyone.

'Squidgy Nanny!' Margaret cried as she clambered out of the car and raced towards Lydia's mother.

Mummy picked her up and invited them in, but Lydia said they had to get going.

Daddy said they were early, but she knew they got up at six

most days. Daddy's hair was greased back – he was proud that he wasn't going bald, at the front anyway – and he was smartly dressed, even though it was the weekend. He helped Dennis out of the car.

'It's a big drop for a little lad,' he said.

Paul shook hands with them both and talked about the journey – Paul much preferred driving to taking the train. No one mentioned Daddy's good news, because it was private and he didn't like talking about it, but Lydia gave him a hug, which she didn't normally. And then Lydia clutched her mummy, which made Mummy sneeze. And Lydia was sure Daddy said, 'Cod you believe they're in such a hurry?' but Mummy didn't respond, she just picked up Dennis and kissed his curls.

Lydia knew she wanted a relationship like her parents': something durable and safe. Whether Paul was capable of that in the long term she had yet to see. She wanted her children to spend lots of time with her parents, too – not just because she liked a break but because they had missed out on bringing up their own children and Lydia knew that her mother thought this was a shame.

'You look beautiful,' Mummy said. She could always be relied upon for a compliment.

Lydia twirled. She was wearing a white fur coat and a pillbox hat, her golden hair was freshly styled and she felt very glamorous.

'Do I?' squealed Margaret, wanting in on the action.

'Absolutely,' said Mummy and Daddy at the same time.

Lydia was proud of how impeccable the children looked. It was important to her that Dennis, even though he might still be a tiny dot, wore top-quality shirts and shorts, and although he couldn't walk yet, wore little leather buckle shoes with grey socks. And it was important that Margaret wore expensive pinafores with soft cotton blouses and that her hair was festooned with bows.

'Romantic weekend away, is it?' Mummy asked, smiling shyly as Daddy put his arm round her. Her parents were closer now than they used to be and Lydia was glad to see it. They had been through a lot, she thought, with a fond swell in her heart.

'No, actually,' she said.

Paul shrugged, giving nothing away as usual.

'It's a reunion,' Lydia explained. 'With Valerie Hardman and Francine Salt.'

'Goodness,' Mummy said. Lydia waited for her to say something else and eventually Mummy added, 'Well, give them my love.'

'Will do.' Lydia kissed the children and instructed them to be good for Squidgy Nanny, then squeezed her mother's arm again. 'It all worked out in the end, Mummy, didn't it?'

A LETTER FROM LIZZIE

Dear reader,

Thank you so much for reading *The Wartime Nursery*.

I don't know if you read Book One, *A Child Far from Home*, or if you leapt straight in here – it doesn't matter, I'm absolutely thrilled you picked up *The Wartime Nursery* and made it to the end!

If you want to be kept up to date with all my latest releases, just sign up at the following link. Your email address will never be shared and you can unsubscribe at any time.

www.bookouture.com/lizzie-page

There have been many wonderful children's books about the British evacuation. *Goodnight Mister Tom*, *Carrie's War* and *The War That Saved My Life* and *The War I Finally Won* are all brilliant. There have been, so far as I know, fewer adult stories about it. In this series I wanted to explore two things in particular: how the mothers involved might have felt, and how it affected the children involved, particularly as they grew up.

I've mentioned previously that I grew up with stories of the evacuation – my dad, his sister, his mother and baby brother were all evacuated from East London separately, and with varying success... I have always felt aware of the good, the bad and the ugly. Dad was the classic last child left in the hall. Beautiful Aunty Nita was one of the first children picked. While researching, this series, I talked to others who had been sent away, and people whose families had hosted.

When Russia invaded Ukraine, I was keen to host Ukrainian refugees – possibly as a kind of pay-it-forward to the families who took in people eighty years ago. Through Dina and then Olga, I've learned a lot about how it is to live in someone else's home – not by choice – and in an unfamiliar town, and that too has very much informed this story.

Poor Mr Davenport is murdered just as he and Mrs Froud are on the cusp of making a new life together.

The murder of politicians is an affront to us all. In recent years, Jo Cox MP and then my MP, Sir David Amess, have been killed. Being a public figure should not be a dangerous job. We need to unite and unequivocally condemn all threats and violence towards those in public office.

The Wartime Nursery took me back – not to the war (my children might be surprised but I wasn't actually there) – but to when my three were little. My husband had a demanding job with long hours (this was long before working from home was a twinkle in anyone's eye), my mum had died when I was young and my in-laws didn't live nearby, so I felt alone when I was looking after the babies.

When they were two and a half, they could get a free nursery place in the mornings and I was so grateful to have a place to send them. It was a lifeline to me and I really did count down the days.

When I read about the wartime nurseries, I was so impressed by the tenacity and practicality of the women who set them up and the lasting legacy they left.

Nurseries are about choice. I would hate anyone to think that I believe children *must* go to nurseries. But I am with Emmeline – it's a great thing that nurseries are there.

I'm currently working on the third and final book in the Wartime Evacuees series. Here, we will find out whatever happened to Francine Salt and about that reunion...

Thank you again for reading; what you bring to the book and what you take away from the book is what it is all about.

Lizzie xx

facebook.com/LizziePage

x.com/LizziePagewrite

instagram.com/lizziepagewriter

amazon.com/stores/Lizzie-Page/author/B079KSR8PZ

ACKNOWLEDGEMENTS

I envisaged this series together with editor Claire Simmonds and worked on this book with editor Lucy Frederick. Thank you both so much for all your hard work: Valerie, Jean, Lydia and Emmeline wouldn't be here without you.

Thank you to copyeditor, Jacqui Lewis – you are an absolute queen – and proofreader and chief error-catcher, Jane Donovan. Your work is so appreciated. Thank you to all those involved in editing, marketing, design, publicity, admin and everyone else working behind the scenes. The team at Bookouture are so brilliant and lovely too. I'm so pleased I get to work with you all.

As always, thank you to friends and family. Your love and patience mean the world to me.

Special thanks to Aunty Becky and Aunty Karen, from the Phoenix Nursery in Leigh-on-Sea, who with love and care and imagination created such a wonderful home-from-home for my children. I don't know what I'd have done without you – but I doubt I would have been writing this today if it hadn't been for you.

PUBLISHING TEAM

Turning a manuscript into a book requires the
efforts of many people. The publishing team at
Bookouture would like to acknowledge everyone
who contributed to this publication.

Audio
Alba Proko
Melissa Tran
Sinead O'Connor

Commercial
Lauren Morrissette
Hannah Richmond
Imogen Allport

Contracts
Peta Nightingale

Cover design
Debbie Clement

Data and analysis
Mark Alder
Mohamed Bussuri